THE AGUNAH

THE AGUNAH

By Chaim Grade

Translated from the Yiddish
And with an Introduction
by
Curt Leviant

A Twayne Book

The Bobbs-Merrill Co., Inc.

NEW YORK AND INDIANAPOLIS

To
Reuben B. Resnik
A Devoted Friend Over the Years

Chaim Grade

Introduction

Sometimes writers are called upon singlehandedly to counterpoint, indeed counteract, the events of history. The writer's creative imagination has to undo, metaphorically speaking, what history has done. If history assumes the guise of a murderer, the writer must revivify the dead. In the case of the Jewish writer: the pen against the sword. Quoting the old adage that the pen is mightier than the sword is nowadays untenable, if not cruelly self-deceptive, for in our time we have seen what the sword of Germanism has done. However uphill the struggle, the re-creation—the attempt to undo physical obliteration—has indeed been the burden of the contemporary Yiddish writer.

Occasionally, a writer even begins the process *benakhat*, in tranquility, and then is driven by thrust of history to become the foil to the historic process. Chaim Grade*, the oft-honored Yiddish poet, novelist and short story writer, is such a counterpointer of history.

As Sholom Aleichem re-created the life of East European Jewry in all its nuances, in a broad geographic spectrum, so Chaim Grade took Vilna, the entire complex and spectrum of Jewish Vilna, and preserved it. In his ten volumes of poetry and five of prose, Grade the literary archivist has re-created, brought back to life, what the Germans and their allies have physically destroyed: the world of Jewish Vilna and its surroundings. The pen against the sword. One man against history. A Jew's fate.

In his prose, Grade has explored the tensions of religiosity in the face of both secular seductions and personal and national adversity. He has displayed his concern for Jews in their individual human struggles, and has also probed his own personal world as extension

---

*In Grade, the two vowels are pronounced like the "a" and "e" in f*a*th*e*r.

of Vilna. Although Grade is steeped in the twentieth century—in outlook and literary technique—he holds all of Jewish traditional values and lore in the palm of his pen.

Chaim Grade was born in 1910 in Vilna, the city known as the Jerusalem of Lithuania. Grade's father was a Hebrew teacher and a *maskil* (an enlightened Jew). From his childhood on, Grade was inspired to follow the paths of Jewish and general learning. He was educated in various yeshivas, but as he himself states, and describes in thinly disguised autobiographical fiction, he was not a keen Talmud scholar. He was more fascinated by that ultimate instrument of the poet, the word and its nuances, than by Talmudic reasoning and pilpulistic achievement.

In 1932, at age twenty-two, Grade finally broke with the yeshiva world and began to publish poetry. His adolescent fascination with the word had prevailed. From his first youthful appearance in print, critics and readers knew that a new force had entered Yiddish literature. His subsequent publication in various Yiddish journals in Europe and America and his books of poetry were enthusiastically received. But of course all this made no impression on yeshiva circles. For among East European religious Jewry there could be no greater gap than between Talmud and secular—even Jewish secular—poetry. Poetry is the very antithesis of time spent in Talmud study; it is considered a purposeful manifestation of *bitul Torah*, waste of time from Torah learning. Yet Grade may have broken with the yeshiva world, but it did not break with him, for his memories of this ambiance, with which he was at odds from a religious point of view, have remained with him.

It has been said of Chaim Grade that he is the most learned of the Yiddish writers. Indeed he is the only *ben-Torah* among them, an ex-yeshiva *bocher* who has portrayed that hitherto unexplored territory that touched tens of thousands of people and influenced almost all of Jewry. The yeshiva and the province of rabbinics have provided Grade with the substantive core of many of his works; and he has been a faithful and objective pointillist painter of this society ever since, presenting its strengths, weaknesses, triumphs and doubts.

In 1941, Grade fled Vilna and, in a tragic turn of events, was separated from his wife, as were thousands who fled to the East in their attempt to avoid the descending German sword. Grade made his way into the Soviet Union, but his close kin, his wife and mother, perished in the Vilna Ghetto.

6

In 1946, Grade returned from the Soviet Union and after a half year in Poland went to live in Paris. There he was a primary force in reconstituting Yiddish cultural life among the vast émigré colony of Yiddish-speaking refugees. He lived and worked for two years in Paris and then came to the United States in 1948, where he has resided ever since.

However, the Yiddish writer's lot is not rooted in space, only in time. Not for a Yiddish writer the luxury of conjoining language, literature and locale, like a French author who needs no more than Paris. There is a unified culture of Yiddishkeit—especially post-Holocaust—all over the world. In addition to language, this culture possesses the same set of values, the same collective memory, the same sacred texts and literary treasures, the same aspirations. With Yiddish literature and Yiddish-speaking people active in many continents, with Jewish communities yearning for a Yiddish word and for contact with Yiddish writers, Chaim Grade has become the modern *maggid* of Yiddish, traveling to many continents on lecture tours.

Until 1950, Grade had only written poetry; that year came a turning point in his creativity when he began writing prose. He has thus far published five volumes of fiction: the two-volume *Tsemakh Atlas*, a magnificent novel portraying yeshiva life and the spiritual vacillations of the protagonist, Reb Tsemakh Atlas, and that of students, teachers, rabbis, townspeople and others in or on the fringe of that society; *Der Mames Shabosim*, Grade's eternal light to his mother, Vella the fruit peddler—symbol of devoted Jewish motherhood—and other down-to-earth Jews who struggle to make ends meet; *Der Shulhoyf*, which contains the novel *Der Brunem* (*The Well* in English translation), as well as a long novella *Reb Nokhemel der Malve*, a work that focuses in serio-comic vein on a one-man free loan society and his relationship to his boorish son and other members of the community; and, of course, *The Agunah*. In addition, Grade also has five more volumes of uncollected prose in preparation.

During his twenty-five years of residence in America, Grade has won all the awards that the Yiddish literary world has to offer, including the coveted Leivick Prize and the Lamed Prize. He was accorded a special prize in literature by the American Academy for Jewish Research, two honorary doctorates (one by the Jewish Theological Seminary, another by the Hebrew Union College), the Bergen-Belsen Memorial Press Award and the Jewish Book

Council's annual literary prize. Grade has been honored in Mexico, Argentina, and Israel, where he was given the Manger Prize. His works, in Hebrew translation, are standard classics in Israel. The Hebrew rendition of *The Agunah*, issued in paperback, was a best seller in Israel, and last year the Hebrew University's Yiddish Department devoted a full year course to the works of Grade.

Chaim Grade now lives in New York City. An increasing amount of his work has recently been available in English: the novel, *The Well*, and the holocaust memoir *The Seven Little Lanes* (which is the final section of *Der Mames Shabosim*). Selections of his poetry have been anthologized in *A Treasury of Yiddish Poetry* and other collections. His short story "My Quarrel with Hersh Rasseyner" originally appeared in *Commentary* and was later reprinted in *A Treasury of Yiddish Stories*.

Of Grade's writings available in English, *The Agunah* is most representative of his epic scope. Set in Vilna between the world wars, *The Agunah* is the story of Merl, a young woman whose husband has not returned from World War I, and the entire town's involvement in her struggle to be legally married again. Since there are no eye-witnesses to the husband's death, according to *halakha* [Jewish law] the woman is considered an agunah, bound to her husband who is missing, but yet unable to marry lest she violate the seventh commandment and commit adultery. (The assumption is that as long as there are no witnesses to the husband's death, he is considered alive and married to her.)

The problem of the agunah has plagued Jewish authorities for centuries and there are hundreds of responsa that focus on it. In the novel, this problem and the ensuing conflict extends via neatly structured sub-plots to other people, and descends into the marketplace and the beer tavern. It reaches the synagogue courtyard, the huge crowded Main Synagogue on Simkhas Torah, and the little side-street shuls. In short, the novel's architecture encompasses almost all the elements of the town's Jewish arena, and the reader becomes a tourist through Jewish Vilna, a place and life-style which exist no longer.

The tragedy of the agunah, a hapless woman caught in a current too powerful for her, is the tragedy of all situations revolving about the strictures of law; that is, its human dimension and implications are more profound. Who interprets halakha? Grade seems to ask. For whose benefit is it interpreted? Are interpretations done in the name of God? Or are human struggles and ambitions and rivalries a part of its fabric?

Grade asserts that Torah words have plasticity in the eyes of whoever is interpreting Torah. Everyone sees himself as a defender of God; everyone considers himself just, selfless, noble. *Others* commit sacrilege. Many, in the name of Torah, subsume compassion to fidelity to law.

In *The Agunah*, we are in a domain that the Jewish fictionist— whether Hebrew or Yiddish—did not usually enter, for its portals were closed to him. Closed either because of lack of training, or lack of interest, for even if a writer *had* the yeshiva training, his rebellion was so complete, he lost or blocked out memories of that experience.

Beyond Vilna, Chaim Grade explores various levels of the Jewish condition. In "My Quarrel with Hersh Rasseyner," he has written what is perhaps the finest dramatic story of ideas in Jewish literature. "My Quarrel" has become a modern classic—outlining the dilemma of the Jewish survivor's struggle between a traditional Jewish life and a life of Jewish service and creativity not linked with religion. In his tale, two survivors meet in Paris after the war. One, Hersh Rasseyner, presents the uncompromising view of the man of faith, whose belief in God has not been shaken by the tragedy; on the contrary, it has been strengthened. The other survivor, represented by Chaim Vilner (the author's alter ego), posits the view of continuing Jewish creativity in a secular sense. Faith has been shattered, Vilner says. "The only joy left to us is the joy of creation, and in all the travail of creation we try to draw near to our people."

Whereas in "My Quarrel with Hersh Rasseyner" the ideational aspects of Jewish survival and choice are presented, in his memoir *The Seven Little Lanes*, the physical aspects of the tragedy are added. In the latter, we see Grade fleeing into the Soviet Union when the Germans come and returning to the ruins of a Jewishless Vilna after the war. Grade goes back to the destroyed ghetto seeking the little apartment where his mother lived, gathering as it were shards of the broken past. The characters are not only individualized, but in Grade's process of selection they also become paradigms of a nearly destroyed people who have enough life energy and will to revive themselves.

The all-encompassing Jewishness of Grade's writings also spills over into his use of language. It is said of Sholom Aleichem that his use of Yiddish covered all known levels of the Yiddish-speaking societies, including various dialects and localisms. One level that Sholom Aleichem did not touch was the Yiddish of the yeshiva, because for him it was an unfamiliar realm. Of Chaim Grade it may be said that his Yiddish covers all levels of Vilna's society. His rabbinic Yiddish, a fascinating linguistic medium, has a preponderance of Torah-weighted Hebrew. Yiddish sentences spoken by scholars contain even more Hebrew than Yiddish. In the hands of Chaim Grade, the Yiddish of the street, of the working classes and their slang, is poetic in choice and precise in usage. In this fashion he may be compared to Israel's Nobel Laureate, S.Y. Agnon, whose Hebrew style was similarly musical and poetic.

Grade's Jews think spontaneously in Jewish images. Thus, when a rabbi is considering whether it would pay to be the only rabbi in a small town or one of two rabbis in a larger town, he says to himself: "It's better to make a blessing over a small whole loaf than over a huge bread that's already been sliced." Or, another example, a man about to rip off a poster from a synagogue courtyard bulletin board looks around like "Moses before he killed the Egyptian." This is immediately followed by the man "shoving his nose into the poster as though into a High Holiday prayerbook."

Chaim Grade has created a gallery of variegated human beings—rich and poor, kindly and mean, pious and freethinking—in poetically conceived works of differing genre and mood. While some writers concentrate on one personality throughout their artistic career—Hemingway kept writing about himself at different stages of his life—Grade has written about one people, an entire folk. Hence, he joins that rare company of writers whose art is national in that it touches every fibre—religious, historic, societal, folkloristic—of a complete civilization.

With Chaim Grade the Jewish world of Vilna of the twenties and thirties comes to life. He shows the continuity of that world, and even post-Holocaust asserts its determined survival in memory, a memory blessed with compassion and with visual and audial precision.

Writers are often singlehandedly called upon to undo, to counteract the events of history. The pen against the sword. One man against history. *Goralo shel yehudi. Der goyrel fun a yid.* A Jew's fate.

CURT LEVIANT

10

Glossary

Agunah—Grass widow. According to Jewish law, a married woman separated from her husband who cannot remarry either because she cannot obtain a divorce from him, or because it is not known whether he is alive or dead

Bar Mizvah—Age 13 when a Jewish boy assumes responsibility for his acts

Cheder—Hebrew school

Dybbuk—Spirit that enters another person

Esrog—Citrus fruit used in services on Sukkos

Eydl—An adjective meaning tender and refined; also a woman's name

Gaon—Great scholar

Gemara—Part of the Talmud

Hanuka—Holiday of Lights celebrating the rededication of the Temple by the Maccabees

Havdala—Prayer said at the end of the Sabbath

Lulav—Palm tree branch used in services on Sukkos

Midrash Rabbah—Volume of commentaries on the Torah and other books of the Bible

Mishna—Part of the Talmud

Mohel—One who performs circumcisions

Quorum—The ten men needed to start a synagogue service

Rebbetsin—Rabbi's wife

Rosh Hashana—Jewish New Year

Sanhedrin—The highest judicial and religious body, or court, during the Roman period, both prior to and after the destruction of the Second Temple in 70 C.E.

Shamesh—Synagogue caretaker (plural: shamoshim)

Shema Yisroel—*Hear O Israel*, the Jew's central affirmation of faith

Shlimazel—Luckless one

Shokhet—Slaughterer of kosher animals or fowl

Sholom aleichem—Form of greeting (Peace unto you). The response is: "Aleichem sholom" (Unto you peace)

Shul—Synagogue

Simkhas Torah—Holiday celebrating the giving of the Torah to the Jewish people

Sukkos—Tabernacles. Holiday celebrating the harvest

Talmud—Body of written Jewish law, made up of Mishna and Gemara

Tfillin—Phylacteries used in morning prayers

Torah—The Five Books of Moses; or, the entire body of Jewish tradition, as in the phrase "to study Torah."

Yebamot—A tractate of the Talmud

Yeshiva—School for the study of the Talmud

Yom Kippur—Day of Atonement

1

When she was single, Merl the seamstress had been carefree and gay. Her eyes flashed dark fire and all the neighborhood boys wanted to kiss her. At nineteen she married the carpenter Itsik Tswilling, one of the anti-Czarist workers who sang "Brothers and Sisters in Labor and Want." Itsik was a nice chap, the girls said, but not much of a provider. Yet this didn't faze Merl, who was a fair match for both his earnings and his courage. When Itsik went out on demonstrations, she marched at his side.

Merl had another suitor, a rich merchant and dandy whom everyone called Moishke Tsirulnik, though he preferred the more modish name, Moritz. Merl's seamstress and glovemaker friends detested him for the way he mocked the anti-Czarist workers, and she herself couldn't stand his despicable character, his thinning pomaded yellow hair, and his unctuous, burning little eyes and piercing laugh. Better a poor boy, but one of my own, she thought, and married Itsik the carpenter.

Itsik was sickly; right after the wedding his teeth began falling out. Merl, however, was always in high spirits, sitting at her sewing machine, laughing and singing all the songs she knew; she couldn't understand why her husband was constantly careworn, gloomily chewing woodshavings as he toiled far into the night.

A year after their wedding World War I broke out. The carpenter was drafted and shipped to East Prussia with the First Orenburg Regiment. For months Merl remembered the women's wailing as they parted from their newly mobilized husbands. Soon news came from the front that the First Orenburg Regiment had been massacred in the East Prussian swamps. Hoping that her husband was among the handful of survivors, Merl waited for the war's end and for Itsik's return from imprisonment.

13

Meanwhile, the Germans had entered Vilna and the great famine began. Merl had to forget her own troubles and support her widowed mother, her younger sister Golda, and her older sister Guteh who had married Motye the barber, a lazy drunkard nicknamed "the speedy turtle."

By nature Merl was courageous. She did not lose her equanimity even when battles raged in the heart of the city and bullets whistled overhead. Nevertheless, when her former admirer Moritz found excuses to visit her and needle her with questions about Itsik's well-being she was always flustered.

Moritz had remained a bachelor whose fondest wish was to have the seamstress tear her hair in regret for not having married him. Merl, in turn, knew that despite her sad and bitter lot, she was still better off than she would have been with the malevolent Moishke Tsirulnik.

At the end of the war, the survivors of the First Orenburg Regiment returned from the German prisoner-of-war camps and reported that there were no survivors from Itsik's company, the 11th, which had been completely annihilated in the first and most furious battle. Merl cried for countless nights, and sat with tear-puffed eyes by her sewing machine during the day.

When the Bolsheviks left Vilna and the Poles entered, Golda married Shaike the tailor, unfortunately as lazy a drunkard as Motye. Merl couldn't stand listening to Golda pleading with her loafer till noon to crawl out of bed, and once, in a fit of rage, hurled her iron shears to the floor to keep herself from throwing them at her brother-in-law. Infuriated, Shaike sprang out of bed, but she fled the house in time. To spite her, he befriended Moishke Tsirulnik, whereupon the merchant no longer needed an excuse to come to the house and tease the seamstress with a new routine:

"The war's over. The Czar's been overthrown. But you're still a little seamstress—and an agunah, a deserted wife, as well!"

Moritz revolted her so much she didn't even reply. Merl decided to move out of her father's cottage at the edge of the forest into her own apartment, and thus be rid of Tsirulnik and her brother-in-law. She wanted to take her mother Kayle, too, for her earnings would suffice for both of them. But Kayle maintained that her daughter should be living with a husband and not with her.

"What's going to be?" the old woman complained. "Your husband went away to war more than fifteen years ago. Other women who had husbands in Itsik's company have all remarried; only you're alone, waiting. Itsik was a decent young man. He would never have run off and left you an agunah. It's as plain as day he's no longer alive. But since I can't have the pleasure of seeing you remarry, I'd rather move into an old-age home and not be witness to your troubles. If you live alone perhaps you'll find someone."

Kayle entered the old-age home and Merl left the family cottage. To avoid being pitied, she purposely moved into an apartment on Polotsk Street, a sparsely settled neighborhood near the Jewish cemetery surrounded by gardens, where no one knew her. The funeral processions crossed the Zaretche River bridge and passed the marketplace; but the mourners returned from the cemetery via Polotsk Street.

It was springtime. Merl sat alone in her new apartment bent over her sewing machine. She thought she could hear the rustling and whispering of countless leaves in the nearby parks. Through the open window a bee buzzed into the room, bumped several times against the ceiling and flew out, as though fleeing withered flowers. Merl had grown so used to the silence that the buzzing of the departed bee vibrated in her brain like a snapped violin string. But she quickly pressed the treadle to drown out the buzzing in her head. The thread in the spool was as endless as her loneliness, infinitely drawn out. Hearing the tread of many feet outside, she realized that Jews were returning from a funeral. She leaned out of her first floor window and watched the mourners until they disappeared. Then, alone again in the sun-filled silence, she listened to the leaves rustling and whispering.

One day Merl chanced upon the funeral of an old girlhood acquaintance. Her former girl friends asked the corpse in the open grave to intercede for them and their families in heaven. After the grave had been filled the women surrounded the cemetery cantor; each one asked him to chant the memorial prayer for her and her family. This astonished Merl: as young girls they had demonstrated against the Czar—and look what had become of them now!

Before they left the cemetery, the women gathered around Merl, and with tear-stained faces asked, "How are you getting along? We're so busy with kids and daily cares we don't even have time to blow our nose! What a pity we meet only at funerals!"

"Merke, what are you waiting for?" they whined. "Get married and give us all one more chance to meet at a celebration."

But Merl only smiled. The women left, but she stayed behind on the pretext that she wanted to visit her father's grave. Alone, she stared at the fresh grave, as though asking her departed friend whether she ought to remarry. On the other side of the hill stood the cemetery cantor, a man in his forties, leaning on his cane and gazing at the seamstress. Having overheard Merl's friends' remarks, he asked if she wanted him to chant a memorial prayer; when Merl nodded, he asked her name and her father's name. He began to chant, then stopped, waiting for Merl to provide the names of her husband and children. He wanted to be sure that he had heard correctly that this woman was all alone in the world.

Noticing that Merl remained silent, he sighed deeply, and devotedly finished the memorial prayer as though it were for the soul of a close relative. When the seamstress offered to pay him, the cantor replied that he hadn't done this for money.

Since twilight had fallen, there would be no more funerals. The two left the graveyard together. As they walked the man introduced himself as Kalman Maytess. He was a housepainter by trade, he said, but since he was unemployed now and could lead prayers, he had recently begun chanting memorial prayers at the cemetery. Frankly, he had actually fallen into the habit of visiting the cemetery since his wife had died. But as soon as he found work, he would give up chanting memorial prayers; perhaps even sooner. He had heard the women say that she was all alone. Where was her husband? Hadn't he returned from the war? Since the war had ended so many years ago, he was amazed that she hadn't asked rabbis if she was permitted to remarry. Since there were no trustworthy eyewitnesses to her husband's death, according to Jewish law she was an agunah who was forbidden to marry without the permission of a Jewish court of law. So why hadn't she made the effort? As for himself, he had been a widower for several years and could no longer stand being alone. She lived on Polotsk Street, didn't she? He always passed her house on his way to the cemetery.

The cantor accompanied Merl to her apartment and parted with the hope that they would meet on happier occasions. In the house, Merl rested her head on the bannister and realized that her mother had been right. Itsik was indeed no longer among the living. Oh yes, she remembered him. But she no longer felt him in her heart.

16

2

A week later Merl heard someone pacing back and forth beneath her window on the quiet Polotsk Street, tapping his cane on the cobblestones and coughing to attract attention. Merl stuck her head out the window and saw Kalman Maytess gazing up at her.

"What are you looking for?" she asked with gypsy-like coyness.

"A cold drink".

As Merl went to open the door for him, a thought struck her: the summer of her youth was over. She was now being courted by a middle-aged graveyard cantor.

Kalman came into the apartment with the walking stick he used at the cemetery, as though he were the demon who raps on the coffin the third day after burial and asks the corpse his name. Forgetting that he was thirsty, Kalman sat down at the table and asked:

"Have you consulted rabbis?"

"There are no prospective husbands waiting for me," Merl smiled sadly.

But Kalman swore that he was absolutely sure that she would have no lack of suitors. She must not be overly pious, he said pleasantly, and began to chant with a Talmudic singsong: "Since fifteen years have passed from the time your husband went away to war; and since there were no survivors from his company; and since he had been sickly and could have died a natural death—you should no longer torment yourself. The rabbis will certainly decide that you may remarry."

"How do you know that my husband had always been sickly?" she asked, astonished.

"Your mother told me."

The seamstress laughed. "Have you seen my sisters, too?"

"No. Just your mother. You once were a very vivacious girl, and even now you're still beautiful. So why don't you go to rabbis and request permission to remarry?"

"When I'm ready to get married I'll look for a man who will take me without rabbinic permission," Merl replied impatiently.

Hearing such sinful talk, Kalman glanced quickly at the corner where his cane stood, as though ready to flee the house. Nevertheless, he did not budge; but the joyful lilt to his voice was muted and he spoke more sedately:

"Of course you'll find suitors, even if you don't request a rabbinic decision. But why should you grieve your old mother? What's more, a playboy who disregards the Torah laws will also disregard people and might very likely cast you aside later. Nowadays if a woman rebuffs a young man's oaths of eternal love, he wishes her the worst. But I'm not the sort to bear ill will toward a woman who rejects my proposal."

Hearing this, Merl realized that her mother had told Kalman about Moishke Tsirulnik, who certainly would not have consulted a rabbi for permission to marry her. Tsirulnik just wanted to marry her in order to torment her for not having married him long ago and for refusing to be his mistress once she had become an agunah.

Merl gazed at Kalman's simple moonface as though seeing him for the first time. He wasn't at all as dull-witted as he looked, she thought. She left the table with the apology that she had some work to finish that day. But he could stay and talk; he wasn't disturbing her. Merl sat down by the sewing machine and ran a piece of linen under the needle. The needle pierced her finger but the pain in her heart was sharper. While Kalman continued talking, she raced the treadle as though attempting to regain the lost years of her agunahood.

Kayle informed her daughter that she wanted to see her without fail on Sabbath at the old-age home. When Merl arrived her two sisters were already there.

"Do something!" her mother wailed. "The joy my three daughters give me I don't wish my enemies. Do something to make the rabbis let you marry."

"But I'm not ready to get married," Merl insisted. "And I won't consult the rabbis when I am."

"Not while I'm alive," Kayle wept. "And if you don't want me to turn over in my grave, don't do it after I'm dead. I've never

18

interfered with the way you did things. You're no rabbi's daughter. But I don't want to live to see the day when they accuse you of violating Jewish law and call you an adulteress. Moishke Tsirulnik the merchant doesn't appeal to me either because he makes fun of you and pours salt on your wounds. But Reb Kalman is a fine upstanding man."

Merl's older sister, Guteh, who lived in the low-rent welfare housing provided by Baroness Hirsch, began swaying back and forth, moaning plaintively:

"I swear Reb Kalman has more decency in his little fingernail than my lush of a husband has in his entire body and soul. Some fault! The bride is too beautiful—Kalman's too pious. If only my souse were as religious, he wouldn't let me and my children suffer so much. What's the good of his being a barber if the only thing he trims is his own curled mustache? He works half a day here, half a day there—until he's fired. By the time he gives one haircut, other barbers have finished ten. One of his employers swore to me that he occasionally leaves customers with lathered-up faces to sneak off for a quick drink. To top it off, he cuts hair like an old Cossack. Today's youngsters don't want their necks shaven like the White-Russian peasants. They like their hair neatly scissor-trimmed down below and bunched up thick near the top."

"You say that your drunkard can't cut hair; can my drunkard sew?" Golda whined. "Even a patchmaker earns more than him. He could have been a first-class tailor, but he doesn't want to adapt to modern fashions. My lazybones considers modern styles sacks and still sews clothes like they did fifty years ago—tightwaisted jackets and narrow lapels. The coat-tails tear and the backs are too tight. That's why the customers throw the suits right back at his face. So take my advice, Merke, and give the housepainter your consent."

While listening, Merl looked around the large room of the old-age home. Emaciated women lay on their beds, groaning. One old woman wearing a bonnet sat at the edge of her bed, her short legs, covered with striped woolen socks, dangling over the side; through the brass-rimmed spectacles on her nose she sniffed at the letters of her Yiddish Bible. In another corner sat a tall woman with a drawn-out expressionless face, chewing a hard crust of bread with her toothless gums.

Lately, Kayle's limbs had become bloated and she could not

move from her bed. Propped up with three pillows, she warmed her blue, puffy hands on a tea kettle as Guteh and Golda, wrapped in shawls as though prepared for a frost, swayed over Merl and gave vent to all their bitterness.

Merl's eyes flashed once more with dark fire. A wild joy came over her. She had met her middle-aged "bridegroom" in the cemetery, she reflected, and the match was now being proposed in the old-age home. All that was needed now to round out the picture was to have the cemetery cantor barge in, graveyard cane in hand.

Merl burst out laughing.

"Look, Mama," Golda clapped her hands. "What do you say to that laugh of hers! She always was and she's still remained a wild goat."

But the next Sabbath when Kalman Maytess, dressed in his Sabbath best, came to visit Merl, she received him as though she had been expecting him. Kalman told her that he had been working on the other side of town all week and had had no time to visit her. Merl invited him to eat and he accepted. He washed his hands carefully, but ate little, his head shyly bowed. At Grace After Meals he felt more secure and with closed eyes began to sing. The sweet melody suffused all of Merl's limbs with warmth. If her old girl friends would now hear such singing, Merl thought, they would probably dab at their tear-filled eyes, as they did in the cemetery when Kalman chanted the memorial prayer. She turned to the window and her glance strayed past the gardens to the forest settlement where she was born and where she spent her youth singing songs entirely different from those that Kalman sang.

Merl suddenly realized with a start that while her guest was saying Grace she sat with uncovered head, not at all like a pious woman. The seamstress donned a kerchief and sat opposite her guest, silent and wrapped in the Sabbath twilight shadows.

3

Kalman Maytess' declaration that the agunah could get rabbinic permission was no idle guess. He had already spoken of the matter with a recluse in the Gaon of Vilna's Shul. Chewing the tip of his beard and knotting his brow, the recluse finally answered that there were grounds for discussion. Although a married woman may not remarry as long as she does not have a trustworthy witness to her husband's death; since this woman had been an agunah for so many years; and since none of the young men who served with her husband's company had returned; and since her husband had been sickly and could have died a natural death—there were indeed grounds for discussion.

But Kalman wanted marriage, not discussion. The recluse replied that if Kalman's intentions were practical and not theoretical, then he should turn to Reb Levi Hurvitz, the Vilna Rabbinic Council's appointed authority over agunahs.

Reb Levi Hurvitz had been a young genius whom Rabbi Yosele, then the eldest rabbinic authority in Vilna, had taken to be his son-in-law. In the town it was rumored that Reb Levi stemmed from Hasidim. He habitually scurried about both at home and in the street; he shouted out his prayers and was the first to finish the Silent Devotion. He detested itinerant preachers and addressed even the older yeshiva students in the familiar form. The anti-Hasidic Vilna Jews considered all this iron-clad evidence that Reb Levi was of Hasidic descent. His neighbors in Shlomo Kissen's courtyard reported that the lights in Reb Levi's rooms burned far into the night. He ran about in his apartment holding a small Psalm book and occasionally wailed so loud that no one in the courtyard could shut an eye.

Reb Levi Hurvitz was a man of great woes. His wife's mind had snapped immediately after her first and only confinement, and she had been insane now for twenty years. Moreover, Reb Levi's only daughter, quiet and melancholic since her childhood, began smashing windows when she grew up. Reb Levi struggled for a long time and kept her locked up at home, but finally agreed to commit her to the asylum. Left alone, the rabbi spent half the night darting through his large, illuminated apartment with a small Psalm book in his hand.

Khiyeneh, an old woman without family, served him. A courtyard resident, she came upstairs every day to clean his rooms, bring water, and prepare a warm meal. Once, Khiyeneh told her neighbors that she had overheard the rabbi's brothers-in-law urging him to marry. They agreed that since not the Torah but Rabbenu Gershom's later edict prohibited bigamy, Reb Levi should get permission from one hundred rabbis and marry again, for his ill wife was beyond hope. Reb Levi's reply to his brothers-in-law, rabbis one and all, was that he would be the subject of gossip. It would be said of Reb Levi that at a time when he had a wife and daughter in the madhouse he wanted to play the young man and marry.

His family, however, kept insisting and repeated the suggestion several times a month. The neighbors, noticing all this, could hardly wait for Khiyeneh to come down from the rabbi's apartment in the evening, eager to know if his brothers-in-law had finally convinced him. But Khiyeneh reported that the rabbi had run circles around the table and even burst into rhyme, shouting: "If the shepherd does as he wishes, the Vilna Jews will say, the flock itself can go astray."

The neighbors shook their heads and concluded that Reb Levi was the type of man who was ecstatic if he lost two of his own teeth so long as his opponent lost one. If Vilna Jews were a flock, no wonder the city detested him. Friday evening he was first in *shul*, they said, and if he saw a woman carrying in a lit candle a minute after the designated time for candle-lighting, he would spring at her, shouting that the Almighty did not need her lights. "Better tell your husband to close his store in time," he yelled. "Better not cook your dainties till sundown. Observe the dietary laws and family purity. Don't send your children to the secular schools which pave the path to apostasy." He apparently could not stand seeing the dozens of candles that the women had set on the prayerstand, for in his house neither his daughter nor his wife lit Sabbath candles. The neighbors assumed that the reason for his brothers-in-law's desire to marry him off was to curb his rancor at people.

But since Kalman Maytess was neither a neighbor nor one of the prominent worshippers, he knew nothing about Reb Levi Hurvitz and went up to him in a thoroughly optimistic frame of mind. But as soon as he saw him Kalman's high spirits sank. Kalman saw a short, broad-shouldered man with a thick square beard who transported himself over the apartment like a stormwind, clomping his shoes and groaning as though his teeth hurt. The rabbi neither offered his hand nor asked Kalman to be seated.

Nevertheless, Kalman plucked up his courage and told the rabbi the entire story concerning the agunah. Not for an instant did Reb Levi slow down his tempestuous pacing. Listening with half an ear, he thumbed through two tomes on opposite sides of the room, as though one glance sufficed to absorb all the truth contained therein. Suddenly, he stopped in front of his visitor.

"There's nothing to talk about. If there are no trustworthy eye-witnesses who have actually seen her husband dead, a rabbi can do nothing."

"But, rabbi, I heard from a recluse in the Gaon of Vilna's Shul that there *are* grounds for discussion. Almost sixteen years have passed since the agunah's husband went away to war. In his company there were no survivors. In fact, he was a sickly man who could have died a natural death. And, anyway, where is it written that the witnesses had to see the corpse with their own eyes?"

"Where is it written?" Reb Levi said, his beard fluttering as though a storm was brewing there. "It's written in the Mishna, it's written in the Gemara, it's written in Alfasi's *Code*, it's written in Maimonides, it's written in Joseph Caro's *Code of Law*," the rabbi launched out against Kalman and cast bits of learning at him, as though they were fiery blows. "It does not suffice if the witness merely saw the man dying, for he could have remained alive and did not wish to return to his wife. The witness must actually see when the man gives up the ghost. It does not suffice if the man was merely seen cut up, or nailed to a board. It does not suffice if a wild beast was tearing at his flesh—except if birds and beasts were eating his marrow, heart or intestines. It does not suffice if the witness had seen him falling into the ocean, for he could have safely reached shore and not wished to return home.

His wife, then, is still considered a married woman, an agunah who may never remarry. If the witness declares that the man was seen falling into a lion's den, it still is no proof that he is dead, for satiated lions do not attack; it is another matter, however, if he fell into a snake-pit, for snakes bite even if they are not hungry. And during a war you cannot take the wife's word that her husband had been killed, for merely hearing that soldiers from her husband's company had been killed might prompt her to assume that her husband, too, was among the slain. And there are some who maintain that in wartime she is not to be believed even if she states that she buried him with her own hands. And now you come with your story that no one from the man's company survived."

But Reb Levi was already talking to the open door, for Kalman had slipped away and gone downstairs feeling as if he'd just been hanged, drawn and quartered. He first caught his breath when he reached the street, then wiped the perspiration from his face and marched off to the recluse in the Vilna Gaon's Shul.

"You said that there were grounds for discussion on the matter, but Reb Levi didn't want to hear of it." Then Kalman told the recluse how Reb Levi had yelled at him, stamped his feet, and cut him to ribbons like a common thief.

The recluse answered calmly that if it was merely a question of talking, the matter could indeed be discussed; however he was no Vilna rabbinic authority and had no business interfering. In any case, he didn't want to start up with Reb Levi, who was an embittered soul, an overly zealous man who could tear a man apart like a herring.

But Kalman had no intentions of giving up. He felt a surge of strength and decided that he would prevail over Reb Levi Hurvitz. Reb Levi should see people whose hearts were as embittered as his. And it was imperative that these be women.

Kalman was afraid to give the seamstress all the details. She might very well assert once more that she would seek a man who would not request a rabbinic decision. Kalman, therefore, went to Merl's sisters and sent them to Reb Levi to give him an earful of their tales of woe. Guteh and Golda didn't have to be asked a second time; they donned their kerchiefs and went up to the rabbi in tears.

Reb Levi Hurvitz, sunk deep in his armchair at the head of the table, heard the women out with bowed head; when he raised his head to reply, his face was contorted, damp and pale, as though he

24

had just snapped out of a fainting spell. He spoke with closed eyes, his voice choking with sorrow:

"Believe me, my heart is torn to pieces. No one understands as well as I what it means to be alone for years on end. How well I know that feeling!" He pressed his eyes shut and did not permit the welling tears to leave his lids. "If you hadn't asked me, I would not have interfered. Nowadays, no one stands in awe of God, so would anyone stand in awe of a rabbi? But since you are consulting me, I must decide according to the law. And the law states that as long as there were no eyewitnesses to the husband's death, the agunah is not permitted to remarry."

Reb Levi sank back in his chair, looking once more as though he had fainted.

Before Merl's sisters left for Reb Levi's house, Kalman had told them that they would be dealing with an intractable man who did not even spare himself. His wife had been in the madhouse twenty years but nevertheless he did not marry, even though rabbis were willing to permit it. Guteh and Golda wanted to vent their rage on the rabbi; if he wanted to do himself in it was his business—but he had no right to kill their sister. However, impressed by the way he heard them out and sympathized with them, they adjusted their kerchiefs and silently left the rabbi's house.

Guteh and Golda went to Merl and reported all the details, adding that if not for their mother's oath not to live to see the day her daughter disobeyed the Torah's laws, they would not mind Merl's marrying without rabbinic permission. Both rage and fear overwhelmed Merl. Had she really lost all hope forever? The rabbi had declared that even more than fifteen years of silence was no indication that her husband was dead. If Itsik was indeed alive and had deserted her, Merl thought, she could surely marry. Had she only known that he was living with someone else, she would have had someone long ago.

But if, as her heart told her, he *was* dead—thousands of signs pointed to it—why should she wither away in loneliness until her dying day? That's why to spite everyone she would begin to look for a husband, a man who stood in awe of no one, not like the cemetery cantor who wouldn't budge without consulting a rabbi.

Kalman realized that he would never meet a prettier woman or a better provider than the seamstress. It was his good fortune that Merl was crestfallen; perhaps she might even consent to marry

25

him. He ought not let a treasure like her slip through his fingers. On the other hand, all his life he had been a pious Jew and had been afraid to disobey the rabbis. He also knew that since he conducted himself in an upright and decent manner Merl's mother was wholeheartedly for him. But if he chose to marry without permission, the old woman would dissuade her daughter from marrying him

Kalman began to dash about again, asking questions, sniffing here and there, until he finally slapped his forehead in realization: he was standing knee-deep in water and was seeking a drink. He would simply go and visit Reb Asher-Anshel, the rabbi of Gitke-Toibe's lane. Reb Asher-Anshel, Reb Levi Hurvitz's brother-in-law, was the appointed authority over divorces, which to a degree was related to agunah matters. Kalman could not understand why these duties had to be split up between two rabbis.

4

Others in Vilna also asked why there was one rabbi for divorces and another for agunahs, then sagely replied that a rabbi would have to have a heart of stone to turn away a weeping agunah who asked him to find a way out for her. Therefore, to handle agunahs the Vilna Rabbinic Council appointed the soul-embittered Reb Levi, who with his cry of despair could have silenced any complaint. But a request for a divorce was another matter. Didn't every couple squabble and then run to the rabbi for a divorce? An impetuous rabbi might immediately acquiesce and grant a divorce. Man and wife would spite each other, marry someone else, and then tear the hair out of their heads in desperation. Vilna would have been in a fine fix if the rabbi in charge of divorces were Reb Levi Hurvitz; and hence, it was commonly held, the Rabbinic Council had appointed the most serene man in the world—Reb Asher-Anshel— to handle divorces.

Indeed, Reb Asher-Anshel felt that in ninety-nine percent of the cases a couple merely came to unburden themselves and not to divorce. Each party to the dispute sought the rabbi's unqualified support. Reb Asher-Anshel, however, knew that siding with one would mean inciting even greater strife; but if he agreed with both they'd consider him a fool. Thus he compromised by remaining absolutely silent. Husband and wife would scream and repeatedly interrupt each other—but the rabbi meanwhile would peruse a book.

Occasionally, his young visitor would want to know what the rabbi was reading with such gusto. And when he discovered that it was the Russian *Jewish Encyclopedia*, he would stand there in open-mouthed amazement. Although the prospective divorcé would have greater respect for the rabbi who also knew Russian, he would still feel somewhat insulted, for he had assumed the rabbi was consulting a sacred text to decide which party was right.

"Keep talking, I'm listening to every word," Reb Asher-Anshel would look up to the complainant, who would suddenly fall silent. "I just want to know when they built the old synagogue in the village of Tiktim, near Bialystok."

Or:

"Keep talking, I'm listening to every word. I just want to know when Jews first settled the Caucasus. One view is that the local Jews came there even before the destruction of the Second Temple in 70 C.E."

Scanning the encyclopedia was a proven means for not losing his temper while the two sides would wrangle. For his part they could scream from today till tomorrow; but then his wife would enter the room and announce with irritation that others were waiting to see him.

Nevertheless, some people preferred Reb Levi's impatience and severity to Reb Asher-Anshel's long-suffering mildness. They noted that the latter was good-natured because he was not as scholarly or as eager for Talmud study as his brother-in-law, Reb Levi; moreover, Reb Asher-Anshel was fortunate in being honored by his wife and in having joy from his children.

Reb Asher-Anshel's son resembled him both in features and character. At eighteen he already had a rabbinic potbelly and knew over a thousand pages of the Talmud with all the commentaries. Reb Asher-Anshel's daughter, too, was tenderhearted; although she had mastered several languages she was not conceited. The neighborhood women for whom she wrote letters to relatives in America said that she washed the floors in her father's house and was pursued by all the doctors in town. Nonetheless, she married a Torah scholar, Reb Fishel Bloom, a student from the Slobodka Yeshiva.

Reb Fishel Bloom had boarded at his father-in-law's table for years. He had not been offered a pulpit because he wasn't a speaker, despite the imposing black beard and the fleshy lips of the fiercest itinerant preachers. Nevertheless, no one ever heard Reb Asher-Anshel complain that his son-in-law had no position. However, jokers said that Reb Asher-Anshel had flared up at his son-in-law only once—when the rabbi's daughter, already the mother of two girls, was delivering her third child. When one of the worshippers congratulated the rabbi, Rabbi Asher-Anshel reportedly snapped: "Another girl!"

This was the only time that anyone had ever seen the rabbi angry. Even Kalman Maytess knew that Reb Asher-Anshel was as patient as the gentle sage Hillel.

Reb Asher-Anshel sat in his study, thumbing through a thick book into which were pasted long handwritten sheets of paper— depositions of the divorces he had arranged. He kept these documents with the names, the familial lineage and the entire proceedings of the divorce, in the event that a couple requested written attestation to their divorce; or wanted to remarry and proof was needed that the man was not a descendant of the priestly class who could not marry a divorcée, not even remarry the wife he himself had divorced; or if there was a dispute over property, or a quarrel among the children concerning the inheritance.

The rabbi paged through the thick book, shrugging his shoulders in amazement. He was famous for his reticence in granting divorces; he prolonged the proceedings for years and used all sorts of ruses to get the couples reconciled; nevertheless, hundreds of divorces had already been granted.

Reb Asher-Anshel had been urged by his brother-in-law, Reb Levi Hurvitz, to examine the depositions. That afternoon at the Rabbinic Council meeting Reb Levi had declared that a separated couple transgressed so many commandments that no rabbi should bear the responsibility of reconciling them; hence were he in charge of divorces, he would grant them more readily.

Reb Asher-Anshel smiled despite his anger. While my brother-in-law admonishes me concerning the couples I didn't divorce, he thought, I have misgivings about every couple I divorced that I could have reconciled. That's my way, and that's why Vilna and I are at peace. Reb Levi says it's no compliment for a rabbi to be on good terms with everyone—it shows he doesn't stand up to any issue. Never mind! I manage to accomplish more with kindness than he with anger. He considers it a shortcoming that my daughter knows foreign languages; in other words, says he, she can read decadent books in several languages. He says I shouldn't have sent her to the Hebrew high school, lest other Jews follow my example and send not only their daughters, but their sons as well.

Reb Asher-Anshel furrowed his brow, as though contemplating whether his brother-in-law's contentions were correct after all.

"It's his fanaticism talking," Reb Asher-Anshel muttered. "Reb Levi is angry at me because his wife and daughter—my sister and niece—are in the insane asylum. But everyone knows that until her confinement my sister had been in good health, as my other sisters are today, thank God. It's I who should complain to him that my sister fell sick by him. He realizes, then, that these complaints are not justified, so he lashes out against my behavior. When our family pleaded with him to get permission to remarry, he replied that people would gossip that he remarried while his wife and daughter were confined to institutions. So he pours out his bitterness on me for having married my sister twenty-two years ago, and for the fact that it isn't fitting for him now to marry again."

Hearing footsteps in the hall, Reb Asher-Anshel grew uneasy. He had no patience to listen to a marital squabble today. He bent down to take a volume of the Russian *Jewish Encyclopedia* out of the bookshelf, then changed his mind: even the fascinating history of the Caucasian Jews would not calm him. As a reminder not to lose patience, he hurriedly immersed himself in the divorce archives. He did not want another deposition of a broken marriage added to the list.

When Kalman saw the rabbi, his hope surged. Even his appearance contrasted with that of his brother-in-law. Whereas the red-bearded Reb Levi was short and broad-shouldered, the silvery-bearded Reb Asher-Anshel was tall and thin. Unlike Reb Levi he did not pace back and forth in his apartment, but sat and bade his visitor to be seated too.

Kalman sat down respectfully at the edge of a chair and began his story, which by now he knew perfectly and narrated in orderly fashion. But as soon as the rabbi heard the subject of the story, he raised his eyes in fright.

"Why have you come to me? Reb Levi is the one who handles agunahs. I only deal with divorces."

"If you can't do anything," Kalman stammered, "then at least try to convince your brother-in-law, Reb Levi, who refused to hear of the matter".

Hearing this request, Reb Asher-Anshel stood, his expression changed, and he retreated a few steps, as though someone had asked him to jump into a furnace.

"God forbid! I won't say a word to Reb Levi about this matter. I dare not meddle. And if indeed there are grounds for discussion here, it must be done by the rabbi from the district where the agunah lives."

Just because Kalman knew Reb Asher-Anshel to be a tender-hearted and extremely patient man, he was frightened more by his quiet trembling than by Reb Levi Hurvitz's anger, and left the rabbi's house confused. He had to support himself with his cane to prevent himself from falling.

5

Deep in despair, Kalman was on his way to the cemetery to chant memorial prayers, something he had not done since he began to hope that the seamstress would marry him. All the way up Zaretche **Street** Reb Asher-Anshel's statement pecked away at his mind: the first person to deal with the agunah's problem should be the district rabbi. The closer Kalman came to Polotsk Street, where the seamstress lived, the more weak-kneed he felt, and a longing came over him, as though he were a youth. So instead of going uphill to the cemetery, he entered the Zaretche *shul*, where the rabbi of Polotsk Street, Reb David Zelver, prayed.

At the table sat an old congregant wearing brass-rimmed spectacles on the tip of his hairy nose, reading a volume of *Midrash Rabbah*. Kalman approached slowly. The old man eyed the visitor from under thick brows and greeted him with a two-fingered handshake. Kalman took the two fingers, discussed the worshippers and the lack of Torah study in the Zaretche *shul*, and concluded by asking what sort of person was Reb David Zelver. The man at the table hardly said a word and constantly looked at the volume of *Midrash Rabbah* before him. It was obvious that he had many things to tell but did not want to speak ill of anyone. So he muttered as though tongue-tied and said:

"If you've heard of the rabbi who gave permission to carry money on the Sabbath to supposedly save the starving Jewish children of Russia, for your information they were talking about Reb David Zelver. If you've heard of the rabbi who of his own accord forbade the *mohel* Lapidus, scion of the Rokeach family, to perform circumcisions, for your information they were again talking about the Polotsk Street rabbi, Reb David Zelver. The *mohel* has even said that the rabbi is a Bolshevik—but I, I don't want to speak ill of anyone, except to add that though Reb David Zelver is a poor man who has troubles with his children, still he should be able to find some time to study a bit of Midrash with some of the congregants."

"What do you mean a rabbi permitted money to be carried on the Sabbath for the sake of the starving children in Russia? What about the other rabbis, are they cutthroats?" Kalman ran his fingers through his beard and approached the man.

The old man's bulging yellowish and bloodshot eyes stared angrily at Kalman. He saw that he would not be able to get rid of his questioner until he had told him the entire story, and the arguments of both the rabbi and his opponents. The old man put both his hands on the *Midrash Rabbah*, sighing over the time stolen from sacred study; nevertheless, he did not omit one detail:

"This is the way it happened. During the war between the Germans and the Russians there was a great famine in Russia. From the pulpits rabbis and communal leaders requested that the Russian Jews be saved. Vilna worshippers heard the sermons, sighed in sympathy, and slowly collected meager contributions, a penny one day, a penny the next. Reb David Zelver said that he felt like shouting in the streets that this was not the way to save people from starvation. But he controlled himself, reasoning that he was neither a son-in-law of a respectable Vilna rabbinic authority nor a member of the great Rabbinic Council; he was only the youngest of the rabbis in the Vilna suburbs. He had seen only one news photograph of starving children in Russia, the rabbi said. Emaciated, skin and bones, with distended bellies and crooked legs. They looked at him, he said, not with eyes but with the eye sockets of their skulls, and yelled 'Bread!' at him. Unable to remain silent any longer, the next Sabbath morning he went up to the pulpit of this *shul* and ordered the worshippers to leave immediately for home and bring back money on the Sabbath. They obeyed and brought back money on the Sabbath. Ever since then the Vilna Rabbinic Council has been infuriated with him. His chief antagonist is Reb Levi Hurvitz, who feels that the entire desecration of the Sabbath had been in vain. Immediately after collecting the money, the *shul's* trustees ran to the communal offices, under the impression that people were packing bundles there twenty-four hours a day for the hungry Jews of Russia. But the offices were closed. The Zaretche Jews then ran to the officials' homes. The latter took the money quite calmly, for carrying money on the Sabbath was a routine matter for them. The officials said that when a large enough sum would be collected, they would purchase food, and that when enough packages were collected they would be sent to Russia. Reb David, so Reb Levi declared, forced the people to transgress God's law, for Reb David had aspirations of being a Reb Israel Salanter, the famous rabbi who had once given Vilna Jewry permission to eat on Yom Kippur during a cholera epidemic."

"Permitting them to eat on Yom Kippur?" Kalman smacked his lips.

The man with the yellowish eyes gazed at his naive, absolutely ignorant visitor.

"A few decades ago Reb Israel Salanter had his yeshiva right here in the Zaretche *shul*, and Reb David Zelver who worships here and who supposedly considers himself a second Reb Israel wants to follow in his footsteps. When a Jew felt his strength ebbing during the cholera epidemic that Yom Kippur, tasting immediately a bit of cake and whiskey saved his life. But here weeks passed before the packages were sent away. And who knows how much time passed before they arrived? And who knows if the food even reached the dying children and was not taken by the fat commissars who have closed all the *shuls* in Russia and uprooted Judaism? And anyway, what a ridiculous comparison! The Gaon of Vilna, Reb Israel Salanter—and some young man named Reb David Zelver, the local rabbi of Polotsk Street!"

Kalman listened attentively and his cheeks flamed. He then urged the old man to tell him the story about the *mohel* Lapidus, scion of the Rokeach family.

"You want to go rummaging in someone else's garbage, do you?" The man tried to brush Kalman away like a pesky fly. "Do you really relish it that much?" Nevertheless, he did his odd listener a favor and told him about the *mohel* Lapidus, scion of the Rokeach family; in *this* story, however, he sided more with Reb David Zelver:

"A man from Zaretche invited Reb David to a circumcision and gave him the honor of holding the child. The rabbi watched the *mohel* circumcising and noticed that his hands shook. A week later the child's father came to Reb David with a cry that the *mohel* had crippled his son. Reb David went to examine the baby and saw that the *mohel* was indeed responsible. Nevertheless, he gave the

34

matter some thought—perhaps there was a children's epidemic in town. So he sent a letter to the Vilna Rabbinic Council requesting an investigation to see if there was an epidemic raging; if so, then all circumcising should be temporarily halted, in compliance with Jewish law. The Rabbinic Council investigated and found that all other circumcisions had been successful. Reb David then sent a second letter to the Council requesting the *mohel* Lapidus' immediate disqualification. Lapidus, however, is one of the oldest *mohels* in Vilna, a very wealthy man of distinguished lineage—after all, he's Lapidus, scion of the Rokeach family! So the Rabbinic Council was in no rush. Lapidus contended that the child's illness was no fault of his; since the child's father had not mentioned anything unusual, he went ahead with the circumcision. Then the Vilna Rabbinic Council began a new investigation, and it turned out that though there were some difficulties here and there, most of Lapidus' circumcisions were successful. While the Council procrastinated, Lapidus continued cutting. Since he was a rich man whose business was managed by his sons, he ran around all day from hospital to hospital circumcising the children of poor families without fee. Sometimes he even brought the mother a bottle of wine for Kiddush. But Reb David felt that if he remained silent, he would be an accomplice to murder. Come what may, he said, and proclaimed in the Zaretche *shul* that whosoever summoned the *mohel* Lapidus for a circumcision was slaying his own children. The Rabbinic Council did not come to Lapidus' defense; the rabbinic authorities even declared that they too had intended to disqualify him, but were still uncertain if he was to blame. And since then Lapidus has become the rabbi's bitter enemy."

Instead of going to the cemetery, Kalman remained in the *shul* till after the Evening Service. The rabbi, wearing a long shabby gaberdine, was the very last to come in for prayers. A short, slender man of about forty with a blond beard and a sad face, he went to his place without saying a word to anyone. As soon as the prominent householders sitting by the Eastern Wall had finished the Silent Devotion, the prayer leader began to say Kaddish. Kalman approached the old man, who had been assiduously pacing to and fro, as if walking on hot coals.

"Don't you wait until the rabbi finishes praying before you begin the Kaddish?" Kalman asked him.

"In that case, we'd have to wait till tomorrow. And besides, our rabbi is so humble he doesn't *want* us to wait for him," the man laughed, and was the first to leave the *shul*.

The next morning Kalman went up to Zaretche via Polotsk Street where Merl lived. He stopped a few times and breathed deeply, plucking up his courage to visit the seamstress, and kept looking over his shoulder, afraid that a funeral might pass by and drag him by force to the graveyard.

The seamstress greeted him with cold impatience. Since he had last seen her, she had become younger and more beautiful, her eyes brighter, her lips fuller. She had also cut her hair, as though she had declared an end to her agunahood and was now preparing to look for a husband to spite the rabbis who were forbidding her to remarry.

After lengthy preludes, Kalman stammered, "Do you know the district rabbi?"

Again a rabbi? she thought, irritated. Nevertheless, touched by his confused look, his humility and devotion, she asked him to be seated. To demonstrate the rabbi's independence of mind, Kalman told her what he had heard about him, and advised her to go to the Zaretche *shul* after the Evening Service when all the worshippers had gone and Reb David Zelver remained alone.

The seamstress looked at the housepainter, her rekindled eyes smiling brightly: "What good would it do even if the rabbi permitted me to marry? You just told me that the other rabbis don't respect Reb David and that you won't marry without the rabbis' consent."

"I'm no saint," Kalman said. "One rabbi's permission would suffice me and your mother, too." Since the knowing smile in Merl's flashing eyes had become sharper, Kalman said in self-justification: "Well, actually you haven't yet promised to marry me and that's not my intention . . . That is, I *do* want to marry you, but above all I want to see you happy and be like everyone else—free to do as you please and marry whomever you wish."

After Kalman's departure, Merl ceased smiling. Nevertheless, she kept postponing going to the rabbi until one day her former admirer, the market-dealer Moishke Tsirulnik, provided the impetus.

Merl had not seen Moishke since she had moved out of her father's cottage, where her sister Golda and her lazy husband

Shaike had remained and where Moishke was a frequent visitor. She had assumed that this old bachelor and spiteful wretch had already forgotten her. But Moishke Tsirulnik still remembered the old injustice: the seamstress had not married him but Itsik, and had not become his mistress since becoming an agunah. Having heard from Shaike that Merl was about to get married, Moritz felt a fire searing his insides and decided to visit her. He came decked out in a white silk neckerchief and an ivory-handled cane. His unctuous eyes and smooth-shaven, wrinkled face had never flared with such rage. His yellow hair had become even thinner— he obviously spent hours in front of the mirror arranging his hair to conceal his baldness. Although Merl did not respond to his greeting and looked at him with open hatred, he sat down quite comfortably on a chair near her sewing machine and laughed sarcastically:

"Since when have you become so religious? Along with all the other raggle-taggle in the neighborhood you used to sing working-songs and shout 'Down with the Czar!' Now all of a sudden you can't marry without a rabbi? Ah woe, look who you've picked— a housepainter! A bungling wall-smearer. Have you ever seen a professional housepainter doubling as a cemetery cantor? He isn't even a cemetery cantor, but a plain beggar. He bleats out a memorial prayer for a dead man, then sticks out his paw for a handout. He looks like an old repainted horse. He reeks of mold. And even *this* dirty little Jew beggar doesn't want to have you unless the rabbis decree their approval. And what will you call him? Reb Kalman? Reb Kalman, come to bed with me, ha ha ha . . . Just tell me this—won't you be afraid of coming near that gravedigger? He even helps the Jews who wash the corpses . . Ech . . . "

Merl felt chills along the nape of her neck. Nevertheless, she made no reply, did not even turn from the sewing machine. But when he pretended to shiver out of fear and disgust at Kalman's washing the corpses, she cast a contemptuous glance at him:

"I'm neither afraid of someone who washes corpses nor of the corpses themselves. I'd certainly prefer sleeping with a corpse to sleeping with you."

"Compared to this Kalman your Itsik was a prince, even though he didn't have a tooth in his mouth," Moishke Tsirulnik snickered displaying a mouthful of golden teeth. "Listen to me, Merke!

I'm sure your husband is alive—he just doesn't want any part of you. He knows what sort of bargain you are, so he's living with some German woman."

"Get out," the agunah jumped up, seizing the pressing iron. "Get out or I'll split your head open. May you be alive like my Itsik is alive."

Moritz recalled quite clearly that Merl was the first to go out on anti-Czarist demonstrations. Neither Cossacks' whips nor bullets frightened her. He knew that she could remain silent for a year, but when she said something, she meant it.

"But I want to marry you," he said, backing toward the door. "I want you to be my wife, not my mistress. And I won't go begging to a rabbi for permission."

"Drop dead, you lying boaster." She stood before him, the pressing iron raised aloft. "You aren't worth a hair of the cantor's head. Yes, I do want to marry him. And to please him I'm going to turn the world upside down in order to get a rabbi's permission. Get out, you low-down worm, or I'll split your skull open."

Moritz slipped out of the apartment, hellfire smoldering in his eyes. That night the agunah donned a kerchief and went to the Zaretche *shul* to see Reb David Zelver, the rabbi of Polotsk Street.

6

The Evening Service in the Zaretche *shul* was over. The worshippers had dispersed and the *shul* was dark, except for a huge memorial candle burning on the prayerstand whose flame twitched and sputtered and twisted to all sides like a sick man gasping for air. Reb David Zelver stood immobile in the corner next to the Holy Ark, blending into the darkness as though the shadows at his feet had nailed him to the floor. He tried in vain to concentrate on the blessings of the Silent Devotion, and imagined that he heard the Torah weeping in the Holy Ark:

"Once upon a time the Zaretche *shul* used to be crowded with Torah scholars. Reb Israel Salanter led a yeshiva here day and night and all the benches were packed with students of all ages. Woe unto men for their contempt of the Torah! Woe unto such a generation! The study-room is desolate, and the bookcase in the little library is covered with cobwebs. And I, the Torah, adorned with my crown and my golden-lettered mantle, like a bride in white waiting in vain for her bridegroom beneath the canopy, am consigned to loneliness and humiliation in the Holy Ark."

Reb David Zelver heard the Torah sobbing and his heart replied with his own troubled sobs. His twelve-year-old son Yosefl did not want to study. He had befriended a pack of street urchins and spent the day with them roaming about the nearby Zaretche market. But Reb David was in greater agony over his infant, who was so ill only God knew if he would live.

"Cause us to return to thy Torah", Reb David whimpered during the Silent Devotion. "Turn Yosefl's heart back to the Torah. Enhance my family's obedience and respect for me, and I'll enhance the honor of the Torah in this *shul*. How can I demand that my congregants spend their time in Torah study, if my first-born son

does not study? Lord of the universe! I begrudge food for myself in order to pay for his tuition. I'd even sell my *tfillin* to pay his teacher. I'd pray in borrowed *tfillin* so long as my boy studies. Help me, O Lord of the universe!"

Reb David's wife had a weak heart. Doctors asserted that she could have heart failure at any time, and ordered him to keep her at a resort. But how could he afford that if he lacked the money to buy a quart of milk for his sick infant? In winter the rooms were so cold his fingers froze when he turned a page of a book, and mornings after prayers he had to hurry to forcibly bring Yosefl to school. Then, after tending to his sick infant, he went shopping. So as not to jostle with the women, he stood off to a side and the market women charged him as little as they possibly could.

"*Regard our affliction,*" Reb David complained through pressed lips. "Isn't it beneath the Torah's dignity for a rabbi to go shopping? The women groan over my misfortune and say that there is no justice up on high, God forbid. They even slander the rabbis who let me suffer. *Heal us, O Lord, and we shall be healed.* Cure my wife and my ailing baby. Strengthen my wife's weak heart and heal her sick soul. She rebels against you out of depths of bitterness and also wants me to rebel against you. So great is her despair that when I chase Yosefl off to school she tells him to run out and play. She says she doesn't want him to be a rabbi and a miserable pauper like his father. Show her your kindness and remove her anger toward your Torah and toward Torah scholars."

Reb David's body trembled, but he neither budged nor sighed. He stopped whispering, as though waiting for the Torah in the Ark to reply. However, there was stillness all around. The scroll within the Holy Ark constricted itself in the darkness to prevent the rabbi's prayers and complaints from reaching it. With his left hand Reb David gripped the back of the chair in order not to collapse with pain, and with his right he covered his closed eyes lest the flame of the sole memorial light on the prayerstand illumine the dark abyss of his thoughts. But no matter how tightly he shut his eyes and covered them with his hand, he could not dispel the contrary thought that prevented him from praying with devotion.

His wife was furious at the Torah and at Torah scholars for being the cause of his bad fortune; but Reb David was angrier at himself for having become a rabbi instead of an artisan like his father. He earned his living from the Zaretche worshippers' donations and from the pittance provided by Vilna's Rabbinic Council. Reb David did not go to the Council for his wages—his son went. Nor did he attend its meetings—he was not invited. He knew the Rabbinic Council would not increase his allowance, for in the *shuls* of the Vilna suburbs there were local rabbis and poor preachers in profusion. But surely the Vilna rabbinic authorities could have come to his aid—if they recognized him as a full-fledged congregational rabbi, he would get wages and not a pittance as charity. But they said they considered him a young man whose leadership had undermined the honor of the Vilna rabbis. Hence, on his account, they were not obliged to listen to the communal leaders' jibes that there were already too many religious functionaries in Vilna. Wouldn't it have been far better, then, to have become an artisan like his father?

Reb David sank into a sea of darkness. The shadows at his feet crawled over his body and pinned back his shoulders. He felt dizzy and weak in the knees. All day long he had run around without tasting a morsel of food, and now he was standing immersed in prayer. Which benediction had he been reciting now? Reb David uncovered his eyes and faced the memorial candle, as though expecting a reply. He had been saying *Heal us*, requesting a cure for his wife and baby, and his thoughts had led him astray to his old dispute with the local rabbis. Reb David continued to murmur the benedictions of the Silent Devotion, but Reb Levi Hurvitz was caught in the web of his thoughts. Instead of the Torah's consoling voice, he now heard Reb Levi's raging, sarcastic shouts coming from the Holy Ark—Reb Levi Hurvitz, who during meetings of the Rabbinic Council had accused him of aspiring to be a Reb Israel Salanter.

"*Restore our judges as in days of old*. Ah, our judges! Cause the Vilna rabbis and Reb Levi Hurvitz to look kindly upon me. Master of the universe, you know the truth! You know that I did not do it out of conceit or pride but only for the sake of starving Jewish children."

He heard the Holy Ark whispering to him, and imagined the Torah parchment within unfolding:

"My son, humble yourself before your rabbinic colleagues. Admit that you have sinned. Admit that you should not have dared to make rabbinic decisions on your own. And then they will forgive you wholeheartedly and accept you into their midst. Then your family and your congregants will respect you. Then you'll be able to convince the worshippers not to neglect me, the Torah, and not let me freeze here decked out in my mantle, and not let mice gnaw at the orphaned books of Reb Israel Salanter's desolate yeshiva. Go to the Rabbis! They have become grey in the judicial chambers; their grandfathers have sat there, and you, the youngest of them, a stranger in Vilna, have sinned against them. Reb Levi Hurvitz too has suffered, perhaps even more than you. You have your family; your wife and child can get better; your Yosefl can still return to Torah studies. But ever since your youth Reb Levi's wife has been in the asylum and his daughter, too, has been committed. For them there is no more hope. So don't carry enmity against him in your heart. Go to him and tell him that you erred. He will burst into tears and be the first to sympathize with your suffering."

"No, no. I won't go," Reb David pressed his lips to steady his trembling jaw. "I won't humble myself and I won't apologize. Truth is on my side. Judgment is on my side. The law, justice and mercy are on my side. I did not err. What I've said and done is as correct as Torah from Sinai. I shall disregard the rabbis *and* Reb Levi Hurvitz. And if God Almighty sides with them, I'll summon them to a trial in the heavenly tribunal. And if they find for the other side, I am prepared to burn in hell for all eternity and still not regret what I have done. If after hearing me proclaim that money may be carried on the Sabbath only one man contributed one zloty more than he intended to; if one bite of bread reached a Jewish child even a minute sooner—I saved not only a Jewish child but also the honor of the Almighty, and also your honor, O Torah. I saved the Torah's honor to prevent people from saying that our Torah is heartless. *I* am the one in the right. If it were only a matter of foregoing my honor, I would gladly grovel in the dust before Reb Levi Hurvitz. But I don't want truth to grovel in the dust before him. His suffering doesn't impress me. His suffering has made him adamant toward others. No, I do not regret what I've done and I shall not ask for forgiveness."

"If you take that much upon yourself," the Torah replied feebly, as though it were floating via a secret path to other worlds, "then you shouldn't be angry at others for opposing you. Since you've crowned yourself monarch of your own world, you must agree to take the pain and insults that you've already endured and will continue to endure."

After finishing the Silent Devotion, the exhausted Reb David sat down on a bench, palm of hand pressed to his forehead, rapt in thoughts.

At least his quarrel with the Rabbinic Council was subdued; even Reb Levi did not openly persecute him; they only withheld further aid. The *mohel* Lapidus complained to everyone in town that Reb David Zelver was a heretic who stood up for Russia and ordered money to be carried on the Sabbath because he was a Bolshevik. Lapidus' remarks were always replete with rabbinic quotations. You can see, he said, who Reb David Zelver is by the way his brat pals around with the young riffraff. Like father, like son, says the Talmud. Some of the people in town sided with the *mohel*; he even had some supporters among the Zaretche residents. The trustees of the Zaretche *shul* looked askance at their rabbi because the Rabbinic Council had washed their hands of him; even the *shul's* worshippers, who had come to his aid at the eve of every holiday, had lately become tightfisted. Nevertheless, this didn't satisfy the *mohel*, who had sworn not to rest until he uprooted the rabbi from Vilna's midst.

The waters encompass my soul, Reb David thought and noticed that his palm was wet with tears. The lengthy prayer had brought him no solace. His heart did not demand a silent prayer; it demanded a heaven-rending scream.

"Hear my prayer, O Merciful One who hears the prayers of the impoverished," he lamented, momentarily stirring up the dark *shul's* silence like an echo spreading over water.

"Answer me, O Merciful One, who answers the brokenhearted," he continued quoting from the penitential hymns.

The flame in the memorial candle sputtered, as if Reb David's cry had awakened some hidden soul in it. A huge black shadow fled from under Reb David's feet and with one leap attached itself to the lamp hanging from the ceiling.

"Answer me, O Merciful One," Reb David swayed with his prayer stand, *"who answers the dejected in spirit."*

Suddenly he heard a thin drawn-out wail, a shy feminine voice opposite him in the darkness. Reb David quickly turned to the Ark to see if the Torah was responding to his cries with one of its own; but the whimpering and sobbing came from the entrance. He saw a shape evolving among the benches, and discerned a woman's kerchief by the scant reddish light of the memorial candle. A thought flashed: perhaps the Torah scroll had donned the black raiments of a rejected bride and was revealing himself to him in the dark and desolate *shul.*

"Who are you?" he cried in a voice not his own.

7

When the agunah entered the night-darkened *shul,* a gloomy stillness hovered before her. As her eyes gradually became accustomed to the darkness, she saw a man standing next to the Holy Ark, facing the wall. Since Kalman had told her that the rabbi was always the last one to leave the *shul,* she realized that this man must be the rabbi. While waiting for the rabbi to finish praying, she thought how unfortunate it was that she wasn't as religious as her mother and never recited the women's prayers of supplication. When one pours out one's heart to God, one undoubtedly feels much better. Kalman was right not to want to marry without rabbinic permission. He was a fine, devoted man whose only wish was to make her happy.

Merl saw the rabbi finishing the Silent Devotion and sitting down on a bench. She wanted to take one step closer to him, but since he hadn't seen her entering she was afraid of startling him. She had better leave and wait for him by the courtyard door. Suddenly, a bitter scream came from the corner. The rabbi had said something in Hebrew, and then in Yiddish. "Answer me, O Merciful One." Merl also felt a cry tearing itself from her throat, like a fire windblown from one hut to another; but she bit her lips and restrained herself. The rabbi, however, cried even louder and tore out of her anguished heart the wail she had suppressed for years. The frightened rabbi shouted, "Who are you?" and she approached him crying:

"I am an agunah, rabbi, an agunah. For more than fifteen years I've waited for my husband to come back from the war. But he has not come and I cannot wait any longer. I can't bear my loneliness any longer, so I've come to you for help. I live right here on Polotsk Street. Help me, rabbi, help me."

Merl spoke without stopping, afraid that the rabbi might run away before she had finished. She rambled on confusedly, repeating herself and swallowing many words with her tears. His hand pressed to his temple, Reb David listened in silence, then finally replied sadly:

"You shouldn't have come to me. I'm only a district rabbi. The Rabbinic Council has given Reb Levi Hurvitz the responsibility for problems like yours. Have you already seen him?"

"Yes," Merl replied dispiritedly, as though the rabbi's voice had extinguished her cry. "Some people I know went to see him, but he refused to intervene."

"Refused," Reb David muttered glumly, as if hearing bad news. "Reb Levi refused because there were no witnesses. If he can't do anything, I surely can't do anything, either. I have enough troubles of my own, and I've suffered enough for others. I dare not impose additional torments on my wife and little children. I have a wife and children, a wife and children," he kept repeating, as though trying to convince himself that he ought not intervene in this affair.

Reb David stood thrust into the dark corner next to the Holy Ark. Merl did not see his face, but sensed the fear in his choked voice. She was sorry for him and angry at her family. What did Kalman and her mother and sisters want of her? She didn't want to marry anyway!

Merl heard someone running quickly in the Zaretche *shul* courtyard. A young lad burst in and cried into the darkness:

"Papa, Mottele's gasping again!"

The rabbi tore out of the corner so quickly Merl scarcely had time to get out of the way. Reb David took hold of the boy and feverishly began to feel him all over, afraid that the boy, too, had lost his breath while running to the *shul*.

"And Mama?" Reb David said.

"When Mama jumped out of bed to help Mottele, her heart began to pound. She told me you should get the doctor."

"Who's with Mama and Mottele?" the rabbi said. "No one?"

"No one," the boy shouted. "Why do you stay away so long? Mama says you stay away much too long."

"What should I do? What should I do?" the rabbi faced the Holy Ark, asking the Torah to help him, then quickly turned to the agunah. "I must run to my sick child and wife. Do me a favor,

46

run down and call the doctor. He lives at the corner of Poplava Street. I can't compensate you, but the Almighty will. Yosefl, go with the lady. Show her where the doctor lives."

"I know where he lives," Merl went to the door. "Rabbi, you go back to your apartment with your boy, and I'll come right back with the doctor."

Merl was the first to rush out of the *shul*, followed by the rabbi and his son. The *shul* was left open and the memorial candle on the prayerstand burned with absolute stillness. The Torah remained forlorn in the Ark and the shadows of the tables, benches and massive lamps stood in mute silence, as though the entire *shul* shared the ominous thought that another ordeal was awaiting the rabbi of Polotsk Street.

The doctor, a friendly rotund man with a trimmed grey beard, had a habit of coughing at the beginning and end of each conversation. He tested his vocal cords as if in addition to being a doctor he was also the assistant cantor in the modern synagogue where he worshipped. If not for his pince-nez, the women wouldn't have had an ounce of respect for this unpretentious man.

When Merl arrived, the doctor was already preparing for bed: he had removed his stiff collar and his suspenders were dangling. Hearing that Reb David wanted him at once, he coughed and grumbled, "It's nothing new that their baby is sick." Nevertheless, he dressed, swiftly gathered his instruments into a little leather bag and with quick small steps marched with Merl to the rabbi's house.

"The poor keep making children, and nothing more. The rebbetsin has a weak heart and she gave birth to a premature, nearly aborted baby."

When Merl and the doctor entered the rabbi's apartment, the terrified rabbi was holding the baby and whispering, "Mottele, Mottele." But the baby, its yellowish mouth awry, uttered no sound. On the bed lay a fully-dressed woman with eyes shut, breathing with difficulty. At her side stood Yosefl, crying, "Mama, mama."

While the doctor was preparing his instruments, Reb David placed the baby on his mother's bed and undid his diapers. Merl meanwhile looked around the large apartment.

They had entered through a long, winding corridor. The rabbi had apparently intended to run a well-established rabbinic household with a large family. But the big rooms were empty, unheated and without electricity. The entire family occupied only the bedroom which also doubled as a dining room. Everything in the room was bare; the bookcase had neither doors nor curtain; the table had no cloth, and even the rebbetsin's wrinkled pillows had no pillowcases.

Poverty peeps out of every corner, Merl thought. Just then the baby screamed—the doctor had given him an injection. The rebbetsin opened her eyes and raised her head, as though her infant's scream had given her new life. She scanned the apartment slowly and stopped when the cold black pupils of her eyes spotted Merl. The rebbetsin sighed and shut her eyes again. The rabbi, with a pathetic smile, whispered to the doctor, who was nervously adjusting the pince-nez on his nose, coughing and grumbling peevishly. The rebbetsin groaned and sighed again, as though seeing through her closed eyes and comprehending the whispering.

"Rest and nothing more," the doctor said, greatly distressed. "Rebbetsin, you must sleep. You and your baby need rest."

He gestured to Merl to follow him. The confused rabbi looked so guiltily at the doctor that he forgot to thank the woman. Once outside, the doctor expressed his vexation:

"They call you in the middle of the night. This time, too, he postponed payment for Friday, when he gets his wages. By then he'll probably call me two more times, but they'll only pay me for one visit and no more."

Merl bade the doctor goodnight and returned to her apartment. The rabbi hadn't given her the permission, but he had shown her that there were people with greater afflictions than hers.

8

The next morning the seamstress returned to the rabbi's apartment to inquire about the sick infant. When she entered, the rabbi was holding his son's hand, attempting to convince him to go to *cheder*. Yosefl stamped his feet and shouted that he did not want to go. "All the other schools are already on vacation. Only the Yavne school is still in session. So we went on strike, and I wrote, 'We want freedom!' on the blackboard. When the teacher found out it was me, he scolded me in front of the entire class: 'At least the other little rebels who plague me are children of well-to-do fathers who pay their tuition. But I don't intend to be plagued by you! Your father still owes me money from last year. I see you're setting out on the same path as your dandy daddy. He opposes all the rabbis and the Torah, too, and you are already following in his footsteps.' And that's why I don't want to study in *cheder* any more!" Yosefl cried, attempting to tear himself out of his father's hand.

"So where will you go? To the marketplace? There you'll grow up a boor!" the father pleaded.

"Let the boy go play," the rebbetsin raised her head from the pillow. "He doesn't have any other pleasures in life. So he'll become a rabbi a minute later."

"That very minute he might miss an opportunity for a position. When a post opens up he dare not be a minute late, for someone else will snap it up."

"That's exactly what I want him to do—miss an opportunity for a rabbinic post. Let him be what he likes, so long as he's not a rabbi," the rebbetsin said, sitting up.

The rabbi was ashamed that the agunah had heard this; but

since the doctor had ordered peace and quiet, he was also afraid of angering his wife.

"Eydl, Eydl," the rabbi pleaded.

"I don't want to be *eydl*.* I'd rather be coarse." Her kerchief slid forward, and her thick beautiful hair—which showed she was much younger than her agonized face indicated—tumbled out on the pillow. "When my mother named me after Grandma Eydl, she didn't know what woes would lie in store for me. Go, Yosefl, play to your heart's content. If the rich men's children are on vacation, you'll be on vacation, too."

Exhausted and embarrassed, Reb David released Yosefl's hand and the boy dashed out of the house. The baby woke up and began bawling in his cradle. The rabbi wanted to put the milkbottle into his mouth, but the rebbetsin pulled it out of his hands:

"I'll do that. Go shopping, David. Other rebbetsins send their servants to the market, and I have to send the rabbi."

"Rebbetsin!" Merl said, not taking her eyes from the rabbi who shrank in humiliation and pain. "That's exactly where I'm going. While shopping for myself, I'll shop for you, too."

"God bless you," the rebbetsin said happily. "Have you come to the rabbi to consult him on a point of law? I'm so flustered I forget that that's my husband's duty. Don't be afraid of me. I'm not so terrible, even though the rabbis. . ."

"Eydl, this is the woman who brought the doctor last night. Don't you recognize her?"

"How could I have seen who was here last night if I fainted?" the rebbetsin said, gazing at the agunah. "May you and your husband and children never know sorrow. Thank God that strangers are more considerate than the Vilna rabbis. David, give the lady some money for shopping."

"I don't have any," the rabbi said. "I'll go myself. The shopkeepers will give me credit until I get my wages."

"Your wages," the rebbetsin laughed drily. "An assistant shamesh in a tiny *shul* earns more."

"Eydl, Eydl!"

"Don't worry, rebbetsin," Merl interrupted. "I'll pay for it now and you can repay me when you have it. What do you need?"

---

* *eydl*: tender, refined

"I won't go along with this," the rabbi said, trembling. "It isn't necessary. Absolutely not."

"Yes, it *is* necessary," the rebbetsin shouted, then pressed her hand to her heart and continued feebly: "Don't be angry. If it were only for me, I wouldn't let my husband go marketing. If it were only for me, I wouldn't borrow money from a woman I don't know, even if it meant my death—for I'm just as good as the other Vilna rebbetsins. But there's nothing in the world I wouldn't do for my child."

Merl quickly left the apartment before the rabbi had a chance to stop her and hurried to the market. What a nonsensical idea had come over her, she smiled. Marrying! She ought rather devote herself to the rabbi and his family. Poor man, he was a tender-hearted soul with an embittered wife. The farther Merl walked the more excited she became. Her mother in the old-age home wasn't dependent upon her, and Merl earned more than she needed for her living expenses. She would tend to the rebbetsin and her child. She would be helping a fine family, have a house to visit regularly, and mitigate her own loneliness.

Loaded with packages, Merl joyfully rushed back from the market to the rabbi's apartment, as though her own family were awaiting her. But the rabbi was not in the house and the rebbetsin sat on the bed tightlipped, gazing at the agunah with wrath in her eyes.

"Thank you," the rebbetsin said coldly. "Since you've already made the purchases, it's too late. As soon as we get our wages I'll send my boy over to pay you back."

"No rush," Merl roamed about the room with homey familiarity. "I'll lend you another couple of zlotys to buy milk for the baby. Then you can repay everything at once. If you don't mind, I'll bring you some pillowcases, towels and sheets. I'm a seamstress and have linen to spare."

"No," the rebbetsin replied crisply. "I don't want to take a thing from you. My husband was right in not wanting you to go shopping for us. If I had known before, I wouldn't have permitted it."

"You're talking to me as if I were an apostate or a loose woman," Merl stammered.

"No, you're just very shrewd. I was wondering why an absolute stranger should pity us. How come the sudden miracle? So it turns out that there are no do-gooders after all. Everyone has something up his sleeve. Not only don't you feel sorry for us, but to top it off you're our worst enemy. You see our condition. It's my husband who's to blame for everything, because he doesn't mind his own business. Some fanatics even say that we're starving because he let people carry money on Sabbath, and that our baby is sick because he disqualified a prominent *mohel*. I don't believe this; I believe my husband is right. But the rabbis and the rich householders are our enemies. Do you want to bring more grief down upon us? All the rabbis have forbidden you to marry, and you want my husband to permit it? The town will stone us."

"I swear I have no ulterior motive," Merl said, scarcely able to restrain her tears, "I didn't dream of marrying again, but I've been persuaded. But now I don't even want to hear of it. I went to the market for you because I saw that the rabbi is a fine person and a truly saintly man. It hurt me that such a noble man has to demean himself and deal with the gentile wagoners and the market peddlers."

"One might think that you had a liking for my husband," the rebbetsin screamed. "And I see that he likes you, too. My sage stood right up for you. He said you didn't run to the doctor last night and the market today in order to get a rabbinic permission from him. God forbid!" she said sarcastically, as if imitating her innocent husband. "You did this, he says, out of pure goodness and compassion. Nevertheless, he says, he shouldn't accept any favors from you, lest it blind him."

"You see, rebbetsin, you see," Merl smiled through her tears. "The rabbi realizes that I had no intentions of tricking him into giving me permission to marry. I swear to you by my life that this was not my purpose. All I wanted was to help you in some way."

"Perhaps. Perhaps," the rebbetsin said with lowered eyes, as though unable to look directly at so brazen a liar. "Perhaps you didn't intend to benefit from this. But I know my husband. He's as stubborn as he is quiet. He'll forgive me, but he'll wage war to the death with the entire world. I see he's already debating with himself whether or not to give you the permission. What a hard time I had getting him to tell me who you are and what you wanted. I know him. I know him well. He's already planning to stand up for you against the whole world. So if you really pity us as much as you claim to, and if you don't want our last few pennies to be taken from us and have my husband removed from his post—don't ever come to see him again. Go away."

The rebbetsin did not tell Reb David what had happened between her and the agunah. Judging by Eydl's look, her silence and her pressed lips, Reb David sensed that his wife had driven the agunah from the house. A few days later, when Yosefl brought the few pennies from the Rabbinic Council, his mother gave him some money and told him to bring it to the seamstress on Polotsk Street.

"Tell her I'm repaying the debt. I ask her forgiveness a thousand times and beg her not to take offense." The rebbetsin looked at her husband with irritation. "It's quite possible that the agunah did everything out of pure goodness. But with a husband like you, one has to be a witch and scare people off."

9

Reb David Zelver knew that he should have been glad that his wife had saved him from another ordeal. But he could not forget how the agunah had wept in the *shul*, nor that it was his fault that his wife had insulted and driven the unfortunate woman away.

Reb David always made a reckoning of the troubles his stubbornness caused him. Nevertheless, he did it with a kind of sweet agony and quiet joy that made all his limbs tremble. Indeed, it was his fear of contention that gave him the strength to wrangle. He would blame himself as soon as he sensed fear impelling him to step aside in order to avoid new troubles. He considered himself cowardly and unworthy as long as he did not stand up both to the majority and to the fear hidden in his heart. During a dispute he never raised his voice and did not seek supporters, for that would be demeaning his own self-respect and integrity. He did what he thought correct, then accepted the persecutions silently and with quiet obstinacy. Now he was in torment because his fear of a new controversy was greater than his fear of becoming involved.

Nevertheless, the fear of aggravating his family's situation was greater than both his hurt pride and his compassion for the agunah. Reb David, however, was a passionate believer; he had absolute faith that God reckoned his every word and thought and weighed his every deed. A man had to find his own way according to the law of the Torah; but on the other hand, he thought, he should not forget that on occasion fulfilling a commandment meant transgressing it. Such subtleties could be explained only through analysis of the Torah's intent, common sense and honesty. One frequently received an unexpected heavenly sign that indicated the course of one's future conduct.

Reb David sought the deeper meaning in the coincidence that his Mottele had fallen ill again just when the agunah had been in the *shul* and that she had played a part in saving the child. Was it a heavenly portent to free her of her loneliness, or was it a test not to be led astray by the desire to reciprocate her help? He did not know whether to listen to his wife, or whether the opposite was expected of him. It seemed to Reb David that when he leaned toward granting permission, his sick baby's health improved; and when the opposing view prevailed, the infant began to gasp for breath. Holding the baby in his hands, he turned pages of volumes in his bookcase. The baby cried and the father, lost in thought, rocked it, as though weighing the decision—in favor of the agunah or against her.

After the Evening Service, Reb David remained in the *shul* even longer than usual. When the worshippers departed, he went into the adjoining library, still full of books from Reb Israel Salanter's time. With candle in hand, he climbed up a little ladder and removed huge dusty tomes devoted to responsa concerning agunahs, and studied them for hours on end.

Reb David remembered everything that the agunah had told him, but since he had immersed himself in this question, he wanted clarification on many points. But until he reached a decision, he did not want the agunah to know, lest she come to complain and perhaps influence him with her weeping. Moreover, he had no way of contacting her. He did not send his son to her, for fear that his wife might find out, and he certainly did not want to go himself.

A few days after Merl's talk with the rebbetsin, Kalman came in to ask her how the matter was proceeding. The seamstress sat by her sewing machine with a stony expression on her face. Sharp lines edged the corners of her compressed lips, as though she had mercilessly indicted herself and decided that it served her right. Merl was more composed now; the crying spell prompted by the rebbetsin's remarks had ceased, but she could not forgive herself for having begged for the permission. I begged for it, I begged for it, the thought pierced her mind like a thousand needles. It served her right. For when she intended to help the rebbetsin, the latter had suspected her of wanting to bribe the rabbi.

Merl calmly told Kalman everything that had taken place and gazed at him coldly: once and for all she was asking him to leave her alone.

Kalman retreated silently. Ah woe, he sighed when he reached the street, he had lost a treasure. No, he would not submit. From Merl's words he gathered that the rabbi had not refused her outright. And even if the rebbetsin feared that her husband would again oppose the rabbis, the matter should not be dropped—not by any means.

Kalman entered the Zaretche *shul* for the Evening Service, waited until the quorum had dispersed, and then introduced himself to the rabbi as the man who wanted to marry the agunah. Reb David's silence encouraged him to relate the entire story and accent the fact that all the other women whose husbands had served in the annihilated 11th Company had remarried. But since the seamstress was a modest woman and had lived happily with her husband, she had wasted away for fifteen and a half years, awaiting her husband's return.

"How do you know they were happy together?" the rabbi asked.

"Everyone knows that. And besides, can't you see we're talking about one of the finest women in the world?"

The rabbi was silent, and Kalman had enough sense to depart and leave him alone in the *shul*. However, he returned the next evening and the rabbi once again inquired about the happy relationship between the agunah and her missing husband. This information was crucial for the judgment, Reb David said, and asked if there were any witnesses that they loved each other.

"If the agunah had not loved her husband, she wouldn't have waited for him almost sixteen years," Kalman said, "for until recently she hadn't been that observant. And it's obvious that he had loved her. First, all one has to do is look at her, and secondly, half the town knows how much he loved her. If her husband was alive I'm sure he would have returned to her on foot, even from behind the Hills of Darkness."

On the third night, Reb David sat once again in the *shul's* crowded little library consulting the works of noted rabbinic authorities; when he grew tired of turning pages and reading he looked at the flame of the candle and whispered:

"Master of the Universe, the responsa do not contain the information I seek—but your Torah bids us to have compassion. My heart, too, is torn to pieces out of compassion for the lonely woman, for I too know the meaning of suffering. When one of the Rabbi of Kovno's children used to get sick he would pray to God to help him because he was occupied with laws pertaining to agunahs. And I have a feeling that whenever I think about freeing her from the bonds of agunahood, my Mottele's health improves; and when I change my mind out of fear for a new dispute, my Mottele takes a turn for the worse. No one quarreled with the Rabbi of Kovno, but me they will persecute. I realize that I'm not as important in Vilna as Reb Levi Hurvitz, the appointed authority over agunahs. So my self-sacrifice will have to be even greater—and I *shall* display self-sacrifice."

Reb David turned away from the burning candle and resumed reading.

He would have to base the permission wholly upon a decision by Mordecai ben Hillel in his volume *Mordecai*, which in turn was based on a decision by Rabbi Eliezer of Verdun. Nevertheless, all the early authorities disputed Rabbi Eliezer of Verdun, and Joseph Caro's compendium, *Bet Joseph*, disagreed with Rabbi Eliezer more passionately than all the others. So should he then use as his precedent one early codifier? Reb David stood and paced around the room. Come what may! If no other rabbi wanted to take upon himself the responsibility, then he, the rabbi of Polotsk Street, would permit the agunah to remarry.

He heard steps in the empty *shul* and shivered. His eyes narrowed. Had someone come again to inform him of trouble in his house? He turned quickly and saw the man who wanted to marry the agunah standing in the other room. Reb David stared at the candle's flame and measured each word:

"Go tell the agunah that she is permitted to marry."

"She doesn't want to anymore," Kalman drawled with a grieved voice. "She told me point-blank to leave her alone."

"Tell her I want her to come see me immediately. I'm asking her to come and save my child."

Kalman left quickly without saying a word. Reb David took the candle and went from the library to the large empty *shul*.

"The rabbi wants you to come see him immediately in the *shul*. His child is in danger again," Kalman burst into the seamstress' apartment with a cry. Lying in a subdued voice was more difficult than shouting; and he was afraid to tell the truth lest the seamstress drive him away.

I've got an assassin's heart, Merl thought, dashing ahead of

Kalman down the stairs. Just because the rebbetsin insulted me, I've stopped taking an interest in her sick infant.

The rabbi again stood by the Holy Ark, but this time he faced the entrance, expecting her.

"Rabbi, what happened to your baby?" she gasped.

"I've given the matter consideration and permit you to marry."

"I'm no longer thinking about getting married," Merl glanced furiously at Kalman, who stood at a distance, as though afraid she would strike him.

"You *are* thinking about getting married," the rabbi shouted. "You've been waiting for fifteen years and I understand you don't want to wait anymore. Will you give me your word that if I don't give you permission to marry you'll continue to remain an observant agunah?"

"I can't promise anything. I'm not going to be a sheep any longer," the agunah's eyes flashed and a dry fire raged in her voice, as though a sinful dybbuk were talking from within her.

"In other words you're going to marry without rabbinic permission, or simply live with a man without getting married. And you'll maintain that the Torah is to blame. Therefore, I'd like you to know that the Torah is not to blame and that you may marry," the rabbi shouted, facing the Holy Ark, as though commanding the Torah within to obey him, too. "I also have suffered and continue to suffer from people's cruelty. But nevertheless I know that the Torah is not responsible, even though Torah scholars are often blind to other people's misfortunes."

"Your wife said that you might suffer on account of me," Merl retreated, frightened. "You might be removed from your position."

"Don't worry about my position," the rabbi shook with anger. "With God's help, I'll take care of my position. No matter how great my suffering will be at the hand of men for permitting you to marry, I'd be punished more severely at the hand of heaven if I withheld permission."

"Your wife will curse me," the seamstress whispered.

"If the matter isn't spread all over town, the rabbi will not suffer," Kalman interrupted, his voice trembling as he approached. "We can get married quietly, without fanfare."

"That's right. If it isn't publicized, the rabbis will remain silent," Reb David replied feebly. "I wish you the best of luck."

Merl let Kalman lead her out of the *shul* as though she were ill.

She said nothing on the way home, and maintained her silence two days later when her sisters visited her. Kalman informed them that Merl had already received permission to marry, praise God, but she was still unwilling. Guteh and Golda then wept on Merl's shoulders again, recounting Kalman's attributes and contrasting them with the faults of their good-for-nothing husbands; they once more invoked their old mother in the old-age home, who daily awaited the good news that her daughter would not have to remain an agunah forever.

Merl realized that her sisters would consider her mad if she told them the truth: that she didn't want to marry now in order to avoid bringing trouble down upon Reb David. From Merl's crushed silence it was clear that she agreed to everything—if only she were left alone.

10

Reb Yoshe, head shamesh of Vilna's Main Synagogue, also performed marriages. Tall and broad-shouldered, he had a white beard down to his belt and a bristly leonine mustache. Reb Yoshe was eating when Kalman Maytess appeared and with assumed formality asked to be married. The head shamesh sized up his visitor with an experienced eye and concluded that this was a poor man's wedding.

"Bring a voucher from a Vilna rabbi that you and the woman are permitted to marry," he grumbled, waving his hand.

The visitor played nervously with the cane in his hand. "I didn't bring such a voucher with me," he stammered, "but if it's absolutely necessary, I can easily bring one from the rabbi of Polotsk Street, Reb David Zelver."

"A note written by him is good for you-know-what," Reb Yoshe said, twisting his bristly leonine mustache, as though gnawing and sucking on a marrow bone. "Go bring a voucher from a real rabbi."

Kalman departed; but he searched and sniffed until he discovered that there was no love lost between the head shamesh and Zalmanke, the assistant shamesh of Vilna's Main Synagogue. Zalmanke complained that Reb Yoshe did not let him go near a marriage ceremony, and that he even kept him away when rich tourists from abroad came to visit the Synagogue. Kalman, therefore, tried to strike up a friendship with the assistant shamesh, and in passing told him that he was planning to get married. He wanted him to officiate and not the head shamesh, for he liked Reb Zalmanke more than that arrogant cutthroat, Reb Yoshe. Kalman also told Zalmanke that his wife-to-be was a prominent woman whose husband had fallen in the last war more than fifteen years ago.

Nevertheless, she did not want to marry just anyone but was waiting for the right man. She had received permission from Reb David Zelver who sided with the poor and with the assistant shamoshim, not like the other Vilna rabbis who sided with the head shamesh. If a note was absolutely necessary, he could bring one longer than the Scroll of Esther. But Zalmanke neither asked nor intended to ask. Showing the head shamesh that the assistant shamesh, too, was somebody, was satisfaction enough.

Kalman hired a gentile woman to clean his apartment, which had been neglected since he had become a widower. He lived in an outlying district and none of the neighbors invited to the wedding knew the bride or her family. Merl's two sisters came without their husbands. The elder, Guteh, didn't want her sot to have an excuse to become soused; and Golda, the youngest, did not take her loafer, because he was Moishke Tsirulnik's pal. Ever since Merl had lifted a pressing iron against Moishke for badgering her, he had become her open enemy.

Because the bride's old mother Kayle had swollen legs, Kalman thoughtfully hired a drozhky for her. Seeing her, Guteh and Golda burst into tears, as though Kayle had come to say farewell before departing for the next world. Merl's bemused silence made her seem younger and more robust, and Kalman's neighbors could not stop wondering how such a two-bit house-smearer who worked but one day a year managed to land such a beauty.

The assistant shamesh wanted the ceremony to be as impressive as the ones at which Reb Yoshe officiated. Short, thin and almost beardless, Zalmanke could not lord it over others like the towering head shamesh. In compensation, he swayed and rocked like Reb Yoshe and devotedly chanted the blessings; and Kalman the widower piously swayed with him, as though he were marrying a woman for the tenth time at least.

Suddenly Golda pinched Guteh and gestured silently to the bride.

Pale, proud and dejected, like a princess among beggars, Merl stared at the slender assistant shamesh and at her bridegroom, the house-painter and cemetery functionary. Her eyes flashed with the old dark fire and her cheeks reddened. In high spirits, she gaily turned her head. Her mouth opened, and her two sisters saw that she was about to burst into laughter. A bad business! The wild goat in her had emerged again. Then the same idea struck both sisters simultaneously. They fell on their sister's neck, wailing:

"Merke, we hope you have better luck than us," and clung to her until they suffocated her laughter.

Merl did not laugh the rest of the evening, but only smiled with moist eyes, stroking her mother's hair. Kayle sat with her swollen hands on her knees and looked on, confused. She sensed an element of haste to the affair. The fact that rabbinic permission had been granted was not at all evident.

The couple agreed that Kalman would move into Merl's Polotsk Street apartment. Actually, Kalman had voiced the decision on his own, and his wife, silent all along, merely nodded her consent. Kalman had reckoned that since Merl had steady customers on Polotsk Street she could not move; but since he always roamed about on the painter's exchange opposite the wood market waiting for a job, he didn't necessarily have to live in his former apartment. Her small place would be rather crowded, to be sure; but that would be no drawback if they were happy. And if they prospered they could always look for a larger apartment on the same street.

Kalman hired a peasant to move his belongings to Polotsk Street. The wagon slogged along for half a day, inching its way from one end of town to the other. Kalman, following on foot, brooded all the while whether Reb David Zelver's permission sufficed, and only when the porter was climbing up the stairs to Merl's apartment did he finally convince himself that it was more than enough.

"If one hundred twenty years from now they won't let us into the Garden of Eden," he joked once all his belongings were inside, "we'll get in by hanging on to the rabbi's coattails. For he'll surely go to heaven and have a place of honor above all the other Vilna rabbis."

Merl stared wide-eyed at her old sage. This she had never expected. Kalman was the one who had whipped up the entire stew with the permission and worked feverishly to make her his wife. What more did he want? Was all this really necessary? She smiled bitterly and went to the window.

Since her second meeting with the rabbi, when he had ordered her to get married, she could not begin sewing until she had seen Reb David, whom she took to be forty or forty-two, leading his son to *cheder*. However, today she had not seen them, and was constantly drawn to the window. Perhaps the infant was sick again, requiring the rabbi to attend to his ailing wife. He had no devoted friends and neighbors, and accepted no help from her because of the permission. She had to be even more careful of the rebbetsin, for if she discovered her husband's deed she would make his life miserable.

Kalman sensed that his joke about hanging on to the rabbi's coattails was improper and sought to justify his remark. But before he said a word, he saw his wife—just two days after the wedding— sitting by the window, tears streaming down her eyes.

11

During his first quarrel with Reb Yoshe, Zalmanke informed
the head shamesh that henceforth he thumbed his nose at him.
He was performing weddings on his own. He had brought under
the bridal canopy a widower and an agunah who had received
permission to marry from Reb David Zelver. So if Reb Yoshe
thought he was riding high because he had the trustees of the Main
Synagogue and the Rabbinic Council on his side, for his information
God was not napping and he, Zalmanke, had Reb David on his
side, as well as the distinguished householder, Kalman Maytess,
and several other prominent persons.

The head shamesh immediately remembered the man who had
a voucher to get married from the rabbi of Polotsk Street; once
he had told him to bring a voucher from an authentic rabbi, the
man hadn't shown up again. Which meant that Reb David, who had
once permitted Jews to carry money on the Sabbath, had now
perpetrated an even greater abomination and given permission
for an agunah to marry. The assistant shamesh he would deal with
personally, Reb Yoshe thought. He'd throw that presumptuous
lout out of the Main Synagogue on his ear. But Reb David would
have to be taught a lesson by Reb Levi Hurvitz, the appointed
rabbinic authority over agunahs.

Lately, however, Reb Levi Hurvitz had ceased participating
in communal affairs, and rarely came to the rabbinic courtroom—
for he had brought his daughter Tsirele home from the insane
asylum.

Reb Levi had given up hope that his wife would ever be restored
to health. From the asylum they had transferred her to a nearby
Jewish village where incurable melancholics were kept. Every
month Reb Levi sent part of his wages to the Jewish villager who

cared for the sick rebbetsin. But his daughter Tsirele's condition had improved lately. Once she had run wild in her father's house, smashing windows and wanting to run out of the house stark naked. Now she had become still as a dove. A faint but clear smile shone on her astonished face, as though after a deep, dream-filled sleep. The doctors had informed Reb Levi that there was a chance she might get well. Deciding to take the risk, Reb Levi removed his daughter from the hospital.

At home, Tsirele's clear smile immediately faded. Reb Levi noted with anxiety that she gazed at the walls, the furniture, and the bookshelves with trepidation. His sad and frightened only daughter looked like a lost soul suspended between heaven and earth. Nevertheless, she was quiet and calm now. Perhaps this was natural, the rabbi consoled himself. A man freed from a dark cell cannot immediately adjust to daylight, either. Perhaps in time she would get used to her home again. Consequently, Reb Levi walked about on tiptoes in order not to disturb or irritate his daughter who continually sat in her room.

Reb Levi's brothers-in-law had many children; in every family there was one Tsirele, named after the old rebbetsin, their common grandmother. During Tsirele's childhood, her best friend had been Reb Asher-Anshel's daughter Tsirele. When his ill daughter had returned home from the asylum, Reb Levi told her that her cousin Tsirele was already a mother of three children. Would she perhaps like to see her or another old friend? For a long while Tsirele gazed uncomprehendingly at her father. Suddenly her eyes filled with mute fear and her small body trembled. Without another word, Reb Levi slipped out of the room.

Despite the fact that the sick girl no longer ran wild, Reb Levi did not leave her alone for fear that she might do some harm during his absence. He never went out unless the cleaning woman, Khiyeneh, was in the house. And even when she was there, Reb Levi was on pins and needles throughout his stay in the *shul*. During prayers he ceased his usual pacing. He apparently wanted to rid himself of this habit in order not to do this at home and frighten Tsirele. At the end of the service he was the first to leave the *shul*.

Accustomed to seeing a light on all night in Reb Levi's house, the neighbors asked Khiyeneh why they were off at night and why it was so quiet.

Khiyeneh stammered and finally sighed that the rabbi had a

guest—his daughter from the asylum. "Why didn't you tell us?" the neighbors said, overjoyed, and began tiptoing about the courtyard, too. They wanted to forget their old irritation at Reb Levi for criticizing the courtyard's lack of piety. Now things were different. When a neighbor returned late at night, he stood in the empty courtyard and looked up to the rabbi's darkened windows, as though knowing that Reb Levi sat there in the dark, his ears cocked for the slightest sound from his daughter's room.

But Reb Yoshe knew nothing of the change that had taken place in Reb Levi's house and in his temperament. On his way to Shlomo Kissen's courtyard, Reb Yoshe imagined how furious Reb Levi would be at Reb David's latest abomination, and how he would hurriedly pace around the rooms. Ah, would he run around! Reb Yoshe chuckled quietly, and swung open the door to the rabbi's apartment. But his greeting stuck in his throat. Before he had a chance to say a word, the rabbi raised himself from his deep armchair at the head of the table, placed his forefinger on his lips and said: "Shh!"

The head shamesh with the long white beard and the leonine mustache looked around the apartment and saw nothing except the closed door to the adjoining room. He shrugged, sat down opposite the rabbi and told him the entire story, relating everything he knew and everything he assumed. Reb Levi, pale and upset, at first listened unwillingly, impatiently, but from minute to minute his glance sharpened and his astonishment grew. When the shamesh had finished his story, Reb Levi once more sank into his armchair and murmured with lowered head:

"A man recently came to me, followed by two sisters of an agunah. It's probably the same agunah. I said it was forbidden." The rabbi sat with hands drooping numbly over the armrests, as he did when the agunah's sisters had pleaded with him.

"Reb Levi!" the head shamesh cried, attempting to bring him to.

"We must remain silent, Reb Yoshe," Reb Levi confided, looking around. "Don't talk about this with the congregants, God forbid. In the name of the Lord God of Israel, I adjure you not to say a word."

"I don't understand," the shamesh looked around, too, as though he were ordered to hush up a murder. "I know you are not fazed by men more influential than Reb David and the man who married the agunah. So why do we have to keep silent about this sacrilege?"

66

"Say nothing!" Reb Levi sprang from his chair, trembling with rage. He did not raise his voice, but seethed quietly. "*You* will not tell *me* what sacrilege is and when it takes place. Do you want to bring misfortune down upon us just because you bear a grudge against Reb David and the assistant shamesh?" His face flaming, the short rabbi raised his clenched fists to the rangy head shamesh who backtracked toward the door. "I know him well, that Reb David Zelver. I know that insurgent well. I also know Vilna and I know the state of our Jewishness. The real sacrilege will take place if this incident becomes known. So if you don't want this to happen, you had better remain absolutely silent. And if you don't obey me, I'll persecute you mercilessly."

Reb Levi is as crazy as his wife and daughter, Reb Yoshe shrugged as he left the house. He, the head shamesh of Vilna's Main Synagogue, had been spoken to like one of the riffraff. However, since Reb Yoshe was usually clever and temperate (except for some moments of occasional rage), he realized he had better not butt in. When he discovered later that Rabbi Levi had brought his crazy daughter back home, he understood Reb Levi's agitation and his frequent glances toward the closed door. Reb Yoshe bit his leonine mustache—and remained silent.

12

Merl too told her husband not to tell anyone who his wife was and how he married her. "If people question you about marrying an agunah, tell them what Guteh and Golda are telling their husbands—that the Rabbinic Council had granted permission. And please don't even set foot in the Zaretche *shul*. The local worshippers there might start asking you questions and learn about your meeting with Reb David. Zaretche, after all, is a small suburb."

Although it was Kalman's plan to have a quiet wedding, he had never dreamed that he would have to lead the life of a hunted thief. He was also quite peeved that his wife thought more about Reb David than about her own husband. At first Merl had declared that when she married she would find a man who wouldn't demand a rabbinic clearance. Kalman fancied that she had married because of the rabbi's request, and not because she had wanted to. And now she constantly feared the possible harm the rabbi might suffer, as though she were in love with *him*. Standing every morning at the window, she watched Reb David Zelver leading his son to school, and then repeatedly warned Kalman: "Be careful to avoid the rabbi, for if he sees you, he might become appalled at what he has done. It would be best if he forgot about us." And only then did she sit down to work at her sewing machine, scarcely saying another word.

For Rosh Hashana, Yom Kippur and Sukkos, Kalman walked over to Reb Yisrolke's Shul, where he stood behind the pulpit, afraid that someone might take hold of him and ask him who he was. Although Kalman knew no one there, that *shul* was still too close to Polotsk Street and he feared the evil eye. It also depressed him that while all Jews would participate in Simkhas Torah festivities in their own *shuls*, he would have to stand forlorn and unrecognized in the back of a strange, crowded *shul*, like a common beggar. One solution would be to pray at the other end of town in his old neighborhood *shul*, where he had been considered one of the prominent congregants. But first of all, one had to have a pair of sturdy legs to tramp that distance; and secondly, the old neighbors might ask him, "What're you doing here? Already divorced your dark-eyed little beauty?"

Kalman decided that for Simkhas Torah he would go to Vilna's Main Synagogue. The distance was not too great, and one needn't be a steady worshipper there in order to feel at home. If he came early enough he might even find a good seat and be able to hear the cantor.

Despite the warm weather, Kalman donned his fur-collared coat—his finest garment—and left for the synagogue. Since he arrived early, he had no difficulty getting in. But by the time the Torah circuits began, more than three thousand people had filled the synagogue and Kalman stood up front by the pulpit, opposite the Holy Ark.

The synagogue was so crowded that—as the saying went—there wasn't even room for a pin to squeeze through. Everyone knew that in a few hours the nine-day Sukkos festival would end. Many weeks would pass before Hanuka lamps appeared in the frosted windows; and by then everyone would be immersed in snow and weekday gloom. Therefore they thronged to the *shul* to rejoice with a great congregation and also listen to a cantor, whose melodic innovations would be repeated in the workshops and the stores.

There was a little *shul* in every corner of the synagogue court-yard, and from each one people streamed to the Main Synagogue. The painters were first to arrive. The walls of their *shul* were decorated with murals based on Torah scenes—Noah's Ark floating on the water, Abraham binding Isaac, Lot's wife turning into a pillar of salt. Proud of their little *shul*, the painters rarely prayed elsewhere; but in honor of Simkhas Torah they went to the Main Synagogue to celebrate with all other Jews.

The artisans of the Workers Society had sparse beards, hunched backs and—even on Simkhas Torah—lifeless pathetic eyes. In their *shul*, no matter how often the shamesh cried, "Now completing the first circuit; the first circuit is now completed," there was no one to hold the Scrolls of Law. Torahs were available in plenitude but not members of the Workers Society—they were dying out each year. Workers of the modern generation were not joining the Society, but forming unions and joining the Bund.

The old artisans with their sparse beards and hunched backs wandered over one by one to the Main Synagogue, and met members of the Burial Society from the Gravediggers Shul who were accompanied by at least a dozen bottles of whiskey. The onlookers retreated, "May we never need their services!"

Then the householders from the Old Shul appeared, old men with milk-white beards and mild silken smiles in the corners of their eyes. Over them hovered the shadowy tranquility of heavy old leather-bound tomes. When they turned pages of the large volumes in the study-room, one could hear the mysterious sounds of past centuries in the pages' rustling and whispering. The Old Shul was even older than the Main Synagogue of Vilna.

The top-hatted landlords of the Old-New Shul arrived rather late, as befitted affluent men; even in the packed synagogue courtyard they proceeded leisurely with their hands behind their backs. They were accompanied by sons and sons-in-law who instead of taking their young wives to the theater were obliged—out of respect for their fathers and fear of their fathers-in-law—to listen to the cantor.

Finally, the old recluses in the Gaon's Shul also finished their services. After the Torah circuits in their cold, dark *shul*, they promptly sat down to rest; for these Misnagdim, opponents of Hasidism, were excellent Torah scholars, but they could neither sing nor dance. After the Musaf Service the recluses wet their mustaches with wine, shook the cake crumbs from their beards, and carefully went down the *shul* steps.

The recluses of the Gaon's Shul were deeply distressed by the Vilna passion for cantorial singing. Instead of praying with devotion, today's young men fulfilled their religious obligations by listening to melodies. Moreover, were these modern, not overly-pious cantors really permitted to lead the congregation in prayers? But in honor of Simkhas Torah the recluses made an exception and listened to the cantor, wondering what everyone saw in all these quavers and tremolandos.

All the *shuls* had by now concluded their services and the worshippers gathered in the synagogue courtyard, except the Koidanov Hasidim whose prayer-room reverberated with the rhythmic sounds

70

of "Bim-bam, bim-bam." They were completely indifferent to the cantor and his choir, but danced and sang with ecstatic enthusiasm until it seemed that the Hasidic prayer-room would tear itself away from the anti-Hasidic synagogue courtyard and fly skyward with windblown beards, billowing gaberdines and dangling belts.

The day was warm and bright, and the sun's rays danced with Simkhas Torah intoxication in the *shul* windows and on the roofs. There was a great crush around the synagogue. The soft hats of the householders rose above the stiff caps of the workers, and the top hats of the rich men towered over them all like long chimneys. At the front door of the Synagogue and at all the other entrances people stood with inclined heads and stretched necks, like thirsty sheep at the watering trough, trying in vain to catch a bit of the melody by cupping their hands over their ears. Since the cantor was not blessed with Adam's voice, which according to the Talmud resounded from one end of the world to the other, the worshippers turned to one another and began to converse. They knew that inside the *shul* they were now distributing the Torahs for the circuits.

In the huge *shul*, there was sudden silence in the area between the Holy Ark and the pulpit, where the Torah circuits were taking place. The stillness spread in broad waves; it rose to the little latticed windows of the women's gallery, filled with shining eyes like nets with goldfish, then turned to deathly silence, paralyzing the chatter in tens of rows, and finally reached the heavy iron doors, and spilled over to the synagogue courtyard like a river freezing over.

Something had happened in the old Main Synagogue of Vilna.

13

Reb Yoshe the head shamesh stood on the steps leading up to the Holy Ark, presenting a Torah scroll to each of the summoned worshippers. The assistant shamesh tagged at his heels, offering suggestions; but Reb Yoshe did not even glance at Zalmanke. Reb Yoshe still remembered that Zalmanke had performed the ceremony for an agunah on the strength of a voucher from Reb David Zelver, and how high and mighty Zalmanke had become ever since. And Reb Yoshe had to bear this insolence without saying a word, for Reb Levi had ordered absolute silence concerning the agunah affair. But now the time had come for Reb Yoshe to become harsh, and when the assistant shamesh told him, "Give Reb Berel a Torah, honor Reb Yankel with a Torah circuit," Reb Yoshe hissed quietly, "Who's asking you?" and presented the Torah to whomever he pleased.

As if to add to Zalmanke's distress, after each circuit the rich men returned the Torahs to the head shamesh and thanked him, while to him, the assistant shamesh, no one said a word. Seething, Zalmanke ran down the steps, confounded with rage. No one noticed him, no one at all. But wait! There, right under his nose, stood a close acquaintance, a friend, a loyal comrade—the very man for whom he had performed the marriage ceremony.

All morning long Kalman had stood up front near the cantor and the choir, in the proximity of the rich near the Eastern Wall; nevertheless, he felt his spirits flagging. Here he'd have to be a Rothschild to be offered a scroll for a Torah circuit. Since he didn't even have a soul to speak to, he was as happy to see the assistant shamesh as the latter was to see him.

"*Sholom aleichem*, Reb Kalman."

"*Aleichem sholom*, Reb Zalman."

"Reb Kalman, why are you standing there like a beggar at the gate? Why don't you take a Torah for a circuit?"

"Reb Zalman, how do I come to get a Torah circuit in Vilna's Main Synagogue? For that one must be a Rothschild!"

"Reb Kalman, I consider a congregant as important as a Rothschild," the assistant shamesh said, glancing at the Holy Ark and noting that God Himself was on his side.

Since Reb Yoshe was chatting amiably with one of the congregants, Zalmanke quietly dashed up the steps to the Holy Ark, removed a Torah and ran back down. But meanwhile Reb Yoshe had turned and seen Zalmanke carrying a Torah for someone waiting with outstretched arms. The keen-eyed head shamesh could have sworn that the man with the kidnapped Torah was the one who had come to him offering a voucher from Reb David Zelver and who was subsequently brought under the wedding canopy by the assistant shamesh.

"You bastard," Reb Yoshe shouted to the assistant shamesh, who once again stood on the steps by the Holy Ark. "How dare you, on Simkhas Torah in Vilna's Main Synagogue, give a Torah to this out-and-out sinner who is living with an agunah, with someone else's wife?"

"Well, what of it? Perhaps you want to hit me, too?" Zalmanke taunted him. "I consider Reb Kalman as fine a man as any moneybags. You're just jealous that I have some of my own clientele. Your glued-on beard doesn't faze me a bit. The policeman on the corner has a beard, too."

By now, the head shamesh was totally oblivious to the Main Synagogue, the huge congregation, and the cantor waiting with prayerbook in hand for the final circuit to begin. Reb Yoshe saw only Zalmanke's half-closed insolent eyes. Spittle gathered at the corners of Reb Yoshe's mouth and his face flamed, as though his beard were on fire. The head shamesh raised his hand and smacked Zalmanke's face so hard with the full force of five outstretched fingers that the assistant shamesh tumbled down the steps leading from the Holy Ark. The chatter at the prestigious Eastern Wall and the facing first row suddenly ceased. Perplexed, the worshippers gaped at the head shamesh standing by the Holy Ark and at his assistant sprawled on the floor. Attracted by the sudden stillness, others also turned to the Holy Ark. The silence moved in cold waves over dozens of rows, until it reached the rear pillars of the synagogue. For sixty long seconds Reb Yoshe heard nothing and saw nothing around him. Lips awry and eyes blazing, he gazed at the assistant shamesh on the floor as though he were the scapegoat offered in Biblical times as atonement for all Israel. Finally, Reb Yoshe became aware of the tense silence and saw the entire congregation staring at him.

Zalmanke, more frightened than hurt, lay on the floor, not removing his glance from Reb Yoshe's murderous eyes, which seemingly smoked in his hairy face. All of Zalmanke's pride and spite had vanished with the blow he had received; now he even feared standing until the head shamesh gave the word. But seeing that Reb Yoshe was looking around nervously, Zalmanke rose slowly and looked around, too. He saw hundreds of wide-open eyes and mouths and immediately sensed that the congregation was on his side. He snapped out of his fear and was overwhelmed by a wild courage and an even greater rage. He jumped up on the steps that led to the Holy Ark and with upraised hands shouted with all his might:

"Fellow Jews! Do something! Why are you standing there? He slapped me and humiliated me in front of the Holy Ark. Me, a father of children!"

And then Zalmanke burst into tears.

A murmur buzzed through the benches by the Eastern Wall and the facing first row, the seats of the very wealthy. Through the other rows, where the storekeepers sat, the murmur grew into a shout, which upon reaching the rear pillars and the gathered crowd had turned into full-scale pandemonium. The trustees had already run to the steps, protecting Reb Yoshe with their shoulders and were waving their hands, attempting to still the excited crowd.

Reb Yoshe felt his knees weakening. Still ringed by the trustees, he gradually backtracked until he nearly came into the open Holy Ark, where the scrolls stood waiting to be removed for the seventh and final circuit. Open-mouthed and enraged bestial forms kept approaching and a sea of hands groped toward him, seeking to strangle him and tear him to pieces. Reb Yoshe shivered and closed his eyes—then trembled even more. He imagined one face floating toward him over the entire crowd—the head, reddish beard and fists of Reb Levi Hurvitz—and forthwith remembered Reb Levi's angry warning concerning the agunah: "Silence!"

That same moment Reb Yoshe heard the entire *shul* thundering:

"Why did he strike the assistant shamesh? If he doesn't tell us, we won't let him out of here alive."

The news of the incident had already reached the courtyard. People didn't believe their ears: had a man actually been slapped in full view of thousands of Jews in the Main Synagogue on Simkhas Torah? "Whoever humiliates his fellow man in public loses his share in the world-to-come," groaned the pious artisans of the Workers Society. But the painters yelled, "We won't wait until the head shamesh loses his share in the world-to-come. We're going to kill him in this world of here and now."

"Reb Yoshe could not possibly have done such a thing without good cause," said a rich man from the Old-New Shul, adjusting his top hat. "Reb Yoshe is a scholar and sage. He studies Mishna with the people in our *shul*."

"The fact that your Reb Yoshe knows the Mishna by heart isn't worth a pinch of snuff," cried a bony-faced, smooth-shaven young man.

"I didn't say he knows the Mishna by heart," the rich man said haughtily. "I've got children older than you, you fresh lout. Who is your father?"

"A tailor, not a leech. And I'm a working man, too."

"Yoshe deserves to be buried alive," the tipsy gravediggers nodded.

"Fellow Jews, what are you talking about?" a white-bearded old man said, trembling. "After all, Reb Yoshe is not an informer, God forbid."

The crowd's fury grew, one man infecting the next with his rage. The courtyard became even more crowded. Those inside the synagogue wanted to leave, those outside sought to enter. Word came that the worshippers were delaying the final circuit and the Torah reading until the head shamesh told them why he had slapped his assistant. The head shamesh replied that if he were to tell what the assistant shamesh had done it would be the greatest sacrilege in the world. They turned to the assistant shamesh, who with a terror-stricken mien looked silently at the head shamesh. Then the word came that the trustees were urging Reb Yoshe not to be afraid to speak up, for it would be a greater sacrilege not to finish the services in Vilna's Main Synagogue, which had not happened since Vilna was founded.

"Well," someone in the courtyard shouted, "have the trustees convinced that conceited ass to speak up?"

"It looks like they did. Although Reb Yoshe is obstinate and arrogant, he's softened up a bit. Who wants to be trampled alive?"

Ears alert, the crowd passed the word that the incident involved an agunah whom Reb Yoshe had refused to marry but who was subsequently married by the assistant shamesh with the permission of Reb David Zelver, despite the opposition of all the Vilna rabbis. And now in the Main Synagogue the assistant shamesh had honored the agunah's husband, that adulterer, with a Torah for the circuits—and that's why Reb Yoshe had smacked him.

"Well, what did I tell you? I told you that Reb Yoshe wouldn't do such a thing without reason," the rich man said triumphantly. The worshippers from the Painters Shul also realized that they had gratuitously suspected Reb Yoshe of humiliating his fellow man. The crowd's sympathy shifted to the head shamesh, and everyone wondered about the identity of that small-time rabbi, that Reb David Zelver who had opposed all the Vilna rabbis. The artisans from the Workers Society shrugged their hunched shoulders. The gravediggers declared that they had never heard him deliver a eulogy. But the smooth-shaven young man was curious and asked the recluse from the Gaon's Shul—a man who had remained silent all along—to describe Reb David Zelver.

"Eh, a rabbi! It's not surprising he opposed the Rabbinic Council. That's his way," the recluse smiled and declined to say any more.

It was clear to the young man that Reb David Zelver and the assistant shamesh favored the folk, in contrast to the head shamesh and the other rabbis. Surrounded by rich nabobs, benchwarmers and fanatic artisans, the young man stood on tiptoe and looked toward the entrance to the Main Synagogue, where the supporters of the assistant shamesh stood. He elbowed his way forward, shouting, "Quit shoving, uncle," and was almost crushed before he finally squeezed his way through the throng.

14

Able-bodied young men were stationed at the main entrance and the rear doors of the Main Synagogue, to prevent the head shamesh from slipping out with the rest of the crowd. With great self-restraint the congregation let the cantor finish the Musaf Service; but in the courtyard the worshippers of the small *shuls* went wild, and the market youths shouted hoarsely:

"They've roped off the Main Synagogue, just like—forgive the comparison—a stable. You can't get a seat there unless you have a ticket. And if you don't have a ticket—stand till your legs swell up! On Yom Kippur Eve they set up hundreds of charity plates in *shul*. And it's give, give, give. For the communal bathhouse, the public privy, the poorhouse. Give for the soupkitchen, the scholars, the recluses in the Gaon's Shul. Give, give, give!"

"Do you contribute for the recluses in the Gaon's Shul?" calmly asked an old man whom the crowd had dragged into the whirlpool of the rebels.

"Sure we do!" The youths of the fish and wood markets pounded their chests.

The residents of the poor courtyards shouted that the communal offices had imposed even greater taxes on them than on the very rich. The rag peddlers reviled the town fathers for not repairing the tottering stores, and the residents of Leib-Leyzer's courtyard complained:

"Chunks of balconies keep falling down on our heads. The walls in the cellars are damp and moldy. The kids develop tuberculosis and the old men cough their lungs out."

"The communal representatives should pay *us* for living in such stench and filth," shouted the residents of Ramile's courtyard. "The privy is right under our nose. Rusty pipes leak on our heads. There's no well, no electricity. There's absolutely nothing."

"Do you think America will look on silently?" the smooth-shaven young man shrieked.

"You moron," the others reprimanded him. "America butts in only during pogroms."

"And I thought that all the Vilna boors had emigrated to America. But it turns out that plenty have remained behind," replied the young man, not one to let the other fellow have the last word. In the tumult, however, his shrill voice was inaudible. The courtyard and the markets tried to outshout one another with their complaints to the community:

How come the old folks weren't taken away to the old-age home? They roamed about in the *shuls* and the corridors. How come the synagogue courtyard wasn't cleared of its madmen? They sleep in the hallways and befoul the steps. How come the beggars and the cripples weren't provided for? Wherever a person turned he was swamped by hundreds of outstretched hands. They stuck to you like leeches, and cursed you roundly if you refused them.

"And all this is the head shamesh's fault?" asked the old man who had strayed into the company of the rebels.

"Of course!" thundered the market youths. "The head shamesh, the trustees, and the rabbis are to blame for everything. Where's the rabbi who gave the agunah permission to marry? We're going to make him chief rabbi of Vilna. You hear what the hunchbacks are saying? They say that Reb David is no son-in-law of an old Vilna rabbi like Reb Levi Hurvitz. In other words, he's nobody special. Just an absolute, rootless stranger. If the Vilna rabbis dare to make trouble for our rabbi we'll scatter them to the winds. We'll make the agunah's husband the first trustee of the Main Synagogue, we'll promote the assistant shamesh to head shamesh, and the head shamesh we'll bury head first."

The worshippers began streaming out of the large synagogue with the force of a tree-smashing current. But like boulders the market youths withstood the crowd. The hot and perspiring throng that had left the synagogue did not disperse. "Here comes the hero of the day," everyone shouted, pointing at the man who had married the agunah. Kalman, completely surrounded by his supporters, walked through the path opened up by the onlookers. Yet after one glance at him, the market youths' enthusiasm cooled and their faces fell.

"Is that him? What's his name?"

"They say it's Kalman Maytess."

The crowd saw that Kalman Maytess had a naive moonlike face, a sparse blondish beard and downcast eyes like a bashful bridegroom. Everyone wondered why he wore a fur-collared coat in such mild weather. The logical explanation—that this was probably his sole holiday garment—brought a smile to everyone's lips. The market youths were stunned. They expected a man among men, the kind that told the world where it could go. After all, he had defied the rabbis. But since he turned out to be a shrunken bit of nothing they immediately nicknamed him: "The clunk."

"You just wanted to make him the first trustee of the Main Synagogue," the old man teased them.

The market youths retorted that they didn't care about this clunkish chap—they cared about the truth. Encircling Kalman like a ring of bodyguards, they shouted to him:

"Don't give in to them, you hear?"

Kalman, scarcely able to stand on his own feet, pleaded wordlessly with frightened, wide-open eyes, as though afraid to let them hear his voice: Fellow Jews, let me pass. I'm dying of shame and you're shouting, Hurrah! And he quickly left the overcrowded synagogue courtyard.

The crush became even greater with the appearance of the assistant shamesh, whose red face was still flaming. Seeing him, the crowd from the suburbs felt even more cheated. The assistant shamesh was thoroughly unimpressive. Someone quipped that this Goliath could be seen only with a magnifying glass. But the market youths snapped back:

"How can the assistant shamesh be big and fat if the head shamesh skims off all the cream? Keep your chin up, Zalmanke!"

"I am, I am," he said, tightening his belt, as though girding up his strength. "How many Main Synagogues are there in Vilna? One! Which means that I'm its only assistant shamesh. So do I deserve to be smacked? Reb Yoshe doesn't let me touch anything, but wants all the money and all the honor for himself. When Americans come to visit, I don't even dare say a word. And I happen to know this *shul* much better than Reb Yoshe. After all, my grandfather was the assistant shamesh here."

"Don't worry, Zalmanke," the market youths exploded with laughter. "We will make you the head shamesh, and our boots will take care of Yoshe."

"God forbid!" Zalmanke trembled. "Without him no one will invite me to perform a wedding."

"But Kalman Clunk invited you to perform the wedding."

"Can I make a living from this? How many agunahs are there in Vilna?" Zalmanke screwed up his face as if about to cry. "They invited me this time because Reb Yoshe refused to go. Without Reb David's permission I wouldn't have performed the ceremony either. But I won't do it again. Don't lay a hand on Reb Yoshe. They'll fire me. Just try to convince him to take me to weddings."

Suddenly Zalmanke became even smaller. Awestruck, he waved for silence, pointing respectfully to the trustees in frock coats and top hats who had come out of the synagogue and were attempting to persuade the crowd to let the head shamesh pass through. The market youths were delighted that others were pleading with them as though with the Kaiser. A tall trustee with a stiff rubber collar on his scrawny neck to prevent his head from wobbling stepped forth. Besides being a synagogue trustee he was also the householders' representative in the Jewish Community Council.

"Gentlemen—" he jabbed his forefinger, and was promptly thrust aside by a short potbellied trustee with a trimmed grey beard. The latter didn't utilize a genteel council-meeting tone in addressing the mob, but immediately commenced with threats: "If you dare to touch the head shamesh, all the synagogue's trustees are going to resign."

"That's exactly what we want," the shaven young man crowed.

"Don't listen to that bathhouse janitor," the pious Jews from the *shuls* outshouted him, "You'll stay trustees till you're one hundred and twenty. The rabble has just come here to stir up trouble. Let them go raise the roof in their own backyards."

Encouraged by his supporters, the short trustee said that anyone who prayed in a *shul* today, received a Torah for a circuit, and recited the blessings over the Torah ought to know what's written in the Torah. According to the Torah, a married woman may not marry until it is positively known that her husband had died or divorced her. Nevertheless, we know of a certain individual who had insisted upon only marrying an agunah; it was to this certain individual that the assistant shamesh had given the holy Torah in the holy Main Synagogue of Vilna. Such desecration Reb Yoshe could not abide and, incensed to his core, he did something foolish for which he would assuredly compensate the assistant shamesh and beg his pardon. But for his zeal for the honor of the Torah and for the honor of Vilna's Main Synagogue, Reb Yoshe certainly did not deserve to be stoned. Lifting a hand against him would be like flinging the Torah to the ground. And besides, Reb Yoshe had a weak heart; if anyone touched him he would immediately drop dead.

The market youths and the residents of the poor courtyards were dumbstruck; the pious Jews from the little *shuls* dabbed at their tear-filled eyes like women. Surrounding the trustees, they demanded that the head shamesh be brought out and declared:

"Whoever lays a finger on him will have to kill us first!"

The market youths began to back down. Why should they lose both this world and the world-to-come over some assistant shamesh? The assistant shamesh was obviously a stubborn, contentious and impudent man, the sort who got under one's skin. So what if you get smacked? A blow is forgotten, but words stick in the memory.

The trustees announced that the head shamesh could now be brought out of the Main Synagogue. Forthwith the procession appeared, led by the head cantor, a broad-faced man whose neck sank into his collar for fear that his voicebox might catch cold. Surrounding him were members of the choir, boy sopranos and old bachelor basses, who were followed by children with tear-stained faces and wrinkled Simkhas Torah flags that had been crushed in the tumult. Finally, the head shamesh himself stepped forth, ringed by the pillars of the community. The trustees had placed him so strategically that to reach him one would have had to step over children and old men. The market youths were astonished to see a man as tall and broad as an oak, with a waist-long white beard. Although supported like a man about to faint, Reb Yoshe stared fiery-eyed at the youths who had threatened him. Now, however, there was no longer any thought of lifting a hand against him.

"How pale he is!" the crowd murmured. "Those boors have probably bruised his ribs. May their hands wither away!"

With the trustees' appearance, the assistant shamesh vanished, hiding in the crowd. But when the head shamesh reached the courtyard gates, Zalmanke crawled after him submissively, as though dying for another smack. Once Reb Yoshe and his entourage were outside, the shaven young man plucked up his courage, put two fingers in his mouth, and whistled smartly at them.

"Moron!" the youths turned to him. "If you don't pipe down we'll put you out of your misery."

Seeing that he could easily become the scapegoat for the abortive revolt, the young man sidled away. The crowd in the courtyard began to thin out, but small knots of people remained, arguing about the rabbi who had permitted the agunah to marry, her clunk of a husband, and the two shamoshim of the Main Synagogue. Only the agunah herself was not mentioned, for no one knew her.

15

The slap in the Main Synagogue was constantly discussed in the poor courtyards and in the streets bordering upon the Synagogue. The market youths also dealt with the matter in their own unique fashion: They didn't give a damn about the agunah affair. They had heard of more intriguing romances. Even Paris had nothing on Vilna. If all the young men and women in Vilna had cast but one-tenth of their sins into the water on Rosh Hashana, the Vilia River would have overflowed its banks and inundated the city. The market youths said that the only thing that interested them was the quarrel of the religious functionaries. The head shamesh had huddled with the trustees like a dog stuck in a bramblebush and refused to say why he had smacked the assistant shamesh. He softened up only upon realizing that he'd be carried away on a slab. And then the whole scandal surfaced. One rabbi had declared that the agunah was permitted to marry, the others said no—and a quiet battle developed between them. So how were the religious functionaries any better than Vilna's rival gangs? The thieves stabbed each other and no one dared ask questions; the same held true for the rabbis.

Nevertheless, the scandal would have been forgotten in a day or two if Moishke Tsirulnik had not butted in. Ever since Merl had threatened him with a pressing iron he had abandoned his most ardent wish—seducing her for a night and then casting her off. Now he sought total revenge. But he did not know what he would do. His pal Shaike had told him that with all the rabbis' permission Merl had indeed married that tattered runt, that gravedigger and housepainter, Kalman Maytess. But it turned out that the rabbis had *not* given their permission at all, and that Golda had deliberately fooled her husband to hush matters up. "In that case, it's a different story. I've got no choice but to do something nasty." Moishke rubbed his hands and neglected his business affairs. He decked himself out in his silk scarf, took his ivory-handled cane, and left for a tour of the butcher shops.

In the aftermath of many expensive meat meals during the nine-day-long Sukkos holiday, the housewives were tightfisted and the meatshops empty. The stony-faced butchers' wives sat behind the tin-plated counters and the bored butchers waited outside the doorways. Spotting Moishke Tsirulnik, one of the butchers said:

"Say, how come you're suddenly all spruced up? Aren't you doing business in the market any more?"

Moritz shrugged. "What business? What market? I've been in business much too long and have been a bachelor much too long. I'm going to marry a gentile girl, a sturdy piece with her own estate, just like a countess. She's been dying for me for years and is going to watch me like the apple of her eye. But I've been refusing her thinking this wasn't kosher. *Now* I know that it's kosher after all."

Everyone knew that Moritz was a liar and a braggart. Imagine a land-owning countess grabbing him! Nevertheless, the butchers wanted to know which fantastic text sanctioned intermarriage. This was the question Moritz had been waiting for, and he offered a lengthy explanation:

"Ever since I was a kid I knew that an agunah isn't permitted to marry until witnesses declared they had seen her husband dead. But lately there's been a tumult in town about a rabbi who permitted an agunah to marry without witnesses. So if marrying a woman who already has a husband is kosher, then marrying a gentile woman is also kosher, especially if the countess is a Karaite Jewess on her mother's side and will have the ceremony performed by the Khakham of Troki. If steer-meat slaughtered by a pious *shokhet* in Oshmeneh is declared not kosher in Vilna because it's considered illegally imported—how come someone else's wife is *yes* kosher?"

The butchers paid scant attention while Moritz talked about agunahs and gentile women; but when he mentioned the meat from Oshmeneh, they saw his point.

The year before when a huge shipment of meat had been delivered from Oshmeneh, the Vilna rabbis had pronounced a ban on outside meat shipments, for these imports were depriving local religious functionaries of a livelihood. Reb Levi Hurvitz ran from one butcher shop to another, shouting to the customers that it was not kosher, and that they would have to throw out their pots, plates and ovens, all contaminated by the non-kosher meat from the Oshmeneh slaughterhouse. The rabbi's cries frightened the housewives and they abandoned the bargains. The butchers wanted to tear the short, potbellied rabbi to pieces—but remained silent. Go start up with the Torah! But the flaming-faced butchers' wives, holding bloodied meat cleavers in their hands, did not bite their tongues: "You're not going to drive *us* crazy like your wife and daughter. We'll put *you* into the nuthouse, not you us." Reb Levi, dizzy and weak-kneed, managed to leave the butcher shops; whereupon the butchers berated their wives for their impudence.

But now the women looked at their husbands and crowed triumphantly:

"Well, what did we tell you? Reb Levi's keeping mum about that adulteress, but he sticks his nose into things that are none of his business. Now our strictly kosher Vilna meat is rotting on the hooks, and the women are running to the butcher shops where there's no rabbinic supervision because it's cheaper' there. The rabbis raised more of a fuss over imported kosher meat than over something that *really* isn't kosher."

Moritz sided with the butchers' wives and laughed at their foolish husbands:

"Reb Levi Hurvitz is keeping his mouth shut concerning the agunah because for that his palms were well greased, whereas for the imported meat from Oshmeneh he didn't earn a penny. If I were a butcher, I'd go to the village tomorrow morning and bring back meat. And you know what I'd say as soon as I heard the first word of complaint from the local rabbis? I'd say: 'Speak to the agunah. First excommunicate her with black candles in the Main Synagogue.'"

Decked out in his white silk scarf and holding his ivory-handled cane, Moritz continued his tour, his unctuous eyes glittering with satisfaction as he formulated new schemes.

The Sabbath Observers Society met to deal with a problem. When they entered the stores individually on Friday afternoons and asked the shopkeeper to close in time they were driven away. Henceforth, they decided, they would proceed to the shops in groups. If one Sabbath Observer were insulted and chased from the store, a second would make his appearance, followed by a third, until the shamed shopkeepers submitted and closed their stores before the onset of the Sabbath. The pious old men implemented the plan and saw that it was successful.

On Friday afternoon the stores were swamped. A Sabbath observer poked his head into a doorway and reminded the owner that it was time to close up. "Go away," the shopkeeper replied, not knowing which housewife to serve first. They had all congregated at the very last minute, shouting for quick service, claiming that their pots were boiling over. A second Sabbath Observer poked his head in. "Go home and kindle Sabbath candles, for fires break out when one violates the Sabbath." A pall fell over the women. A third man now appeared in the doorway. "Because Jews violate the Sabbath wild beasts attack and devour little children."

Hearing such talk the women became white as sheets, and the shopkeepers saw their sales melting away. Some of them ran out to see why this delegation of God's attorneys was larger than usual today, and were alarmed by what they saw: two rows of Sabbath Observers stretched along the length of both sidewalks, just like the beggars who traveled in packs from door to door. The shopkeepers shouted that there was a remedy even against locusts: fires were lit around the fields. They would deal in like fashion with these fanatics by calling out the firemen who would hose them down until they were soaked to the skin. This time, however, the pious old men, feeling the strength of their numbers, hurled back abuse at the impudent louts until the street became black with onlookers. But then Moishke Tsirulnik appeared and with his harangue silenced the Sabbath Observers as though the roof had caved in on them.

"If you religious Jews want the Sabbath to be observed, go smash the windows of the Vilna rabbis for permitting an agunah to marry. If those hunchbacks hush up such a sin, they shouldn't even dare say boo to someone smoking on the Sabbath in the Main Synagogue courtyard. I tell you, the world's full of thieves and crooks," Moishke concluded, walking away with head held high.

In one of the second-hand clothing stores Tsirulnik bought a satin jacket and chatted with the salesman. In Reb Leib-Leyzer's courtyard he had an old friend, and in Ramile's courtyard he was pals with everyone. He turned up everywhere and every place heard his laughter.

"Fellows, you've always been a bunch of asses and you're still a bunch of asses. Where should the community get money to white-wash the cellars and repair the steps, install electricity and water, and clean up the filth if all the money is used up to support the rabbis? For their benefit taxes are taken from the living—and even from the dead for a cemetery plot. Fellows, do you have an inkling how many rabbis there are in Vilna and how much they cost us? And what about all the little rabbis of the suburbs, the preachers in the *shuls*, the recluses in the Gaon's Shul, the poor students at Ramile's Yeshiva, and the benchwarmers at the other *shuls*. Do you know what a rabbi is good for? A rabbi is good for declaring what's not permitted. But if everything *is* permitted, if even marrying some-one else's wife is permitted, why do we need so many freeloaders?"

"And if the rabbis force the agunah and her husband to divorce—will we be any better off?" asked one of the residents of the poor courtyards.

Moishke's fiery eyes gleamed and he screwed up his face with contempt: "Do you think I want to see man and wife separated? My only concern is the truth. I consider the entire agunah affair as worthless as flypaper," he laughed. "I'm going to marry a Jewish countess with her own estate. She's head over heels in love with me and will care for me like the apple of her eye. After a magnificent wedding, the celebrations will begin at her estate. So what do I care about a slattern who married a slovenly Kalmanke under a canopy provided by a raggedy Zalmanke."

16

Years ago, a slender young man named Kasriel Zelinger once came to the *mohel* Lapidus with a request to teach him his sacred calling, for he wanted to be a *mohel* in his village. Lapidus acquiesced and the young man departed. Years later Lapidus learned that Kasriel had moved to Vilna, opened a dry goods store, and was performing circumcisions. Both *mohels* met one day and Lapidus was vexed that this once-slender young man had developed a hefty paunch. His vexation increased when Vilna sang this *mohel's* praises for having a pair of golden hands. Lapidus sniffed several times, like an animal who senses danger, but nevertheless retained his composure. Since he did not take any money for his services and there was no lack of poor childbearing mothers, both *mohels* would have sufficient circumcisions.

But from the day Reb David Zelver had proclaimed in the Zaretche *shul* that anyone who invited the *mohel* Lapidus for a circumcision was slaying his own children, Kasriel Zelinger's star rose and Lapidus' descended. Knowing that Reb Levi Hurvitz hated Reb David Zelver like poison, Lapidus ran to Reb Levi crying: "Why did the Vilna Rabbinic Council let Reb David independently put a ban on me, the *mohel* Lapidus, scion of the Rokeach family?"

But to his absolute astonishment, Reb Levi Hurvitz had replied, "The Rabbinic Council dares not intervene in this matter, lest people say that the rabbis hold the honor of the *mohel* Lapidus dearer than the lives of little infants." But even a blind man would have noticed that in retrospect the rabbi was pleased with the Polotsk rabbi's ban.

"Everyone agrees that I'm a scholar and philanthropist who never takes money for the performance of my sacred calling." Lapidus lost his self-control. "I'll become the laughingstock of Vilna if my word isn't taken over that of Reb David Zelver's, some shoemaker's son who permitted Jews to carry money on Sabbath not out of compassion for hungry children in Russia, but because in his heart he's a bit of a Bolshevik."

"The rabbis have always suffered more from your kind of God-fearing scholars than from the ignorant non-believers," the infuriated Reb Levi shouted. "Despite the fact that the Vilna Rabbinic Council has great grievances against Reb David, it is nevertheless an unheard of injustice to say of him that in his heart he is a bit of a Bolshevik, God forbid. What's more, I consider it very suspicious that you were not at all alarmed when you heard that the condition of the infant you circumcised was critical. It just shows that this is not the first time something like this has happened."

Lapidus ran out of the rabbi's residence in a rage. "I will never forgive him!" he swore, and wanted to pour his heart out to Reb Asher-Anshel, a man whose temperament was worlds removed from his brother-in-law's. Nevertheless, the *mohel* decided not to say a word to Reb Asher-Anshel about Reb David Zelver or Reb Levi Hurvitz. He realized that no matter how much the rabbis poured fire and brimstone on one another, they all joined forces in brotherhood against a layman.

One morning, Lapidus stopped Reb Asher-Anshel as he returned from *shul.*

"Is this the reward of piety?" the *mohel* asked him. "For more than thirty years I've been running around from one woman in confinement to another without ever getting a penny in return, and I even provided a bottle of wine for Kiddush wherever it was needed. And look how many converts I've circumcised and then arranged their weddings. All the *mohels* from Vilna and Grodne and their environs are my disciples. My one foolish move was to teach Kasriel Zelinger the art of circumcision. I know that in the world-to-come I'll have to give a reckoning for instructing such an absolute ignoramus in this sacred calling. My one excuse is that my intent was holy and divine. I couldn't have known that Zelinger would move to Vilna and keep his dry goods store open until after the onset of the Sabbath. But now that it's common knowledge, how can Zelinger possibly be permitted to be a *mohel* for Jewish children?"

Reb Asher-Anshel was used to people stopping him occasionally on his way back from prayers to reveal the secrets they could not tell him when they came to be divorced. But now Reb Asher-

Anshel had already turned into his street, hoping that today he had been spared. But he had no luck. Still, a pest like this he had never expected. His eyes downcast, the rabbi in charge of divorces picked his beard and bobbed up and down on his toes—which was his way of suppressing impatience when his Russian *Jewish Encyclopedia* was not within reach. The more the *mohel* Lapidus reviled his disciple Zelinger, the quicker and higher Reb Asher-Anshel bobbed.

"Do you have a cigarette?" he finally asked.

Lapidus opened his silver cigarette case, offered one to the rabbi, and struck a match for him. While the rabbi smoked, the *mohel* continued slandering Zelinger:

"Zelinger's a bankrupt. He signed his merchandise over to his wife and thumbed his nose at his creditors. He flays to the bone the poor young men who come to him to study circumcision, charging no less than five hundred zlotys and demanding the money in dollars. He makes the rounds of the hospitals and grows rich. He doesn't even circumcise poor children unless he's paid. With this extorted money he buys goods in Lodz, whose weaves, forbidden by the Torah, are a mixture of wool and linen. And this cloth he sells until after sundown on Friday."

"Do you have another cigarette?" the rabbi asked.

Lapidus was overjoyed that Reb Asher-Anshel was prepared to hear him out in exchange for a bit of tobacco. So he offered him another cigarette and continued: "Calling him a bankrupt is one of the nicer things that can be said of Zelinger. What's worse, he's said to have dealings with gentile women, heaven save us! If Vilna had zealots like the Biblical Pinhas, the grandson of Aaron, he'd spear Zelinger for adultery and whoredom."

"Do you have another cigarette?"

"With pleasure," Lapidus replied, noticing that the rabbi was very nervous. Still, what a difference between him and his brother-in-law, Reb Levi Hurvitz! Lapidus quickly brought out his cigarette case—and saw that it was empty.

"Then never mind," Reb Asher-Anshel said with irritation.

"Don't worry," the *mohel* said. "I'll run to the kiosk and buy another pack."

"Smoking on an empty stomach isn't healthy," Reb Asher-Anshel said gloomily.

The *mohel* was dumbstruck. "Haven't you eaten breakfast yet?"

"How could I have eaten breakfast if I'm on my way back from morning prayers?" Reb Asher-Anshel—famous for his even temper—exploded angrily. "You know Talmud and quote the sages, but you've forgotten the rabbinic statement that a man should not envy his son or his pupil. You've also forgotten that even a Tatar can be a *mohel*."

The irate rabbi turned and went away, and Lapidus felt a sudden pain in a filling, as though there were an abscess beneath his golden crown. Seeing that he could make no headway with the rabbis, he went to the householders. First he proceeded to the Zaretche *shul* and asked the local worthies if they realized that the entire town was laughing at the Zaretche *shul* for keeping that Bolshevik David Zelver as their rabbi. The Zaretchers replied that they knew of the dispute between their rabbi and the Rabbinic Council, and complained that he never studied Talmud or Mishna with them. But on the other hand, he was an unassuming man and had a sick wife and an ailing infant. So he couldn't be blamed for not studying Talmud with the worshippers.

Lapidus even tried to strike up friendships with the poor people of his own *shul* and gave vent to his wrath for Reb David and the *mohel* Zelinger. His listeners nodded in agreement, but when they celebrated a grandson's circumcision, they did not invite the *mohel* Lapidus, scion of the Rokeach family, but indeed that ignoramus, bankrupt and lecher, Kasriel Zelinger. "Very nice!" Lapidus reproached them. "Didn't I circumcise all your children without taking a penny?"

"Perfectly true," they replied. "We respect you for having circumcised half the Jews in town. But word has it that now your hands shake."

Lapidus felt depressed. He had never imagined that performing circumcisions could become a passion. "I'm no longer needed. No longer needed," he would mutter to himself. But he snapped out of his spell after the slap in the Main Synagogue on Simkhas Torah. Lapidus discovered that Reb David Zelver had perpetrated another scandal—permitting an agunah to marry; and since the rabbis were looking the other way, the masses wanted to throw off the yoke of their Jewishness.

Sabbath morning the *mohel* went to pray in Reb Shaulke's Shul, the fortress of the ultra-orthodox Agudah party. Beneath the windows the butchers shouted that they would go to Oshmeneh to import meat, and the worshippers felt like a small island in the midst of a tempestuous sea. Hence they were doubly pleased with the unexpected guest.

"Is it true that in your *shul* there's no quorum for Sabbath morning? Nowadays anything is possible."

Lapidus didn't reply at once. He covered his head with his prayer shawl, then wrapped it around his shoulders and began to mumble verses. Having said a few prayers, he stroked his beard and fixed his gaze towards the ceiling.

"I don't know if there will be a quorum without me. But I had to flee because the worshippers kept throwing it up to me that Reb David had consecrated the marriage of a married woman, a deed to which the rabbis were closing their eyes."

"So what's to be done?" the Agudah people asked.

"I know exactly what's to be done," Lapidus said. "But I don't want to hold up the service. There'll be plenty of time to chat later."

Their hearts at ease, the worshippers began to pray, calmed by Lapidus' sense and confidence. During the Torah reading he offered a generous donation, which increased their esteem of him; and after the service listened respectfully as Lapidus declared: "The Vilna rabbis are to blame. With all due respect to them, they're extremely arrogant men who tell a householder to mind his own business when he offers them advice. And, therefore, you ought to send a delegation to Reb Levi Hurvitz and demand that he place a ban of excommunication on Reb David Zelver. The butchers will then see that Judaism still preserves law and order, and they'll stop clamoring about their intent to import meat."

Pleased with the *mohel's* suggestion, the worshippers asked Lapidus to accompany them to Reb Levi and be their chief spokesman.

"God forbid!" Lapidus shivered. "I'd rather jump into a lion's den. I've already warned Reb Levi once that Reb David is a secret Bolshevik. And I wouldn't want to experience another one of his outbursts. Not on my life! And that's why I won't go to Reb Levi under any circumstances. But a delegation from the *shul* should by all means go. Tonight! After the Sabbath. Now's the time to act. For the glory of God. And your delegation should not leave Reb Levi's house until he tells you on whose side he's on. Does he support the Agudah party which is devoted to the Torah, or the Mizrachi party, which appeases heretics and always kowtows to them? Let Reb Levi proclaim once and for all where his sympathies lie!"

During the Sabbath Afternoon Service Lapidus sidled into the Old Shul. The *shul's* steady worshippers, the old people of the Sabbath Observers Society—their milk white beards glowing dimly in the twilight—conversed apprehensively about their failure to close the shops yesterday afternoon. The *mohel* intruded with a rabbinic epigram and said: "Open desecration of the Sabbath in Vilna began when Reb David Zelver permitted Jews to carry money on Sabbath, supposedly to aid the starving Jewish children in Russia. That's all the boors needed—for they deduced from this that desecration of the Sabbath was altogether permitted. And now that Reb David has permitted a married woman to marry, everything previously forbidden is now sanctioned. And that's why you should go to Reb Levi Hurvitz and tell him that as long as the storekeepers see that the rabbi who permitted a married woman to marry was still a rabbi in Vilna, nothing can be said against the Sabbath violators."

For the Evening Service Lapidus went up to the Old-New Shul, where the landlords and the trustees of the communal courtyards prayed. Coming up the stairs he already heard the raging voices of the rich trustees. He silently opened the door and saw the pillars of the community, Jews with wrathful faces and puffed-up beards outshouting one another.

"We've just put down the Simkhas Torah revolt, and now we've got another one on our hands. The tenants of the communal court-yards are refusing to pay rent until their cellars are renovated like the duke's palaces."

"None but the rabbis are to blame," a quiet, temperate voice was heard.

The trustees saw the *mohel* Lapidus, scion of the Rokeach family, and realized that he certainly was not supporting the rebels. They stretched their hairy necks to hear him, and he spoke without restraint:

"In bygone days the rabbis used to wield the whip and command absolute respect, but nowadays the modern rabbis fear the rabble of the Vilna sidestreets. And that's why you should go—tonight, after Sabbath!—to Reb Levi Hurvitz and tell him that Vilna is on the brink of strikes. The streets are rising up against the *shuls*. And if the rabbis continue to maintain their silence, the householders will certainly not intervene and Vilna will become a city of heathens wherein a Jew is forbidden to live. So if Reb Levi doesn't want this to happen, he and other Vilna rabbis should proclaim and announce far and wide that Reb David Zelver was a Bolshevik, not a rabbi. And Reb Levi should promise that this Bolshevik from Polotsk Street would be placed under the ban with his salary terminated, decree to the Zaretche *shul* that he should be excluded from a quorum, not be permitted to enter the *shul*, and not . . . "

The *mohel* Lapidus, a froth of white foam edging his lips, voiced his dream of revenge against Reb David Zelver and in his extreme agitation forgot his bundle of rabbinic epigrams.

That night the three *shuls* that Lapidus had visited during the day sent delegations to Reb Levi Hurvitz.

17

Tsirele roamed about behind closed doors in the innermost rooms. In order not to disturb his daughter, Reb Levi ate his third Sabbath meal on the bare hall table. He had not yet recited the Saturday night Havdala prayer, but remained sitting in his frayed armchair, enveloped in the evening shadows and immersed in gloomy thoughts.

At first, upon noting that Tsirele had sunk into her former depression, he had fleeting hopes for God's compassion; perhaps she would regain her reason and not be melancholic like her mother. At that time Reb Levi would still occasionally leave the house. But lately he feared stepping outside, even when Khiyeneh was cleaning the apartment. For Tsirele's insanity had returned.

Several times, while sitting in his chair studying a sacred text, the door would suddenly open behind his back and Tsirele would appear in the doorway stark naked. Seeing this his hands would become completely debilitated, and he would feebly thrust his daughter back, gag her, and restrain himself from shouting for help. With threats, tears and pleas, he would manage to push her back to her room, and then sit at her side, calming, stroking and kissing her, until her rage would abate and she would sink once more into her depression.

Were Tsirele the victim of another sort of madness, Reb Levi would not have feared her screams; he too would have succumbed and screamed, too. But her mania for running out naked was not only disgraceful but sacrilegious. A man like Lapidus, scion of the Rokeach family, would call it measure for measure. He'd say that since the modesty of Reb Levi's house was false and artificial, he was punished with a daughter who in her madness displayed her father's essential attribute. Our sages teach us, Lapidus would say, that the walls of a house are stricken with leprosy to let the world know the secret sins of its owner. For Lapidus never uttered slander without the aid of a Talmudic quotation. Hypocrites who belittled their neighbors were in plentiful supply in Vilna.

Perhaps it was indeed a punishment, Reb Levi thought. The doctors' statement that Tsirele was improving and could be taken home had taken him by surprise. And now the plague had returned. For what sins was he being made to repeatedly suffer the same agony?

Reb Levi looked out the dark blue window, as though waiting for the starry sky to reply.

Perhaps it was a punishment for being a strict zealot all his life. Hence the divine omen to show him what he himself had wrought— a daughter who wanted to run out of her father's house naked.

Reb Levi pressed his hand to his forehead: The All-Knowing who read man's thoughts knew the truth. He had never stood up for his own glory, but always for the glory of God. He could have been easygoing like his brother-in-law, Reb Asher-Anshel, and be beloved by the masses like his other brothers-in-law. The Creator knew that even his neighbors did not commiserate with him and did not sympathize with his woes, for he had punished them for desecrating the Sabbath. During the summer months he would stand for hours at the window in his study and look down into the courtyard to shame his neighbors into not hanging laundry on the Sabbath or watering the flowers or going out with a lit cigarette. Instead of looking into a book, he looked out the window. But did all this merit having his Tsirele attempt to smash these very windowpanes?

Reb Levi turned toward the closed door, as though afraid his daughter were standing on the other side listening to his thoughts. He settled deeper into his chair and bit his lips in irritation. In his daydreams he was contending with Reb David Zelver, the rabbi of Polotsk Street.

Reb David Zelver had complained that he had not been made a member of Vilna's Rabbinic Council. But the communal leaders did not want to enlarge the Council. All the suburbs had rabbinic judges, and every little *shul* its preacher. And they all had aspirations like Reb David. Were they any less worthy than he? Was he such a profound preacher, that rabbi of the Zaretche *shul*? He was no more learned than the Vilna rabbinic authorities, and moreover, he was the youngest of them all. And despite this, he had once permitted people to collect money on the Sabbath for the starving children in Russia because he wished to be a second Reb Israel Salanter. And besides displaying the saintliness of a Reb Israel Salanter, Reb David wanted to show that he feared no one. He was a proud and conceited man with a twisted mind. He even enjoyed his wife's and children's ordeal, for he could presume that he suffered for the sake of truth, that he was the persecuted one, and that Reb Levi Hurvitz was his cruel tormentor.

But the Almighty was his witness that he was not persecuting Reb David, that proud man of affliction and woes. On the contrary! When Reb David had permitted the agunah to marry, he had not intervened and had also ordered the head shamesh to hold his tongue, because excessive talk would only increase the sacrilege. At that time, too, he had brought his daughter Tsirele back from the hospital, and feared the accusation that if he did not show compassion for the agunah and for Reb David who had an ailing infant, heaven would not show compassion for his sick Tsirele. In brief, despite his jurisdiction over agunahs, he decided to forego his prerogative and hoped that the town would not learn of the incident.

But he was bitterly mistaken, even though he had known that the scandal would eventually surface. He wanted to ask Reb David: What had he accomplished with his permission? How did he and the agunah feel being the center of an entire city's attention? And what was her attitude toward her husband who dared not show his face in public? Wherever Reb David Zelver turned, he brought trouble upon himself and upon others.

"Papa, why don't you recite Havdala?" Reb Levi heard a soft voice.

He jumped up as though his chair were on fire. God be praised! Tsirele stood before him, fully clothed.

"My child, would you like to hold the Havdala candle?"

"Yes, papa," she said. By the dark blue light that streamed into the window he saw her small, pale face illumined with a childlike smile, tranquil, delicate and modest.

"Behold, God is my salvation; I will trust and not be afraid," Reb Levi chanted softly, and from under his arched brows looked at his daughter holding the braided Havdala candle. But the words remained stuck in his throat. Tsirele's face had the astonished look of a person who awoke in strange surroundings and could not imagine how he got there. Her numb expression showed that she

was not even conscious of the Havdala candle in her hand. Reb Levi considered his words carefully. He did not want his remarks to draw the tears gathering in his throat. But the tears were already rolling through his reddish grey beard, on their way to the brimming glass of wine in his hands. Reb Levi looked at his daughter, afraid that she might see him crying. But Tsirele stood there apathetically, seeing nothing and hearing nothing.

Reb Levi finished the blessing, annoyed at himself for crying so readily. He sat down, sipped a bit of wine, and swallowed his tears. After Havdala he switched on the light and remained sitting in silence.

"Papa," she asked, sitting next to him, "why am I called Tsirele?"

Tsirele wore a white-collared black batiste blouse with long finger-length sleeves, he noted. Her satin-soft black hair was swept up from her thin neck into a flat bun. Her hair is still wet and shiny. She washed it on the Sabbath. She's the image of her mother when she was young. If during the signing of the engagement contract I'd taken a closer look at her, I would have seen that she was deranged and spared myself all this agony. The thoughts tumbled in Reb Levi's head and he winced as though aroused from a dream. His daughter had asked him a question.

"Why are you called Tsirele? You're named after the old rebbetsin, your grandmother Tsirele, my child. Grandfather Yosele's wife . . . It is forbidden to wash and comb one's hair on Sabbath," Reb Levi groaned, but immediately stopped so as not to antagonize her.

"And why is Uncle Asher-Anshel's daughter named Tsirele?" she wondered, smiling like a blind man guessing colors.

"She too is named after the old rebbetsin," Reb Levi said, pleased that she had not heard his reprimand. "Uncle Zelig's middle daughter is also called Tsirele. And so is Uncle Reuven's daughter. All told there are four Tsireles in our family."

"Four Tsireles?" she shook her head, gazing wide-eyed at her father. "And how come the other Tsireles weren't locked up in the hospital?"

"My child, you won't have to stay in the hospital any longer, either," Reb Levi felt his heart turning within him. "If you don't scream and run out of the house naked, you won't have to go back to the hospital."

"Papa," she continued, as though oblivious to his remarks, "If

I'm named after grandma like all her other grandchildren, why didn't she ask God not to lock me up in the hospital? When I meet her in the world-to-come, I'll say to her: That wasn't very nice, grandma. That wasn't very nice at all."

"It is forbidden to talk that way," Reb Levi seized the corners of the table, lest in despair he tear the hair from his head. "It is forbidden to talk that way. Whatever God does is right and his judgment is right."

"He's not right, papa, and you don't believe he's right, either. You know when I had my first fright?" Tsirele bent over the table and whispered in his ear. "When grandpa Yosele died. You don't know, papa, you don't know," Tsirele said, as gay as a little girl splashing barefoot in a pond. "You assume that I became sick when I grew up. The truth is that I became sick when I was still little. When grandpa died, you woke me up and took me to him. There were many candles burning around him and men with beards as long as yours were chanting Psalms and all the aunts were crying. I too wanted to cry. Now grandpa won't be able to stroke me any more, I thought. You always were so strict. You either yelled or didn't talk to me at all. You always yelled at the people who came to see you, too. I stood next to grandpa thinking, now no one will stroke me. Then we went outside and I saw a woman with flowers in her hair standing by grandpa's window. When she saw us she shouted, 'I'm a bride. My bridegroom ran away and I have no place to hide my face in shame.' Then you chased her from grandpa's window and called her a madwoman. She screamed more passionately that she wanted to be buried with Reb Yosele. I began to cry. 'No! No! I won't permit it.' And she cried, 'Yes, that's just what I want! Reb Yosele was to have performed the ceremony. That's why I want them to bury me with him. If you don't permit it, you won't live to stand under the wedding canopy.' That's what she shouted at me. So I ran and you, papa, ran after me, angry at me for being frightened. But I was afraid that the deserted bride with flowers in her hair would get her wish and be buried with grandpa. Also, after grandpa's burial I didn't want to leave the grave. So you took me by the hand and led me away by force. Since then every night I tremble that the bride with flowers in her hair will dig up grandpa's grave and ask him to stroke her hair like he used to stroke mine. And when I grew up and you didn't let me go to the Hebrew high school, I said to myself that the deserted bride with flowers in her hair had put the curse on me to run about in the streets like her—why are you crying, papa?"

"I'm not crying, my child . . . I'm . . . not . . . crying." Reb Levi patted her hair, as if to compensate her for his lack of tenderness during her childhood. "Forgive me, Tsirele, for being strict with you. Do you know why I shouted at you when grandpa died? My heart grieved me that now there would be no one who would hug you, my child. Your mother was in the hospital then, and I was still a very embittered young man. But I had a tutor at home for you to teach you to write. I didn't send you to the Hebrew high school because there boys and girls studied together, and they studied Bible bareheaded. I wanted you to grow up pious."

"But I was pious, even more than Uncle Asher-Anshel's Tsirele. So why did she get a husband and not me? No one took me because you didn't let me go to the Hebrew high school together with boys."

"Your cousin Tsirele didn't marry a boy from the high school either," the broken Reb Levi defended himself as though before a judge. "She married a Torah scholar, a religious young man. If you keep up your good behavior, I'll get you a husband no less worthy than your cousin's. I'll assign my rabbinic post over to your husband and thank God Almighty that you have been cured."

"No one will take me. I've been in the hospital and I'm an old maid," Tsirele laughed hollowly and fell silent.

His eyes lowered, Reb Levi fell silent, too. He had been pondering why he deserved such punishment from heaven. Now he realized that it wasn't God, Tsirele's mother, or his unfortunate daughter who were to blame. He alone was to blame. He should not have kept Tsirele in isolation. He should have let her go to the Hebrew high school. Reb Asher-Anshel's daughter had gone and had remained religious. So why then had he been so fearful that his only child would become promiscuous if she were educated and would have girl friends? Because he had been afraid that his daughter might inherit his character. He was afraid that she might stumble just because she was his daughter. And perhaps his zealousness stemmed from a fear of his own secret desires. He felt that he had to be more devout and stricter than his brothers-in-law, because he was more likely than they to go astray, especially since he had lived so many years without a wife.

"Papa, you told me that cousin Tsirele has three daughters. Isn't she ashamed?"

100

"Why should she be ashamed?"

"Since she has children, everyone knows what she does with her husband when they're alone," Tsirele suppressed a giggle. "Everyone knows and she's not ashamed?"

Startled, Reb Levi gazed at his daughter. Who was she, an angel or a demon? Her madness evidently sprang from her contempt for her modesty. That's why she raved and stripped herself naked.

"Papa, people are coming," Tsirele jumped up.

"Who is coming?" Reb Levi shivered, hearing the heavy tread of footfalls. "Who can it be?"

"It's the bride with flowers in her hair who stood by grandpa's window. Papa, I'm afraid," she said, backing into her room.

"Don't be afraid, my child," Reb Levi pleaded, terrified by her mad notion. "Have you forgotten that our house was always full of people? Lately, I've stopped participating in communal affairs, and don't even go to the meetings any more. You'll soon see that these are good people. But for your sake I'll tell them to leave at once."

"No, don't tell them to go, and don't shout at them like you once did. I'm afraid when I hear shouting. I'll come out of my room when they leave. Don't say a word," she said, and with the silence of a shadow disappeared behind the door.

The footsteps approached, but Reb Levi still faced the door to his daughter's room and mumbled with burning lips, "Oh, God Almighty! You rescued Abraham from a fiery furnace; you sent your angel to rescue Hananiah, Mishael and Azarya from the fiery furnace. Merciful Father! I too am in a fiery furnace, beset by flames day and night. Send your angel to cure my daughter."

"A good week, rabbi!" Reb Levi suddenly heard voices and saw a host of people in his study.

18

Reb Levi fidgeted in his chair for an hour, his hand over his eyes, rubbing his forehead and listening to the Agudahniks from Reb Shaulke's Shul. These pious souls did not care about the butchers' complaints that if marrying someone else's wife was permitted, they'd import meat from Oshmeneh. Let them go ahead and do it. If there wouldn't be kosher meat, religious Jews would eat fowl. The Agudahniks only cared about one thing—what would the rival Mizrachi organization say? And what about members of other parties, damn them, what would they say?

The congregants of the Old-New Shul weren't as proficient in politics as the Agudahniks; hence their remarks weren't as clever. "Rabbi, we're in a sad fix," they began indignantly, as befitted trustees who neglected their own affairs and concerned themselves with the public good. "If the tenants of the courtyards won't pay rent, there won't be money to pay the rabbis' salaries. And there won't be enough money to fix the ritual bath. The rabbis, however, are silent and it's the rich householders who must swallow this bitter brew to the dregs. The *mohel* Lapidus is absolutely right when he says we ought to shout it from the rooftops that the Vilna Rabbinic Council is afraid of some puny rabbi from Polotsk Street who permitted a married woman to wed."

"Is that so? Has the *mohel* Lapidus been to see you?" Reb Levi muttered into his beard. "Now I understand. Now I understand."

"What's the fuss?" an Agudahnik from Reb Shaulke's Shul intruded. "The *mohel* Lapidus, scion of the Rokeach family, cherishes the honor of the Torah. That's why he's storming against Reb David. For the glory of God."

In his mind's eye, Reb Levi constantly saw the closed door behind his back. Tsirele had asked him not to yell at his visitors, for shouting frightened her; but Reb Levi could no longer tolerate the phony piety of the Agudahniks and he answered sharply:

"That quarrelmonger Lapidus is doing this for the glory of God? Either you're just pretending or you simply don't know that he's been carrying a grudge against Reb David Zelver ever since he disqualified him. You young men here undoubtedly studied in the Mussarist *yeshivas*, so you know what Reb Israel Salanter said about those who fired a *shokhet* after suspecting him of using a faulty knife. 'Who knows,' Reb Israel Salanter declared, 'how many faults are in the hearts of those who slew the *shokhet*?' And when the head *shamesh* slapped the assistant *shamesh* for snatching a wedding ceremony from him, didn't he claim that he did it solely for the glory of God? And when you young men love to stir up a stew and play politics, don't you also claim you're doing it solely for the glory of God? Everyone acts solely for the glory of God."

"And the rabbis who ordered the *shamesh* to keep his mouth shut about Reb David's decision to let a married woman marry— did they also act for the glory of God?" a representative from Reb Shaulke's Shul flared up.

"Which rabbis?" Reb Levi looked at him, flustered, as though his head were suddenly spinning. "It was *I* who ordered the head *shamesh* to keep silent."

"Rabbi," sighed a Sabbath Observer from the Old Shul. "I don't know how to say it, but we're in a sad fix, a very sad fix."

"Why sad?" Reb Levi asked, his eyes glazed, obviously unaware of what he had just said.

The old man groaned and nodded; and his words fell sadly like the monotonous ticking of an old grandfather clock:

"Till now I willingly accepted the insults hurled at me by the shopkeepers when I reminded them to close their stores on Friday afternoons before the kindling of Sabbath lights. Even my own children didn't want to obey me when they were little, but when they grew up they realized I had meant it for their good. Likewise, in the world-to-come, the shopkeepers will thank me for having kept them from desecrating the Sabbath. But last Friday, when the shopkeepers declared that if marrying a married woman was permitted, then desecrating the Sabbath was permitted, too, I decided that from now on I would no longer visit the stores. I saw that the shopkeepers won't obey me anyway. The sages state that a man is even forbidden to punish his own children, if he knows they won't obey. Isn't that so, rabbi?"

The delegates exchanged frightened glances. What had happened to Reb Levi? He sat with lowered head, immobile, as though in a dead faint. Was he sick, or did he simply not hear what was being said? The enraged visitors stood, ready to depart.

"Where are you going?" Reb Levi perked up, seizing one of the men by the elbow. "Sit down, gentlemen, sit down. And now . . . now *you'll* be my judges for a while. What's the matter, gentlemen? I really mean it—I want you to be my judges for a while. I've been thinking about one thing all evening, but I can't make up my mind." He glanced uneasily at the closed door behind his back and spoke more softly. "I ordered the head shamesh to remain silent, for I foresaw that it would lead to sacrilege. If only I'd been proven wrong! The same mob that previously shouted that Reb David Zelver was right and that he should be made Vilna's chief rabbi is now clamoring for just the opposite. Now you come to me, demanding that I declare my opposition to Reb David Zelver. But since this Reb David is a frightfully obstinate man who enjoys suffering for his stubbornness, he will not withdraw his permission. If we publicize the dispute, the sacrilege will be even greater, for then the mob will truly see that disobeying the rabbis is permitted. Consequently, I suggest silence until passions abate and the entire incident is forgotten. Jews who stand in awe of God will continue to obey the Torah; and as far as the others are concerned—well, they're beyond help. The power the rabbis once had exists no longer."

"So where should we get the strength to wage war with the impious Bundists?" asked a trustee of the Old-New Shul.

"And who will struggle with the Bundists and the Zionists in the communal council? Who will stand up for the *cheders* and for the Yavneh religious schools?" one of the Agudahniks sang out. "If the great Torah scholars are no generals, the plain Jews are no soldiers. Vilna is becoming a city of heathens."

"God forbid," said the old Sabbath Observer with the milk-white beard, his hands trembling. "Vilna is still the Jerusalem of Lithuania. But we're in a sad fix, rabbi, a very sad fix. My children always ask me: 'Papa, do you get paid for dragging your old ailing feet from store to store every Friday afternoon? Let the Vilna rabbis do this.' I scold them and continue to do as I please. But if a rabbi has permitted a married woman to marry, I don't know what to tell my children."

"Send whoever you want," Reb Levi pleaded. "Go to other Vilna rabbis. I'm afraid of the agunah's tears. She's been without a husband for many, many years. I know full well what it means to remain alone. Look at me!" he groaned to the old men of the Old Shul, hoping that perhaps they would understand him.

"May the Almighty help you, rabbi," an old man sighed. "May He help us all. Both the agunah and the shopkeepers deserve to be pitied. All week long they wait for the brisk Friday business. 'What have you got against us, grandpa?' they shout. 'Talk to the housewives who come shopping just when candles should be lit.' And the poor housewife has to wait until Friday afternoon when her husband brings her his earnings. There are no bad Jews—we should always find something good to say about every Jew."

"Reb David's wife will curse me," Reb Levi whispered more to himself than to his visitors. "She has a sick infant and she herself is ill. Her husband, Reb David, will not retreat from his position. So I'll be the tormentor and he—the persecuted, the man of anguish who will ask God Almighty to take his part. And the curses of the persecuted will fall upon me."

"Come," one of the young scholars jumped up. "We didn't realize that we had to fear Reb David's anger. And if Reb Levi is afraid of his anger, there's nothing more to talk about. Let's go, gentlemen!"

All the visitors stood, their chairs scraping the floor.

"I'm puzzled by two things," said a trustee of the Old-New Shul. "First, why did you ask us to stay when we wanted to leave? Secondly, why all this indecisiveness? Either—or! Since Reb David has freed an agunah, the rabbis should declare their assent to his decision and then no one will have any complaints. But if Reb David had no right to do this, why should he be spared? And why are you telling us to go to other rabbis? It's you, and no other rabbi, who has jurisdiction over agunahs."

"We too studied the tractate *Yebamot*, and we're no strangers to the early codifiers. Still, we've never heard of an instance where an agunah could be freed without the testimony of a witness," one Torah scholar from Reb Shaulke's Shul addressed another, as though Reb Levi weren't even there.

"Fine! I'll summon Reb David to the rabbinic courtroom," Reb Levi said between his teeth, and his eyes, glinting with hatred for the scholars, burned with a yellow flame. "If he refuses to admit that he erred, the Rabbinic Council will have to proclaim this. But the responsibility for the consequences will fall—"

"On us all," Reb Levi wanted to—but could not—conclude. One of the visitors who had turned to the door behind Reb Levi's back suddenly screamed. Another stood open-mouthed, absolutely dumbfounded. The trustees from the Old-New Shul covered their faces, as though acid had been cast at them. Reb Levi saw everyone withdrawing in fright. Something exploded in his mind and he jumped up. Tsirele, smiling secretively, had partly opened her door and quietly made her way through the narrow opening—stark naked.

The short, heavyset Reb Levi sprang toward the door, stumbled and fell on the **threshold.** Tsirele, intending to slip by unnoticed, saw that she had been spotted and flung the door wide open. Her nakedness flashed in the rabbi's study: she had a small slender body, protruding hip bones, shadowy abdomen, and stocky legs; her thin shoulders were snow-white, and her breasts were small and round. Her eyes glowing slyly, she stepped over her father with lightning speed. The fallen Reb Levi jumped up and pushed his daughter so furiously she flew back into the open room. Reb Levi slammed the door and, helped by others, leaned his entire weight on it, as though supporting a house that had collapsed on him.

"Let me out," a childish voice whimpered from within. "I want to go to the bride with flowers in her hair. Her bridegroom left her and during grandpa's funeral she put the curse on me that I should not live to get married. Now her bridegroom has returned and she is no longer an agunah."

"My child," Reb Levi pressed his head to the door, as though nestling against her shoulders.

"Let me out," she pounded. "I want to tell the bride with flowers in her hair to run away with her bridegroom."

"Call the neighbors!"

"Call the first-aid wagon!"

"No need," Reb Levi groaned, pressing with all his might against the door. "She'll calm down, she'll calm down."

"I won't calm down, I won't calm down," Tsirele raged. "You cut-throat, I won't calm down. You want to separate the bride with flowers in her hair from her bridegroom and lock her up in the madhouse, like you locked me up and like you locked Mama up. Cutthroat!"

"I'm afraid she'll jump out the window!" someone shouted.

"Let her jump. Let her jump," Reb Levi too began to pound the door, as though infected by his daughter's madness.

"I won't jump. I don't want to die. I want to live and dance naked in the street," she burst into laughter. "I want to dance naked, naked, naked. I want a man. A man! Get me a man!"

"Tie her up! Gag her!" Reb Levi screamed, wet with perspiration. "She's no daughter of mine. She's a bastard. A bastard! No daughter of Reb Levi would want to run out of the house naked."

"I'm your daughter. Yours!" she laughed. "The bride with flowers in her hair is your daughter. The agunah is your daughter. And I'm your daughter, too. Your daughter wants to dance naked with boys. With boys."

The two old men who had hitherto remained dumbstruck, now regained their presence of mind and knew what had to be done. They opened the window, stuck their heads out into Shlomo Kissen's courtyard, and shouted into the night: "Jews, help, help!"

"Don't call Jews, call gentiles. Get the wagon of the insane asylum," Reb Levi shouted, his lips foaming. "She's driven me mad. I can't bear it any longer. Day and night I stood guard to prevent her from running out naked. But I can't bear it any longer. Take her away from me. It's all her fault. It's because of her that I didn't want to intervene. But God has punished me for permitting this sacrilege. Take her away from me, and I'll be your rabbi again. The agunah remained alone almost sixteen years. I've been alone for twenty."

People came running up the stairs. Broad-shouldered, vigorous men filled the apartment. They pushed aside the trustees and the delicate young Torah scholars who held the door. But the father could not be pushed away. Reb Levi stood with outspread hands and feet, his back pressed to the door, facing the crowd.

"Call the asylum's wagon and take her away from me forever . . . Call my brothers-in-law. Let them see what their niece has inherited from their side of the family. It's not my blood, and it's not my father's blood. Summon Reb David here, summon that rebel. It's his daughter. His! Assemble the great rabbinic court. I'll uproot him, I'll excommunicate him. It's his daughter—his!"

"Water. He's fainting," everyone shouted.

From the other side of the door came a laugh which turned into a sharp, thin wail.

"*Your* daughter. I'm *your* daughter. String a necklace for Tsirele, a necklace for Tsirele."

19

One fall morning Merl the seamstress went down the Zaretche hill into town to see Reb Levi Hurvitz, covering her face with her kerchief to prevent acquaintances from stopping her.

Three weeks ago, when Kalman returned from the Simkhas Torah service at the Main Synagogue and told her about the scandal, Merl had turned white, dropped into a chair, and, wringing her hands, murmured:

"Reb David Zelver has brought a calamity down on his head."

"You always act as if you married me not of your own free will but because Reb David ordered you to," Kalman complained, losing his patience. "Even now, when I'm telling you that I was so humiliated I wanted to bury myself with shame, again you're thinking about Reb David and not about me. In that case, by rights I should be the first to regret having married a woman who causes me humiliation."

But Merl's cold-blooded stare crushed him completely.

For weeks Merl had not slept at night. She wanted to run to Reb David, apologize for the anguish she was causing him, and ask him what she could do for him—yet she was afraid to appear before him. Since Kalman had revealed the secret in such a foolish manner, the rabbi had surely concluded that the agunah had repaid him evil for good. But Merl feared the rabbi's wife even more. The rebbetsin would refuse to believe that her husband had practically forced the dispensation upon Merl. And even if she believed it, who knows what other doubts she might have.

Nevertheless, Merl trusted that the tumult would gradually subside. But the scene in Reb Levi's apartment caused more of a stir in town than the slap in the Main Synagogue, and shattered her hopes that Reb David would be able to avoid catastrophe.

The incident concerning Reb Levi's daughter terrified and saddened everyone. The story was spread by the market peddlers, the butchers, the tenants of the courtyards and the storekeepers, who said that it was all the fault of God's thieves, the pious hunchbacks who had pestered the rabbi for hours on Saturday night to settle the matter of the agunah.

"All along you've been shouting that Reb Levi and Reb David Zelver were members of one gang," said one of the *shul* Jews, risking his life. But the bystanders hooted him down and the market youths slapped their heads and said:

"How should we simple working people have known that Reb Levi had a crazy daughter? And how come you're mixing us into your crooked business? Never mind what we've said. We've got tongues, so we talk."

The women peddlers in their wide aprons and the red-faced butchers' wives dabbed their wet eyes:

"There's good reason for the saying that God prepares the cure before the illness. Luckily the rabbi fainted, so didn't hear his daughter screaming when the asylum wagon took her away."

"The *shul* Jews who had pestered him ran away from the confusion in the apartment like mice into their holes. Those who did remain were the tenants of Shlomo Kissen's courtyard who over the years hadn't gotten along so well with Reb Levi."

"The rabbi, God forgive us for our words, is hot-tempered and fanatic. But if misfortune strikes, our people don't carry grudges."

"They doctored him until he opened his eyes and saw that his daughter was no longer there. He didn't shout or cry, but quietly asked the neighbors to leave him alone."

"Well, don't Reb David and that slut deserve to be run out of town?"

"Then we'll run them out of town!" the men consoled their women of valor. "And that'll be the end of that wretched upstart and that brazen slut who couldn't go to bed with her husband without that crooked rabbi's permission. Nothing else was good enough for that clunk but carrying a Torah in the Main Synagogue on Simkhas Torah, that baggy-kneed, raggedy wall-smearer."

The news surged along Polotsk Street and broke in Kalman's ears, who cringed even more with fear and humiliation. But when Merl heard the aspersions, her black eyes flashed with their old fire and she laughed crisply. If not for her ninny of a husband, she would have walked arm-in-arm with him in those very streets where they gossiped about them and laughed right into the slanderers' faces. But as soon as Merl remembered Reb David the light in her eyes expired. She hastily put on her kerchief and ran to Reb Levi Hurvitz.

But the closer Merl came to the rabbi's house, the more leaden her feet became. She was afraid of standing before the rabbi whose daughter, folks said, lost her reason when she had heard about the agunah. They also declared that the rabbi himself did not want to intervene. They said he had begged his visitors to leave him alone, for he feared the agunah's curses and tears. "I won't weep in his presence and I won't even curse him in my heart. I'll do anything he says, so long as no harm comes to Reb David," the seamstress said to herself, and her thoughts leaped to Moishke Tsirulnik.

She had heard that Moishke Tsirulnik was busily inciting the Jews in town against the rabbis for not firing Reb David Zelver and not excommunicating him. This was Tsirulnik's way of taking revenge. Merl bit her lips and, as if suddenly feeling warm, removed her kerchief. Instead of going to the rabbi she'd find Tsirulnik and throw a bottle of acid into his miserable face. But she changed her mind, quickly donned the kerchief again and proceeded to the rabbi. If she took her revenge upon Tsirulnik, it would only make matters worse for Reb David.

The door to the rabbi's study was open, as were the doors of the inner rooms, like a house from which a corpse had recently been removed. Merl waited at the **threshold** until she saw the rabbi—short, broad-shouldered, his face swollen from weeping and lack of sleep—coming from the other room.

"What do you want?" he snapped.

"I'm the agunah."

"Which agunah?" he retreated, startled.

"The one Reb David Zelver gave the rabbinic permission to."

"Ah, sit down," he said and dashed into the adjoining room, looked about as if still seeking his Tsirele, then stormed back to the agunah. "I heard you've been without a husband for fifteen years. Almost sixteen!" he shouted and collapsed into his armchair at the head of the table.

He's much older than Reb David, Merl thought, moving her chair closer to the table. The rabbi is about forty, while Reb Levi is over sixty. He's old enough to be Reb David's father.

"Rabbi, I'm prepared to divorce my husband."

"Divorce your husband?" the rabbi arched his eyebrows. "Of course you must divorce your husband. You are forbidden to remain under the same roof with him even one day. As long as you do not bring trustworthy witnesses that your first husband is no longer alive, Jewish law considers you a married woman."

"I'm certain that my first husband is no longer alive. My heart tells me that he's not alive. But, nevertheless, I'm ready to divorce my husband."

"That's precisely what you must do," Reb Levi grumbled and looked down at his beard, as though amazed to find some red hairs among the grey ones. "How old are you?"

"Thirty-six."

"And you remained without a husband for almost sixteen years? I see . . . You've probably heard of my daughter. She's twenty and her mother has been ill these past twenty years. Her mother fell ill when she was in confinement with her," he said sadly, addressing the strange woman like a sister, and was momentarily dumbstruck. A thought flashed. Where the woman was standing now, only last Saturday night Tsirele had stood and kindled his Havdala candle.

"And if I divorce my husband, no one will suffer on account of me?"

"What do you mean?" he said, snapping out of his spell of weakness and gazing at her with fire in his eyes. "Who is suffering on account of you?"

"Everyone is suffering on account of me." Against her will Merl felt her eyes brimming with tears. "My husband is suffering on account of me, my mother and my sisters are suffering on account of me, and even Reb David Zelver is suffering on account of me. He's not at all to blame. My sisters and I wept before him until he consented to let me marry. Now that I see what has come of all this, I don't want him to suffer on my account. I feel sorry for his wife and children."

"Of course his wife and children are to be pitied," Reb Levi sprang out of his chair and began pacing around the room. "If Reb David admits his error, we'll proclaim it in all the *shuls* and he won't have to suffer. The Rabbinic Council will defend him against all his enemies. Go see his wife and tell her that you are prepared to divorce your husband, and then both of you should try to convince him to admit his error."

Merl felt herself flushing down to the shoulders. For a moment she stood speechless. She didn't want to tell the rabbi that she was ashamed and even afraid to show her face to the rebbetsin.

"Why should Reb David humiliate himself and admit his error?" Merl asked with almost childish concern. "He's gentle, but very proud."

"He is gentle, but very proud," the rabbi laughed wearily. He walked about the room with increased tempo, the words seemingly flying forth from his beard, his eyes, his pockets and his sleeves. "Do you think that the entire tumult in town stems from your living with a man illegally? These things are a daily occurrence and the rabbis don't say a word. No one consults us and no one obeys us. Your affair has stirred up the entire town because a rabbi permitted something forbidden. Now everyone contends that if one agunah may marry, so may other agunahs. In brief, everything is now permitted! That's why the rabbis have no choice but to declare war against Reb David and proclaim before Vilna and the entire world that the Torah is still the Torah, and that an agunah is forbidden to marry as long as she doesn't bring trustworthy witnesses concerning the death of her first husband. So if you want to spare Reb David needless anguish and humiliation, try to convince him to admit his error. And do it today. Right now! Tomorrow the rabbis will assemble in the rabbinic courtroom and Reb David has been invited to attend. Woe unto him if he does not come! You say you feel sorry for him and his family. But if you had weighed the consequences of your act, you would not only have spared Reb David anguish, but me and my only child as well," Reb Levi said, running into the adjoining room and slamming the door behind him.

Merl stood terror-stricken, then walked downstairs like someone entering an abyss. Besides having Reb David on her conscience, Reb Levi sought to blame her for his daughter's madness. She stood at the gate, firmly holding the edges of her kerchief as though the rabbi's shouts were still fluttering about her and tearing off her head covering. Hurrying back to Zaretche, Merl mused that she was now between the fire and the frying pan. On the one side was Reb Levi Hurvitz, and on the other, Reb David Zelver. To Reb David she would talk tonight, when he remained alone in the *shul* after the Evening Service. Perhaps she would succeed in convincing him after all to withdraw his permission and thus save himself.

20

Reb David Zelver sat in his usual place near the Holy Ark, trying to formulate his reply to the meeting of the Vilna rabbis. But he could not concentrate and had no strength to return home. His wife's shouting made his mind go blank.

The rebbetsin never ceased cursing the day she was born, the hour she was married, and the minute an ill wind had swept in the agunah. The rebbetsin's fear that a new controversy with the rabbis would make her family suffer more, was overshadowed by her anger at her husband for hiding this from her and for having learned about it from Yosefl. The boy returned from *cheder* in tears: "The teachers are humiliating me. The minute I don't behave, right away they bring up the unpaid tuition. They don't consider me a rabbi's son, because Papa said the agunah could marry. I swear I won't go to *cheder* any more."

"Don't go to *cheder*," his mother agreed. "Don't go! Grow up to be a horse trader, even a thief—anything but a rabbi."

The rebbetsin had bluntly told her husband that if he wrangled with Vilna's rabbis on account of the agunah, it meant there was something between them. Reb David did not reply to her accusation. He thought that perhaps God had decreed that he too have an insane rebbetsin, like his antagonist Reb Levi Hurvitz. Everyone opposed him. He could not show his face in the Rabbinic Council. The *mohel* Lapidus went from *shul* to *shul* inciting the worshippers against him. The head shamesh of the Main Synagogue was now his eternal enemy. The mob was clamoring for his removal from Vilna. The Agudah group—fire and brimstone against him. And just plain respectable Jews said he should be excommunicated. Even the Zaretche congregants were displeased with him and would gladly have seen him dismissed. Heaven, too, opposed him. While granting the permission, Reb David thought that in return for easing the burdens of a troubled woman his Mottele would become well. At first it appeared that way; his baby's health improved. But lately his condition worsened from day to day. He could not sit next to the infant, for his wife's wailing drove him from the house. The only one who had remained silent thus far was his old adversary, Reb Levi Hurvitz. Now the latter had suddenly notified him to present himself before the rabbinic court.

"Rabbi!"

Reb David could not believe his eyes. The former agunah stood before him now as she had the first time when she poured out her misfortune, and the second time when he told her to get married.

"What do you want?"

"Forgive me, rabbi," she said, feeling his sharp voice cutting into her heart. "My husband did not do it intentionally. He didn't dream that the assistant shamesh giving him a Torah would cause such a tumult."

"I realize that myself," Reb David said impatiently.

"I want to divorce my husband," she murmured, confused by his unfriendliness. "I don't want you or your family to suffer on my account."

Merl's remark was said with such compassion and tenderness that Reb David felt sorry for himself. But his wife's words immediately flew through his mind—if he stood up for the agunah, there was something between them ... And he quickly moved away from Merl to the pulpit, hoping that the verse inscribed on the marble tablet, "I constantly think of the Lord" would protect him from strange thoughts. The seamstress followed and stood opposite him, as if she were the incarnation of the Evil Impulse. But when he saw her face by the light of the memorial candle on the pulpit, his fear vanished. Her eyes glowed with goodness and devotion. Reb David felt a twinge of pain in his heart for having received her coldly.

"You want to divorce your husband in order to spare me anguish?" he asked in a soft voice which made her tremble with joy.

"Yes, rabbi," she whispered.

"That won't help. The rabbis couldn't care less if you get a divorce or not. The main thing is that I retract and admit that I was mistaken."

"Do it, rabbi," she stretched her hands to him, then quickly withdrew them. "Have pity on yourself and your family. My hus-

114

band won't have any qualms about getting divorced. He's sorry he married me. He can't show his face in the street and is ashamed to go to *shul*. And if my husband regrets the marriage, and I regret it, why don't you regret it too? And then the rabbis will make peace with you. They'll treat you better than before and defend you against all your enemies."

"How do you know?" Reb David's eyes darkened like the panes in the night-cloaked *shul*.

"Reb Levi Hurvitz told me."

Reb David's nostrils quivered. The rabbis wanted to come to terms with him, but on condition that he retract his decision. And Reb Levi was so compassionate! He seemed to be so magnanimous and was prepared to condone Reb David's impudence, if only he would capitulate and publicly proclaim his transgression.

"I will never retract my decision," Reb David whispered stubbornly. "If you want to divorce your husband in order to do me a favor, you will only cause me harm. You will only show the entire town and all the rabbis that even *you* don't consider me a rabbi and have little regard for my decision. And you can tell your husband that I told him to take courage. He *should* go out into the street. He *should* go to *shul*." Reb David's slender body twitched with anger and he clenched his fists to keep himself from shouting that her husband was no man. "Tell your husband that I consider you a saintly woman. Yes, a saintly woman! But don't you dare meddle in my affairs any more. Your going to Reb Levi was a bad move, extremely unfortunate. And the more you intervene, the more harm you'll cause me. If people see you running around defending me, they'll say I was bribed to give you the permission. And they might even say nastier things. Which my wife is already saying. . . And if you do divorce your husband, the entire town will say what my wife is saying. I'm prepared to suffer all kinds of torments and humiliations—except that one." Reb David looked directly at her with frightened eyes, his jaw and sunken cheeks quivering, as though afraid that his wife's suspicions weren't groundless.

"True, true," Merl whispered, unsure if she was assenting to the rabbi's order not to meddle or to his wife's remark. For a moment she gazed at him with sadness and mute admiration. Suddenly she shivered and backed away from him, lest she fall at his feet. Reb David's eyes glowed with fear, amazement, and suspicion.

Even after the seamstress had gone, he stood with his hands clasping the pulpit behind him, as though forcibly restraining himself from running after her.

Reb David tore himself away from the pulpit, ran up the steps that led to the Holy Ark, and wiped his eyes as if wiping away the image of the married woman. And as though still afraid that the seamstress had remained in some dark corner of his thoughts, he switched on one lamp after another until the *shul* was bright with light like on the night of Yom Kippur.

Merl, outside, suddenly saw the courtyard and a part of the street up to the Zaretche market sown with rays of light, as though the windows of the *shul* were showing her how to return to her house and to her husband.

21

Reb Shmuel-Munye, the rabbi of Glazers Street, was a slightly-built man with a willowy white beard and a thick nose dotted with root hairs like an overgrown radish. His imperial beard and his behavior continually amazed the town. He had three sons and two daughters. Reb Shmuel-Munye's wages sufficed for only three days of the seven; the remaining four, including Sabbath, the family lived by borrowing. Creditors constantly streamed into the house. Today, the butcher, the grocer, the landlord and the recluse who tutored his sons all met in his house as though for a wedding. The postman entered with a letter. Reb Shmuel-Munye put on his glasses and glanced quickly at it.

"Gentlemen," he smiled to his creditors, "everything will turn out well."

The creditors did not know the contents of the letter, but judging by the rabbi's confident smile, he had apparently won the grand prize in the lottery or inherited a rich American uncle's fortune. The shopkeepers and the recluse left, appeased, and Reb Shmuel-Munye called in the rebbetsin who had hidden in the kitchen.

"Your son David-Moshe wants to know how we all are."

"What else does he write?" the rebbetsin asked, her face dark and gloomy.

"He quotes the Torah and asks for money. I'll write to the head of the yeshiva that he should give David-Moshe what he needs and charge it to my account."

Her hands folded on her chest, the rebbetsin looked anxiously at her husband: "On your account? You think that the head of the Mir Yeshiva will trust you on your smile alone? Other rabbis' sons are supported by the yeshiva, so why do you consider it beneath your dignity to accept money from them? Is it nicer to request a loan from the head of the yeshiva and never repay it? And why do we have to have a tutor for the younger children instead of sending them to Ramile's yeshiva? And why do you insist on scholars for sons-in-law when you know that you don't even have enough of a dowry for someone mediocre?"

"No congregant has such little respect for a rabbi as his own wife," Shmuel-Munye answered all her questions at once and ran out of the house.

Reb Shmuel-Munye never had any time to spare. He managed the politics of the Rabbinic Council, the peace-loving Ahdut movement, the Yeshiva Council, and the Agudah organization which held that pious Jews should never befriend freethinkers. Although Reb Shmuel-Munye was the big wheel in all the great conventions of Lithuanian rabbis, he himself remained inconspicuous—he was never the chairman—and the young men did not even rise in respect when he passed by.

In Vilna itself, nothing—whether wedding or funeral—took place without him. During a rabbinic wedding, he whispered to the father of the bride to whom to give the honors. When a great man died, Reb Shmuel-Munye determined which rabbi would eulogize at the Main Synagogue, which at the cemetery, and which rabbi would return home without having delivered his prepared tribute. Not a few scholars who traveled great distances to attend a wedding or a funeral remained his lifelong enemies. But he did not mind; he always rushed to conventions smiling.

His sarcastic smile made everyone feel that Reb Shmuel-Munye held him in contempt. For every subject discussed, he maintained that he was its greatest expert. If it pertained to laws of women, he stroked his white beard, counseled the other rabbis not to argue with him, and always declared: "Just leave it to me. It's my specialty." Even on the eve of Sukkos, when the small-town rabbis gathered in the stores, fingering the *esrogs* and *lulavs*, Reb Shmuel-Munye adroitly inspected the tips of the *lulavs* and proclaimed, "Rabbi, take this one. And you, rabbi, take this one. Just leave it to me. It's my specialty." The rabbis were dying to ask him how he could possibly be such an expert in everything if he never even picked up a sacred text. However, they bit their tongues and controlled their impulse. After all, he was a rabbinic authority in Vilna, and he did manage the affairs of the Rabbinic Council. The only one who did not stand in awe of him was Reb Levi Hurvitz.

When Reb Shmuel-Munye began to say, "Just leave it to me. . . "
Reb Levi cut him off with, "Your specialty is politicking."

Reb Shmuel-Munye's two daughters were also graced with his endearing character. Upon hearing that one of their girl-friends had become engaged, they smirked with half-closed eyes: Look who she's marrying! Reb Shmuel-Munye's eldest son was even more disdainful than his father. In the new interpretations to Talmudic texts that he sent home from the yeshiva, he mocked a dozen rabbinic authorities and then modestly concluded with a request for funds. Even the two younger boys, who studied with the recluse in the Gaon's Shul, contradicted everything their teacher taught them. The only one in Reb Shmuel-Munye's family who didn't scoff at the entire world was the rebbetsin. The more her husband and daughters smiled with half-closed eyes, the more her face darkened and her shoulders stooped.

While running to the rabbinic court that would judge Reb David Zelver, Reb Shmuel-Munye was preoccupied with more important matters. He had been offered a rabbinic chair in Levoneshok and in Vashileshok. Where should he go? In Levoneshok he'd be the town's only rabbi; Vashileshok, however, already had a rabbi, and the two of them would have to share the honors. Although Vashileshok was four times the size of Levoneshok, it was far better to say a blessing over a tiny whole loaf, than over a huge one, already cut-up. So the decision, then, was Levoneshok, where he would make a comfortable living. It was high time to marry off his daughters, remit his debts, and have some peace from his wife who always looked at him with a corpse-like countenance. On the other hand, Levoneshok was tinier than a pinhead. And how could he leave Vilna? Who would run the affairs of the Rabbinic Council, the Yeshiva Council, the Kashrut Committee and all the other committees. Levoneshok, Vashileshok—where had he wandered off to?

In order to get to the courtroom from Glazers Street, he had to pass German and Vilna Streets. But he turned into Gaon Street, then strayed into the gentile quarter. This so frightened him his sarcastic smile disappeared into his beard like a sunray in a thicket. Only when he finally disentangled himself from the camp of the uncircumcised and found his way to the Jewish communal offices, did the sarcastic smile return, as though he were arming himself against Reb Levi Hurvitz.

Reb Shmuel-Munye could not understand why Reb Levi was either always sour-tempered or sniveling like an old woman. Once, when the Hasidic Lubavitcher *rebbe* had visited Vilna, Reb Levi told him in the presence of the Rabbinic Council that he stemmed from Hasidim and began bawling like a baby: "*Rebbe*, bless me! My wife and only child are sick."

The Vilna rabbis, iron-clad *misnagdim* vehemently opposed to Hasidism, were thunderstruck: was it possible that this keen scholar and irascible man, a rabbinic authority in Vilna—where the Vilna Gaon had put the Hasidim under the ban—was it possible that this selfsame Reb Levi Hurvitz should request a blessing of a Hasidic *rebbe*?

Reb Shmuel-Munye hurried to the courtroom in the Jewish communal offices, confident that everyone was waiting there for him. He quickly opened the door and saw only Reb Levi sitting at the head of the table. Reb Levi grumbled a reply to his greeting and, scarcely fulfilling the custom that scholars rise in one another's presence, rose slightly from his seat. Reb Levi did not turn from the huge tome before him, but sat there gloomily, lost in thought, absolutely mute, as though he'd been there for days. His face was strained and hard, and his silence was so foreboding that Reb Shmuel-Munye's words remained stuck in his throat. Reb Shmuel-Munye removed Joseph Caro's *Code of Law* from the bookshelf and, in passing, glanced at the open book on the table. Reb Levi was immersed in Maimonides' laws concerning insurgent scholars who defied the law of majority rule. Reb Shmuel-Munye sat down at the other end of the table, turning pages in the *Code of Law* thinking: Reb Levi wants to place Reb David under the ban for being an insurgent scholar. Placing someone under the ban is *not* my specialty.

22

Reb Asher-Anshel, the rabbinic authority over divorces, agreed with all the other rabbis that Reb David Zelver had done an unheard of thing. Nevertheless, Reb Asher-Anshel would have given a fortune to have been spared the appearance in the courtroom today and meeting his brother-in-law, Reb Levi Hurvitz.

Reb Levi had always kept himself aloof from his brothers-in-law, an attitude they reciprocated with even greater fervor. During a family celebration, when there was no choice but to invite him, and he had no alternative but to attend, he sat radiating gloom and enmity. He stared at his nieces—the trio of Tsireles—and sighed so loudly that everyone sensed what was taking place in his heart. Disgruntled with himself for not displaying a pleasant mien, he would become even more depressed and leave in the midst of the celebration.

The family had been constantly frightened and grieved ever since Reb Levi had brought Tsirele back from the hospital. They weren't really convinced that she had been cured and were insulted that Reb Levi did not let any relatives come near her. When Tsirele was taken back to the hospital, her aunts descended upon their brother, Reb Asher-Anshel, wringing their hands and declaring that Reb Levi was a cutthroat. If he had let them tend the sick girl, they complained, she would not have run out of the house naked. Now Tsirele, like her melancholic mother, was doomed forever, the sisters asserted, and rebuked their brother for his silence. But Reb Asher-Anshel replied that he would rather meet an enraged bear than contend now with his brother-in-law.

Reb Levi's request that Reb Asher-Anshel be present in the courtroom during the judgment of Reb David caused all of Reb Asher-Anshel's peace of mind to vanish.

That day he rose late, lingered over his prayers, and bobbed up and down in agitation. He had put on his coat, stroked his beard—but did not budge. His granddaughters, his daughter Tsirele's children, crawled about his feet, as though between huge pillars, saying, "Grandpa, grandpa." They knew their grandfather enjoyed their pulling his beard and tugging his earlocks. But today he didn't pick them up. Suddenly Reb Asher-Anshel decided that his son and son-in-law should accompany him. Despite their astonishment, the young men dressed and waited, as did Reb Asher-Anshel's wife and daughters. He looked down at his grandchildren and then stared at his son-in-law, Fishel Bloom.

Fishel was a young man with thick lips, full cheeks and a dense black beard. His big round eyes were always smiling and happy. Reb Asher-Anshel could see no reason for his son-in-law's perpetual contentment. Was it because he had three girls and not even one son? Or was it because he hadn't even received one offer for a position? A man with such thick lips probably could not say one word from the pulpit. A modern rabbi also had to be a good preacher, Reb Asher-Anshel thought and then looked angrily at his son.

His eighteen-year-old son, Yosele—named after his grandfather—had a long pale nose, curly black hair and a rabbinic potbelly, as befitted a young man who knew more than a thousand pages of the Talmud by heart. Taciturn by nature, he kept his eyes lowered like his father. Reb Asher-Anshel had nothing, absolutely nothing against his son. But today he gave vent to his anger at his son-in-law by shouting at his son:

"Why are you picking your nose?"

In awe of his father, Yosele actually jumped with fright. His blonde, blue-eyed sister Tsirele, a stocky girl with a wide, peasant-like snub nose, looked angrily at Fishel, having immediately sensed that her father's irritation was directed at him. The only one who preserved her presence of mind was the old rebbetsin, a thick-set, broad-shouldered woman, whose face was distorted by arthritis and whose marriage-wig was always down over her eyes.

"What are you afraid of?" she asked her husband, adjusting her wig. The rebbetsin wasn't fazed by her irascible brother-in-law, Reb Levi. His wife's mettle usually pleased Reb Asher-Anshel; but now he shouted to his son:

"What are you staring at? Let's go."

Flanked by his son and son-in-law, Reb Asher-Anshel proceeded as though he were Isaac, bound for the altar. His wife, daughter and grandchildren accompanied him to the door; from the looks on their faces it seemed as if he and not Reb David Zelver were to stand before judgment. On his way he kept up his hesitant bobbing pace, like a lid on a boiling pot, and said nothing. But when he approached the synagogue courtyard he suddenly cheered up, having seen Reb Kasriel Kahana, who was also on his way to the courtroom.

Reb Kasriel Kahana was a tall, clever, red-bearded man who walked with a cradle-like shuffle. Owing to his good business sense, his office was always packed with merchants. As an arbitrator he earned more than the combined wages of three Vilna rabbis. He delivered no sermons, taught no Torah; no one even knew whether he belonged to the Mizrachi or the Agudah. It was said that wholesalers took him as partners because of his knowledge of merchandise and his good counsel, and that by reading the paper he could predict the fluctuations of stocks and currency. Reb Kasriel Kahana was annoyed that instead of arbitrating a business dispute he would have to sit in judgment of Reb David Zelver. Hence, he was as glad to see Reb Asher-Anshel as the latter was to see him. Both men had moderate temperaments and hated disputes.

Seeing his two colleagues of the Rabbinic Council entering the courtroom, Reb Shmuel-Munye jumped up as though they were two angels. But Reb Levi did not tear his eyes away from his book and scarcely rose from his seat. His face became even more incensed and puffy. Reb Shmuel-Munye, who had been sitting by himself, depressed because of Reb Levi's stubborn silence, quickly whispered to the two rabbis that by handling Reb David diplomatically they would persuade him to submit of his own accord. Reb Kasriel shrugged and Reb Asher-Anshel coughed. Both agreed that a dispute should be avoided; still, they had no desire to contend with Reb Levi if he decided to impose the strictest severity of the law.

Immersed in the Maimonides volume, Reb Levi wondered why Reb David had not yet arrived. He knew the rabbi would keep his word, even if he had to go through fire. If he weren't so obstinate and proud there would have been no need for this meeting. One couldn't even compare Reb David with his judges. They didn't even come up to his ankles. Reb Kasriel devoted himself to arbitration. Did one have to be a rabbi for that? A clever merchant could have done an even better job. Reb Shmuel-Munye applied himself to politics. A rabbi's first responsibility was to take care of the Jews on his street and to see that they didn't violate the Sabbath, and that they observed the dietary laws and the laws of family purity. But Reb Shmuel-Munye dispensed Judaism to all of Lithuania, all of Poland, the entire world—consequently he didn't have time for the Jews of his own street. Reb Levi noted that his brother-in-law, Reb Asher-Anshel, had brought his son and son-in-law as watchmen. He should also have brought his daughter Tsirele, who wrote letters for all the neighbors in various languages. Oh yes, all the women in Gitke-Toibe's Lane praised his brother-in-law's daughter. She was pious *and* educated.

Reb Levi pulled at the wiry hairs of his eyebrows and glared with foreboding silence into the open text before him. His gloomy silence spread over the room, seeped into the rabbis' beards and sealed their mouths as though with clay.

The door opened. Reb David Zelver stood at the ' threshold, out of breath, as though he had been running. Reb Levi, who had hardly risen when his venerable colleagues entered, now stood erect for his adversary, the youngest of all the assembled rabbis.

"You're late," Fishel Bloom declared.

Does that dandy son-in-law of mine have to tell it to him? Reb Asher-Anshel thought. It struck him that the Divine Providence that had given the cat soft-cushioned paws to hide its claws, had graced his son-in-law with a great thick beard to hide his fleshy lips and cheeks. Reb Asher-Anshel looked furiously at Fishel and at Yosele, who sensed his father's glance and quickly removed his finger from his nose. The eighteen-year-old master of more than one thousand pages of Talmud reviewed in a flash all the laws pertaining to women in the Talmudic tractate *Nashim*; it was beyond him how Reb David could possibly have decided in favor of an agunah who had no witnesses to her husband's death.

Reb David Zelver arrived late because he had to fetch the doctor for his ailing infant. He felt that he should offer an excuse, lest the elderly rabbis suspect him of being disrespectful. But he didn't think it was proper to arouse their pity.

"Sit down, Reb David," Reb Levi said, not in the least irritated that the rabbi had let the court wait.

Reb David sat at the far end of the table, his hands still in his coat pockets, as though only sitting down for a moment.

124

"Why don't you take your coat off, Reb David?" Reb Levi said sadly and amicably. "Don't you even want to talk to your friends in the Council?"

Reb David removed one hand from his pocket and wrinkled a piece of paper—the doctor's prescription, which he wanted to show the rabbis and justify his lateness. He wanted to tell them that in his rush to get here he hadn't filled the prescription, and that he would soon have to run back to the pharmacist. But instead of speaking, he removed his coat, sat down again, and placed both hands on the table, as though eager to show that his hands were clean.

23

His hand pressed to his huge furrowed brow, Reb Levi was steeped in a melancholy silence and did not quite know how to begin. He had a host of prepared accusations—a barrelful of gunpowder, but no fire to kindle it. Reb Levi sighed and, owing to his weakness, began softly:

"God above knows that I've done everything in my power to suppress the agunah affair. But the incident in the Main Synagogue brought the matter to light and, as everyone knows, stirred up the entire town. So the Rabbinic Council had no alternative but to summon you, Reb David Zelver, and ask you about the basis for your permission. A sound basis will please us, and we will publicly proclaim that the agunah's marriage was indeed legally sanctioned, whereupon there will be peace upon the house of Israel."

Reb Levi gazed at Reb David Zelver with an angel-pure countenance, as though confident that Reb David would soon provide all the answers and everyone would depart contented. The other rabbis also looked at him with great anticipation. Excitement made Yosele's pale long nose even paler and longer; he was expecting to be astounded by brilliant Torah discussions.

Reb David responded quickly: "There is no doubt in my mind that the agunah was permitted to marry. More than fifteen years have passed since her husband has gone to war and he has not returned. Most people who do not return from a journey can be presumed dead, and most people who do not return from war can *certainly* be presumed dead. In our case, the man was in the 11th Company of the Orenburg Regiment stationed in Vilna. Everyone knows that this regiment was sent to the Prussian front and wiped out almost to a man in the very first battle. Very few escaped unscathed. The few who did, reported—and maintain unto this very day—that of the 11th Company there were no survivors. Therefore all the widows have long remarried."

"The women who married without permission are not the subject under consideration," Reb Levi exploded, his voice hardening. "What is under consideration is whether you, a Vilna rabbi, had a sound basis for granting permission to the agunah. If a woman comes and declares that her husband fell in the war, according to law she is not to be believed, even if we know that the couple was happily married. Our assumption is that she might have heard about the death of other soldiers in her husband's company and then fancy that her husband too was slain. She is not considered a credible witness even if she declares: ' I buried him with my own hands.'"

That point is disputed by the codifiers, Yosele thought, and owing to his great excitement that the entire Torah stood revealed before him, he winced nervously like his father.

"In our case too the woman didn't state with absolute confidence that her husband was dead." Fishel Bloom spread his ten stubby fingers to show his father-in-law that he was not boarding at his table in vain, but was immersing himself in learning. "There was not even a letter from the company that the soldier had fallen."

"In brief," Reb Levi wrinkled his brow, "we don't know whence you've derived the basis for your decision."

"From the Torah," Reb David Zelver said, raising his head. "Mordecai ben Hillel, the author of the legal code *Mordecai*, cites Rabbi Eliezer of Verdun's decision that if a man falls into the ocean his wife may not remarry as long as he can be presumed to have been saved, yet was unable to return home. But if some years pass and he does not return, we assume that he is dead. On this basis, Eliezer of Verdun granted permission to a woman who had been an agunah only four years—while the woman whom I permitted to marry had not heard from her husband for *fifteen* years. Many of the great medieval codifiers granted permissions without witnesses, but merely on the basis of conjecture and judicious assessment. Even Rabbi Asher ben Yehiel quotes a responsa of Rabbenu Gershom, the Light of the Exile, on the necessity of being lenient during wartime."

"What are you talking about, Reb David?" Reb Levi said. "For a thousand years our early and latter sages tormented themselves to find ways of permitting agunahs to marry; so if what you say

127

can be used as a precedent, why were all these sages wracking their brains? The law is *not* according to Eliezer of Verdun, who ordains that an agunah should wait only several years. Joseph Caro, the author of *Bet Joseph*, thunders out against the author of *Mordecai* and cites one early authority after another who dispute him. Rashi and the Tosafists dispute him, too, as do Nachmanides and Rabbi Shlomo ben Abraham Adret. All the early and later rabbis dispute him and maintain that if the woman doesn't bring trustworthy witnesses who saw her husband dead, she can never remarry." Reb Levi grabbed his head, as though his brain would burst.

But the louder Reb Levi screamed, the firmer and more obstinate Reb David became; he lowered his voice and did not retreat: "Even the rabbis who disputed Eliezer of Verdun and held that the husband's non-return is not proof that he was dead would have had different views today. Many of the later sages stated that in the old days with highwaymen and no postal, rail or telegraph service—a missing man could have been presumed alive. But nowadays when there *is* postal, rail and telegraph service, one can't possibly imagine so many years passing without the husband letting his wife know that he is alive."

"Just the opposite is logical," Reb Asher-Anshel raised his watery blue eyes. "The lenient sages of long ago would not be lenient today. In these days of moral anarchy, young people don't care about a Rabbenu Gershom's ban against bigamy. In handling divorces I learned of young men who hid from their wives in far-off places and remarried there."

"I heard that the agunah's husband was a socialist, and socialists don't take much stock in Rabbenu Gershom's ban against bigamy," Fishel came to his father-in-law's aid.

"The agunah's husband was very much attached to his wife, and he would not have done such a thing," Reb David Zelver replied.

Reb Kasriel Kahana looked down at his red beard and spoke quietly and logically in his resonant bass voice: "The young man could have done it out of poverty, not out of defiance of traditional law. People say he was a poor carpenter. Quite possibly he met a woman somewhere who supports him and now he doesn't want to come home and start over again."

"I'm not interested in conjectures," Reb Levi snapped at the merchants' arbitrator, Reb Kasriel Kahana. "I rely on the law. Rabbi Eliezer of Verdun is a lone dissenter, and his decision is not law, for the pillars of rabbinic authority oppose him. And Reb David Zelver versus the Rabbinic Council is also a lone dissenter."

"Eliezer of Verdun is not a lone dissenter, and even if he is, it makes no difference," Reb David retorted. "The Mishna, tractate *Eduyot*, explicitly states that the opinion of a lone dissenter is cited—even though the law is according to the majority—to teach us that in an emergency a court may even decide according to the opinion of a lone dissenter. And there can be no greater instance of emergency than this agunah—especially if she has already married and if we consider Maimonides' declaration: 'If you've married, stay married!' If I hadn't given her permission to marry, she would have married anyway and considered God heartless."

The eighteen-year-old Yosele saw that he knew each and every codifier who had been mentioned. He smiled to himself, musing that he was more learned than Reb David Zelver. As to Maimonides' decision that the woman's marriage was irrevocable—in that context Maimonides was referring to witnesses who weren't sufficiently trustworthy. But here there were no witnesses at all. So what was Reb David babbling about?

"Not so," Reb Levi jumped up. "The present husband of the agunah visited me before the wedding, and I saw that he would not have married her without permission. The agunah, too, came to see me, and I know that she is even prepared to divorce her husband. But we want you to retract and admit your error."

"God forbid!" Reb David stood and retreated several steps, hunched over and trembling. "I will never declare that I erred."

Reb Levi saw such unnatural obstinacy and self-confidence in Reb David's motions that he could scarcely keep from jumping toward Reb David and pushing him into the adjoining room, as he had pushed Tsirele when she tried to run out of her room naked.

"Reb David," Reb Levi pounded the table. "You are bringing down misfortune upon us, the Vilna community, and all Israel. You are causing the greatest sacrilege. And all because you put your honor and pride above all."

"That's not true. I've done this for the sake of Heaven," Reb David whispered and straightened up, standing stiffly erect. "It's *you* who put pride and honor above all, because I've entered your domain—deciding the problems of agunahs."

"God is my witness that I don't care a bit about my honor," Reb Levi raised his hands. "I've done everything I could to suppress what you've done, because I know you from your previous deeds. I didn't want to start up with you. But now that your decision has become generally known, you must openly proclaim your error. If you refuse, the consequences will be terrible. You will be tried as a rabbi who defies the majority and be placed under the ban," Reb Levi pointed to the open volume of Maimonides. "We will excommunicate you."

"Go right ahead," Reb David answered with pressed lips and clenched fists.

"What's going on, gentlemen?" Reb Shmuel-Munye rose. He had remained silent all along, waiting for the rabbis to turn to him for aid. Now that both sides had amassed scores of early and latter authorities and the cry of excommunication had remained hanging in the air like an ax, Reb Shmuel-Munye felt that the time had come for him to demonstrate his diplomatic skills.

Just leave it to me, that's my specialty, Yosele mimicked him silently. The eighteen-year-old master of Talmud knew that the display of codifiers was over. He stopped tugging at his tightly-curled earlocks—and the great Vilna Talmuds, whose pages had unfolded in his memory, sank into the depths of his mind like into a huge closed bookcase.

24

Reb Shmuel-Munye quickly left his seat, intending to take Reb David aside and, in his usual manner with adversaries, gently persuade him to agree. But Reb David stood with a furrowed brow, his silence serving strict notice that he wished no secret negotiations. Reb Shmuel-Munye then immediately changed his tactics and spoke loudly, for all to hear.

"What good are arguments? The affair can be settled to everyone's satisfaction. Reb David will sign a statement that he has erred and the agunah will do whatever she thinks right."

"I have no intentions of signing anything," Reb David asserted.

"In that case, there's another way out," Reb Shmuel-Munye gestured with his thumb. "You won't actually have to sign, but you'll convince the woman to divorce her husband."

"I don't want her to divorce," Reb David replied.

"Then how have our sages helped us?" Fishel said. "The important thing is for Reb David to admit his error. What good, then, would it do for the agunah to divorce, if Reb David will not withdraw his permission?"

"Just leave it to me, that's my specialty," Reb Shmuel-Munye gazed at him with his sarcastic smile and turned once more to Reb David. "If you don't want to order the agunah to divorce, then don't. You don't want to admit your error? We won't force you on that matter, either. But what then?" Reb Shmuel-Munye fingered his long white beard; the thoughts could be seen buzzing in his head. "What then? Announce in your *shul* and in the other *shuls* that you're not intervening. Your decision was based on Rabbi Eliezer of Verdun. But since all the early and latter rabbinic authorities dispute him—you are no longer intervening."

"I *am* intervening," Reb David replied.

Reb Kasriel coughed twice to contain his laughter. Fishel Bloom opened his big round eyes, smacked his thick lips, and struggled to keep the naive look on his face. He rubbed his fat neck, scratched his throat beneath his thick black beard and felt a cramp in his stomach—in no time he'd burst out laughing. Yosele, the rabbi's son, winced and picked at the hair of his chin. He had never heard anything like it in his life. He was and he wasn't intervening. Even Reb Asher-Anshel kept lowering his head until his beard lay flat on the table like a piece of silver.

Reb Levi Hurvitz, who had sat seemingly lifeless for a while, roused himself and asked drily: "Well, what's the decision?"

"He's terribly stubborn," Reb Shmuel-Munye shouted and looked around as though he'd been doused with cold water. He had never had dealings with a man as obstinate as Reb David Zelver. Yosele laughed at Reb Shmuel-Munye and curled his earlocks: He specializes in everything, but the upshot is that he can't even manage politics. Yosele looked longingly at his uncle, Reb Levi— perhaps he would again begin to hurl quotations from the early and latter rabbinic authorities. Reb Levi, however, had already lost all hope of acting on strength of the *Code of Law*, and his eyes seethed like a pair of burning lamps:

"Reb David Zelver should remember that we will proclaim that he is no longer a rabbi but a man who publicly commits sacrilege. Transgressions must be punished! We will mention that he once permitted the carrying of money on Sabbath."

"And I was right in doing so. I saved Jewish children in Russia from starvation."

"Absolute lies!" Reb Levi stormed. "The money that the Zaretche worshippers brought on Sabbath was used three weeks later. Unto this very day no one knows how long it took your Sabbath bundles to get to Russia and whether they were even delivered to the Jews."

"How should I have known that the trustees had hearts of stone and would wait weeks on end until they gathered more money? And even had I known that the trustees would delay the sending of the packages, I would have done it anyway. By this I sanctified the name of God—to prevent people from saying that we have a heartless Torah that lets Jewish children starve."

"You are taking too much upon yourself, Reb David," Reb Kasriel Kahana's face became as red as his beard. "The Torah permits violation of the Sabbath in case of danger to life. But it's unheard of to violate the Sabbath to prevent people from saying that our Torah is heartless."

"You are still a young man," Reb Shmuel-Munye flared up, too. "It is we, the rabbis of the council, who managed to find a way to appoint you, a young man, as a Vilna rabbi in Polotsk Street."

"The agunah scandal is also causing me lots of trouble," Reb Asher-Anshel groaned, describing his habit of postponing the issuance of a divorce, as was the law, and as had been his wont all these years. The couples had already become accustomed to his postponements, and in most cases they reconciled. Lately, however, they were complaining that if there was a rabbi who had freed an agunah, they would find a rabbi who would grant a divorce on the spot.

Reb Asher-Anshel then posed two questions to Reb David Zelver: "First, your soul joined all of Israel at Sinai during the Revelation of the Torah—why then did you accept the Torah in which one of the severest sins was the violation of the Seventh Commandment, living with a married woman? Secondly, why did you become a rabbi? Did you think that you *would* be able to accomplish those things that the great rabbis from the 11th century Rabbi Isaac Alfasi to the contemporary Rabbi Isaac Elchanan had *not* been able to accomplish?"

Seeing that his father-in-law was also involved in the dispute, Fishel Bloom set to work to extricate himself from the straits that had inhibited him. In his anxiety to express his opinion, he burst into perspiration: "King Saul had wanted to be more compassionate than the prophet Samuel and disobeyed Samuel's order to slay King Agag, grandson of Amalek, eternal enemy of Israel. The sages tell us that during that one extra night that Agag was permitted to live until Samuel slew him, he slept with a serving maid from whose seed eventually sprang the wicked Haman. Compassion at the wrong time is cruelty," Fishel Bloom concluded and looked at his father-in-law, the rabbinic authority over divorces.

Well! Well! So he can speak prettily after all—that son-in-law of mine! But he's too lazy to look for a job. Sitting and freeloading at my table is much easier, Reb Asher-Anshel thought, looking down at his white beard, asleep on the table.

Reb David Zelver's silence in the face of the questions and complaints directed at him from all sides, momentarily took the edge off the angry altercation. Reb David stood and walked to the window where his coat lay. He felt that he ought to explain to the older rabbis that he was leaving first because he had to fill a prescription for his ailing baby. But he said nothing, in order not to stir up pity, just as he said nothing when he had entered late. He put on his coat and searched his pockets with a worried look until he felt the prescription for Mottele. But Reb Levi's voice stopped him on his way to the door.

"Reb David, we will stop your wages. And you, not we, will be to blame for your hungry children's tears and your wife's curses."

"You've been holding this threat in your bag and now you cast it at me." Reb David's pinched cheeks quivered, as though his hungry children's fingers were already plucking pieces from them. "Not I, but *you* will be to blame for my children's tears and my wife's curses."

"You! You!" Reb Levi shouted furiously. "I am already cursed. I am already cursed! And you, not I, will also bear the responsibility for the torments of the agunah. She visited me and told me that her husband is sorry that he married her. Everyone in town considers him a leper. He can't show his face in the street or go into a *shul*. I want you to know that the troubles and humiliations that the agunah will have to bear now will even be greater than before. And you will be the one responsible for all this, not I. You, who pretend that your heart is being torn asunder by compassion. And the agunah has even been taken in by your false saintliness!"

"What do you know about compassion?" Reb David smiled sadly.

"I have more compassion than you; and I suffer more anguish than you," Reb Levi jumped up, speaking quickly, as though afraid Reb David might leave before he had a chance to reply. "You *want* to be persecuted. You've convinced yourself that you are suffering for being a man of truth. But the fact is that you suffer for your pride. You're ready to sacrifice all for the sake of your pride."

"Ah, woe unto the world that has lost its leader, and woe unto the ship that has lost its captain. If Vilna's rabbis weren't such cowards, they would excommunicate you for persecuting a tormented woman." Reb David left and Reb Levi had no one to reply to. He ran about in the courtroom so quickly that Yosele crept into a corner to avoid being trampled by his uncle.

"Under ban and excommunication! We'll put up posters in the synagogue courtyard and proclaim in all the *shuls* that the former rabbi—I repeat, the *former*, for he will no longer be a rabbi in Vilna—is henceforth excommunicated," Reb Levi said pacing furiously in the room. "During Temple times when the Sanhedrin sat in the Temple courtyard pronouncing judgment, the rabbi would have been sentenced to death by strangulation."

"According to Maimonides, Reb David Zelver should not be judged as an insurgent scholar and he is not deserving of the death penalty," the excited Yosele said out loud. "Reb David should be judged as a heretic or a Karaite who denies the Oral Law. He should be cast into a pit and not be taken out."

"What are you saying?" Reb Levi turned to him angrily. Yosele fell silent and Reb Levi continued storming about the room. "Reb David pities the agunah. One is forbidden to pity even a poor man if the judgment of the law is against him. Let justice take its course! Excommunication! . . . Well, why don't you speak up?" he roared at the rabbis who sat with lowered heads. "Are you frightened?"

"Who's frightened?" Reb Shmuel-Munye attempted to flash his sarcastic smile. "I certainly am not frightened. But as far as I'm concerned, excommunication is much too severe."

Reb Levi opened the Maimonides volume on the table. "Excommunication too severe? For the Babylonian Talmud and the Jerusalem Talmud it is not too severe, for the *Code of Law* it is not too severe. It is too severe only for the Vilna rabbis!" Reb Levi snapped the pages furiously and told his colleagues to look into the text. "According to the Talmud there are twenty-four deeds for which a person is to be excommunicated, and Maimonides lists all twenty-four: for insulting a scholar after his death—and Reb David insulted scholars even during their lifetime; for not accepting the decision of a rabbinic court—and Reb David laughed right into the face of the Vilna rabbis; for committing sacrilege—and who has caused more sacrilege than Reb David Zelver? For putting a stumbling block before the blind; that is, leading someone astray—and he ordered a pious Jew to marry a married woman. And if that doesn't suffice you, Rabbi Abraham ibn Daud also concurs! You see? You see?" Reb Levi pointed at the volume and showed his colleagues that the Divine Spirit had graced Rabbi Abraham ibn Daud. "Having foreseen hundreds of years ago that in Vilna there would be a Reb David Zelver who would permit an agunah to marry. Rabbi Abraham wrote to Maimonides that one must excommunicate a scholar who permitted an agunah to marry without witnesses. And Joseph Caro's *Bet Joseph* goes even further, referring to a scholar who disputes the majority. Reb David Zelver should be uprooted. Excommunicated!"

"But a ban isn't quite excommunication; it doesn't mean exclusion from the community," Reb Asher-Anshel said, not raising his eyes from the book. "And even a banned person cannot be deprived of his livelihood."

"If the Court deems it necessary, it may even decide not to circumcise the children of the one excommunicated and upon death even bury him behind the cemetery fence," Reb Levi cast his remarks at the assembled rabbis, as though lightning had struck the table.

"Rabbis no longer have the power they used to have. We're now living in Exile," Reb Kasriel Kahana roared, his bass voice rippling the pages of the volume.

"Reb David might find an ally in the non-religious elements and then the matter will reach the Warsaw papers," Reb Shmuel-Munye addressed his colleagues. "Our enemies will describe us as narrow-minded reactionaries who want to reinstate excommunication, whipping and the stocks."

"Of course they will! Are you surprised?" Reb Levi mocked them as though relishing the insults that the non-religious would heap upon the religious. "But we have to consider the *shul* Jews who complain that there is no longer any rabbinic leadership in Vilna. Consequently, we have to show them that we are not silent, but proclaim: He shall not come among members of the congregation! Otherwise, we must proclaim that *we* were in error and not Reb David, and declare that the agunah *was* permitted to marry. Are you ready to do this?" Reb Levi laughed with wild abandon, as though enjoying the fact that his Council colleagues were so impotent they were afraid to make a decision. "There is only one way out: to exclude him from the community. Do you agree, Reb Shmuel-Munye?"

"I agree only to a public reprimand, but not to exclusion from the community."

"He should not be reprimanded publicly," Reb Kasriel Kahana muttered. "We will merely proclaim that the Vilna Rabbinic Council opposes Reb David's decision."

136

"But will we continue to pay his wages?" Reb Levi jumped back, as though to avoid the proximity of the other rabbis. "It would be the height of duplicity to proclaim our opposition to his decision and then quietly pay his wages. Once this becomes known in town they'll call us hypocrites."

The rabbis sighed and agreed not to pay Reb David's wages as long as he persisted in his obstinacy. Reb Asher-Anshel sighed louder than the rest. "It's a pity. He has a sick wife and an ailing baby."

"Is he more to be pitied than I, who have been without a wife for twenty years?" Reb Levi pounced upon his brother-in-law, as though ready to kill him.

Reb Asher-Anshel looked anxiously at his son and son-in-law. For this very reason he wanted to absent himself from the judgment. He knew that Reb Levi's complaints against the family were likely to burst forth even in the courtroom.

"The family has repeatedly asked you to get married—to ask for permission to marry," Reb Asher-Anshel stammered.

"Of course I can get married with the consent of one hundred rabbis, for my wife isn't of sound enough mind to accept a divorce. You gave me your crazy sister for a wife, and a crazy woman cannot even be divorced according to law. I know that Rabbenu Gershom's ban against bigamy is not applicable in my case. But the mob is looking high and low to find the slightest fault in a rabbi. Even though I am permitted to, I did not marry, to prevent agunahs from saying to me, 'You can and we can't?'"

Reb Levi moved in a whirlwind, as though his shouts and swift pacing sought to compete with each other in intensity and reckless-ness. "For me there's no pity, even though I spent twenty miserable years without a wife and had to commit my only child to the insane asylum! But everyone commiserates with Reb David Zelver. Go, gentlemen, go! The meeting is over. We'll follow your wishes. We will proclaim that the Vilna Rabbinic Council opposes Reb David's permission, but we will neither excommunicate him nor exclude him from the community. Go!" Reb Levi roared and sank back into his chair with closed eyes, as though not wanting to look at anyone.

The rabbis, astonished and agitated, shrugged their shoulders and rose one after the other. Reb Levi had scolded them like school-boys or assistant *shamoshim*. Nevertheless, they had had their fill of quarreling and wanted no part of another dispute. Reb Shmuel-Munye and Reb Kasriel Kahana were the first to slip out. Thanking Divine Providence that his brother-in-law's eyes were closed, Reb Asher-Anshel hurried silently to the door, followed by his son-in-law, Fishel Bloom. The last to leave was Yosele, who directed a glance full of hatred and scorn at his uncle. Who does he think he is, Maimonides? The Gaon of Vilna? I know more than him and Reb David Zelver put together.

Reb Levi leaned his head on the back of the chair, his perspiring face distorted with contempt. My colleagues don't even come up to Reb David's ankles. Reb David remained firm in his opinion, while their only wish was to be left alone and to avoid stirring up tumult in town. Which is why Reb David considered them cowards and had not the slightest respect for them.

Reb Levi opened his eyes, looked around at the empty courtroom, and pounded the table.

"But me he'll have to defer to! Otherwise, I'll persecute him mercilessly."

25

The *mohel* Lapidus poked his face, pointy beard and all, into the poster displayed in the Main Synagogue courtyard. The Vilna Rabbinic Council was proclaiming its disagreement with Reb David Zelver's decision to permit the agunah to marry without witnesses. The learned Hebrew text was very brief, as though the rabbis had written it with fire and feared burning their fingers.

Disagreement! Lapidus thought. Is that all? Nevertheless, he was pleased that the proclamation ordered all preachers and rabbis to announce the decision in their *shuls*.

A tall wide-set man with a waist-length white beard suddenly materialized next to the poster—Reb Yoshe, the head shamesh of the Main Synagogue, smiling contentedly into his leonine mustache. Aware that the *mohel* Lapidus was on his side, he whispered to him:

"Zalmanke's been given the job of pasting this poster in all the *shuls*."

The *mohel* was surprised. The slapped assistant shamesh himself had to put up the poster which in effect sanctioned Reb Yoshe's smacks? "Excellent. Wonderful! But how can we be sure that he'll carry out the task?"

"If he were ordered to, he would even paste it in Reb David's house—as long as I take him to weddings," Reb Yoshe smiled, departing, his hands behind his back. He knew that the mood in town had shifted in his favor and that henceforth no respectable Jew would arrange a wedding without him.

The *mohel* followed him with his glance. Reb Yoshe was a sly man, he thought. Now that he got what he wanted, nothing else concerned him. But he, the *mohel* Lapidus, scion of the Rokeach family, was still not being invited to perform circumcisions. In that case, he had to make sure that the proclamation was posted everywhere. Once everyone realized that Reb David had permitted a married woman to marry, perhaps it would become clear that the rabbi had disqualified him without rhyme or reason, and he would once more be invited to circumcisions. After all, he had never taken a penny for his services.

The *mohel* ran from one *shul* to another and saw the proclamation at every entrance. However, the worshippers did not gather to discuss the matter.

"Have you read about Reb David Zelver's excommunication?" Lapidus asked them.

"Excommunication involves black candles, the blowing of a ram's horn, and the curses of the Chapter of Admonition," they replied. "The rabbis just proclaimed their disagreement with Reb David's decision. And no more!"

Seeing that the proclamation had not accomplished very much, Lapidus ran with a complaint to the preachers of the *shuls*: "Why aren't you declaring in your sermons that the proclamation's intent was indeed excommunication? The only reason the rabbis are afraid to go through with the formal ceremony in the Main Synagogue, complete with black candles, ram's horn and the Biblical curses, is that Jews are now in Exile."

One preacher replied that Reb David was not so wrong. Another washed his hands of the affair: Not him! He would have no hand in helping Reb David's wife and children go hungry. A third grumbled that the Rabbinic Council paid him pennies; hence he wasn't obliged to be their errand-boy. A fourth sighed that he agreed with the Council and had mentioned the proclamation in his recent Sabbath sermon. But he was afraid to accent it because in his *shul* prayed many progressives who would side with Reb David Zelver. Finally, Lapidus met a sharp-witted preacher who explained that the proclamation's wording suggested that the rabbis weren't particularly eager to make a fuss over the incident.

"Really?" Lapidus asked innocently, reflecting that he *was* eager to make a fuss over it. He saw that all his efforts had been in vain and that the excommunication had crumbled under his fingers like cobwebs.

He ran down the street and up to the Zaretche market to look into Reb David's *shul*, then returned to the courtyard of the Main Synagogue boiling with rage. There wasn't even a trace of the proclamation on the door of Reb David's *shul*. Who, then, would announce to the congregation that the rabbi had been excommunicated? The rabbi himself?

Lapidus wandered about in the courtyard, waiting for Jews to gather in front of the proclamation and begin to argue. At that point he would step forth and explain the entire matter. But it was a cloudy autumn day. A light rain was falling and the weekday worshippers were rushing to their *shuls* to say Kaddish. No one stopped to look at the proclamation. Who's to stop me? Lapidus thought, looking around like Moses before he killed the Egyptian. When it grew dark, Lapidus shoved his nose and beard into the poster, as though into a High Holiday prayerbook—and swiftly tore it off in order to hang it on the door of the Zaretche *shul*.

On his way home he was still not certain he had done the right thing. Every day hosts of Jews marched through the gates of the courtyard, and sooner or later everyone glanced at the posters on the billboard. On the other hand, the Council's proclamation had been placed in every *shul*, except the one in Zaretche. In brief, he *had* acted wisely. Lapidus felt a pain in his teeth, as though his conscience had burrowed beneath his gold crown and tormented him for persecuting an impoverished rabbi who had little children to support. Lapidus sucked his pain-ridden tooth. He persecuted *me* and disqualified *me*. I've even come to consider myself superfluous.

The following morning Lapidus went straight to Reb David's *shul* in Zaretche.

Tsalye the trustee was a tall man with bent shoulders. His long legs were so bowed that a ten-year-old could have slipped between them while he stood for the Silent Devotion. His dirty beard looked like unmelted snow and his blue face like a hunk of spleen. On his long bony index finger he habitually turned a huge ring of keys to his house and the Zaretche *shul*. The bewildered congregants said it was understandable that Tsalye kept all the chests, clothes closets, pantries and wall closets at home under lock and key. He had married for the fifth time, and it would be a fine state of affairs indeed if every stranger who became his wife would be snooping in his drawers. But why did he put locks on all the prayerstand drawers? What could be stolen from there—the tattered old prayerbooks? The congregants were annoyed that Tsalye considered the Zaretche *shul* his private domain; but they realized that without him there would be no quorum in midweek. The *shul* had declined the last few years and didn't even employ a shamesh. Tsalye summoned the worshippers for the Afternoon and Evening Services and if a tenth man was missing for the quorum, he stood by the gate and collared passersby.

Tsalye's house next door to the *shul* had a porch that faced the Zaretche cemetery. Each time a funeral passed he went out and asked but one question:

"How old was the deceased?"

If he was forty, fifty, sixty, even seventy, Tsalye stood calmly on his long crooked legs, turning the ring of keys, not even bothering to ask if the corpse was a man or a woman. But if he was in his eighties, Tsalye's thin fingers trembled and the ring of keys almost fell from his hand. He could not budge until the very last mourner of the silent funeral had disappeared from view. "What did they say?" he groaned. "May no younger ones die! they said. Ah, woe is me, woe is me."

His odd behavior was understood only by the Zaretche residents. Tsalye, it was said, was in his eighties. Strong as an ox, he believed that the Angel of Death had forgotten him and took only those between forty and seventy-nine. But when he saw a corpse in his eighties, he realized that the Angel of Death did not forget.

Out of great disdain for Reb David, the generally taciturn Tsalye did not even exchange a word with him. When the rabbi addressed him, Tsalye spread his long crooked legs, stuck out his flat belly, and, turning the ring of keys, looked with scorn upon the rabbi— because of his short stature and his golden beard, and above all because he had a wife with an ailing heart, while he, Tsalye, had already buried four wives. But Reb David was dependent upon the trustee, for Tsalye had the library key, and also locked up the *shul* when the rabbi departed late at night. As Tsalye inspected the locks, he cursed the rabbi. Just because he can't stay at home with his miserable wife, I have to become his errand-boy and lock up after him.

Monday afternoon, when Tsalye left his porch to open the *shul* for the Afternoon Service, he met a stranger in the courtyard who greeted him and introduced himself as the *mohel* Lapidus, scion of the family Rokeach. Tsalye, not at all impressed by familial lineage, asked: "What do you want? Did you come to pray?"

"Yes," Lapidus tugged at his beard and sighed. "Ah, what's

become of the Zaretche *shul*! Locked up all day! Closed! Once Reb Israel Salanter conducted a yeshiva here and people studied Torah day and night."

Tsalye no longer heard him; the eighty-year-old trustee with the bent shoulders and long crooked legs despised groaners and weepers. He strode slowly into the *shul*, not looking at Lapidus, who stole in after him.

"Doesn't the rabbi come for the Afternoon Service?" the *mohel* asked.

"He comes for the Evening Service." Tsalye inspected the locked drawers to see if no one had broken into them. "The rabbi's got a bedridden wife and sickly kids, so he can't leave the house during the day."

Confident that he wouldn't meet Reb David here, the *mohel* complained about diminishing piety. "What with Reb David Zelver as the rabbi here, it's no wonder the Zaretche *shul* is in a state of decline. I didn't even see the proclamation that's been posted in all the Vilna *shuls*."

"What proclamation are you talking about?" Tsalye looked at him suspiciously.

"This one." Lapidus pulled the proclamation from his pocket. "Here it is black on white that the Vilna Rabbinic Council disagrees with Reb David's decision to permit the agunah to marry. You see, they had to formulate the proclamation carefully because Jews are in Exile. But their real intent was to excommunicate Reb David and exclude him from a quorum."

"Exclude him from a quorum?" Tsalye looked around the empty *shul* as though reckoning if he could assemble the necessary ten men without the rabbi. "So he's the sort that can't be included in a quorum! And he poses as such a poor, innocent chap who can't even put two plus two together, and who drags out the Silent Devotion for an hour."

The angry Tsalye turned his back on Lapidus and talked over his shoulders. "I can't understand why I wasn't invited to the rabbinical gathering. The trustee of the Zaretche *shul* ought to know what the city rabbis are saying about the rabbi who prays here. What's more, the agunah is also from this neighborhood. The proclamation's been posted in all the *shuls* except here in Zaretche."

"I know very well why the Rabbinic Council skipped over the Zaretche *shul*," Lapidus replied. "The rabbis were sure that the people on Zaretche hill agreed with Reb David, for when he gave the permission to carry money on the Sabbath, that miserable deed caused a fuss down in town, but up here on the hill they looked the other way. On the other hand, if a proclamation were posted, would Reb David permit it to remain? He runs the *shul* as though it were his own private backyard."

"Meantime, I'm boss here." Tsalye took the proclamation out of Lapidus' hand and measured it against the billboard at the entrance. "For this we need either paste or tacks. Spit alone won't do."

"If you need tacks, I've got them." Lapidus quickly brought forth a paper bag with broad tacks.

"Oho! So you've prepared tacks, too, eh?" Tsalye looked at the visitor with an expression that seemed to ask if he were doing all this out of pure piety.

Lapidus saw that he could talk freely. "All the years I've been a *mohel* I've never charged for circumcisions or for teaching dozens of young men to be *mohels*; then one day a former pupil of mine named Zelinger became my adversary and paid off Reb David to disqualify me. This Zelinger is a bankrupt, a pork gobbler, a lecher who chases skirts and runs after gentile girls."

"There's nothing wrong with that."

"Nothing wrong with what?" Lapidus stared at him.

"Nothing wrong with Zelinger being a skirt-chaser," Tsalye said calmly. "Your pupil knows a good thing when he sees it."

"We're not talking about Zelinger, damn him! We're talking about Reb David," Lapidus screamed, as though Tsalye were totally deaf. "And what's more, your so-called rabbi probably even took money from that harlot, that adulteress whom he gave the permission to."

"She isn't bad either," Tsalye said, cool as a crook. "She passes by quite often, and I tell you she's a good-looking woman. Before I married my present wife, I often thought that the agunah would suit me much better. But I understood she was looking for a young man. And besides—as you said—she's a married woman."

"She's a married woman beyond saving," Lapidus said hastily, biting his tongue to keep himself from quoting the sages. He saw that he was dealing with a coarse lout who despised a scholar; quoting the Talmud might even earn him the boor's enmity. So Lapidus helped the trustee round up a quorum, and flattered him by declaring that the youth of today was absolutely worthless. Never-

144

theless, before he left he blurted out a verse from Lamentations. "How great the decline! The Zaretche *shul* has sunk so low, that from the heights of a Reb Israel Salanter it had fallen into the hands of Reb David Zelver."

26

When Reb David came in for the Evening Service he saw a lamp lit over the entrance and people congregating before a poster on the door. But as soon as the worshippers saw him, they scattered over the large half-dark *shul*. Reb David looked at the poster and stood petrified. There was no mention after all of the excommunication with which Reb Levi had threatened him, but only that the Rabbinic Council disagreed with his decision. Nevertheless, Reb David's knees and lips trembled. Where would he gather strength to withstand these new persecutions?

His head lowered, he walked toward his corner by the Holy Ark. He would have to summon the worshippers and justify himself, telling them everything. He would have to round up supporters to side with him against the Council that persecuted him. But first of all, he did not usually justify his actions; and, secondly, because of his preoccupation with his sick family he was never close with his congregation. Despite this, some worshippers helped him out before holidays, and occasionally on Fridays, too. They were gentle souls who practised silent charity; upon shaking hands with them, he would find money in his palm. And now he would lose even his few supporters.

On the other side of the Holy Ark some men surrounded Tsalye and sought to calm him down. But Tsalye purposely raised his voice for Reb David to hear: "If we had a real rabbi, our *shul* would be packed. Mourners returning from the cemetery look for a place to pray and hear some words of consolation from a rabbi. But the Zaretche *shul* is always closed. Our rabbi has more important things to think about. He's too busy giving married women permission to marry."

"Let's begin the Evening Service," a merchant also shouted to drown out Tsalye's remarks. "I'm in a hurry. I left my store wide open."

"Who cares?" Tsalye outshouted him. "Who am I, your assistant shamesh? Go out and find a tenth man for the quorum."

"There are ten of us," another man pleaded with the trustee, and to avoid the evil eye counted, "Not-one, not-two, not-three . . . "

"I only see nine," Tsalye insisted. "The rabbi is forbidden to be included in a quorum."

The worshippers pounced upon Tsalye. "You ought to be ashamed of yourself for talking like that! We've had enough of your high-handed manner. We're not the drawers that you lock up. You won't lock up our mouths."

"I'm boss in the *shul*," Tsalye screamed, "and if I say the service won't begin, the service won't begin. The *mohel* Lapidus told me that from now on the rabbi is to be excluded from a quorum."

"Lapidus?" one of the worshippers leaped towards Tsalye. "He's a thief with a skullcap. A butcher! He mangled a little baby and our rabbi disqualified him. So he's seething and boiling like a potful of fat. Well, there's a fine how-do-you-do, that plaster saint Lapidus!"

"You've buried four wives, and now it's high time for the fifth to bury *you*," a Zaretche market peddler shouted. "Eighty-five-year-old men die, too. You still haven't danced your quadrille with the Angel of Death."

"Rabbi, don't pay any attention to this," said the merchant who had left his store wide open. "You are our rabbi and you will remain our rabbi."

Shrunken and perspiring, Reb David straightened up and went from his corner to the group of worshippers. The men stood still and Tsalye turned to him out of impudence and fear. The rabbi wanted to shout to the tall, thin trustee: You wicked wretch, *you're* excommunicated, you wicked wretch! But he could not utter a word. His lips moved, his teeth chattered, but he was unable to produce a sound—as though the ban had cursed his voicebox, too. The confused congregation gathered round Reb David, but his silence made them uneasy: perhaps he *was* to blame. Tsalye noticed their helplessness and looked down at the rabbi with a twisted smile. Turning the ring of keys on his index finger, he silently teased Reb David: I won't open the library for you any more. I won't let you use the *shul* till after midnight as a refuge from the constant weeping in your house.

Reb David gazed at Tsalye wide-eyed and his body trembled. He mustered his strength to summon back his dead voice, but the muteness reigned within even more intensely. Without saying a word, he went to the door. When he passed the proclamation, illumined by the lamp, the thought flashed that this was a death poster and the lamp his memorial candle.

Reb David's twelve-year-old son Yosefl had returned several times from the Yavneh school crying that he would not go back because the teacher was humiliating him. Using anger and kindness his father had convinced him to return to school. But the day after Tsalye had refused to include Reb David in the quorum, Yosefl came home in tears again.

"I had a fight and the boy tattled on me to the teacher and the teacher asked me in front of the whole class why I was picking fights with children of respectable families. He said that he pays tuition and I don't and that the rabbis put up proclamations against you and that I'd be better off not studying and not becoming a rabbi like you. And that's why I'm not going back to school any more."

The rebbetsin Eydl fell into the bed in a half faint. As Reb David tried to revive her he thought of going to Reb Levi, smashing his windows and plucking out his beard. Even if they excommunicated him they were forbidden to deprive his child of an education. But he immediately realized that it would be ridiculous to demand justice from his adversary and bitter enemy. When the rebbetsin finally came to, Reb David consoled himself with the thought that he would tutor Yosefl.

"The teacher is right," the stunned Eydl murmured. "Better for him to be a horse-thief—anything but a rabbi. Then his wife won't have my troubles and won't have to curse the day she was born."

Suddenly she sat up and fixed her large eyes on her husband:

"What sort of proclamation have the rabbis posted? You're taking advantage of my being bound to the house and never tell me anything."

Reb David had constantly postponed telling his wife about the judgment in the rabbinic courtroom. Now that he could hide it no longer, he described everything, including the humiliation in *shul* the previous night, with a strange apathetic calm. Eydl was more astonished than frightened. Fearing the moment when pain would replace astonishment, Reb David swiftly left the house and walked quickly, attempting in vain to outstrip his thoughts:

What should he do now? His only haven was the empty *shul* at night, where he could hide in the huge shadows and let the stillness cool his feverish mind. If only he could have remained there forever, forgotten and unseen in the darkness. Now the trustee had deprived him of his last place of refuge. Had he stood up to the trustee, some of the worshippers would surely have sided with him; but fighting such vulgar persons was against his nature and beyond his strength.

Reb David saw that he had mistakenly gone up Polotsk Street to the wooded hills. He returned and ran past his house, as though afraid his wife might stretch her hand out the window and drag him in; and his long, loose, frayed gaberdine became entangled between his feet, like Satan in his thoughts. The seamstress he had permitted to marry lived in the vicinity, he reflected. Did he want to meet her? Perhaps he should tell her that if she insisted upon divorcing her husband he would not mind. Indeed, she had mentioned her husband's regret about the marriage. Reb Levi Hurvitz, too, had accused him of holding his views out of obstinacy and pride, and not out of pity for the agunah. Perhaps she had concocted the story about not getting along with her husband in order to save him and his family. She was a wonderful person, who in order to save him would have chosen to remain lonely and rejected.

On his way home Reb David brooded: It was no concern of his if the seamstress and her husband got along or not. In any case, he would not retract, for his decision had been rendered according to the law, and his recanting would only cause him further trouble. If he would submit now, he would expose himself as a boor and a liar.

In his desire to stretch the distance, he walked slowly as he approached his house. He thought about Reb Levi's threat to stop his wages. Having left the courtroom before the end of the meeting, Reb David did not know what the rabbis had decided. The wording of the proclamation showed they had avoided harsh words and left the door open for a peaceful solution. Only fools and his sworn enemies could interpret the proclamation as an edict of excommunication. On the other hand, though they did not excommunicate him, they might stop his wages, as Reb Levi had threatened. As much as he had told his wife, he didn't have the courage to tell her that. The day after next Yosefl was to go for the wages. Perhaps he himself should go down to town and find out what had been decreed against him.

But deep in his heart, Reb David knew that he would not go.

The rebbetsin ceasing crying, cursing and complaining. For days on end she lay in bed, breathing heavily, either staring at the ceiling or watching her husband tending their sick infant. From time to time she glanced tightlipped at the door, waiting in vain for a housewife to come and ask her husband a question pertaining to ritual. "What did you expect? The congregants would rather send their wives to town than consult the rabbi on their own street."

In order to avoid humiliations in his *shul*, Reb David went to pray in a *shul* on the other side of the bridge.

Thursday morning, when Reb David was at prayers, the rebbetsin sent Yosefl to the Rabbinic Council for the rabbi's wages. When Reb David returned from *shul*, his wife's silence and her countenance told him where Yosefl had gone. The rebbetsin, fully clothed, rocked the ailing infant's cradle, her face darkened as though waiting for a sentence of life or death. At noontime, Yosefl stuck his head in the door and shouted:

"The cashier told me that they won't pay Papa's wages anymore."

Yosefl did not even enter the house, afraid that his father would force him to study. The rebbetsin came down from her bed, and with hair disheveled, ran to the door.

"I'll scratch her eyes out. It's on account of her, that slut of an agunah. It's all her fault. Because of her my children will die of hunger."

"It's not her fault, it's mine," Reb David murmured. "She visited me in the *shul* and said she was ready to divorce her husband. But I asked her not to divorce him under any circumstances."

"Is that so? You meet her and I know nothing about it?" the rebbetsin's dark eyes flashed with wild rage. "I had a feeling there was something between you two. She's younger than me, she's prettier, and she earns her own living."

"Be still!"

The rebbetsin trembled and gaped at him with amazement, never having heard him shout in such fashion.

"You don't think about your own wife and children!" she said.

"You're crazy! The agunah was afraid of coming here because you once chased her out. So she came to the *shul* to tell me that to spare us further troubles she is prepared to divorce her husband. But I told her that instead of benefiting me this would only harm me. It would mean that even the agunah did not consider my permission valid. And I want to show everyone that I stand behind my decision. Let them chase Yosefl from school, let them exclude me from a quorum, let the rabbis stop my wages—I still won't submit."

"But how will we live and pay rent? The doctor doesn't want to visit Mottele because we still owe him for previous calls. And where will we get money for milk? Yosefl will soon come crying that he's hungry. Oh, God in heaven! People with sounder hearts than mine collapse and never get up again, and with my weak heart I live on and suffer . . . Where are you going?" she yelled at her husband, who had put on his coat.

"I'm going to get a loan. Compassionate people are still to be found. The God who helps all the persecuted will help us too, and then I'll pay my debts."

"Don't go to her, you hear? Don't you dare borrow anything from her!"

Reb David withdrew; he shrugged, as though certain his wife had gone mad. Astonished at his wife's suspicion, he even managed to smile. How could she possibly imagine that he would borrow money from the woman to whom he had given the permission to marry. It would be the equivalent of taking a bribe. He would turn to one of the congregants who had sided with him when Tsalye had insulted him. Reb David stopped for a minute, concerned. "A loan?" he muttered to himself. "Of course I'll request a loan, but on condition that if I can't repay it, it should be considered a donation."

"A donation?" the rebbetsin wailed. "You're willing to take a donation, but you're not willing to submit to your colleagues, the rabbis."

"The finest people have requested donations. Accepting donations is neither illegal nor shameful. But I won't submit to them. Under no circumstances will I submit!" Reb David shouted, suddenly feeling weakened, crushed. Small and shrunken, he stood with hands lowered like a helpless man caught alone in a downpour in a shelter-less plain.

27

Merl remembered Reb David Zelver's warning that if she divorced her husband, people would say that even the agunah did not consider Reb David a rabbi. As a result, she drew closer to Kalman, treated him more tenderly, and smiled sadly at him, as though to placate him for her former apathy. She rebuked herself for being a stubborn mule. If she took a dislike to someone, her initial feelings persisted, and this attitude had made Moishke Tsirulnik her sworn enemy. She had sized him up correctly—he really was an unprincipled fiend. It was he who had stirred up the town to put Reb David on trial. But the gentle Kalman was her husband. Abiding by her request, he had done his best not to publicize the marriage. And how many humiliations he had suffered on Simkhas Torah in the Main Synagogue! And yet she completely disregarded him. Thus Merl indicted herself, knowing how hopeless was her desire to stir up non-existent love toward Kalman. Exhausted from the strain of make-believe affection, the black gleam in her eyes vanished, wrinkles lined her face and the edges of her lips, and her shoulders stooped as though she had suddenly aged.

Usually laconic, Merl now talked ceaselessly and swiftly ran her sewing machine to conceal her feigned high spirits from Kalman. Suddenly she stopped sewing, piously donned her kerchief, and in a trembling voice asked her husband to chant some table-hymns for her, as he had that Friday evening when he was courting her. But Kalman no longer thought of singing. He no longer sought to be appealing to her and did not even notice the change in her attitude. Ever since the scandal in the Main Synagogue, he had been ashamed to set foot in a *shul*, and went neither to the painters exchange nor to the cemetery to recite memorial prayers.

One day after Merl had gone to deliver some dresses and shop in the Zaretche market, she came home deathly pale and stunned; she sank into a chair and could scarcely catch her breath.

"The rabbis have ordered posters hung on all the *shuls* proclaiming their disagreement with Reb David Zelver," she told Kalman. "And the trustee of the Zaretche *shul* has chased him from the synagogue. And you know what else I heard from the wife of a shopkeeper who lent the rabbi some money? That his wages have been stopped and he is going from door to door borrowing money, saying unashamedly that if he can't return the loan it should be considered a donation."

"Measure for measure. He has it coming to him," Kalman said.

"What?"

"Till now I couldn't enter a *shul* because of him, and now he himself can't enter a *shul*." Kalman gazed innocently at his wife.

"Coward! Jellyfish!" Merl snapped, springing at him like an enraged wolverine, her black eyes and white teeth gleaming. "What sort of man are you? You're a dishrag! Anyone else in your shoes would have risked his life for the rabbi, just as he risked his for you. And you have the gall to say that he has it coming to him? If I didn't have so many troubles of my own, I'd go scratch Tsalye the wife-killer's eyes out. But I dare not plead the rabbi's cause. I dare not. But you ought to be turning the world upside down. A *shlimazel* bungler like you should never have married!"

As Merl shouted, Kalman stood dumbfounded and petrified; then he slowly edged to the door until he slipped out of the house. After his departure, Merl realized that she shouldn't have said a word to him. She should have kept him locked up in the house and stuffed him like a goose. Oh, how he disgusted her! But she had to remain with him—for that was the rabbi's wish. Merl laughed bitterly: no fear, her runaway husband would return. Perhaps her scolding would prompt him to go down to the city to convince people to stop persecuting Reb David. Merl pressed her head to the wheel of the sewing machine and bit her lip. She would even have pleaded on bended knees before that dog Moishke Tsirulnik, if only he would stir up the town in the rabbi's favor. But the rabbi, fearing his wife and gossip that there was something between them, had told her not to intervene. If he were alone and she single, she would gladly have become Reb David's housemaid.

After running down Polotsk Street, Kalman stopped to catch his breath. Was that the sort of person she was? A blind man could have seen that she loved the rabbi and not her own husband. She had continually rejected him and married him only upon order of Reb David Zelver. When he came home on Simkhas Torah and told her how he had been humiliated, she wrung her hands and cried that Reb David had brought misfortune upon himself. She still looked out the window daily to see him walking with his son. Now she had cast away the mask altogether and driven him out of the house to brew up a storm for the rabbi.

Kalman went down to town and passed the Zaretche market. Tugging at his long ears, he pondered: Had he no sense? He had known that Merl was not religious. He hadn't even considered what kind of family he was marrying into. Her mother was a common woman, her sisters had married lowlifes, and Merl herself had been an anti-Czarist revolutionary in her youth. He had met her at the funeral of an atheistic glovemaker or stocking-knitter. Why had he been in such a rush? When work was available, he painted houses; when it was not, he was a cantor at the cemetery. And now the devil had prodded him to marry one of that circle who had no fear of God and scorned the Torah. He had made a mistake; he had been blinded; but the real culprit was the rabbi who had fooled him and talked him into marrying a married woman. "He's made me miserable, miserable," Kalman sighed and followed his feet up Zavalne Street to the painters exchange.

"What's the good word, clunk?" a group of youths surrounded him, bored by waiting for some householder to summon them to work.

"My name isn't Clunk, it's Kalman. My name is Kalman and my family name is Maytess."

"Rubbish!" laughed Isaacl Barash, a lanky young man with long hands and feet protruding from his short sleeves and trousers. "Everyone in town calls you Clunk, so we'll call you Clunk, too."

"Since when do people call me Clunk?" Kalman looked around, as though seeking a corner to hide.

"You were called Clunk in your mama's belly, but you never told us your real name," Isaacl Barash declared. "When you came out of the Main Synagogue with the slap marks on your face—that's when everyone discovered your real name."

"It wasn't me who was slapped. It was the assistant shamesh."

"Rubbish!" the painters snorted, their broad barrel chests crackling with laughter. "Since the assistant shamesh was slapped, you were slapped too; and since your clever rabbi was excommunicated, so are you."

Kalman shivered. "What do you mean I'm excommunicated?"

The youths were delirious with glee. "Excommunicated, pal, excommunicated! No one's allowed to talk to you or stand near you. We're supposed to scoot away from you like from a bad smell. But since we're your pals, we're taking the risk of chumming up with you. And anyway, how come you don't know you've been excommunicated? Where've you been, in confinement? If so, then you really are a clunk. But your wife from Novgorod is no clunk at all; she's a cutey-pie!"

Kalman's eyes widened and he said gloomily that his wife was not from Novgorod but from Polotsk Street. But the painters shouted, "Rubbish! Your wife's from the underworld of Novgorod—she just happens to be living in Polotsk Street now. Can't you see for yourself that she's from the Novgorod underworld the way she pulled the wool over your eyes?"

Kalman saw that he was the laughingstock of the town. He felt as though he had descended from a ladder and instead of placing both feet squarely on solid ground, he put one leg into a pail of paint and the other into a pot of glue. He groaned and poured his bitter heart out to his friends:

"Reb David Zelver has made me miserable."

"Then say the hell with him and with a wife like that . . . Some saint! Ask Moritz and he'll tell you what sort of gem your wife is. She used to be quite cuddly-wuddly with him," said Isaacl Barash, whose short jacket and trousers looked as though they'd been swiped from a laundry line. Kalman tugged at his long ears and replied that his wife had never been cuddly-wuddly with Moritz. Moritz had wanted to marry her even before she married her first husband, but Merl had refused him.

"Then you *are* a clunk. Ask Moritz and he'll tell you a thing or two. He's often asked about you—in fact, he wants to meet you. Come on, let's go!" The painters took Kalman by the arms and told him that Moritz was always to be found at the wood market, where he had his wholesale business.

"Leave me alone. I don't want to have anything to do with that roughneck Moishke Tsirulnik." But the painters turned a deaf ear to Kalman's pleas. Tsirulnik had promised them whiskey and a meal if they brought the cemetery cantor to him. So they pinioned him and carried him like a sacrificial chicken.

"You've got nothing to be afraid of. Moritz is your pal. After we all guzzle a quart of whiskey we'll all feel much better."

28

Moishke Tsirulnik stood next to a wagon laden with bags of onions, carrots and potatoes. In order to get the peasant to agree to a price, he used the market dealers' proven method of slapping the peasant's palm until it stung and the peasant struck a bargain, if only to avoid further pain. Moishke looked up and saw the painters leading a short man and yelling, "Moritz!" He immediately left the peasant with the swollen palms and narrowed his small unctuous eyes.

"Here's Kalman," the painters thrust him forward. "You-know-who's husband."

"Whose?" Tsirulnik couldn't for the life of him remember.

"The agunah's husband, your mistress' husband," said Isaacl Barash.

"The agunah's husband," Moritz shrugged unconcernedly, and shouted at Isaacl: "Drop dead! How come you're saying the agunah was my mistress? Don't listen to him, Reb Kalman. He's just teasing you."

The youths exchanged glances. Tsirulnik was playing his role excellently. Kalman, his fear gone now, looked at him with greater confidence. But when Moritz invited him to a restaurant for a hearty meal, Kalman became confused:

"I don't eat non-kosher food."

"And do you think I do?" Moritz asked in astonishment, his hand on his heart. "You choose the place. If you prefer, we can go to the Savoy, where eating is a sheer delight. But if you're very hungry, we can go to a restaurant where you don't pay for the food, but only for the time you spend there."

"I'm not hungry."

"Not hungry? Then we won't go anywhere. Just into the cellar opposite the market where you can order only jellied calves' feet, chopped liver, gefilte fish, meatballs, beer and whiskey."

157

Before Kalman could say a word, the gang once more took him by the arms and led him down into the steam-filled cellar. Crowded around the tables were porters and market peddlers, youths wearing sackcloth shirts and high boots. They smoked, spat on the floor, guzzled whiskey with open mouths, and swore and cursed at the top of their lungs. The newcomers, frequent visitors here, swiftly set six stools around a table and gave Moishke Tsirulnik the place of honor. Since he would foot the bill, he was king. They shoved Kalman alongside of Moritz, and everyone pressed tightly around him. Even if he were a bird he couldn't have flown the coop. The youths turned their hungry faces to the buffet; a moment later, waitresses with flushed faces and filthy aprons appeared. Moritz winked to them and the painters ordered whatever their hearts desired.

Soon the table was covered with bottles of whiskey and beer, goblets, water glasses and potbellied mugs.

"Marinated herring in cream sauce. A herring loves to swim in cream," shouted one.

"Chopped liver!"

"Jellied **calves'** feet—with lots of meat and garlic!" called a third, rubbing his mustache as though sharpening a knife.

"Here's to your health, Moritz." The gang poured whiskey into water glasses. "And ours!"

"Drink hearty," Moritz said glumly, with the tone of a rascal who knew he was being taken advantage of. He had promised these ragpickers a drink and a meal if they brought him the clunk—and here they were eating him out of house and home. But even though it galled him, he had to keep still to impress the cemetery cantor and wall-smearer with his generosity. Isaacl Barash had a bottomless pit for a stomach. He ordered everything under the sun and snatched the full platters out of the waitresses' hands as though he intended to swallow the plates along with the chubby hands that held them. He chomped and chewed until he was dripping with perspiration; and in between bites he kept flattering Tsirulnik.

"Moritz, how come you didn't wear your silk scarf today? Moritz, we heard a rumor that you lost your diamond-studded cigarette case. You hear, Kalmanke? If you travel the length and breadth of Vilna, you'll never find a better buddy than Moritz." Isaacl poured himself a mug of beer and immediately gulped it down. "Why aren't you drinking, Moritz? How come you're not eating?"

"I'm waiting for Reb Kalman," said the market dealer.

"I told you before that I only eat kosher food," Kalman said, shrinking as though a wolf had invited him for a meal.

"And I thought you didn't want to eat hot, cooked meat for fear that it isn't kosher. But what's not kosher about cold chopped liver?" Moritz poured Kalman a thimble-sized tumbler of whiskey and measured three-fourths of a water glass for himself. He poured all the whiskey into his mouth without flinching and took no chaser, but merely sniffed at the fresh black bread and looked contemptuously at his drinking partner. "Well?"

Kalman muttered a blessing and to show his skill drank up the minute contents of his glass. But he pulled a face as though it were codliver oil and groaned. One sin leads to another, he thought. He had begun with an agunah and now he was boozing in a tavern with a gang of youths.

"Let's have some more," Moritz poured another thimbleful for his guest and half a water glass for himself. He looked at Kalman like a sergeant at a recruit who didn't know how to hold a rifle. "Bottoms up! If you marry a young woman you have to know how to drink, too. He who can't drink can't do other things. You probably haven't had a drop of liquor since Simkhas Torah."

"He wasn't thinking of liquor on Simkhas Torah. That's the day he was slapped on account of your mistress," Isaacl Barash shouted to Moritz.

"I wasn't the one who was slapped. It was the assistant shamesh," Kalman said.

"Drop dead!" Moritz cursed Isaacl once more. "It wasn't Reb Kalman who was slapped. The assistant shamesh was the one who was slapped. Don't pay any attention to him, Reb Kalman. Listen to me. I'm your friend."

"How come you're my friend?" Kalman bit into a dry biscuit and nibbled at it quickly, like a squirrel.

"Because I'm a man who has suffered, that's why I'm your friend," Moritz answered dejectedly. "May I drop dead if you understand me! If a dog licked my heart he'd croak. Poisoned."

"If your wife could have turned Moritz's head, Kalman, she'll screw your clunkish head off with one turn," the lanky painter said, flattering Moritz again.

"This chap doesn't have a clunkish head, just a chicken's heart," one of the gang laughed.

159

But Kalman either hadn't heard or was just pretending. Although the table was heaped with all kinds of dishes, he pecked at the biscuit crumbs on the table and even teased Moritz.

"This one says that Merl was your mistress, and that one says that she just turned your head. So who's telling the truth?"

In a flash all of Moritz's gentility vanished. He pressed his forehead up to Kalman's until the latter felt his skull backing into the wall, and his hands dropped to his sides. The crumbs fell from his lips to his sparse little beard, and his mealy face became terror-stricken at the thought that this gangster might crack his skull.

"Have no fear, there'll be no shortage of troubles," Moritz stared at him with his tiny eyes, and laughed venomously. "Merke the seamstress was going with me for years. But on the side she also had that toothless carpenter, Itsik Tswilling. So I told her: either me or him. Once she saw she couldn't lord it over me, she chose the toothless carpenter. He was made to order for her. He didn't even inspect the merchandise. And once he discovered the truth, he was already under her thumb. But when he left for the front he said, 'So long, folks,' and never returned. In Germany he married a gentile woman."

Kalman felt Moritz's head pressing his like an iron bar. Nevertheless, he risked his life and replied, "If Merl's first husband were alive, he would have returned. Reb David had given her permission to marry because her husband's not returning from the war after fifteen years was a sign that he was dead."

At this Moritz laughed so uproariously he threw his head back, enabling Kalman to remove his head from the wall.

"And during the fifteen years she remained an agunah do you think all she did was modestly mumble prayers?" Moritz asked the astonished cemetery cantor, and then turned to the gang. "What do you say, buddies, do you think that all she did was modestly mumble prayers?"

The gang laughed lewdly. They pressed their heads together, gazing admiringly at Moritz. Moritz closed one eye to indicate that he could talk from personal experience if he chose to. Then he attacked Kalman from another side.

"All right, let's assume that her husband is dead. So how come you were the one she picked?" He poured Kalman another glass to appease him.

"That's right. How come you were the one she picked?" the

160

painters shouted in unison. "Because you're a cemetery cantor? She chose you as a cover-up, pal. As a cover-up, so that behind your back she could do as she pleased. You pray with your eyes toward heaven. That's exactly what your modest maiden wants you to do— pray with your eyes pointing up."

The youths snickered at Kalman's innocence, and he, out of great despair, downed his third tumbler and had a coughing fit—the drink had gone down his windpipe.

"Bring a knish for Reb Kalman," Moritz ordered, and the gang, overjoyed at the new treat, shouted gleefully: "Knishes! Knishes!"

Moishke Tsirulnik felt a stab in his heart. The more he slandered the seamstress the more his blood boiled. He couldn't comprehend what was happening to him. For almost twenty years now he had been chasing after her despite her continual rebuffs. By all rights, he should wish her dead, treat her like a dog and not give a damn. But nevertheless, she was driving him to apoplexy; that cold firebrand was sucking the marrow from his bones. With him she didn't want to sleep, yet she married this wall-smearer. Moritz looked at Kalman with a rage-distorted face. Moritz was sure that Merl had done this just to spite him and make him burst with envy. But all in due time! If he kept on his toes, he would be able to get her more easily than before. And in order to extinguish the fire in his guts, Moritz ordered another quart of whiskey.

Kalman, also immersed in gloom, watched the painters glutting and swilling, hugging and kissing one another, while he sat there depressed. Why indeed had she married him? The liquor suddenly whizzed in his head: she'd married him to cover up her love for the rabbi. Kalman saw before his glazed eyes two Moishke Tsirulniks, then three—all laughing at him with wide-open mouths. Moritz, dead drunk now, held Kalman by the lapels and shook him:

"She's got a heart like a chunk of marble, right?"

"Throw up a bit, Kalman, throw up!" Isaacl Barash slapped his back so hard that Kalman shook like a broken tree. "Talking eases one's heart and so does vomiting."

Kalman no longer heard what was being said to him. The tavern swayed before his eyes; he could hardly move his thick tongue. The rabbi had made him miserable, absolutely miserable.

29

Their faces steaming, the painters left the tavern in high spirits. They sucked in the crisp air and stood rooted on steady legs. After the three whiskies, however, Kalman tottered like a broken-legged porcelain doll. Moritz looked at him with the grieved expression of a nobleman obliged to deal with a common Yid.

"Knock it into his head that if he doesn't divorce her, it'll be too bad for him. I promise you another quart and a meal," Moishke Tsirulnik muttered to Isaacl Barash and departed, his heart gnawing. The gang had made him squander so much money, and the agunah was sucking the marrow out of his bones.

Spurred by the promised whiskey and the meal, Isaacl Barash agreed to deliver the tipsy wobbly-legged Kalman to his house. The painter put his bony hand under Kalman's hat and scratched his head with his sharp nails, as though with a rake. Kalman coughed and sniveled, straightened up carefully, and looked at his friend who was dragging him home and shouting in his ear:

"Moritz is a man of his word. If he says it'll be too bad for you if you don't divorce your wife, he really means it. Come, let's go. I live near the fish market. I'll bring you home and then I'll turn in on Poplava Street."

The climb and the steep descent to the Zaretche market made Kalman tired, but it sobered him up. The closer Isaacl Barash got to his street the more uneasy and depressed he became. He scratched his scalp, blew his nose loudly, and shouted to Kalman:

"I wish things were as bad between me and my wife as they are between you and your wife. 'You drunken bum, where's your pay?' she yells at me. Since she wasn't an agunah when I married her, I don't have any excuse to boot her out. You have it good, buddy.

162

Yours is an agunah, so you can kick her out. A wife's got to be beaten up."

"Do you beat yours?" Kalman asked.

"The apartment is so tiny if I shove her she's got nowhere to fall," Isaacl Barash said, pushing Kalman up the stairs. "Remember! Moritz is a man of his word. If he says it'll be too bad for you if you don't divorce her, he really means it."

Isaacl left quickly, afraid that the seamstress might drive him away with a broom. Kalman slipped into the house guiltily. He saw Merl sitting bent over the table, sewing by hand. The lamp illumined her fingers and half her face, spreading a bright silence and a cozy warmth that encompassed him, too. "Ah woe, what has become of me!" Kalman sighed silently. Drinking in a tavern with drunkards! Never mind what Moritz had said. Moritz was a crook and Merl was a pious Jewish woman. Kalman waited for his wife to ask him where he had been. Now that he'd left the house for the first time in weeks, she should surely want to know where he had been and what he had done. But Merl didn't even look up. Her needle flew across the cloth, as though racing the shadow of the swiftly moving hand on the wall. Kalman was annoyed with himself for not being a man like Moritz.

"I was at the painters exchange today drinking with my pals," he said indignantly, removing his coat. "But I didn't ask anyone to support the rabbi. I don't care about him. I'm worse off than him."

Merl rose, but sat down at once. She realized that by driving him to side with Reb David she had made matters worse. So she didn't even want to ask him why he had been drinking. But in order not to anger him with her silence, she said simply:

"And you're not drunk at all?"

Confused by her lack of interest, Kalman didn't know what to do or how to reply. Moritz threatened that it would be too bad for him if he didn't divorce her. But if he divorced her, he would be worse off. Where would he go? His apartment at Lipuvke Street had already been rented. He had been a widower—now he'd also be a divorcé. What's more, unlike Isaacl's wife, she didn't call him a drunkard and didn't curse him for not earning money.

The next morning Kalman rose with a worried look. Throughout his prayers he kept staring at the cane he always held while reciting memorial prayers at the cemetery. After breakfast and grace, he grumbled a belated reply to her question of the previous evening, as though it had kept him awake all night.

"Actually, I didn't drink enough last night to make me really drunk." Seeing that Merl was smiling goodnaturedly at his apology, he added testily: "There's no work to be had. I'll have to become a cemetery cantor again."

He was waiting for his wife to assert that she did not want her husband to work at the graveyard. But Merl merely nodded her head in assent. Kalman picked up his cane and left the house vexed. On his way to the cemetery he saw the trustee of the Zaretche *shul* standing on his porch surveying the marketplace. Struck by an idea, Kalman stopped in front of Tsalye's house.

Earlier that day, Tsalye had seen a funeral passing and asked his usual question. Hearing that the corpse was only in his sixties, Tsalye felt better and looked triumphantly at the store of the shopkeeper who had shouted that eighty-five-year-olds died, too. I'll see him buried first. I'll stay right here on my porch and watch his coffin passing the house, Tsalye thought, turning the big ring of keys on his index finger. The storekeeper had threatened to have him fired; now let that dog see that he was still the trustee, with the *shul* keys still in his possession. A year ago Tsalye had married his fifth wife, who until lately had been a quiet woman. But recently she had begun talking his ear off, saying that other men who married in their old age signed over a part of their property to their wives, yet he kept everything under lock and key as though she were his maid. I'll see her buried, too, Tsalye thought, swaying on his feet as though testing how solidly he stood on the ground.

"When are you opening the *shul*?" asked a man walking in front of his porch with cane in hand.

"I open it for the Afternoon and Evening Services. What do you want to do in the *shul* now?" Tsalye asked suspiciously.

"What do I want to do? I want to look at my troubles," the man moaned, hiding his head in his hunched shoulders. "I want to look at the proclamation concerning Reb David Zelver. I'm the agunah's husband."

Tsalye gazed at Kalman with his bloodshot watery eyes. His blue splotchy face darkened and the bags under his eyes puffed up. He turned his back to Kalman, an indication that he was expecting trouble. Tsalye was waiting for the agunah's husband to pick a fight with him over the rabbi, as the shopkeepers in *shul* had done. Instead, the man complained and groaned that the rabbi had made him absolutely miserable. Tsalye turned the ring of keys, a contemptuous expression on his face. He compared himself with the agunah's husband and thought: the agunah doesn't know what she's missing. He was certainly far better suited for that young woman, and she for him, too. His present wife, number five, was an old creep.

"If you're so nosey about how the rabbis besmirched you, go read the poster in the Main Synagogue courtyard."

"I don't have any time. I have to go to the cemetery to recite memorial prayers." As Kalman stepped up to the porch, Tsalye blocked the way, as though fearing that the agunah's husband might defile his porch.

"If the rabbi who permitted you to marry someone else's wife has been excluded from a quorum," Tsalye said, "do you think that you, the adulteress' husband, will be permitted to recite memorial prayers at the cemetery?"

Kalman retreated, frightened, but a wild rage immediately swept over him, and he shouted, "No one can scare me—I'm also a house-painter."

"And who'd let you into his house to whitewash his walls?" the trustee said, gazing at him with his bloodshot, watery eyes. "Take my advice. Instead of going to the cemetery, go to the rabbi's wife and let her tell you what all of Zaretche knows already. She tells Reb David that he supported the agunah because he and the agunah were having a secret affair. Even the miserable bastards who opposed me in *shul* for excluding the rabbi from a quorum are keeping their mouths shut. This so-called rabbi used to meet your wife in the *shul* on the sly. I would have to stay up till after midnight and then drag myself over to lock the *shul*, for I assumed he was sitting there studying. The fact is he used to meet your wife there. If I had a wife like that I'd sooner see her in the grave than with a strange man, damn you!"

Tsalye stalked into his house and locked the door; Kalman stood momentarily thunderstruck, then left the porch, following his tapping cane, as though suddenly blinded. He knew that his wife was crazy about the rabbi; now he had heard that the rabbi's wife was saying the same thing. In that case, Moritz's statement that Merl had been his mistress was certainly true. But Moritz had dropped her because she had had another lover on the side, the man she eventually married. Kalman decided not to go to the cemetery, for there he might have to bear even greater humiliations than those he had suffered in the Main Synagogue; he would go to the painters exchange instead. The painters would look for Moritz again, and everyone would go into a cellar tavern for a snack and some conversation. The painters were his loyal friends and, despite Moritz's boorishness, he too was an honest man. And how open-handed he had been—Moritz alone had footed the bill for the entire party.

When Kalman came to the painters exchange, he found his pals in a completely differently mood. Moishke Tsirulnik's orders had been to drive Kalman off with sticks so that he would be scared to show his face in the exchange. If the painters disobeyed, he would henceforth drink with dogcatchers and not with them. When Kalman appeared, a pall of angry silence fell over the group. They did not even look at him. After staring at them in wide-eyed amazement, Kalman asked softly for his best friend, Isaacl Barash. Where was he? Had he gone out on a painting job?

"His old lady probably conked him one with a two-by-four, or knocked his eye out, and he's lying flat on his back, with broken bones, suffering like a dog," said one of the group. "Well, Kalman Clunk, have you divorced your wife from Novgorod?"

"My wife's not from Novgorod," Kalman told them again. "And my name is Kalman Maytess, not Kalman Clunk."

But they pounced upon him heatedly: "If you don't divorce that vixen of yours, don't dare show your puss here at the exchange. It's beneath our dignity to hear people saying that a housepainter is a dumb dishrag. So get a move on, you dumb dishrag, go to the cemetery, or join the rest of the beggars in the synagogue courtyard. Scat, beat it," they yelled.

Kalman retreated as though from a pack of wolves. He turned into the first sidestreet, raised his eyes and murmured with wan lips:

"God in heaven, I'm deeper in the ban than Reb David."

He stopped by a little red church surrounded by a stone fence, gazed at it for a while and then reeled back—what was he doing looking at the cross? Did he want to convert, God forbid? Kalman looked about and saw that he was in Gitke-Toibe's Lane, where the rabbinic authority over divorces, Reb Asher-Anshel lived. If Merl gives me a divorce it'll be my salvation, the thought buzzed, but he pressed close to the wall, as though afraid that Reb Asher-Anshel would read his thoughts and through the window order him to divorce his wife. No, no! He was already a widower; he didn't want to be a divorcé.

Kalman looked up and saw the assistant shamesh of the Main Synagogue stepping smartly along the street, carrying a wedding canopy on his shoulders. Kalman caught him by the arms. "Oho! So they're taking you for weddings already?"

"Who are you?" the small, swarthy Zalmanke asked irately.

"Kalman Maytess! You made me miserable when you married me to the agunah."

"You're the one who made *me* miserable, not me you," Zalmanke leaped toward him. "You've sucked my blood by the barrelful. I'm the one who had to go to all the *shuls* pasting up the Rabbinic Council's proclamation against Reb David Zelver. But thank God my atonement is over, and now I'm being invited to weddings again."

Nevertheless, Kalman had no intentions of forgiving the assistant shamesh. He aimed all his bitterness at Zalmanke:

"You're not a man. You're a coward, a jellyfish, a *shlimazel,* a dumb dishrag. You were smacked in the Main Synagogue and you go pasting up proclamations against yourself."

"You're the dumb dishrag, not me," Zalmanke laughed into his face. "Even the agunah who hooked you at first wants to get rid of you—she wants to divorce you."

"Liar," Kalman approached, cane in hand.

"Don't tell me you aim to hit me! If you so much as lay a finger on me, you'll wind up in a shroud. Everyone knows that at the rabbis' meeting in the courtroom, Reb Levi Hurwitz threw up to Reb David Zelver the fact that even the agunah was now sorry she had married. But the rabbi answered that he had no regrets about his permission and that he would not let the agunah divorce her husband. So then which one of us is the dumb dishrag?" Zalmanke asked and hurried away.

Kalman's head swam; his knees buckled, as though he were more intoxicated today than yesterday. He tapped the cobblestones with his cane and shook his head. He wasn't even permitted to spend another day with her.

30

Once, at the cemetery, Kalman had seen an amputated leg being carried for burial. Realizing that no mourner would permit some stranger's leg to be placed into his relative's grave, the gravediggers waited until a lone beggar was brought in, then sought to bury the leg in the charity plot. But the dead beggar's only kin and the sole mourner—himself a beggar—raised a fuss. Kalman remembered how the gravediggers joked that instead of raising a fuss the kinsman should be overjoyed. At resurrection the corpse would be a sensation—with three legs he'd get more donations than any other beggar.

"I'm like the lonely beggar without relatives. I too have been given something that doesn't belong to me . . . They put a married woman in my bed," Kalman said to himself, wandering about the streets feeling depressed and superfluous. He returned home in the evening, his insides grumbling with hunger, aware that he would have no strength to pack up and leave.

The table lamp was lit. Merl stood in the kitchen, cooking supper. Kalman placed his cane in the corner and asked: "What's for supper?"

"Your favorite, a meat borscht."

"I don't like that," he growled. "I like lentils and noodles and meat fried with small potatoes."

"Tomorrow I'll prepare lentils and noodles and meat fried with small potatoes," Merl answered calmly. "Go wash and eat."

Kalman washed his hands, recited the benediction, and chewed the bread as though it were straw. When Merl served him a full platter of soup, he raged once more:

"I eat meat before soup, not soup before meat. How come you're suddenly wearing a kerchief? You always go about bareheaded."

All day long Merl had been thinking about Kalman with compassion and concern. Although he was suffering and was ashamed to appear among people, he still sought to earn a livelihood. Yesterday he had gone to the painters exchange and today to the cemetery. Consequently, she put aside her work at twilight and went to prepare a hot supper for him. Hearing him coming up the stairs, she quickly donned a kerchief. After all, he was a religious man and it was high time for her, too, to begin to act like an older woman.

"The wife of a cemetery cantor should not go about bareheaded," she smiled and tied the edges of the kerchief under her chin, as though she were already a grandmother.

"I didn't go to the cemetery," he scowled, petulantly breaking pieces of bread into the soup and pushing them deeper into the plate with his spoon. "I've been told that no one will let me into the cemetery to recite memorial prayers. All my life I've earned money and now I've become played-out, like your mother in the old-age home."

"I'm not asking you to go out and work, but if you insist on going to the cemetery, you should talk to people and ask them to side with you and with the rabbi," Merl said and immediately bit her lips. It had slipped out again, although she had promised herself never again to mention Reb David.

"You always talk about the rabbi as though *he* were your husband and not me. Yesterday morning you attacked me for not doing anything for him. But today I heard that even those who once sided with him don't support him any more."

"Who told you this?"

Kalman saw that her hands were trembling as she served him the meat.

"Tsalye the trustee of the *shul* told me. The rebbetsin, Tsalye said, was pestering the life out of Reb David, claiming that he gave you permission to marry because he was in love with you. Tsalye said that you used to meet the rabbi in the Zaretche *shul*. The entire market knows this and so does the rebbetsin. That's why the store-keepers don't want to support the rabbi any more."

"Kalman, do something!" Merl grabbed his hand and prevented him from stuffing more meat into his mouth. "You yourself sent me twice to see the rabbi in *shul*. Go out into the marketplace and tell it to everyone. Tell them that the rebbetsin is sick and confused. If you don't care about the rabbi, you have to care about me. How can you permit your wife to be slandered?"

"You don't care that much about being slandered," Kalman tore his hand out of hers. "I know you went to the rabbis and told them you're ready to divorce me, but Reb David openly said in the courtroom that he forbade you to do this. And you say you only went to see him twice."

"It's true I went to see him once more," Merl looked him straight in the eye, "and he told me that if we divorced it would appear that even we were against him."

"Aha, so it's true you visited him?" Kalman was on the verge of tears. "And I refused to believe what people were saying. It's all a lie, I thought. You didn't say a word and you wanted to divorce me. You only pretended to be true to me."

"You promised Reb David not to tell anyone about the permission. But since everyone found out anyway, I concluded that the rabbi should not suffer on account of us. I saw that you, too, were sorry you married me. So I wanted to set you free," Merl smiled weakly. But Kalman sullenly pushed the empty plate away.

"I never said I'd divorce you. And if you wanted to free me, why did you change your mind when your rabbi told you that it would be unpleasant for him? No, I don't believe you anymore. I'd rather believe what the rebbetsin said and what Moritz told me."

"What did *he* tell you? Where did you meet him?"

"Moritz invited me and all the painters to the tavern yesterday," Kalman answered with a sulking air of triumph, pleased at having hidden this from his wife. "Moritz told me that you were his mistress even before you married your first husband, and that the years you were an agunah you didn't just sit and modestly mumble prayers."

"You were drinking in a tavern with him?" Merl said incredulously. She sat down on a chair next to the table and laughed bitterly to herself. "And what did you say to this Moritz when he claimed I was his mistress?"

"I told Moritz, the painters, and Tsalye the same thing—that Reb David Zelver has made me miserable," Kalman groaned. "But the painters who drank with me the other night chased me from the painters exchange today. 'Scat, beat it!' they shouted at me and told me not to show up until I had divorced my Novgorod vixen. I insisted over and over again that you're not from Novgorod, but they kept repeating that you're of the Novgorod underworld," Kalman moaned, and then began to say grace, swaying back and forth. Suddenly he noticed that his wife had thrown off her kerchief and was pressing both hands to her temples. Since he was in the midst of murmuring his prayers, he didn't want to stop, but merely shrugged his shoulders: a while ago she had donned a kerchief, and now, just when he was saying grace, she removed it. A Jewish girl—yet she knew so little about Judaism.

Merl sat with a numb smile on her face, thinking: How strange! The fact that that her husband believed Tsirulnik didn't bother her. If she had only the slightest affection for Kalman, she couldn't have abided the insult that she had slept with such a despicable dog like Moritz. She herself had not hitherto known how little she cared for Kalman. Then why was she living with him? Simply because the rabbi had ordered her to. But Kalman had just told her that he had been going around telling everyone that Reb David had made him miserable; with such talk he was making matters worse for the rabbi. She would divorce Kalman and no one would be able to blame Reb David for the fact that a married woman was living with another man. Perhaps then Reb David would recant and make peace with the rabbis.

When Kalman opened his eyes after reciting grace, he saw Merl standing by the clothes closet, putting on a long coat. She approached the table and said softly: "I know you have no relatives and nowhere to go to sleep. I'm going to my older sister's for a few days until you you find an apartment and remove your belongings. I don't even want to spend another hour under the same roof with you."

Kalman shrieked and lifted his hands, as though she had threatened him with an ax. But Merl continued, her face hard and dispassionate:

"Pleading with me won't do any good. I'm going to tell everyone that we have separated and you're to do likewise. Then you'll be accepted once more; you'll be able to recite memorial prayers at the cemetery and the painters won't drive you from the exchange." Merl stared at his round face and frightened, popping eyes and continued: "Kalman, even after we divorce we'll still be best of friends. But since you're a religious man, you must tell everyone that the rabbi is not to blame. I want you to know that there is nothing between us. He is a saintly man and would sooner die ten times than touch me."

When she reached the door, she turned once more to Kalman and smiled at him through tear-filled eyes.

"I don't have to account to you as to whether or not I was Moishke Tsirulnik's girl friend. I wasn't your wife then. But the truth is that just as the rabbi would sooner die ten times than touch me, I'd sooner have my head chopped off than let Moishke Tsirulnik touch *me*."

She left quickly, running down the stairs, as though afraid that his silence, loneliness and fear might draw her back.

31

Motye the barber, Merl's older brother-in-law, didn't give a damn about anything. He shaved his full smooth face until it gleamed blue and twirled his silver mustache. He was always the last to show up for work; and while lathering and shaving customers, he paid more attention to his own mustache in the mirror. And since he didn't give a damn, he hardly talked to his customers who quickly became bored in his chair. But he cared least of all about his family. He squandered his daily earnings on food and liquor, and even took money from his daughters who worked to support themselves and their mother. His employers always sought an excuse to fire him, but he didn't give a damn about that, either. When he lost one job, he looked for another, until finally he had exhausted all the barbershops in Vilna. Motye then packed his tools in a suitcase and became an itinerant barber, cutting hair and shaving beards in the countryside.

His wife, Guteh, on the contrary, took everything to heart. When her children were small she was grieved at having to turn to Merl for support. When her youngest sister, Golda, married the lazy tailor Shaike, Guteh again wrung her hands in despair. And when Merl married Kalman, Guteh really became despondent. Her misery began even prior to the wedding, for the permission had been given by only one rabbi and this fact would have to be concealed from enemies. And when the slap in the Main Synagogue echoed throughout the town, Guteh's knees buckled and her arms went limp. She sensed a worse disaster impending and her intuition proved correct: one evening Merl brought the news that she had separated from her husband and would live with Guteh until Kalman found another apartment.

"It's my fault," Guteh keened, rocking back and forth, "I shouldn't have talked you into marrying him."

Startled, Merl quietly replied that if her sister would not cease her weeping, she would leave and spend the night outdoors.

172

"I want to forget about everything," Merl burst into tears. "For just one week I'd like to be the forgotten agunah I've been the past fifteen years."

When she calmed down, she asked if Guteh had received letters from her husband and how her two daughters, Zelda and Freidke, were faring. Guteh complained that there were no letters from her husband and that she had not an ounce of joy from her daughters.

"Why? Aren't they both working?"

"You'll see why for yourself," Guteh sighed, and suddenly clapped her hands in fright. "Merl, don't breathe a word to Mama. She is getting senile and doesn't even remember that you married. She still thinks you're an agunah. If she got wind of the tumult surrounding you, she won't survive it. Thank God she doesn't remember."

Merl felt a chill in her bones. The rabbi is still worse off than I, she thought. "I won't say a thing to Mama," she replied, "but you can spread the word that I've separated from my husband. That's my wish and that's what should be done."

Merl then went to the old-age home to see her mother Kayle, who was mired in her swollenness like a man stuck in a swamp. Merl recalled that it was in this room that her mother and sisters had convinced her to marry. On the beds lay women whom Merl did not recognize from her previous visits. Kayle emerged momentarily from her daze, groaned, "God has taken my former roommates, and I'm still suffering here," and once more regressed into her daze.

Then, forgetting the fifteen years of Merl's agunahood, she stammered and asked, "How is your husband Itsik?"

On her way back from the old-age home Merl laughed to herself. If Kayle and her daughters suddenly vanished, who would miss them? They were as essential as boulders in a wheat field. Reb David Zelver ought also to ask the same question of God, but he would not utter such a thought.

Guteh's elder daughter, Zelda, had a soft pale face, dark hair and misty grey eyes, full of yearning. After taking one look at the short, chubby, full breasted girl, any worldly-wise young man would swear that she would conceive on her wedding night and have at least a dozen children. Her only trouble was that she fell in love with every boy who hugged her once. She clung to him with her soft, heavy body, and looked trustfully into his eyes, waiting for him to propose. But while waiting, she snuggled up to him with half-open expectant lips. Zelda was crazy about kissing.

Her younger sister, Freidke, was her antithesis in character and appearance. Tall, slim and well-built, the blue-eyed, blond-haired Freidke had broad shoulders, and strong arms. With her well-proportioned face, unflinching gaze and wry smile, she resembled a show window mannequin. The boys nicknamed her "the plaster statue" and tried their best to warm her up, make her melt, drive her wild. But when a boy attempted to kiss her, she stuck out both elbows and no one could get near her.

Guteh, who lived in the low-rent welfare housing, had a kitchen and one large room, a third of which was partitioned off with an old clothes closet; from it curtains were strung on both sides to the wall creating a bedroom for the entire family. Before going to sleep, they pushed the curtains aside to permit some light to enter as they undressed. In the evenings when the curtains were closed, the room belonged to the girls, who sat there with their boy friends on alternating days.

The evening Merl returned from the old-age home, the room was Zelda's. Merl found a tattered old note-book containing love and work songs, and recalled how she used to enjoy singing. She sat at the table, her back to the bedroom, and turned pages, immersed in her thoughts. Guteh was busy in the kitchen; her daughter Freidke, spiting her ten boy friends, did not leave the house, but sat fixing her hat, fuming at her sister.

In the curtained-off room, the boy laughed heartily, while Zelda whispered, "No, no." But soon enough sighs, panting and kisses were heard. Zelda laughed ecstatically and cried in a faltering voice, "Oh Azrielke, Azrielke."

"She's fallen in love again, that goose," Freidke said, her large shining eyes blazing with fury.

"Keep still," her mother said, standing next to her, waving her hands as though extinguishing a fire. "You know Zelda's a good girl and only likes to kiss. Is there anything wrong with that? If she does this at home, she won't shame me."

Merl listened with half an ear, turning the pages, looking at songs about couples in love. She thought of her mother in the old-age home. Earlier she had asked herself who would miss Kayle and her daughters if they all vanished. But her nieces had no such thoughts. They wanted to live. She too had been a wild young thing who loved to laugh and kiss the boys. But after her marriage to Itsik everything changed. At night he was tired from the day's work, and when he had no work, he walked about depressed. Nevertheless, although no one believed her, she had waited for him for more than fifteen years. She had remained faithful to him during the first few years when she was sure that he was yearning for her in some prisoner-of-war camp, and had continued to remain faithful even later, when she doubted that he was alive, for her only desire was to support her mother and sisters. Meanwhile, however, the years passed and her blood cooled.

And when she finally married, she took a man for whom she hadn't the slightest affection. She had married Kalman for his honesty and his devotion to her; she had married out of loneliness, and because she wanted to spite Moishke Tsirulnik, and because the rabbi had told her to . . .

"That goose is already talking marriage to him," Freidke interrupted Merl's reverie.

"Quiet, quiet," her mother pleaded softly and whispered to Merl. "Besides not having any joy from my husband, I don't have any from my daughters, either. Wait, you still don't know half of it."

From behind the curtained-off room Zelda led her boy friend out through the kitchen. A while later she returned with red blotches on her cheeks—aroused, pinched, and kissed. But Freidke did not look up from her sewing and did not say a word. No matter how irritated she became at her sister's instantaneous falling in love, she abided by their agreement not to meddle in each other's affairs.

32

The following evening Freidke sat in the room with a boy who joked loudly: "Don't be a little village teaser," then begged and whispered passionately. But Freidke's reply was a stubborn silence felt in the rest of the room, as though a cold wind had blown through a broken pane. Zelda, restless and impatient, poked her aunt Merl who was once more looking into the songbook.

"What do you say to Freidke? She thinks she'll lose something if she lets herself be kissed."

Perhaps Zelda's right, Merl thought. One should enjoy life with a vengeance. How strange! During the two evenings that young couples sat behind the partition, she was flipping pages of a songbook. Then, as though suddenly abandoning all hope of recalling the songs of her youth, she closed the book, stood and looked around. She felt cooped up in her sister's apartment.

Behind the partition the quiet pleading became a struggle. The boy grumbled, sighed, and rasped out a tormented laugh. But not a sound was heard from Freidke. The household knew that though the boy moved heaven and earth Freidke would rebuff him with her long powerful arms.

"You hellcat, why are you so stingy with a kiss?" Zelda screamed. Her mother ran in from the kitchen and implored her daughter:

"Don't butt in! You agreed not to meddle in each other's affairs. Should she let herself be kissed by every boy?"

"A hug and a kiss and no further, miss," Zelda said, worried, knowing that Freidke would not forgive her. Soon enough, the boy left via the dark kitchen, apparently having heard Zelda's shout and embarrassed at his failure. Freidke entered the room, her eyes blazing and her lips awry:

"Damn his eagerness!"

176

Zelda was silent, but her heart grieved. She noticed that the more adamantly Freidke repulsed the boys, the more they were attracted to her; yet from her, the devoted and easy-going Zelda, the boys fled after the first meeting and kissing session. Freidke settled accounts with Zelda by telling her aunt Merl that this boy had previously gone out with Zelda and was now running after her—and Zelda wanted her to kiss that bargain hunter.

"Because I wanted him to see that you're nothing more than a cold plaster statue," Zelda jumped up, furious. "Otherwise he might have thought that you're God-knows-what kind of a bargain."

Without intending to, Merl burst out laughing. She had never imagined that the chubby and perpetually amorous Zelda could be so clever. That's the way to live! Merl threw her hair back. But her laughter didn't please Zelda, who feared that her aunt sided with Freidke.

"Freidke has someone to take after," Zelda shouted at her mother. "She takes after her aunt Merl. *I* wouldn't have left the man I loved."

"He would have left on his own," Freidke snapped.

"Quiet, quiet," the mother pleaded with Freidke and lectured Zelda: "When you fight with your sister, must you bring in your aunt? She's our guest now."

"And what would you do if your husband told you every day that you made him miserable?" Merl asked Zelda.

"I'm not talking about that greasy bit of antiquity. I'm talking about the man who's been chasing after you since you were a young girl," Zelda replied. "I'm not a plaster statue. If a man had run after me all these years, I wouldn't have pushed him away."

"I wouldn't push away a boy who has serious intentions either," Freidke said, her arms akimbo. "My name isn't Zelda and I don't let everyone paw me. I'd have some reputation!"

"And who have I rejected that has run after me all these years?" Merl looked from one niece to another. "Are you by any chance thinking of Moishke Tsirulnik? Do you think I'd marry a Moishke Tsirulnik?"

"I swear my daughters don't even know what they're talking about," Guteh interrupted. "There isn't a decent person in the world who thinks well of Moritz. No wonder he's remained an old bachelor."

"I'd thumb my nose at the entire world," Zelda stood in the middle of the room, as though demonstrating how she would oppose everyone. "With a husband one has joy; from others one gets nothing but slander. I see what's happened with aunt Merl."

"If a man runs after a woman as many years as Moritz has run after aunt Merl, there's no doubt that he's really in love," Freidke agreed with her sister this time. "But to get used to every boy and then suffer? Let *them* rather suffer!"

Merl smiled to hide her confusion. Apparently she was already old-fashioned and did not understand girls of the modern generation. Her friends, poor stocking-knitters and glovemakers, had also despised Moritz. But her nieces thought otherwise. One was easy-going, and the other seemingly repulsed the boys, but each in her own way wanted to get a man—even if he were a Moishke Tsirulnik. They apparently wanted to use her experiences as an example and then do exactly the opposite. Merl was happy that at least her family knew nothing of her crazy thoughts about Reb David Zelver.

Unlike her two older sisters, the short, agile Golda was a loud-mouth. She arrived when Guteh and Merl were alone in the house, and immediately raged at the latter.

"Divorce that husband of yours! Men like him should be thickly sown and sparsely grown. You've always been and you still are a wild goat. Almost sixteen years without a husband and when you finally married, you got yourself a good-for-nothing, a cemetery cantor and wall-smearer."

"You were the one who talked me into marrying him."

"How should I have known that he's a *shlimazel*? What's the matter, was he too tender to go out and work? Too scared to go scratch the rabbis' eyes out? That bearded goat saw the whole town buzzing about his wife and yet he went around blubbering and complaining that he'd been made miserable."

"You can't blame him. What with everyone dragging his wife through the mud, it's no wonder he crumbled away," Guteh vindicated Kalman.

"Goody-goodies like you, Guteh, the worms eat," Golda yelled at her. "Your Motye never provided for you or your children, but since he went out into the countryside to cut hair, you eat your heart out because he doesn't write. I'd have your husband crawl on his knees, and Kalman I'd sweep out of the house the next morning."

"And is life a picnic with your Shaike?" Guteh wondered. "You always seem to be whining that since your husband has palled up with Moritz you fight every day."

But Golda grimaced and began grinding away: "Some comparison! Your Motye, Kalman Clunk, and my Shaike! My husband has always been a hard-working man, except that he sometimes gets lazy and loses his spunk. But since his pal Moritz has given up drinking, Shaike too has turned over a new leaf. He's become quiet as a pussycat. He never leaves the house and sits and works constantly."

"Moritz has given up drinking? Your husband is working? Miracles upon miracles!" Guteh shrugged.

Merl said nothing, but stared at Golda who hitherto had always cursed Tsirulnik; now she rather offhandedly declared that Moritz had given up drinking. Merl waited for the mill to start grinding again, but Golda stopped as suddenly as she had begun, and left the house. Two days later, however, she barged in again.

"Well, Merke, what're you dilly-dallying for?" she shouted. "Divorce that *shlimazel* of yours. Time marches on. Before you turn around you'll be an old granny. Enjoy yourself and let your enemies burst with envy."

"Who should I rush out and get a divorce for? Is anyone in a hurry to grab me?" Merl asked, her eyes flashing.

"Moritz will grab you," Golde snapped, unable to contain herself.

Merl expected this reply, but Guteh spat out: "I wish such good fortune on my enemies. He's treated her worse than an anti-Semite, so how can you even utter the thought that Merl marry him?"

"Really?" Golda scoffed, the smart comeback burning her lips: "I've heard of worse things. I've heard of men who killed the women they loved. Everything Moritz has done was done out of pure love for you, Merke. He's been head over heels in love with you all his life, and you've always rebuffed him. Bitterness drove him to drink, to cause scandals, and even to corrupt Shaike. But now Moritz is a changed man; he neither touches a drop nor lets Shaike touch one. He's been roving about as a bachelor long enough. Now he'll be a model husband."

"And how do you know he'll marry me?" Merl asked, as though she were perfectly amenable. "Isn't he afraid of the rabbis and of the entire town?"

Golda talked so quickly she could hardly catch her breath: "Moritz laughs at all the rabbis in town. 'Go tell Merl,' he said, 'go tell Merl that even after all the heartache she caused me, I swear to God I love her more than ever.' He beat his chest and wept like a baby. It was a pity to look at him. 'Go tell Merl that though everyone is dragging her through the mud, I love her with all my soul and would fight like a lion to protect her. If we can't settle in Vilna,' he said, 'we'll flee abroad. I have plenty of money. I just want to see who's going to dare say boo.' Now that's what I call a man. Moritz isn't Kalman. If gloves are a gown then Kalman's a man.''

When Golda finished, Merl slowly rose and said with deliberation:

"It's time to go home. If Kalman hasn't yet found an apartment, I'll continue living with him.''

She wanted to add that she was even prepared to live with the devil—anyone but Moishke Tsirulnik. But Golda pulled out of her purse the key to Merl's apartment and declared:

"I had enough sense to go see what the hero Kalman was planning to do. I found the door locked and the key at a neighbor's.''

"Did you really find the key at a neighbor's, or did you chase Kalman out of the apartment?" Merl asked her sister.

"What, me chase him out?" Golda screeched, clutching her heart. "I was only there once to ask him when he was moving out, and when I came a second time, I found the key at a neighbor's.''

"Sister, you've done a terrible thing," Guteh lowered her hands, wailing.

"You silly goose, why are you crying?" Golda burst into tears, too. "I wasn't the one who separated them. But now that Merke has left him, I wanted her wound to heal as quickly as possible.''

Merl could neither cry nor reply to Golda. Again Moishke Tsirulnik, she thought. It was he who had sent Golda to drive Kalman from the house. If that callous fiend had been able to dupe her sister who had known him all these years, no wonder he was able to dupe the innocent Kalman into believing that she had been his mistress. Her thoughts had been centered so much on Reb David Zelver, she had forgotten that her husband deserved to be pitied, too.

33

Isaacl Barash, a veteran of the Russian army, lived on his past glory. He loved to tell about his capture by the Germans, his natty artillery corps uniform, and his heroism at the front lines. The painters, however, laughed at Isaacl's stories. He talked about uniforms while wearing his battered, paint-smeared hat, and his ludicrous short jacket and narrow trousers. He bragged about his Samson-like deeds in the war, but when he took a drop, his wife beat him black and blue. He rarely went to look for work at the painters exchange because the painters' taunts about his wife's beatings mortified him. Since his wife was a peddler in the market and came home only toward nightfall, Isaacl lay in bed all day, staring at the ceiling and talking to no one. But since lounging in bed for days on end bored him, he was overjoyed when Kalman Maytess paid him a surprise visit.

"I'm divorcing my wife and I'm looking for a corner in someone's apartment, because I don't have enough money to rent an apartment all for myself."

"Move in, pal, move right in," Isaacl said happily, sitting up in bed. "We'll be two bodies and one soul. In the barracks I also had a buddy like that. We shared one pack of tobacco and ate out of one pot."

"I'm a little short of money, but I'll pay you whatever you ask," Kalman said morosely. "But what will your wife say. Won't she say no?"

"And what if she does? You think I'm scared of her? Listen to this, Kalmanke, when I was a soldier I had an overcoat as hard as tin. Wherever you put it, it just stood there."

"Perhaps you can convince your wife to let me live here."

"Of course I'll convince her, pal, of course I'll convince her. Listen to this, Kalmanke, once I had guard duty and was ordered not to let anyone pass. Well, an order is an order. I saw a chicken strolling by. Halt, who goes there? I shouted. But it played dumb. So I speared it with my bayonet. Come tomorrow, Kalman, and meanwhile I'll talk to my Jezebel."

As soon as Kalman left, Isaacl put his hairy feet on the ground and began looking for his shoes. He dressed, set the paint-smeared hat on his head, and went to the wood market to look for Moishke Tsirulnik. Moishke had still not given him the promised quart of whiskey and the meal for convincing Kalman to divorce his wife. Now a quart didn't suffice him; he had visions of an entire tavern full of bottles that Moritz would order for all the buddies, who would celebrate for seven days and seven nights.

Isaacl found Moishke at the wood market and brought the good news that he'd convinced Kalman Clunk to divorce his wife. Now the way to the agunah was free and clear. Moishke Tsirulnik closed his right eye and his left grew larger.

"So who are you telling this to, me? Everyone knows that as soon as my onetime fiancée divorces that clunk, we'll get married. And he's telling me that the way is clear!"

Seeing that Tsirulnik was reneging on his promise, Isaacl played dumb: "Give me a bit of advice, Moishke. Kalman asked me if he could come live with me. If I take in the clunk, I might have troubles with my Jezebel. But if I don't take him in, Kalman will have to stay in the agunah's house, and your former fiancée will be as available as a fortress. So what should I do?"

Moritz opened his closed eye and narrowed his open one: "As far as I'm concerned you can do as you please and both go to hell. If the clunk won't move out of the agunah's apartment of his own free will, he'll be carried out feet first. As long as I was single I let myself be milked dry by the painters. Now that I'm about to get married, I've got better things to waste my money on. And, anyway, it's beneath my dignity now to deal with those barefoot bums."

Moritz turned his back on Isaacl, who realized that it wouldn't pay to start up with him. Isaacl left the wood market for Zavalne Street and watched the bored painters slapping one another's backs to keep warm. Snow had not yet fallen, but the cobblestones were white with frost. The sky glittered blue, like ice on a lake. Isaacl gazed down at his short, narrow trousers and at the leg bindings protruding from his crooked shoes, then glanced back at the painters exchange. Since no one was looking for a painter, he didn't want to just stand there and be ridiculed like Kalman Clunk. So he pulled his hat down over his forehead, stuck his long hands into his pockets, and went back home.

When Kalman returned the following day, Isaacl's attitude had changed radically. "My Jezebel won't hear of me having a friend of mine in the house. I told her my friend wasn't one of the drunken painters but a pious man, the one who married the agunah and was now separated from her because the rabbis decided she wasn't permitted to marry. My Jezebel said that a husband who left such a quiet, noble and faithful wife wasn't worthy of crossing anyone's threshold. Let him drop dead, she said . . . And you know what else she said?"

"What?" Kalman said with the look of a condemned man.

"She said if she'd had the good luck of me not coming back from the war, she would have danced in the streets and not waited fifteen years to remarry like the faithful agunah did. You know what else that Jezebel of mine said?"

"What?" Kalman asked, thoroughly smitten.

"She said that Moritz's talk is like a dog's barking. If there's any truth to his claim that your wife had been his mistress, and that he didn't want to live under one roof with her because she had other men behind his back, why is he going to marry her now?"

"Who is going to marry her?" Kalman said, feeling the ground beneath him tottering like a ship in a stormy sea. "Is Moritz going to marry Merl? But she's still my wife!"

"That bastard says that as soon as you divorce her, he'll marry her. You know what? Now he doesn't want to have anything to do with people like us! I don't care about the quart of whiskey he still owes me. What bothers me is—why should a man be a swine?"

"But you told me that if I don't divorce my wife it'll be too bad for me!" Kalman said, his eyes popping.

"I told you what I heard. How should I have known that Moritz—damn him—was purposely knocking your wife just to make you leave her so that he could marry her? Lister, Kalmanke, I have a wonderful idea. Play dumb and don't leave the house."

"She was the first to leave, and she's expecting me to leave," Kalman looked down at the floor.

"Stay there, and when she comes back, play dumb. My Jezebel fights with me day in and day out and always asks me the same question: why did I come back from the war while so many nice quiet soldier boys did not? I hear this and play dumb. Do likewise, Kalmanke, and it'll be to your advantage. And if for once in his life Moishke Tsirulnik is telling the truth about his engagement, then don't give her a divorce and let her burst."

"I *will* give her a divorce." Kalman raised his head as though deciding to look fate right in the eye. "That's precisely what I will do. But the question is where will I sleep?"

"Don't give her a divorce and don't leave the house, and then you'll have a place to sleep," Isaacl answered apathetically, and once more longed for the bygone years when he served in the army. "Once on my way home on leave, I boarded a droshky at the train terminal like a regimental commander and told the coachman to take me home. When I approached the house, the entire street ran up to see the tall man with the shiny new boots and long overcoat. And that tall man in the shiny new boots and long overcoat was none other than me."

His head lowered like a scrawny nag in a downpour, Kalman mused: Perhaps the painter and Tsirulnik had purposely slandered Merl. But if everything they said was a lie, then it was probably a lie, too, that Merl was intending to marry Tsirulnik. In that case, he should obey Isaacl and not leave the house. He would wait for Merl to return and then apologize that he was just an old-fashioned man and didn't realize what liars those slanderers were. But perhaps she wouldn't want to be reconciled? She was very stubborn and proud. Kalman knew that Isaacl Barash was in no small measure responsible for his misfortune. He gazed at him with his troubled eyes and said sadly:

"Some people are not as bad as the deeds they do. If you had considered the troubles your big mouth would cause me, you might have been more careful to keep it shut."

34

The pantry was full of food, but Kalman felt so strange and superfluous in his wife's apartment he went hungry and touched nothing. Nevertheless, he continually wondered if Moritz was only boasting about Merl marrying him, or if she had really agreed—until Golda barged into the apartment and screamed: "When are you planning to move out? But don't think that Merl will remain an agunah once more if you disappear! She's no longer alone—she's got a friend now called Moritz who'll drag you out from under the ground by the hair and force you to give her a divorce."

"I'll give her a divorce, I'll give her a divorce," Kalman retreated, as though before a snake spitting venom. "Till now your sister didn't even want to hear about Moritz."

"That's just the trouble. My bright sister never even looked at Moritz, who has remained an old bachelor for her sake; but you, a good-for-nothing beggar, a complete stranger, knocked her off her feet. One would think you're a clunk, but you seem to have had enough sense to pull the wool over my sister's eyes."

Kalman retreated even further into the corner. "This Moritz slandered Merl all over town, and in my presence, too."

"Moritz was only testing you," Golda waved a finger under his nose. "What sort of man are you to let people say such terrible things about your wife and even believe them yourself? And who are you, anyway? A greasy Jew, that's what you are! And a widower to boot, who looks old enough to be Merl's father. Instead of giving the skin off your back to treat her like a queen, you became a burden on her. And while the entire town was sucking her blood, you hid under the bed as though bombs were falling, and then went around complaining how miserable you are. And now it's all over—by tomorrow I don't want to see a hint of you in the apartment. All right, I'll give you one more day, till the day after tomorrow, because I don't want you to have an excuse to go around mewing that you weren't even given enough time to find an apartment. And don't forget to remove all your stinking junk."

When the shrieking harridan had left and Kalman had regained some of his composure, he realized that it would be best to find a corner in some *shul,* which was preferable to a corner in someone's house. Living with a family meant dealing with landlords who might even pour salt on his wounds. But if he were to get a corner in a *shul,* no one would say a word to him, and he would not have to think about himself. Weren't there plenty of poor men sleeping in the *shuls,* thinking of nothing? If they thought too much about themselves they might commit suicide. He too, then, would be a pauper, and eat dry crusts and drink boiled water instead of tea. Men more respectable than he had become impoverished.

Kalman thought of a plan that both pleased and frightened him. He would ask the trustee Tsalye to let him sleep in the Zaretche *shul.* Hordes of poor people looked for lodging in the courtyard *shuls,* but the Zaretche *shul* was still empty. True, there everyone knew him and knew what had happened to him. But what was there to be ashamed of? It was better than finding a *shul* where no one knew him and where people might suspect him of being a thief. The Zaretche *shul* had the advantage of being close to Polotsk Street and Kalman would be able to carry his things over in half a day. The main thing, however, was to win the trustee's favor.

Kalman waited anxiously for Tsalye to open the *shul* and addressed him humbly:

"You can include me in a quorum now. I've separated from my wife."

The entire Zaretche market had heard of this and so had Tsalye. He looked down at Kalman and said nothing. A young woman like that, he thought, would be far better suited for him than his creepy old fifth wife. On the other hand, the seamstress was still considered an agunah; and, besides, there was a brawny chap, her one-time fiancé, to reckon with.

"Have a heart, I don't have a place to sleep," Kalman pleaded. "I'll stand on the street and round up a quorum. I'll bring the congregants the prayer shawls and prayer books. And if there's no one to lead the prayers, I'll lead them, for I'm a cantor."

Tsalye spread his long crooked legs, looked over his shoulders

186

at the man and said nothing. Kalman crept to a corner and waited for the decree. If the trustee included him in a quorum, it meant there was some hope; if not, then he was in God's hands. But apparently heaven wanted Kalman to suffer a while longer, for just this once a full quorum had gathered and Kalman had no hint of the trustee's decision.

During the Afternoon and Evening Services Tsalye carefully reckoned that it would be worth his while to let the man into the *shul;* he would have a free assistant shamesh and would show the congregants, who had reviled him for chasing out the rabbi, that he was more compassionate than they.

Tsalye assembled a few of the householders and talked with them. Kalman understood that they were discussing him, and to avoid disturbing the trustee while he was making up his mind, retreated to the farthest corner of the *shul.* Tsalye beckoned him with his finger, like a teacher summoning a naughty pupil, and the ring of keys in his hand looked like an iron whip. Kalman approached and the curious worshippers regarded him sympathetically.

"I won't pay you a thing," Tsalye gazed down at him. "And even if the householders want to give you something you are forbidden to accept it. If people contribute to the shamesh, they give less to the *shul.*"

"I'm not asking for any money," said the delighted Kalman, still terrified lest he lose favor in the trustee's eyes. "I earn my money at the cemetery. From now on they'll surely let me recite memorial prayers there."

"No good!" Tsalye turned the ring of keys under Kalman's nose. "Since you bury corpses, the worshippers will feel disgust at taking prayer books and prayers shawls from you."

"Why should they feel disgust?" someone said softly, clearing his throat to make his voice ingratiating. "We're in God's hands. No one will feel disgust, God forbid."

"I'm not asking you," Tsalye shouted. "I'm not thinking about you. I'm thinking about myself. Knowing that he washes corpses, I'd be afraid to take the *lulav* and *esrog* from his hands on Sukkos."

"Hanuka hasn't even come yet, and Sukkos is a long way off, almost a year away," another man interrupted. The congregants saw that Tsalye was aching for another fight, but realized that the first victim would be the downtrodden newcomer who wanted to be the assistant shamesh.

187

"I'm not a gravedigger," Kalman said, trembling. "I come after the burial and only recite the memorial prayer."

"Well, that's another matter," Tsalye said, pleased at showing the congregants that decisions here were made by him alone. "But you're a housepainter, too. Woe unto you if you smear up the *shul* with your paint-stained clothes."

"When I come from work I immediately change my clothes," Kalman whispered, as though his strength were ebbing. "And besides, there's no work now anyway."

"Well, that's another matter. You'll have to sweep up the *shul* and fill the water-tub."

"I'll sweep up and bring in water. But where will I sleep?"

"You'll sleep in the library. Since I chased out your rabbi, Reb David Zelver, no one enters that little room, and everything is covered over with cobwebs. You are to keep everything clean and remove your bedding every morning. If not, I'll chase you out, too," Tsalye concluded and headed for the door, followed by the other congregants.

"A man has to get used to everything, God save us," a worshipper sighed. At this Tsalye turned and blocked the exit.

"And when will you divorce your wife?" he asked Kalman, pointing to the door. "Here hung the rabbi's proclamation which said you had no right to marry the agunah. As long as you haven't divorced her, she's still your wife, and I won't keep an assistant shamesh who lives with a married woman."

One man hastily chewed his beard, as though silencing himself thereby. Another exchanged fiery glances with his neighbor, seemingly asking: Should we overlook this? A fourth looked around the *shul*, as though searching for a blunt object with which to crack Tsalye's skull. Nevertheless, everyone bit his lips and held his tongue. Each one thought if he were the one involved, he would rather be chained in prison than forgive Tsalye. But since it concerned a man who might remain without a roof over his head, he dared not intervene. Standing tall with stooped shoulders, Tsalye stared at the angry faces around him. His gaze remained fixed upon Kalman, who looked as though he had fallen asleep on his feet. The trustee's remark that he would sleep in the little library stuck in his mind like tacks. In that very room the rabbi had pored over his books before permitting him to marry Merl. Why, then, had the other rabbis forbidden it? Did they have other books?

188

"Well, I asked you something," Tsalye shouted at Kalman, as though he had been his lifelong provider. "Will you or will you not divorce your wife?"

"I'll divorce her, I'll divorce her. I'll give her a divorce as soon as she requests it. In fact, I won't even wait until she asks for one, I'll run after her and demand that she divorce me."

"You won't have to demand anything. She'll grab that twelve-line bill of divorce with both hands. A young roughneck is waiting for her, someone on the fringe of the underworld," Tsalye grimaced. The worshippers stared at him and at the cowering assistant shamesh who looked more dead than alive. The Jews wanted to know the identity of this young roughneck who was about to marry the agunah. But just because they wanted to know, Tsalye didn't say a word; he drove everyone from the *shul* and told Kalman:

"You can move in tomorrow. I keep the keys to the *shul*. I'll lock you in after the Evening Service and open up in the morning."

A prison! Kalman thought as he walked along the street. A week ago he had been an independent householder, had slept in a clean bed, and had been served whatever he wanted by his wife. Now the master of the house would be Moritz, while he, Kalman Maytess, would sleep on a hard bench in the library, in the very room where the rabbi had learned in the books that he and the agunah could marry. Why, then, had the other rabbis forbidden it? Did they have other books?

35

When she returned home, Merl set to work assiduously. The weather had grown cold and the women who had placed orders with her were waiting for their winter garments. During the week with her family she had noticed that her sisters and nieces needed winter blouses. Now that she would no longer have to care for her husband, she would visit her old mother more frequently and be a better daughter, sister and aunt.

But Kalman did not leave her mind. Just as she had considered him small and pathetic when he could not stand up for her—so did he grow in stature by his manner of departure from the house. She fancied that his silence remained hanging in the air. Golda had told her that Kalman had immediately agreed to grant a divorce. She knew that he had already moved into the Zaretche *shul* and, in order to vacate her house, had become an assistant shamesh there. He had taken all his old things away and touched nothing of hers. Before his departure he had cleaned the house as though sweeping himself out of her life, wiping away every trace behind him to make her forget him all the sooner.

Merl began to hate Golda for having driven Kalman out. But Golda, confident that she had done Merl a favor, came up to visit her, dragging along Guteh, too. Golda renewed the discussion concerning Moritz and determined that if Merl rejected him now, she'd be the most detestable woman in the world.

"If you marry him, Mama won't have to lie in bed like a hunk of clay. He'll bring her the best doctors, he'll help Guteh and give dowries to Zelda and Freidke."

"I don't need his help. The children provide for the household expenses," said Guteh. "But it would do no harm if he'd bring doctors to Mama and pay for my daughters' wedding expenses."

"And I *certainly* don't need his help," Golda yelled. "Moritz has sworn that he won't drink anymore. If he keeps his promise, my Shaike won't drink either, and he'll stop being lazy and earn more than enough for both of us."

Merl saw that Golda had even won over Guteh, who had previously opposed Tsirulnik. "You've got memories like cats," Merl shrugged. "The one sweet smile that Moritz gave you made you forget everything he's done. In fact, he was even responsible for my marriage to Kalman. He came to me and sneered that Itsik was still alive but didn't want to come back. I couldn't stand it any longer and ran down to the rabbi and pleaded tearfully with him to set me free."

"And you still think you're right?" Golde filled the room with her raucous shouts. "You threatened Moritz with a pressing iron and wanted to kill him for a little joke he had made. Who *wouldn't* have gotten angry? Your Kalman, who got you with no more effort than plucking a hair, didn't even lift a finger for you; and Moritz, whom you've been torturing for twenty years in a row, is ready to lay down his life for you."

Merl stopped the sewing machine and walked to the window. She looked toward the forest settlement where she had lived in her youth when Moritz courted her. Through the branches of the naked trees on her street she had a view of the entire area up to the blue stretch of late fall woods. The gardens had already been harvested, and the fields plowed and covered with piles of withered leaves. From the distance came the white glow of slender birches, bending to and fro in their struggle with the wind. Here and there on the frozen ground solitary bushes still blazed, their red leaves flaming. The needles of a fir tree glittered in the yellow light, and the cold sun hung immobile between the clouds like an ice-trapped ship. Wherever she looked she saw only frost and desolation, like that in her heart. The earth, the piles of leaves, and the naked trees were waiting for the snow to cover the shame of their nakedness. By being an agunah she too had remained seemingly outside, her loneliness on public display and the subject of city-wide gossip.

"I'll marry Moritz Tsirulnik when the moon turns to cheese," she told her sister, still staring through the window. "I'm surprised you don't realize he only wants to marry me to get even for all the years I didn't let him come near me."

"I'm afraid that's true, too," Guteh blurted out.

"Silly goose, what have you got to be afraid of?" Golda pounced on Guteh, who had ruined her plan. "He's forty-four already. Do you think he has nothing better to do than get even with you? There are plenty of pretty and healthy young girls who would be delighted to get him. But Moritz says that old love doesn't rust. Did you hear that Merke?"

Merl's face was pressed to the pane. She fancied that she saw Reb David Zelver outside. Yes, it was him, walking up the street to his house. She tore herself away from the window and ran to the door.

"Where are you off to?"

"I'll be right back," Merl said, running down the steps. The rabbi had told her not to visit him any more to avoid gossip. But now she had to see him. Her steps echoed through the empty street, and even louder in her heart. She pressed her breast with both hands to prevent her heart from leaping forth, and finally caught up to Reb David near the end of Polotsk Street.

"Rabbi, I've separated from my husband," she called behind his back, afraid that otherwise he might not stop.

Reb David hesitated for a moment, not sure if he was being addressed, then turned slowly. Merl's gaze fell on his blond, now-greying beard; since she had seen him last he had aged ten years and looked fifty now. He stared at her as though he were in another world.

"Rabbi, I've separated from my husband. We couldn't get along anymore."

"I know," he said coldly.

"You told me that if we separated it would mean that we had no faith in you. But my husband believed all the rumors about me and continually complained that he had been deceived. I couldn't stand it any longer. Now, rabbi, you have no more reason to oppose the other rabbis. Withdraw the permission you gave me and the town will make peace with you."

"In other words, it's true," the rabbi smiled bitterly. "At least you say you want to do me a favor. But he came right out and threatened to beat me."

"Who?"

"The man you're intending to marry. He came and told me that if I don't openly admit that you and your husband weren't permitted to marry, he would beat me." The rabbi looked at her

192

sadly for pretending total ignorance. "The fact that my wife has a weak heart didn't even bother him. She nearly died of fright."

"Moishke Tsirulnik!" Merl said, shuddering. "Was it he who threatened to harm you? Rabbi," she struggled with her choking voice. "I swear I know nothing about it. I didn't know he came to see you, and I never thought of marrying him, despite my sisters' urging. He hates me because I always rejected him. *He* stirred up the town against you and against me, and *he* told my husband the most dreadful things about me. Now, since Kalman and I have separated, Tsirulnik is spreading the word that I'm going to marry him."

"He's a vulgar person. In my wife's presence he had the nerve to say that I gave you the permission to marry because there was something between us." Reb David looked around, afraid he might be seen standing with the agunah. But the street was empty and the only passersby were the residents of the nearby gentile quarter.

"Rabbi, have pity on yourself, your wife and your little children, and do as the rabbis asked." Merl wrung her hands. "I've separated from my husband and I will not marry anyone else. I have been an agunah and I shall remain an agunah."

"I didn't grant the permission as a favor, but because such is the law in the Torah," he said. "Even if you divorce your husband—and that would be a pity, a great pity, for he is a fine man, despite his weakness—even if you divorce him and want to marry the man who threatened me, I still won't change my mind about the permission. And my making peace with the rabbis won't save the life of my child. They took the baby to the hospital. The child is dying."

He stared at the dumbstruck seamstress; then his clouded face brightened and a troubled smile hovered on his lips.

"I considered you honest, even saintly. Therefore, I couldn't imagine that you would want to leave your upstanding husband in order to marry someone else. But this man spoke in your name, too. 'I and the agunah don't need a rabbi's permission,' he said. 'We need precisely the reverse. We want you to withdraw your permission so that Kalman Maytess will leave her.' Therefore, I thought it over and concluded that perhaps it's true, perhaps you're doing this out of despair and anger at your husband who had become frightened by the tumult in town. But I see that I had suspected you in vain and I ask your forgiveness."

Reb David again stared at her for a while and suddenly shivered.

"You're standing here without a coat. You'll catch cold and get sick." He stretched out his hand as though intending to take her arm, then immediately withdrew it. "Go back home and don't be afraid of that man who threatened me. There is a God in heaven. I'm very glad that it wasn't you who sent him to me."

With his hands in the pockets of his frayed gaberdine, he drew closer until she felt his breath, as though he wanted to warm her.

"I see how grieved you are over me. Don't blame yourself for my tribulations. It's I who am to blame for yours. I should have warned you that I have enemies and that they wouldn't remain silent. But God is my witness that I meant for the best and pronounced my decision according to the law. Help can yet come for my child and for you as well. God's help comes instantaneously."

Reb David went away and Merl followed him with her glance until his small shrunken frame disappeared into the gate of his house. She returned home, wide-eyed with astonishment. Moishke Tsirulnik had threatened to beat the rabbi and told him in the rebbetsin's presence that she was the rabbi's mistress. And her sisters were expecting her to consent to marry him.

"You crazy loon, where did you run off to without a coat?" Golde clapped her hands as Merl entered.

"To a neighbor's," Merl answered with a lifeless voice. "I've made up my mind. Before I decide to marry Moritz, I want to have a talk with him. Tell him I want him to come up to see me."

"You always were and you still are a wild goat," Golda said softly, as though talking to a naughty child. "Our advice you don't trust. But when a neighbor tells you it's the proper thing to do, you take her advice over that of your own flesh and blood."

On their way back home, Guteh wondered aloud at the stubborn Merl's quick change of heart. But Golda crowed, "Some girls are pretty—she's smart. Moritz knew what he was talking about. Old love never rusts."

36

At first Merl thought that she might persuade Tsirulnik not to torment the rabbi. But she soon changed her mind; if that louse saw that she was interested in the rabbi he would cause him more trouble. Merl could not understand why she had precipitated a storm over a permission she didn't need, even if she *had* wanted to marry once more—after all, she had neither been, nor become, religious. Anger at herself, hatred for Moishke Tsirulnik, and despair at her impasse prompted an oft-recurring thought that she did not repulse: she had never been afraid of death; why, then, should she hold on to her fruitless life? If she decided to put an end to her suffering, she would also be doing the rabbi a favor. Seeing how far she had been driven, people would commiserate with Reb David as well, just as they had commiserated with Reb Levi Hurvitz on account of his crazy daughter. But Merl felt that she wasn't ready yet for this extreme act.

The seamstress had stopped working and no longer thought about her customers and her sister Guteh; she no longer thought about her nieces for whom she was supposed to sew winter blouses or her mother in the old-age home. She paced back and forth in her apartment, touching her temples in feverish expectation.

Golda had come to inform her that with great difficulty she had finally persuaded Moritz to come to see her. He said that since Merl had raised a pressing iron at him, she was supposed to come and apologize to him, and not vice versa. Nevertheless, he would swallow his pride and come up at noon tomorrow.

"Merke, be nice to him. Be friendly. You've sucked his blood long enough."

A chill passed over Merl, but she said nothing and hastened to send Golda home. Golda was certain that bliss had befuddled Merl.

Once alone, Merl looked around the apartment and decided she would flee—to a village where no one knew her and where she would earn her livelihood. A moment later, however, she already laughed at the idea. But could the rabbi run away from his heartsick wife and his dying child?

Merl looked at the second bed which she had brought in for Kalman. Upon seeing the additional, now-empty bed, Moritz would chuckle to himself and his unctuous eyes would crawl over it like worms. So as not to give him an opportunity to feel revenge, she angrily and swiftly pulled the bed away from the wall, but a minute later—even more angrily and swiftly—pushed it back. And even if she removed the bed, didn't he know that she had separated from her husband? She wanted to give his filthy fantasy full reign—and let him burst. She wanted to see if she were still woman enough to make him writhe on the floor at her feet. She would regale him with food and drink in order to heat up his blood. And in order to keep up the role without feeling nausea, she would drink with him, too.

Merl went shopping and returned even more agitated than before. The storekeepers had already heard that the seamstress was divorcing her husband to marry her one-time lover, and their faces expressed anger, curiosity and scorn. She lay down to sleep earlier than usual, but could not shut an eye. Feeling hot, she removed her night-gown and lay naked under the quilt, running her hands over her small, full breasts, the silky smooth skin on her belly, her firm hips and legs.

Merl had always noticed that besides Moritz, other men too devoured her with their eyes. The young men thought that her clever smile and her ability to maintain silence until she suddenly burst out with a merry laugh indicated well-concealed experience in the ways of love. The truth was that she had to keep watch over her body, like people who scrupulously turn off all fires before leaving their house. "I was a fool," she said to herself. She could have picked a young man who was not a Moritz Tsirulnik. But yet when she did marry again, she chose an honest but pathetic man, who pleased neither her body nor her soul. Kalman complained and asked why she thought and worried more about Reb David Zelver than about him. But Kalman did not even realize that her body was like a chunk of clay in his presence. Frankly, her love for Itsik hadn't been deep enough either to let her enjoy his embraces to the point of pain and intoxication. Her capability for intense love was greater than her hatred for Tsirulnik, but her life had come to naught.

Merl was somehow ashamed to think of Reb David Zelver while feeling the painful sweetness of her nakedness, and she pulled her hand away, as though from burning coals. In order to put a greater distance between herself and her body, she wrapped herself in a sheet and thrashed about like a huge silver fish on the shore. Nevertheless, she felt her body not only under the quilt, but also behind the skin of her forehead. Her body, that huge silver fish, had filled her mind and was glowing there in the dark, quivering and twitching. She felt that she loved her body to the point of madness. Merl tore off the cover, jumped out of bed and ran to the mirror.

A dark blue light filled the apartment, and in the mirror above the chest her shoulders and breasts shone like ice. She stepped back in order to see her entire body, but from that distance it blended into the depths of the polished glass, as though her body had ceased to exist and only she herself lived on. Merl remembered the reports about Reb Levi Hurvitz's crazy daughter jumping out of her room naked. The rabbi's daughter probably loved her body, too. Merl returned to bed, her body aflame, shivering with cold and fear. What was happening to her? Was she saying farewell to life? She listened carefully, as though awaiting an answer, and heard the wind moaning outside.

The piercing post-Hanuka December cold crept into her fingernails, but snow had not yet fallen. The fierce wind tore at the roofs on the sparsely settled Polotsk Street, shook its row of naked trees, and, swirling in the emptiness, brought snow clouds that aimed to cover and bury everything. Merl heard the storm raging against the walls of her apartment, like waves crashing against sea boulders. It seemed that the storm was an enormous, frenzied monster, some kind of destructive demon with a will of its own. It wanted to smash her window and drag her naked out of the house, through the gardens, over the lake, to the mountain near the forest settlement where she had spent the summers of her youth—and cast her down to earth there, and cover her with pine needles, moss and rotted leaves.

She fell asleep toward dawn, when the dark blue light gradually turned pale grey. The light of day filtered into the room, as sparse as smoke wafting in place. She awoke late in the morning; the wintry sun was shining through the window, cold and yellowish, like a lamp through a smoky glass. Merl wearily lifted her head from the pillow and saw that it was snowing.

Instead of being cheered by the blinding whiteness, she felt her heart turning over with pain, as though afraid that the snow would cover her, too. The round potbellied alarm clock on the chest showed 10:45, and Moritz was due at noon.

She quickly rose, made the beds, washed, and dressed in front of the mirror. Behind her back she nimbly adjusted her brassiere to the last clip to make her full breasts appear even rounder and firmer; she put on a short skirt, a white silk blouse with a high collar, and a knitted wool jacket. Her full figure, tight brassiere and high heels made her taller and more supple. Holding the hairpins between her teeth, she combed her stiff black hair before the mirror and inspected her pale face, the pinched corners of her mouth, and the blue circles under her tired, lifeless eyes. Merl could not understand why she said she loved her body last night. She rubbed rouge into her cheeks, applied lipstick, and sprayed herself with eau-de-cologne. "Old love doesn't rust," she laughed bitterly. "The bridegroom is coming. The bridegroom is on his way."

"Finished! I'm ready to receive him." She looked at the door, then turned immediately to the window. A few days ago she had seen Reb David walking outside, and on account of him had invited Moritz to see her. If by some divine miracle she would learn that the rabbi's child had improved and that he had made peace with his antagonists, the rabbis—she would perhaps accept her fate with greater equanimity.

Merl pressed her lips to the cold pane, as though reverently kissing someone's hand, or touching her lips to a sick baby's forehead. The small and feeble Reb David was a hero. No wonder his wife was so jealous of him. As embittered and despondent as the rebbetsin was, she knew that she had a prince of a husband. Merl's eyes filled with tears. "But me the rebbetsin must be cursing. And with a vengeance! If the baby dies, the rabbi will curse me too. He had hoped that by helping me he too would be helped and his baby would become well. Perhaps the rabbi won't curse me, but I myself will curse the day I was born."

The door creaked and Merl shuddered. She wanted to turn from the window and welcome her guest, but she felt as though her neck had turned to concrete.

37

He stood in the doorway wearing a black homburg, a well-tailored black overcoat with a white handkerchief in his breast pocket, and pointy lacquered shoes. His snow-white silk scarf billowed over his collar. In one hand he held his ivory-handled walking stick, and in the other a pair of pressed leather gloves. He glowered at Merl, who still had not turned from the window. Moritz approached her with measured steps and over her shoulders whispered into her ear:

"Did you invite me over to throw the pressing iron at me?"

She quickly turned and met his menacing stare. "If you don't insult me I won't lift a pressing iron at you."

"Insult?" he glared at her again. "Who insulted whom? I never heard of a woman rejecting a man twenty years in a row. A dog in front of a stranger's door is beaten once, twice, and if he still doesn't go, the tenants finally get to like him and throw him a bone. But you always rebuffed me."

He spoke with the composure of a man whose anger had not developed recently, but, inbred and stubborn, had seeped into his bones and become part and parcel of his entire being.

"I didn't want to be unfaithful to my husband."

"No one can blame you for remaining true to your husband who went to war," Moritz said, his hand on his heart. "But I never imagined that when you decided to marry you'd reject me and take a Kalman Maytess. It didn't suffice you that on account of you I remained an old bachelor; it didn't suffice you that I began to drink in order to drown my sorrows; it didn't suffice you that you toyed with me for so many years—but to top it off you married a Kalman in order to give me apoplexy."

Merl saw that Moishke Tsirulnik, confident of his triumph, was already beginning to settle accounts for her continual rejection of him. Her hatred for him pressed her heart, as though someone were standing with one knee on her abdomen. But she summoned up all her strength—and smiled. Then she turned on her high heels and charmingly, almost coquettishly, said:

"Have you come here to quarrel with me? We've quarreled enough over the years."

On the cloth-covered table, Merl placed liquor and soda bottles, assorted glasses, plates of lox, marinated herring, dried fish, goose salami, fresh tomatoes and sour pickles, crackers, a wicker basket filled with white bread, and a big bowl of fruit. Merl set the dishes and silverware with the speed and efficiency of a housewife; Moritz watched her nimble movements and scrutinized her well-developed body, her shoulders and her profile. Her face, he noticed, was somewhat wizened but well made-up, and her back was slightly rounded from perpetually sitting at the sewing machine. But her shapely legs beneath her billowy skirt seared him and he eyed her with the experienced look of a veteran patron of bawdy houses.

Moritz knew the addresses of whores who received their clients in their well-appointed flats. There one could have dinner, spend an evening, and feel perfectly at home. Moritz always wondered when one of his friends complained about wife-trouble: for twenty-five gulden a beautiful woman would throw herself at his neck; and if he brought some gift, she would kiss his feet as well. Why, then, did one need a wife with all the headaches? But the obstinate, teasing Merl was the only one he was prepared to marry, if only to bring her to her knees. Yet he still could not envision a woman who could not be bought. Looking at Merl's lithe body he was plagued by the thought: was she really that modest, or had she been play-acting all along?

Her eyes lowered, Merl moved about the table silently, as though giving him the opportunity of looking her over. Suddenly she glanced at him, her black eyes sparkling impudently, as though she had read his thoughts and was mocking his belief in her modesty.

"Why don't you take off your hat and coat?"

"Who's this beer-hall spread for?"

"For you. Afraid I'll poison you?"

"I've got nothing to be afraid of," he said, stepping up to her. "I know that you're not foolish enough to play with fire."

"Are you fire?" she laughed ambiguously, as though doubting that he were man enough for her.

200

"Try me and find out," he said lewdly, affecting a languid air. But her suggestive laughter was like a spray of sparks. Moritz put down his walking stick, removed his hat and coat and remained in his black suit and white silk scarf which, as was the custom among stylish young dandies, he had not removed. His shiny shoes squeaked as he slowly approached her. She leaned against the table and gazed at him.

"Smoke?" He took out his large silver cigarette case, famous among his friends, whose cover was studded within and without with brightly colored precious stones.

"Give me a light," Merl said, taking a cigarette and maintaining her cool and ambiguous smile.

He held the cigarette case open to let her notice its expensive gems. But seeing that she ignored it, he snapped it shut and slipped it into his pocket. He lit Merl's cigarette, blew out the match and struck another one for himself, as befitted a true gentleman. He watched Merl blowing thin lines of smoke from her nose, keeping silent with the dispassionate skill of a bought woman who would soon quietly begin to undress. Moritz, too, was silent, his smooth-shaven, wrinkled face seemingly angry and apathetic. He curled his tongue and blew smoke rings, like actors in American films. She's unmasked herself, he thought. Perhaps she had been modest because she thought she'd catch—a lord! But once she realized that all her plans had gone down the drain, she decided to live it up. He wouldn't even have to promise to marry her; her heart wasn't set on that at all. But what if she were just teasing him?—the lit cigarette seared his mind.

"You're too smart to play with fire," he threatened again, placing his hand into his pocket, as though he had a loaded pistol there. "And how's your mother? I heard she was quite sick," he sympathized, his mien indicating that if she were kind to him, he'd be kind to her mother.

"Yes, she is quite sick," Merl looked over his shoulders, as though expecting someone to come toward her from the distance. "Mama won't hold on much longer."

"She knows nothing, right?" he insinuated with a vexed smile. "See to it that she doesn't find out."

Merl immediately divined his intentions and sucked in her breath. The three sisters thanked God that their senile old mother was oblivious of the scandal in town. But Moritz might very well go to the old-age home, wait for one of her occasionally lucid moments, and then reveal everything. It would be just like him!

"Do you know what your brother-in-law calls Golda?" Moritz blew smoke rings in the air, his wrinkled shaven face still smiling. "Goat feet! Shaike wants to leave her, but I put my foot down. He idolizes me."

Golda, who had told her sisters that Moritz had stopped drinking and didn't let her husband drink either, had said nothing about her husband wanting to leave her. Now Merl realized why Golda had so insistently promoted the match with Tsirulnik, who surely had a share in Shaike's wanting to leave his wife. And that's why Golda tried to prevent this by bringing Moritz into the family.

He's right. I *am* playing with fire, Merl thought. The world wasn't big enough for both of them; it was either him or her. She ought to stab him in the heart with her shears. It was senseless to have invited him. But if she were to throw him out now, she would make matters even worse. He would take revenge not only upon Reb David, but also upon her mother and sisters, who would end up cursing her— all thanks to Tsirulnik. Consequently, she would have to use kindly persuasion.

"What are you thinking of?" He crushed his cigarette in the ashtray, having given her enough time to digest his intentions.

"What am I thinking of? I'm thinking of old times." She also crushed her half-smoked cigarette. "We met so many years ago, and yet it seems like only yesterday. A person begins to look old before he feels old, and if others wouldn't let him feel his age, he'd be the last to realize it."

Merl looked at him ruefully, as though regretting all the unwarranted anguish she had caused him throughout the years. Her eyes widened, became misty, overflowed. She breathed quickly and panted, as though scarcely able to control her burning passion.

38

In her high heels, Merl stood taller than Moritz. She glanced down at him, looking like a person at the edge of the abyss deciding whether or not to jump. Suddenly she folded her hands around the back of his neck, closed her eyes and kissed him so hard he lost his breath. The sweet weight of her body ignited his blood, and he tore her hands away from his neck, brutally twisted them behind her back and pressed himself to her. Her eyes lowered and her mouth contorted with pain, Merl thought quickly. An idea hammered at her temples. The only feasible kindly persuasion would be offering herself. And that's precisely what she would do. Who was she, a saint? Let him rot along with her body.

"Yes, you are fire. Playing with you is like playing with fire," she said and nimbly slipped out of his hands.

Moritz stood there confused, momentarily seeing nothing around him, as though in a fog. He had never had such a woman. And she too had never had the sort of man she needed. If she weren't starving for a man she wouldn't have kissed him with such wild abandon.

"Even without a girdle you still have the figure of a young girl," he breathed heavily. "Let's see, you must be thirty-five or thirty-six. But since you didn't have any children, you're not all played out."

"Don't mention my age," she snapped. "Do you want a drink?"

"I'll have one for the sake of our friendship," he sat, then jumped up at once. "No. I'm not drinking any more. You know I've stopped drinking and made Golda's husband stop, too."

"With me you can have a drink." She pushed the platters of food toward him and began to pull the cork from the bottle.

"You should have told me you wanted to have a drink with me. I would have taken you to the finest restaurant in Vilna," he said, taking the bottle out of her hands. Moritz slapped the bottom once and the cork shot out with a bang. He filled Merl's tumbler and poured himself three-fourths of a water glass. Like a sophisticated drinker, he didn't down his drink straightaway but held the glass in his hand.

"Here's to you! Health to all!" he said and the liquor slowly burbled down his wide maw.

Merl drank her tumbler at once and the whiskey seared her from her abdomen to the top of her head: for fifteen years she had lived like a nun, preserving her chastity for—Moritz Tsirulnik! She began to laugh.

"Why are you laughing?" he asked, his mouth stuffed with salami and crackers.

"I've smeared you with lipstick," she said, bending over him and wiping his lips with her handkerchief. He felt her body and her firm breasts leaning against him, and pressed his head into her abdomen, like an angry beast banging its hairy head into a tree trunk.

"I like women who have bodies like a steel spring," he said and tried to put her on his lap. But she jumped away and spun about in the apartment with outspread hands, as though rehearsing a quadrille for a forthcoming wedding. Her dress swirling and billowing, she stopped again in front of his chair.

"Do you really want to know why I just laughed? Because I reminded myself how Kalman came home drunk. He told me that he had been drinking in a tavern with you and the painters."

"He's got a chicken brain. After two-three little tumblers he fell smack on his nose. Let's have another drink. *You* don't have a chicken brain."

"Bottoms up, bottoms up," she shouted as if in a fever, and as soon as he poured her a glass, she finished it, without waiting for him to drink. The two glasses of liquor and the spinning around the room made her dizzy; another wave of hysterical laughter swept over her at the thought that she had remained chaste all these years only to fall into the hands of a Moritz Tsirulnik. Moritz sipped down his drink and sat with lowered head, heavy and drowsy, plagued by the thought that she had had many men. She doesn't even take a chaser after her drink, like a veteran lush. And she laughs much too slyly, that experienced wench. Merl embraced him and sat on his lap, as though to drive away his melancholy and keep him awake. Moritz unbuttoned her woolen jacket and the top of her blouse, and with nostrils flaring inhaled the scent of her flesh.

She didn't resist, but merely gazed at him intently, as if curious to see if he'd be repelled by the wrinkles on her neck, hidden by her high collar; then she rebuttoned her blouse and jacket and sat on a chair opposite him.

"Tell me, Moritz, why did you drum the lie that I was your mistress into Kalman's head?"

"Stop tormenting me," he whispered, and huge drops of perspiration appeared on his head of thinning yellow hair. "Your Kalman was howling like a jackal to everyone that you made him miserable and fooled him, so I pulled his leg. You ought to thank me that I helped you get rid of him."

"You told my sisters you're prepared to marry me, but I know you'd rather remain an old bachelor. However, I won't force you to marry me," she said with calm indifference, looking straight into his eyes. "But how can I be sure that after I'll be yours you won't tell my sick mother that I've separated from my husband? And how can I be sure that you won't persuade your friend Shaike to leave my sister? After all, you threatened me."

Moritz chuckled. "Why should I persuade Shaike to leave his wife and bring even more suffering down upon a sick woman in the old-age home? You're not a streetwalker taken for a night. If you'll be mine, I'll lie at your feet forever." Moritz took her by the elbows and pushed her back to her bed.

Merl did not resist, but looked about the room for help, until her glance fell on the window. Before Moritz had come, she had been standing there, her lips pressed to the pane, thinking about the rabbi. She imagined that Reb David was standing outside, looking up at her apartment, aware of what was happening there.

"Save Reb David Zelver! The unfortunate man is being persecuted by the entire town. Do something for him. Find some people who will come to his support. You, you were the first one who stirred up the town against him."

"I was neither the first nor the only one," Moritz sat down on her bed, and with feverish fingers searched for the hooks of her dress. "Your rabbi has enough enemies without me. All the religious functionaries are against him. But if I so much as touch him, you can chop my head off."

Merl saw that he had loosened her dress. His head was hanging over her like an animal standing on all fours over its victim. Soon the beast, Moritz, would devour her. A shudder serpentined down her back; but it was sweet and warm, and intoxicated all her limbs.

She felt only disgust and revulsion for Moritz, and yet she wanted him to hurt her. Disgrace her, ravish her. She glanced to the window and her lips moved, as though praying to the snow-silent day to cool her blood. Let him take her. Let him have her. So long as she wouldn't desire him. Her body wasn't hers; she would leave it and run away, flee to the rabbi . . . Once more she thought the rabbi was standing outside, looking up at her apartment, aware of what was happening there. She had sworn to the rabbi that she would never marry Moritz, and now like a streetwalker she was offering herself without marriage. No, he would not even have her body.

"Please, Moritz, have some pity. Leave me alone," she stroked his face, his hair, trembling and weeping. "I don't like you. I can't be yours. You have other women far prettier than me. I'm old already, old and faded."

"Me you don't like," he said breathlessly, his mouth foaming. "But you like that loafer rabbi. While you're in my arms you're thinking of him. And I wasn't putting any stock into people's remarks that you're his mistress! Now I see that it's true."

"It's a lie. It's absolutely untrue," she looked at him with terror-stricken eyes. "I just feel sorry for him. You threatened to beat him and told his wife that I was his mistress."

"And how do you know I talked to him and to his wife? Who told you? Ah, I understand! He himself told you. You meet with him and you're both afraid his wife might find out," he said, purposely frightening her to silence her opposition.

"The rebbetsin curses me and the rabbi will curse me, too," Merl whispered with closed eyes.

"Leave the rabbi and his wife alone. They're not thinking about you anymore. They have worse troubles. Their baby died."

Merl lay with closed eyes, not moving, as though she had already plunged into the abyss. It took a while for his words to penetrate her numbed consciousness. She slowly moved her head, opened her eyes as though from a dream, and pushed him with all her might. She sprang from her bed and retreated, wild and disheveled.

"Died? How do you know the baby died?"

In his drunkenness and rancor he had blurted it out to depress her all the more. Now he saw that he had ruined things for himself. She tied her belt and buttoned her blouse. Anger cooled his passion, like a smoking firebrand in water, and a murderous rage swept over him.

"Why're you so scared? It's true the rabbi's your lover, but the child is from his wife. It was his wife who told me that her baby died."

"Did you see the rabbi again?" Merl could hardly utter the words. "Did you threaten him again?"

"If I blow at him once, he's finished," Moritz moved from the bed to the table and rinsed his parched throat with a glass of soda-water. "I went to see him today and told him: 'Listen to me. The agunah has sent for me. We're going to get married and we don't give a damn about rabbis. But we don't want to have anything to do with Kalman Clunk. So it's either or: Either you publicly announce that the agunah doesn't need a divorce, or you force that clunk to divorce her right away?'"

"And you didn't hit him?"

"You're ridiculous," Moritz laughed scornfully, and drank another glass of water. "I didn't hit him and I didn't threaten to hit him. I just pulled his hat down over his nose," he snickered. "The hat covered his head like a night pot. Then he pulled the hat back up and just kept looking at me without saying a word. But his wife opened her mouth up at me. Boy, did she raise the roof! 'Aren't you ashamed to touch my husband? Aren't you ashamed to touch a rabbi?' she shrieked. 'Our baby died, my little baby is still freezing in the morgue and you want to hit my husband,' she yelled. 'Take your slutty bitch and do what you want with her.' How should I have known that someone croaked on them and that that frump is as jealous as a cat of you? She called you a slutty bitch." Moritz licked his lips with the joy of revenge, squinting as though sunblinded.

Merl stood with lowered head by the table. The shears are on the sewing machine, flashed through her mind. But if she dashed over there, he'd have enough time to jump away. So she grabbed the neck of the whiskey bottle and quick as lightning smashed it with all her might against his skull. Shattered glass, blood and whiskey poured over Tsirulnik's face as he fell back, his head split open.

"H-e-l-p!"

"I always wanted to do this for my Itsik and now I've done it for the rabbi," she shouted wildly, grabbing her kerchief from a corner and running to the door and down the stairs, followed by his groans:

"Help! Save . . . me!"

"Don't help him! Don't help!" she shouted and ran out to the street.

39

Merl ran down the Zaretche hill, turned into Paplava Street, crossed the Vilenke Bridge, crying with a choked voice into the kerchief around her disheveled hair. "Now he won't hit the rabbi any more! Now he won't tell the rebbetsin I was her husband's mistress. He's lying there with his skull cracked. Serves him right."

She stopped at a large courtyard, looked up to a window and ran further, as though there were a bullet in her. That's where Guteh and her daughters lived. If she were to hide there, they would catch her immediately. God in heaven! She hoped they would not find her until she had taken her life. She had already known that there was no other way out. Death would be redemption for her, true salvation.

She stopped again. At the top of the path stood the family cottage where Golda now lived with Shaike, Moritz's friend. If her brother-in-law discovered what she had done, he would be the first to call the police. Merl turned aside and entered the forest.

In her high heels she kept turning her ankles and her stockings became soaked in the snow. She wanted to climb up a little hill and kept sliding down. Taking hold of a bush, she clambered up on all fours. Finally, she found a shelter beneath a thick pine tree where the ground was sticky and greenish. Her neck hurt and her skull rang and pounded, as though the sound of the glass shattering on Moritz's head had remained in her ears. She sat on a huge gnarled root which looked like a knot of snakes.

Gradually the ringing in her skull abated and her tense nerves calmed down, like strings that had ceased vibrating. She put out her hand, caught some snowflakes and watched them melting on her palm. The wind, as though discovering a corner not yet snow-covered, began to blow snow sharply at her face. Her eyebrows and lashes became studded with diamonds; patches of light danced before her eyes and she was as happy as a child. Snow stars, snow stars. The branches could no longer support the weight of the snow and clods rained down on her shoulders. The clouds thinned like white balls of unraveling thread, and the snow covered one remaining green bush and a young tree to whose branches some dry yellow leaves were still clinging. Everything in view was white and still as a graveyard. Weariness swept over her and she felt herself sinking into a numb daze; but after a while her nerves tensed once more and she felt refreshed and wide awake. The muteness, loneliness and desolation of the winter scene encompassed her.

Merl was terror-stricken at what she had done, but felt neither regret nor pity for Tsirulnik. That fiend had humiliated Reb David. If that cold-blooded extortionist had ten heads covered with thinning yellow hair, she would have split open all ten of them. Her only regret was that she had enjoyed her life so little.

Merl saw a squirrel climbing down a tree. The little animal came down the trunk head first and fixed its eyes on her, full of fright and amazement. "Are you hungry, poor little thing?" she stretched her hand out. With its claws gripping the tree, the squirrel looked momentarily at her, then scampered up the tree again until its bushy tail disappeared in the branches.

"I'm even more miserable than the squirrel; at least it's at home here," the runaway Merl thought and her eyes filled with tears. Kalman! Him she had forgotten altogether. He was fainthearted, downtrodden and satisfied with little, like a squirrel—a mute soul, even though he sang with heartfelt sweetness. Perhaps he was even more to be pitied than the rabbi, because he did not know why he suffered. Were it not for the fiend Moritz and the other demons, she would have been able to live with Kalman in a secluded corner, like the squirrel on the tree. Kalman was still her husband, they weren't divorced as yet, but he would no longer need a divorce from her. He would be a widower for the second time. Would he at least say Kaddish after her? She wasn't thinking of the world-to-come, but merely wanted to be remembered with kindness. But to Kalman she had not been kind, and perhaps not even honest. She had married him without even telling him that she didn't like him. And when she smashed the bottle over Moritz's skull, she had not even thought that she was getting even for Kalman, too.

Fatigued, she closed her eyes, but her senses were wide awake. She heard a wagon rumbling on the road. The driver swore and whipped the horses, but the wheels moved slowly. The peasant had probably left his village last night, before the snow, and had not taken the sleigh. How good it would be if the peasant would take her along, hide her in the straw, and bring her to his village. She would sew clothes for his wife and family, help in the house, and thank them for a dry crust and a bed to sleep.

Merl lowered her head, dozed off, and heard two people talking loudly in the nearby path behind the row of trees.

"How could you have let my daughter remain an agunah all these years?" a woman said. Merl recognized her mother's voice and wondered: Mama no longer lives in the forest settlement with Golda but in the old-age home. With whom was she talking?

"My leg was amputated and I use a wooden leg, so I was afraid that Merl might chase me out," she heard a man replying in a loud sharp voice. Merl recognized her Itsik's voice and wondered why it had not changed after so many years. "Don't tell her right away that I have a wooden leg. Since I wear long pants she won't notice it until we go to sleep," Merl again heard Itsik talking to her mother, and she laughed in her hiding place: You silly thing, I'll cover your wooden legs with kisses.

"And where is she?" Itsik's voice rang out. "Is she still a wild goat? Does she still run around in the forest laughing like she used to when she was young?"

"Yes, yes, I'm still a wild goat, and I'm hiding so that you won't find me," Merl was as happy as a naughty young girl in her hiding place. Suddenly she heard her mother groaning as though it were a death-rattle.

"She got married and wolves are tearing pieces from her flesh."

"Was she unfaithful to me? I'll split her skull open with my crutch!" Merl heard Itsik shouting and running toward her. Her heart pounded and quivered. "I've waited almost sixteen years for you," she wept. His steps came closer and closer. "Oh, he'll split my skull open," she yelled and snapped out of her nightmare.

It was twilight and the snow had stopped. The cloudless sky was clear and blue. Billions of gems sparkled in the snow-covered distance, and Merl fancied that she was in fields sewn with white blossoms. The fright of the nightmare had vanished and only the echo of Itsik's voice remained, a sweet memory that surrounded her like a silver mist around the moon. She smiled at a long-gone spring. Years ago she had gone for walks here with her friends. Her lips moved and she sang wordlessly, the tune vibrating in her mind.

Let's have a love affair,
Let's be man and wife;
I'll wait for you a year or two,
I swear this by my life.

A year or two I'll wait for you
And even five will be worthwhile;
I'll send you money to your fort,
I'll suffer, sew and smile.

She heard voices. People walking on the path. Perhaps they were looking for her, she shuddered. For the murderer. She had never been afraid of death. She had bravely gone out on anti-Czarist demonstrations despite Cossacks' whips and swords. While the Poles and the Bolsheviks battled in Vilna, she had run under fire to get bread for her mother and sisters. But now she realized that she did fear death.

She came out of her hiding place and shook the snow clods from her kerchief. All she had to do was walk across the path and she'd be in her father's cottage, where her sister Golda now lived. No, she wouldn't go there, for Shaike was Moritz's friend. She would go to Guteh. Nevertheless, she stood rooted and looked at the snow-covered branches that hung motionless in the dark blue. Merl imagined that the forest had seized her, enchanted her, as though she had been born here in a cave and nourished by roots and grasses. She feared going back to the company of people; she could no longer bear the troubles that she had borne until now.

If Moishke Tsirulnik was alive—and he probably was, for he was one of those brawny knife-wielding roughnecks—he would take his revenge upon her, her sisters, Reb David, Kalman, all of them. If not, she would be jailed and brought to trial for murder. Her sisters would avoid her; Kalman would thank God that he had run away from her; and the rabbi would consume himself with regrets over having helped a murderer. Then they would really begin to persecute and torment him for having violated the Torah for the sake of a whore who during a quarrel had murdered a gangster. She did not want to live and had no right to live. The rabbi had hoped that by setting her free, God would have mercy on his child. But God didn't consider her worthy enough of having compassion on the rabbi's baby for her sake. The baby died and she would die, too.

Merl saw a big black crow sitting on the tip of the tree where the squirrel had hidden. The crow did not utter a sound, but spread its wings and beat them, beat them, as though in pantomime inviting the human form below to come up to the tree. Merl looked at the lowest branch and already felt a choking sensation in her throat. She approached the tree with her head high and whispered that she would hide where the squirrel had hidden. She hoped that God would protect her eyes, for she wanted to look directly at Him, and not let the crow pick out her eyes, her black eyes.

40

Upon hearing that Mottele had died, the rebbetsin Eydl, her heart thumping wildly, fell back on her bed with a pain-wracked face. But she soon recovered from the attack and told her husband: "I'm all right. Don't worry, I'll live."

Later that morning Moritz Tsirulnik visited them and caused the tumult which he later related to Merl. After his departure, the rebbetsin's distress over her husband numbed her grief. A vulgar boor had humiliated her gentle husband and there was no one to stand up for him. The rebbetsin had no doubt that the slutty agunah had sent that roughneck. Eydl no longer wept or sighed, but merely lay on her bed, not removing her hand from Yosefl's head. The twelve-year-old, always misbehaving and contentious, now sat on the edge of his mother's bed and let himself be stroked, as though understanding that henceforth he would have to take the place of his younger brother Mottele. Reb David continually paced in the room, stopping only once by Eydl's bed to ask if she wanted to eat. But when she refused, he did not insist and again resumed his pacing, as though he were all alone in the large empty *shul*.

The incessant snowfall imposed the mood of cemetery stillness and weariness upon the couple. In the evening when the thick snow had stopped falling and the windows were covered with blue frost, Eydl and her boy were huddled close, sunk into a lethargic sleep. The next morning, when the rebbetsin awoke, Reb David was once again pacing back and forth, as though he had not gone to bed. Yosefl too rose, serious and calm, suddenly grown-up. For the first time his father did not have to tell him to recite his morning prayers. Yosefl took out his little Siddur and began turning the pages.

"You don't have to pray today, for your little brother hasn't been buried yet," his father said. He approached his wife's bed and said

213

softly, "It's freezing outside and it will be dangerous for you to go to the hospital where the baby is and then accompany the coffin to the Zaretche cemetery. I decided to tell the relatives to take the child and that just I would attend the funeral."

"I want to go," Yosefl cried.

"Don't cry, Yosefl, I won't let them take Mottele away; for then I won't even know where he's buried." Eydl turned to her husband. "Don't leave me alone."

Knowing that Eydl would not approve, Reb David did not argue with her. While giving Yosefl whatever food he found in the pantry, he told him: "I have a two-fold errand for you. First, go to the communal offices in town and tell them that Reb David Zelver's baby has died and that I'm asking them to arrange the funeral for tomorrow. If the cold spell continues tomorrow, ask them to postpone the funeral for the following day, for the baby's mother is sick and can't withstand the cold. On your way back, step into Reb Shmuel's shop in the Zaretche market, tell him everything, and say that I'm requesting one final loan of another few zlotys."

Yosefl nodded. His father tied a scarf around his ears to protect them from freezing. His mother lay in bed, in her clothes since yesterday, and did not say a word. When Yosefl was about to leave, she called him back, unbound and re-tied the scarf so that the edges also covered his throat under his coat, and spoke to him even more gently than his father:

"Don't be ashamed to tell the shopkeeper and his wife that we're freezing here without a piece of bread in an unheated apartment."

After the boy had gone, the rebbetsin did not say a word, and Reb David once more began to pace around, burrowing in his thoughts.

"Eydl," he stopped by her bed, "I beg you, Eydl, if a congregant from the *shul* or a neighbor comes, don't say anything against the rabbis or against the Almighty, God forbid."

"No one will come here, neither worshipper nor neighbor. Don't run around back and forth. It's making me dizzy."

Reb David stepped back from his wife's bed and burrowed deeper into his thoughts. The agunah had not behaved properly. At first, her tears and pleading had prompted him to accept new tribulations so that she could marry Kalman Maytess; and later she sent the market merchant to demand that he annul her previous marriage. When the agunah had caught up to him on Polotsk Street and sworn that she had not sent Tsirulnik and had no intentions of marrying him, he believed her. But this morning that vulgar creature had come all dressed up and declared he was going to see his bride. "If you don't believe me, come with me and you'll see me going up to the seamstress' house," he laughed. And he was obviously telling the truth. I searched long enough in all the early and latter rabbinic texts until I found a precedent for the permission, but I did not investigate sufficiently whom I was freeing, he thought, forgetting that his wife had asked him to stop pacing. He ran back and forth, from wall to wall, from corner to corner, seeking an exit from the maze of his thoughts.

"Eydl, Eydl," he stopped again by her bed and trembled, hovering over her as though seeking salvation at her side. "Our Mottele was born prematurely with a weak heart. It's a miracle he lived till now. Abraham was ready to sacrifice his only son, Hannah sacrificed her seven sons to prevent them from bowing down to idols, and we can't find solace that the Almighty has taken a child from us."

"What are you saying?" Eydl looked at him, confused, as though the cold and the agony had muddled her brain. "Are you comparing me with Hannah and her seven sons? For hundreds of years Jews have talked about Hannah and her seven sons, but who will mention my little infant? I'm not considered a saint. I'm not a saint and don't want to be one."

"Then we are to blame," Reb David bent over her. "If we both had accepted the decree and uttered no complaints to God, our Mottele's death would have been a sanctification of God's name, too, as it was with Hannah's children. Jews would have seen our humility and learned how to have faith in God."

"No one will learn from our experience," she smiled bitterly. "You're not Abraham and I'm not Hannah. You're not even considered a rabbi any more. We're excommunicated." She closed her eyes and murmured as though in a dream. "Hannah was able to sacrifice her children, but she could not live without them, because afterwards she threw herself off a roof. But I have to continue living."

"You have another child," she heard David's approaching voice and felt his breath on her face.

"And my husband is still a child, too. He has remained a child who trusts everyone," she murmured, sensing that her husband too now doubted if the agunah had merited all his efforts on her behalf.

"You understand, Eydl," he pleaded with her, "when a Jew suffers and does *not* lovingly accept his suffering, his torments are even greater. But if we both gladly accept our suffering and realize at least that it's on account of our sins, we would not suffer so much."

"I've committed no sins either against God or people," she hissed, opening her eyes. "Why do you keep talking about sins? How have you sinned?" she looked at him terror-stricken, afraid he was about to confirm her suspicions about him and the agunah.

"I haven't sinned, either," he concluded and left her bedside, deep in reverie. "God is my witness that when I gave the permission to the agunah I had the purest intentions." He stopped by the bookcase, as though summoning the books as witnesses; his self-vindication prompted the thought that the agunah had not fooled him either. After all, she had asked him twice to withdraw his permission and make peace with the rabbis. Her statement that she had no intentions of marrying the market merchant was probably true, too. Had she been a promiscuous woman, God forbid, she would not have troubled herself to get permission to marry the poor working man, Kalman Maytess.

But what would happen from now on? The market merchant who had visited him twice would surely come a third time. Hitherto he had been satisfied with threats; the next time he might resort to blows as well. The shock of witnessing such an outrage might kill Eydl. Reb David knew that he had no other source of loans or even donations. People had spread the lie that he had been intimate with the agunah, and even the worshippers who had previously sided with him were abandoning him. How would he be able to survive this, and how would Eydl? the rabbi asked himself, and the entire store of bitterness within him spilled out in a wail:

"Answer us, God who answers in time of distress, answer us! Answer us, merciful and gracious God, answer us!"

"David. stop crying." the rebbetsin wept, stunned by her husband's despair. "If you cry, I'll . . . I'll . . ."

The rabbi sprang toward his wife, who had suddenly stopped speaking, as though struck by a heart attack. Her mouth was open, and her eyes, where terror, rage and astonishment mingled, were fixed on the door. Reb David turned and saw Reb Levi Hurvitz standing in the doorway.

216

41

In his sable hat and long fur-lined, fur-collared coat, Reb Levi looked like a wealthy nobleman. His face was marked by sleeplessness and his beard was unkempt and perspiring. He strode quickly into the room, staring at the rebbetsin.

"What I have, I wish on you," Eydl yelled, covering her face.

"I've reached that stage already. Isn't a wife and a daughter in the madhouse enough?" Reb Levi sat down at the uncovered table and looked at Reb David Zelver, as though comparing whose troubles were greater.

"My baby died."

The weeping behind Reb Levi's back pierced his flesh like needles. "I know. I knew everything all along. Whatever one wishes to know, one finds out." Reb Levi leaned his perspiring forehead on his hand, as though he had come to Reb David's house to rest after his sleepless nights at home.

"And did you also know that my husband was driven from the *shul* and my boy from his *cheder*? Did you know this and remain silent?"

"Yes, I knew," Reb Levi addressed Reb David who stood opposite him, his lips pressed.

"And did you also know and remain silent when our enemies said that the agunah is my husband's mistress?" the rebbetsin shouted.

"I bear no responsibility for this," Reb Levi once again addressed Reb David, as though he had asked him the question with his wife's voice. "The Rabbinic Council did not order the teacher to drive your boy from *cheder*, and we did not order the trustee of the Zaretche *shul* to humiliate your husband. We did not excommunicate you! We merely posted proclamations stating our disagreement with your decision. Reb David, the sacrilege in this town has reached terrible proportions. Admit that you erred and save the honor of the Torah and the honor of Torah scholars. Rebbetsin!" Reb Levi faced the bed, as though realizing that he would not convince the rabbi. "Rebbetsin, try to persuade your husband—beg, plead, weep before him—to admit his error, if not in his heart, then at least in public, and thereby prevent everyone from saying that the rabbis themselves trample upon the Torah."

"If you've come to speak about peace now, you're too late." Her tears turned to sparks, and her face kindled with wrath. "If you were able to look on while my child was dying without coming to help us, then you are a murderer, an out-and-out murderer. It was *you* who incited everyone against my husband."

"I didn't incite anyone against your husband," Reb Levi approached the rebbetsin's bed and spoke with heartfelt, fatherly tenderness. "I have witnesses, too, that I told the head shamesh of the Main Synagogue to keep silent. But he did not keep silent. Consequently, I had no alternative but to summon your husband to a meeting of the Rabbinic Council. We pleaded with him and warned him that his enemies and the mob would go much further than we. But your husband paid no attention either to our warnings or our pleas. So we had no other choice but to stop paying his wages."

"And if my husband is a wilfully stubborn man, do my children have to suffer? But you're even worse; you're a murderer. You tormented your wife and daughter and then packed them off to the insane asylum."

"Let's assume that I'm to blame for my wife's and daughter's illnesses, but I'm not to blame for your troubles." Reb Levi stepped even closer to the bed and spoke even more tenderly. "For me there's no longer any hope of improving my condition. I'm an old man and I won't marry again, just as I didn't marry during the last twenty years that I have spent without a wife. And I certainly won't live to bring up another twenty-year-old daughter. But both of you are still quite young. God will help you. Your life is before you, not behind you. You have a son of bar mizvah age, and you will no doubt send him to a yeshiva. Do you want your son to be ashamed of his father for having permitted a married woman to marry? If your husband admits his error, we will pay him all his unpaid wages for the past weeks, and we will support him against all who speak evil of him. But if your husband continues to be obstinate, the persecutions will not cease. It will not be we rabbis who will do this but the mob, and we will be unable to help. Because if we come to his side, the people will say that all the rabbis are just like Reb David Zelver and scoff at the Torah: they permitted a married woman to marry. So have compassion, rebbetsin, on your boy, on yourself, and on your husband who has no compassion for himself."

"What should I do if he doesn't listen to me?" the rebbetsin wept. But despite her despair and bitterness, she saw that Reb Levi sincerely sympathized with her, even though she had reviled him.

"The rabbinic authority over agunahs must be jesting. He should not be talking about compassion, for he does not know what compassion is," Reb David emitted a dry laugh, as though it had torn itself from him.

"I'm more compassionate than you," Reb Levi turned to him, his face flaming. "But I cannot be more compassionate than the Torah and do not wish to be."

"You believe in the Torah but not in God," Reb David said scornfully.

"I believe in God *and* in the Torah, but you, Reb David, do not believe in the Torah. You are not quarreling with me, but with all the early and latter rabbinic authorities. With the most renowned sages and scholars of the Middle Ages—Maimonides, Shlomo ben Adrat, Joseph Caro, and all the codifiers. At the meeting of the rabbis we demonstrated that you base your support only upon the argument of Eliezer of Verdun, a lone dissenter. And the law is not according to his interpretation. In the world-to-come you will have to contend with all the codifiers whom you have insulted. They won't let you into Paradise."

"I'll accept the responsibility," the short Reb David straightened up. "I won't retreat in the face of the early and latter rabbinic authorities, just as I didn't retreat in the face of the Vilna Rabbinic Council. And if they don't admit me to Paradise, as you claim, then I'll calmly go to Hell. It's all the same to me. I won't suffer any worse tortures there than I'm suffering here. You, Reb Levi, probably won't have to contend with the rabbis, but instead you'll have to contend with an agunah. She'll stand by the gates of Paradise, tearing the hair from her head and crying to heaven that Reb Levi had tormented her. He persecuted her and harassed her and wanted her to spend the rest of her life without a husband, just as he spent twenty years without a wife. Since he did not marry, he didn't want the

219

agunah to marry either. And if the agunah refuses to let you enter Paradise, you will not be able to enter, because she—and not you— is the real saint."

"That's a downright lie," Reb Levi slammed his fist on the table, enraged. "A married woman who lives with another man without a divorce from her first husband is no saint. I've suffered more than you. And if you think that you don't have to fear Hell because you've suffered enough, then I surely don't have anything to fear. My decision was based upon the decisions of the codifiers. Therefore, your agunah won't be able to block my way to Paradise. And if as you claim she'll stand by the gates, then all the sages and codifiers will move out and will prefer to be with me in Hell than remain in Paradise with you and your agunah."

"Whose part are you taking, a whore's?" the rebbetsin shouted at her husband, wild with anger. "You don't take your wife's part, or your dead baby's, or our remaining son's—but you take the part of that slutty bitch, as if our enemies' remarks about you two were really true. Get out of here," she turned to Reb Levi. "My baby is still freezing in the hospital morgue. We are so torn and tattered we can't go out in the cold to the funeral—and you have the nerve to threaten us that things will go worse for us? Get out of here!"

Reb Levi retreated mutely, as though he had seen in the rebbetsin a reincarnation of his crazy daughter. Standing at the threshold, ready to depart, he was thrust forward by the door opened by Reb Shmuel, the merchant from the Zaretche market. Reb Shmuel, a man with a woolly grey beard, wearing a big winter hat and short fur coat, led Yosefl by the hand; behind them stood Reb Shmuel's short, stocky wife holding a basket.

"We just heard that your sick baby died," Reb Shmuel said, confused and agitated. "Ah, woe, rabbi."

"We brought you something to eat," his wife pushed him aside, set the basket down on the table, and wrung her hands. "Rebbetsin, don't ask what's going on outside. Vilna has never seen the like. May God preserve us all! Last night the market merchant Moishke Tsirulnik was found at the agunah's place with a cracked skull and today they found the agunah in the woods hanging from a tree."

A dead silence hung in the room. Suddenly the rebbetsin left her bed and stretched out both her hands to her husband, as though the floor beneath her were collapsing and she were awaiting help.

"David, it's not my fault. I didn't drive her to this, David," she called, covering her mouth with both hands, as if afraid that her cry might kill her stunned husband. Reb David did not even see his wife fainting on the bed, or hear Yosefl crying, "Mama, Mama!" Reb Shmuel rushed to revive the rebbetsin, but the rabbi stood petrified, staring piercingly at Reb Levi Hurvitz, his lips scarcely moving. But his voice was not heard, as if the rope that had strangled the agunah were around his neck, too. He pointed his index finger at Reb Levi and finally summoned all his energy to groan out:

"Murderer!"

The confused merchant, holding on to the door for support, looked on as the fur-clad rabbi slipped out of the room, admitting a draft of cold air.

"You are the murderer, not I," Reb Levi yelled from the other side of the threshold and slammed the door, as though afraid that Reb David's pointing finger might extend to the stairs and the street, and like a spear stab him in the back.

42

It began in the Zaretche *shul*.

Along with all other neighbors, Tsalye heard the news about Tsirulnik, the agunah, and the death of the rabbi's infant. "So what! They're all cut from the same cloth," he said and entered the *shul* for the Afternoon Service holding his ring of keys. But this time he didn't have to wait for the people to gather one by one for the quorum. A group of Jews stormed into the *shul*, tore the keys out of Tsalye's hand and shoved him with such fury he rolled to the door. In discussing the incident later, the worshippers said that the over-eighty-year-old Tsalye with his bluish face and long spindly legs obviously had ten lives to have been able to rise again. Tsalye got up from the floor, dumbstruck with terror. The quorum surrounded him and said, choking with rage:

"You wife-killer! You eighty-year-old cadaver! It's your fault that the agunah hanged herself and that the rabbi's baby died. Drop dead yourself! May your fifth wife bury you limb by limb."

And once more they pounced upon him. They scratched his lean, hard body, lifted him like a clod of rotted straw atop a pitchfork, and chucked him out of the *shul*.

"At least we accomplished one thing," one man said, slapping one palm against the other. "When the agunah will be brought to the cemetery, Tsalye won't go up to his porch and ask how old the deceased was."

The impassioned men regretted the fact that the trustee offered no resistance and thus prevented them from breaking all his bones. They sought a victim upon whom they could vent their pent-up anger, and one worshipper accused the other:

"I was the only one who stood up to that miserable wretch when he excluded our rabbi from the quorum. All of you suddenly lost your tongues."

222

"First of all, you weren't the only one. Secondly, you believed that bastard when he accused our saintly rabbi of having dealings with the agunah. But I was the only one who didn't believe it."

"You can't compare that to financial support. When the rabbi began looking around for a loan, you shied away; and when the rabbi bluntly asked for a donation, you suddenly became totally deaf."

The men argued and raged until one of the group noticed the new assistant shamesh of the Zaretche *shul*.

"He's the one to blame."

All along Kalman had been immersed in his troubles, hiding among the cobwebs of the library. Only now, when the worshippers attacked the trustee, did he gather from their shouts what was happening. He stood there, eyes protruding, mouth open, mute, pale, and covered with perspiration. The entire congregation swooped down upon him:

"You're worse than Tsalye, a thousand times worse. Our rabbi risked his life for you to let you marry. But you cast your wife aside and became the assistant shamesh of that wicked Haman who threw our rabbi out of the *shul*."

"You deserve to be drowned in a gob of spit," a worshipper spat, and the others followed suit. "Only a beaten dog can lick the hand of his oppressor the way you licked the hand of the man who kicked you."

The pulpit, the Holy Ark, the lamps—everything swayed in front of Kalman's eyes. Terrified, he ran out into the courtyard, as though sure that the swaying *shul* would soon collapse.

The painters and the wood merchants gathered at the painters exchange to talk. Moishke Tsirulnik's pals who had sworn eternal friendship hated him in their hearts for tyrannizing them and for his perpetual boasting and arrogance. When he was high and mighty, they flattered him and kowtowed to him. But now that he had suddenly fallen into unanimous disrepute, everyone turned his back on him and denied that Moritz had ever treated him to a drink. They gleefully repeated the report describing how all the neighbors came running upon hearing Moritz's unearthly cries, which sounded like the squeals of a butchered hog, and how they found him lying in a pool of blood and brought him to the Jewish hospital to stitch up his split skull.

"He's lucky," Isaacl Barash laughed loudest of all. "If he wouldn't have been taken to the hospital, he would have been torn to pieces, just as the agunah's kerchief was torn to pieces, for the rope of a hanged person brings good luck. In the hospital, doctors with white cloaks guard him so that no evil eye will harm him. No one knows better than me what Moritz has done."

"What else did he do?" Isaacl was surrounded by the market peddlers, youths in large boots, felt-lined trousers, and caps with stiff leather vizors.

The lanky Isaacl Barash, in his short jacket and narrow trousers, whose war stories bored everyone, now had the opportunity to tell how Moritz had put a knife to his throat to force him to persuade Kalman to leave his wife, and how Kalman then came asking him for a place to sleep, a request he could not comply with on account of his wife, that Jezebel.

"You dumb ass! And you're boasting that you were buddy-buddy with Moritz?"

A stony fist slammed an uppercut into Isaacl's chin, and he heard all of Vilna's church bells ringing in his ears.

"Smack him black and blue and douse him with red paint. He and Moritz are to blame for the agunah's suicide."

"How am I to blame?" Isaacl felt his chin, which immediately swelled up. "Was it only *me* who drank with Moritz? *All* the painters drank with him. They dragged Kalman into the tavern and poked fun at him for living with the agunah."

"You down-and-out wretch! *We* buddied up to Moritz? *We* dragged him off to a tavern?" the painters pounded their chests, aroused by Isaacl's slanderous accusation. "Go to hell! You think we don't know that when Kalman Clunk wanted a place to sleep in your house, you rushed off to Moritz to collect for having convinced Kalman to leave the agunah? But Moritz told us that all he gave you was the short end of the stick. It's your fault that the agunah hanged herself. Yours and Reb Levi Hurvitz's!"

"Reb Levi Hurvitz is to blame," the youths howled. "He ought to be fried in oil."

"We ought to pull his guts out and throw them to the dogs."

"He killed one of our poor sisters."

"Let's go to the Main Synagogue courtyard. Things are popping over there. The hell with work! Let's go to the *shul* courtyard!"

In the Main Synagogue courtyard they didn't need any excuses for whipping up scandals like those at the painters exchange. Rage burned like fire, and the news spread. The agunah had fashioned a rope out of her torn kerchief and hanged herself three steps from her sister's house. She was found and immediately recognized by neighbors who went to the forest to gather wood. Her lonely death stirred everyone and the wrath was expressed in glittering eyes and clenched fists. People recalled the head shamesh who after slapping the assistant *shamesh* on Simkhas Torah had escaped the crowd's wrath because like little lambs they had submitted to the trustees.

"Where is that crook? We'll take care of him now."

But this time, too, Reb Yoshe was saved. He had sniffed out the danger in time and disappeared. This further whipped up the crowd's temper and they pounced upon Zalmanke the assistant *shamesh*, who had just then appeared in the doorway to summon a quorum.

"There he is, Yoshe's lackey! Yoshe smacked him and then he went out pasting up posters that the agunah wasn't permitted to marry."

"Would you be happier if Reb Yoshe didn't take me to weddings and if my wife and children died of hunger?" Zalmanke wept.

"Damn that flea!" the crowd said, turning from him.

In the communal courtyards the bitterness was even greater, and their complaints clashed in the wild pandemonium: The fear of the long icy winter; the anxiety over lack of wood, coal and light in the apartments, and outside illumination for the broken steps; the women's curses and the children's wails; the miserable life in the cellar dwellings with ice on the walls and freezing privies; the mold in the bones and the ashen faces.

"Reb Levi Hurvitz is to blame. All the rabbis are to blame! If the community will continue to pay the rabbis their salaries, we'll make mincemeat of the community organization. They're God's crooks. Those pious hunchbacks shouldn't get a penny from us."

"The crazy Reb Levi is to blame!" was the cry in the butcher shops, where the women in their broad aprons and large pockets sat without a penny's worth of sales. "It was he who issued the ban forbidding us to import kosher meat from Oshmeneh. It's his fault that the agunah hanged herself."

"And perhaps he's not to blame?" a flayer in a leather apron sought to defend him. "Moritz probably promised to marry her and later laughed in her face. That's why she split his skull open and hanged herself—because he refused to sleep with her."

"Why don't *you* go to sleep and don't bother waking up?" the older butchers roared. "Don't you remember how Moritz stirred up the town against the agunah and against the rabbi who married them? Everyone knows that Tsirulnik crawled after her for twenty years and she couldn't get rid of him. So she decided they'd both die."

"And he bragged that no woman ever refuses him," the cold-blooded flayer wondered. "In that case, we have to wait until Moritz recovers and then nail him down to his coffin."

But the butchers decided that if Tsirulnik didn't stretch his legs and croak in the hospital, they'd have ample opportunity to settle accounts with him. Meanwhile, they should not forgive Reb Levi Hurvitz who stormed and raged and cursed the world and made everyone miserable.

"We'll make mincemeat of him."

Someone said that the agunah would be subjected to an autopsy, for the police wanted to know if her death was due to suicide or rape and murder. The news tore at the hearts of the merchants on Shavel Street like the wind that tore at the doors of their little shops; among the butcher shops the news spread that the agunah was going to be dissected by the medical students, God preserve us!

"You oxen! Why don't you speak up?" the butchers' wives cried to their husbands. "Go raise hell among the communal leaders. Smash their windows and knock their teeth out. They're going to cut up one of our sisters."

"What?" the men echoed their wives. "Let them perform an autopsy on the rich men, and let them hand Reb Levi Hurvitz over to the medical students."

The butchers went out to stir up the town. The women peddlers, standing next to their fire pots with glowing coals, looked at the butchers trustingly and saw in their broad manly shoulders a guarantee that someone would take up the cause of the poor and the oppressed. Noticing that they were regarded as deliverers, the butchers marched shoulder to shoulder and strode solemnly, gloomily, not even greeting acquaintances. Only one flayer pretended to tie his boot, and smiling slyly to the crowd, flashed his long gleaming knife. Then he slipped it back into his boot and straightened up with a cold glance, as if to say: During our chat with the city fathers there'll be no need to use the weapon, but there's no harm in taking it along, either.

The empty Old-New Shul in the synagogue courtyard huddled next to the surrounding *shuls*. Its windows, frost-decorated with scenes from the Bible, glowed darkly and screened the flickering Eternal Light. The wealthy householders had remained at home, not overly anxious to show their faces on the street. But the two old men with milk-white beards from the Old Shul who had accompanied the delegation to Reb Levi Hurvitz did go out. They were on their way to the *mohel* Lapidus to ask him if despite his anger at Reb David Zelver he considered it just that the rabbi had been excommunicated and that a Jewish woman had taken her life. But the old men had no chance to ask their question, for the *mohel's* son informed them that his father had gone to Warsaw to visit his sister; and he advised the two old men to hurry home so that people won't think they were sent by those robbers who looted stores under the pretext that they were siding with the agunah.

In Reb Shaulke's Shul, where the Torah scholars and the orthodox Agudah members worshipped, the commotion was even greater. Since two young scholars who still boarded at their fathers-in-law's houses had joined the delegation to Reb Levi Hurvitz, neither of them could sufficiently make amends for having butted into the agunah affair. One father-in-law publicly reviled his son-in-law by saying that had he known in time he would have invested the large dowry in a dentist for his daughter; while the other yelled at his son-in-law: "When I was at *my* father-in-law's table, I sat and studied and didn't stick my nose into other people's affairs." The young men justified themselves by saying that they had done it for the glory of God, but that Reb Levi had gone too far because of his grief at his crazy daughter's running naked out of her room. At that moment Reb Levi Hurvitz appeared on the threshold of Reb Shaulke's Shul. The worshippers immediately fell silent, uncertain if the rabbi had heard them. Reb Levi strode to his seat by the Eastern Wall and shouted:

"What sort of holiday is it? Why aren't you reciting the Evening Service?"

Instead of talking moderately and humbly, as they had expected him to, he sounded more belligerent than ever. After prayers, when he approached the doorway, both sons-in-law stopped him and said:

"The Rabbinic Council should put up proclamations stating that the *shul* Jews are not responsible for the agunah's suicide."

"The Rabbinic Council and the *shul* Jews must indeed take the

227

responsibility for what has happened," Reb Levi replied, striding out of the *shul*.

The tenants of Shlomo Kissen's courtyard know that the darker Reb Levi's mood, the brighter were his windows at night. The rabbi usually ran about in his room reciting Psalms. But after they had taken his daughter back to the insane asylum, his apartment became dark at 10 p.m. Apparently losing all hope that his daughter would be cured, he ceased praying. But suddenly, the lights again began to burn all night. Khiyeneh, the cleaning woman, had heard from the shamoshim of the rabbinic court that Reb David Zelver's baby was in the children's hospital; and she herself was present when the rabbi had chased the shamoshim to the hospital to find out how the child was faring. Reb Levi ran about in the room with his Psalm book in hand, reciting Psalms ceaselessly even during the day. Khiyeneh had a strange thought and went down to a neighbor:

"You know what? My rabbi is saying Psalms day and night for Reb David Zelver's baby."

People shrugged their shoulders. Everyone knew that Reb David's main antagonist in the agunah affair was Reb Levi Hurvitz; and yet here he was reciting Psalms for the well-being of Reb David's infant. That he was a contrary person everyone knew too by his appearing in *shul* on the very evening the town was seething over the agunah's suicide.

Late in the evening the butchers returned from the communal headquarters. "We gave the trustees such a fright, they dashed right out to try and stop the autopsy. Tomorrow the agunah will be brought from the general hospital to the Jewish one, and she'll be buried the day after tomorrow. What's more the funeral carriage is going to be drawn by two horses."

When the butchers were told that Reb Levi Hurvitz, the person to blame for all the troubles, still had the gall to show his face in the streets, they replied with satisfaction: "Excellent! It's obvious that he's dying to be brought to the cemetery along with the agunah. We'll make his wish come true."

"His assistants scattered like mice to their holes—but never mind. All the other religious functionaries are little sardines, but the big fish—that's him."

"Until the funeral he's liable to get cold feet like his other assistants and run away, too."

"Then we'll make a shambles of his house," the butchers said.

228

43

Reb Asher-Anshel sent his son Yosele to Reb Shmuel-Munye, and his son-in-law Fishel Bloom to Reb Kasriel Kahana with the request to meet at Reb Levi's house. But Reb Asher-Anshel himself had to shout and even stamp his feet until he tore himself away from his wife and daughter, who didn't want to let him go out to the tumultuous streets. In Reb Shmuel-Munye's house, Yosele was witness to the same scene that had taken place in Reb Asher-Anshel's house. Reb Shmuel-Munye's two daughters, whose eyes always expressed contempt for the entire world, shouted that on a day like this a rabbi would be well-advised not to show his face outdoors. But the general factotum in Reb Shmuel-Munye, the man who conducted all the rabbinic conventions, was awakened, and he left immediately for Reb Levi's. To Fishel Bloom's surprise, he did not find Reb Kasriel Kahana's house full of merchants seeking arbitration. Reb Kasriel weighed the tip of his heavy copper-red beard in the palm of his hand, considering whether or not to go, then finally consented. Everyone stared at the rabbis as they walked along the street. Their heads lowered, they hurried by, huddling close to the walls of houses as though walking in a downpour.

All three rabbis urged Reb Levi to have the Rabbinical Council proclaim that the agunah had taken her life not because they had forbidden her to marry a second time, but because her former fiancé, a market merchant, had attacked her, and also that Reb David Zelver was not being persecuted by the rabbis but by his old enemies. Reb Levi, who always ran about in his apartment, now sat calmly at his table, sipping tea and eating, and even seemed to be enjoying his colleagues' agitation.

"We can't have the town holding us responsible for this tragedy," Reb Asher-Anshel leaped up excitedly.

"Do you think that one can continually cast off responsibility by declarations?" Reb Levi twitted his brother-in-law, who had given him a crazy sister for a wife.

"My hand has not spilled this blood." Reb Asher-Anshel refused to remain silent this time. "I was against imposing the full severity of the law against him. Since I had no choice, I agreed that Reb David's wages should be temporarily suspended. I never imagined that such a tragedy would result."

"And I certainly opposed it," Reb Kasriel Kanana boomed. "But Reb Levi insisted throughout that Reb David be persecuted mercilessly."

The trembling Reb Shmuel-Munye was absolutely frantic. All traces of his nasty sarcastic smile had vanished. The root hairs on his thick nose moved and his white beard was soaked with perspiration.

"All the troubles came about because I wasn't given the chance to settle the matter. Everyone agrees that politics is my specialty. But no one wanted to depend on me. Now you see the results."

"Of course, I see," Reb Levi drummed his fingers on the table and looked at his colleagues from under his raised brows. "I went to Reb David and pleaded with him to change his mind; his wife pleaded too, but he remained adamant. Against the Torah, against all the rabbinic authorities, against the Vilna Rabbinic Council and against public opinion. But we, the Rabbinic Council, we have become frightened of the mob, like a *cheder* lad afraid of a rock-throwing peasant."

"You expect us to swallow the stew you whipped up?" Reb Shmuel-Munye seethed.

"The town considers you responsible and we risked our lives to come here in order to save you," Reb Kasriel Kahana grumbled.

"In order to save yourselves," Reb Levi interrupted, and, throwing fiery glances from one rabbi to another, added: "You're afraid that the community will stop paying your wages."

Reb Kasriel Kahana was by nature a man of great deliberation who did not utter a superfluous word. If during an arbitration one merchant introduced irrelevant remarks about another, Reb Kasriel bent his head, seized the edges of his beard, and uttered a long "Y-e-s!" His subdued angry roar reminded the merchant not to babble so much, whereupon the latter respectfully fell silent. Reb Kasriel now roared the same reply in order not to respond to the insults. Since Reb Levi's obstinacy prevailed over his logic, there was no point arguing with him. But Reb Shmuel-Munye refused to pass over this in silence.

"You care neither about the honor of the Torah nor the honor of the Vilna rabbis. You only care about one thing: that Reb David should not prevail. That's your one and only objective."

"Yes, that's my one and only objective. That that refractious rabbi should not prevail, that's my one and only objective." Reb Levi leaped up and like water bursting out of a dam his suppressed anger overwhelmed his affected calm. "The entire town knows that the agunah did not commit suicide on account of us. Nowadays there's no lack of couples who live together contrary to the Torah's commandments. And, besides, everyone realizes that as long as the refractious Reb David doesn't withdraw his dispensation, the Vilna Rabbinic Council cannot consider him a member and pay his wages. But what most pleases the mob who supports him is the fact that he had permitted a married woman to marry in opposition to all the rabbis. Therefore, we have to insist that *we* are right, not he. We must insist upon the law of the Torah."

"It's sacrilege," Reb Asher-Anshel groaned. "Everyone in town feels that we don't have an ounce of pity in our hearts."

"Let them! And by our displaying cowardice we'll add to the sacrilege." Reb Levi stormed across the length of the room, and suddenly stopped in front of Reb Shmuel-Munye. "Leave before the agunah's funeral comes here."

"The agunah's funeral?" Reb Shmuel-Munye touched his soft white beard with trepidation, as though it had suddenly turned to barbed wire.

"The mob wants to settle accounts with me," Reb Levi laughed bitterly, but without a trace of fear. "Haven't you heard? I heard it this morning in *shul*."

The rabbis, shocked and frightened, looked with astonishment at Reb Levi who paced around the room with his hands behind his back, in a festive mood, as if he were expecting honored guests.

"The cleaning woman told me that she asked the neighbors to lock the gate, but the tenants were afraid that the mob would break it down and make a ruin of the courtyard. As far as I'm concerned, well—*I* bear the responsibility, but *you* don't and you are not at all to blame, so you're not obliged to suffer. Go away before the host arrives."

"The crowd might even turn into Glazers Street and smash my windows," Reb Shmuel-Munye said nervously.

"Reb Levi, it would be best to leave the house now, too," Reb Kasriel Kahana said, heading for the door.

"Go, go. The quicker the better," Reb Levi urged them on. "And if the funeral blocks your way, say that you are not to blame. Say that Reb Levi Hurvitz is to blame for everything."

Reb Kasriel Kahana played deaf to these gibes, but Reb Shmuel-Munye could not bear Reb Levi's derision and shouted in an unnaturally loud voice, as though he wanted to overcome the fear that possessed him:

"It's true that you bear the responsibility. You created all this tumult, not us. You would have had us excommunicate Reb David Zelver in the Main Synagogue with the blowing of the shofar and the kindling of black candles. Nevertheless, if you promise to let me talk to the crowd and show them that we are not responsible, I'll stay with you . . . Yes, I'll stay with you."

"Now it's too late to start talking to the crowd," Reb Kahana spread his hands. "Now the best thing to do is to avoid them."

"Even now it isn't too late," Reb Asher-Anshel held the rabbis back. "Simkhas Torah morning, when the crowd wanted to break the head shamesh's bones, the trustees went out and pacified the crowd. Now, when the mourners see old rabbis talking kindly to them, they'll calm down too. We have to tell them how gingerly we handled Reb David Zelver despite his violation of the Torah's laws, and that we certainly are not responsible for the agunah's death."

"I will not attempt to justify myself," Reb Levi ran about the room with dizzying speed. "I will not permit that Zelver rebel from Polotsk Street to prevail. On the contrary, I'll tell them that *I* was the one who insisted that he be excommunicated."

"Let's go. He's out of his mind," Reb Shmuel-Munye pushed Reb Kasriel Kahana to the door.

"Let's not go, gentlemen. We dare not leave Reb Levi alone," Reb Asher-Anshel pleaded.

"He's your brother-in-law, not mine. And according to the law, I'm not obliged to risk my life for his madness. I should have listened to my daughters and not come," Reb Shmuel-Munye shouted and ran to catch up with Reb Kasriel Kahana, already on his way down the stairs.

"You go, too," Reb Levi told Reb Asher-Anshel, who had

remained in the room. "You weren't even one of the judges. We're relatives, and according to the law, we are not permitted to sit as members of one court. You were just an observer and bear no responsibility. I carry the entire responsibility, and I take it all upon myself."

Nevertheless, Reb Asher-Anshel did not leave. He closed the door and slowly approached Reb Levi.

"I know why you want to risk your life and face an impassioned crowd. You are disgusted with life, God save us, and you want to become a martyr."

"True, I'm sick of my life," Reb Levi sat down in his chair, breathing with difficulty. "I can no longer bear a life among people who shake off responsibility, like a man who at the Rosh Hashana *Tashlikh* ceremony symbolically shakes the sins out of his pockets. As a believer I know I was appointed to suffer on account of my wife and daughter, and I blamed no one. But you, Reb Asher-Anshel, were always afraid that I'd blame you for giving me a sick sister for a wife, so you continually say that you're not to blame. In other words, it's my fault that first your sister and then your niece went out of their minds. Therefore, in moments of despair I often blamed you for giving me a sick sister in marriage; but when I am alone I know that everything that has happened to me and is happening to me comes from God Almighty."

"You take upon yourself more than a Jew is permitted to," Reb Asher-Anshel whispered. "You want to drive enraged Jews to commit murder, God forbid. Excuse me for telling you this, but Reb Shmuel-Munye is absolutely right. You refuse to permit Reb David to prevail, even if it costs you your life, God forbid."

"True, I don't want that rebel to prevail, even if it means my life. He doesn't act like the atheists or the hedonists—for they don't have the power to withstand temptation. But he violates the Torah—in the name of the Torah. He is a pious-eyed rebel, supposedly compassionate, who permits Jews to throw off the yoke of Judaism. The time has come for rabbis to die for the Sanctification of God's name—not among the gentiles but among the Jews. The people believe in Reb David Zelver, for they see that he is prepared to bear any anguish and not retreat. These same people, then, should see that the rabbis with an opposing view are also ready to sacrifice themselves for the Almighty and for the Torah. Only then will they believe our assertion that the agunah was not permitted to marry."

"I'll stay with you," Reb Asher-Anshel said after a moment's thought. "Since you don't want to receive the crowd with kindness— you have the choice of either leaving with me, or having me remain with you. Come what may! I don't want you to say once more that I'm avoiding responsibility."

"That's all I need is to have your wife and children blame me if something happens to you. Leave at once!" Reb Levi jumped up, infuriated like a wounded beast.

Reb Asher-Anshel was familiar with his brother-in-law's wrath, but he had never before seen such wild rage. As he left the house a thought shared by everyone in town flashed unwillingly through his mind: given such abnormal fury, no wonder his family went out of their minds.

44

It was a cold and cloudy day. The biting wind stirred up snow gusts and blew them into the faces of passersby. The market women, delivery girls and embittered housewives from the poor courtyards wrapped themselves in their shawls and glumly slogged through the snow to the funeral. The men, wearing scarves and hoods, covered their ears with the brims of their high winter hats, and trod to the Jewish hospital where the agunah now lay. The funeral was scheduled for 3 p.m., but the people came early from outlying areas and the Vilna suburbs. Fishermen, cattle-dealers and bargemen appeared. In the lanes around the hospital, the shopkeepers still remained in their stores, the artisans stood by their worktables, the butchers' wives looked for customers, and the porters waited on the corners for a job. But everyone discussed the agunah and kept glancing toward the hospital in order not to miss the funeral. What a cruel world it was! Every movie ended with the hanging of the villain, but in real life the robust young woman hanged herself, and the villain remained—the villain.

In the meantime, the residents of Zaretche Street arrived, and they felt like mourning kin. Reb David Zelver was their rabbi and the agunah was their neighbor. They reported how they got even with the trustee Tsalye, who had excluded Reb David from the quorum.

"Excluded the holy rabbi from a quorum?" the brawny youths asked in astonishment, and the shopkeepers and their wives sighed. "And Reb Levi Hurvitz caused all this?"

Then someone retorted that the Zaretche Street people weren't as tenderhearted as they pretended to be. When the Vilna rabbis stopped paying Reb David's wages, even his own congregants stopped supporting him. Hearing this the youths were even more astonished. "If you're such kindly souls," they told the Zaretche residents, "then go to hell with all the religious functionaries." But in self-justification the Zaretche residents replied that since Reb David had been falsely accused of having dealings with the agunah, they washed their hands of both of them. Who could know? Slander had brought destruction upon Jerusalem.

The rumor soon spread that Reb Levi had invented the report that Reb David was living with the agunah. Had the rabbi of Polotsk Street not been a saintly man used to tribulations, he would have hanged himself like the agunah. But a Jew who committed suicide lost his share in the world-to-come, and Reb David didn't want this to happen to him.

"Our rabbi would have been here for this funeral, but he's busy with a sorrow of his own—the funeral of his child," said the Zaretche residents. "While Reb Levi Hurvitz was at Reb David's house trying to pick a fight with him, a man suddenly brought the news that the agunah had hanged herself, and Reb David called Reb Levi a murderer."

"If Reb David called him a murderer, he is a murderer, and we'll tear him to pieces," the youths said and told the Zaretche residents. "And what's more, Reb Levi threatened Reb David to forbid the burial of his baby in the cemetery."

"They say that those who commit suicide are buried next to the cemetery fence."

"Is that so? We'll see about that!" the youths gritted their teeth and hitched up their belts. "Reb Levi Hurvitz will be buried next to the fence. The agunah will be buried next to Dvora-Esther, Vilna's greatest saint."

From Zavalne Street came the ornate horse-drawn carriage that the community had promised. The hospital street became crowded with mourners. Several broad-shouldered youths went into the wide-open entrance of the morgue to bring out the body. When they came forth with the black coffin swaying over their heads, the women broke into wails and even strong men sobbed; and when the pall-bearers approached the carriage with the coffin, hundreds of voices cried:

"Carry her to the cemetery. On your shoulders."

"Past Reb Levi Hurvitz's house. Let him see what he's done."

A wail echoed through the hospital street. "Merke, what will we do now?" shouted Golda. Behind her walked the two nieces who

236

supported their mother. Guteh was silent, her face as yellow as wax. Whispers passed through the crowd:

"You see that loudmouth? She came without her husband because he's Moishke Tsirulnik's best pal and is afraid to show his face. Even the older one, the one walking between the two girls, came without her husbuand. He ran away from her."

"The agunah even has a senile old mother in the old-age home. She can't move and she's more dead than alive. She doesn't even know that her daughter hanged herself."

"And how come the agunah's husband isn't here?"

"That two-legged ass? He chucked her off. Lucky for him he hasn't shown up. Otherwise he'd be clobbered with cobblestones."

"We ought to scratch her sisters' eyes out," the women spat and hissed. "They shouldn't be permitted to go near the coffin. The poor agunah is more kin to us than to them."

The louder she wailed, the more Golda felt the mood of hostility surrounding her. At a funeral one usually found hosts of friends and relatives. Strange women supported mourners, wept and comforted them—yet around her people stood with cold, stony faces. Some turned their backs on her, some pushed her away, supposedly by accident. In the silence around her, Golda heard only one voice— a voice from within the black coffin: "You wanted me to marry my worst enemy as insurance to hold on to your own husband. But you killed me and who knows if you've saved yourself. Now your husband can throw you out all the quicker."

Golda fell on the stunned Guteh's neck and wept softly. "I didn't mean any harm. I just wanted Merl to be happy and not to remain an agunah myself. I didn't want all three of us to be agunahs."

The funeral of Reb David Zelver's baby also took place that morning. With the money that Reb Shmuel had lent him, Reb David hired a droshky and drove to the children's hospital with his wife and Yosefl. When they brought the coffin, the black-caped driver was amazed to see no other mourners besides the parents and a boy.

The Zaretche residents had gone to the agunah's funeral. They concluded that there was no comparing the death of a weak-hearted premature infant to a young woman who had committed suicide. Nevertheless, some of the congregants would have come to the funeral for the sake of Reb David. But in reply to questions about the time of the funeral, Reb David merely mumbled, making it obvious that he didn't want anyone to attend.

The rebbetsin Eydl, too, had no regrets that there were no mourners. In her heart raged an anger against all the rabbis and against the Zaretche congregants who had neglected them until the agunah's suicide and their baby's death. She realized that the agunah's suicide had changed the atmosphere in her husband's favor. She had noticed Reb Levi Hurvitz's fright, and had seen the merchant and his wife coming to comfort them, bringing food and lending them money; and that same evening she heard that the Zaretche congregants had beaten up the trustee Tsalye, her husband's gratuitous enemy. But this neither calmed nor comforted the rebbetsin. She no longer had the slightest doubt that her husband loved the agunah—and even during the baby's funeral these thoughts ran through her mind.

When David argued with Reb Levi Hurvitz in their house, he did not talk about her or Yosefl or even about their dead infant— David talked about the agunah and called her a saint. And when Reb Shmuel brought the sad news about her suicide, David was stunned, as though his life had already ended. True, the seamstress was a gentle, patient and kind-hearted soul, attractive and independent, while she, Eydl, was a sick, wrinkled, perpetually screaming woman who spent most of her time in bed. No wonder that David liked *her* more. Still, she could not believe that there was anything between them. The rebbetsin gazed at her husband. She felt that he had become hard and impatient because now there was no need for the pretense of make-believe affection. If it weren't for my Yosefl, who would remain an orphan without me, I would do what the agunah did, the rebbetsin thought, seemingly catching her husband's stupor.

When the small coffin was put into the funeral carriage, Reb David told his wife and son to remain in the droshky. Eydl had wanted to follow the carriage on foot like her husband, but to avoid a quarrel she immediately submitted. She ascended the hired droshky, covered the warmly dressed Yosefl with her shawls, huddled next to him, and remained silent all the while. The short Reb David, wearing a long, frayed black overcoat, walked behind the funeral carriage, followed by the droshky with his wife and son.

In order to avoid more gossip about himself, the rabbis and the agunah, Reb David asked the driver to bypass the Zaretche market and drive to the cemetery by way of the bridge along the Vilya River. Once more the driver was amazed: that was the Christian quarter, and even plain Jews, not to mention a rabbinic family, always asked him to drive their dead through the Jewish streets.

A wind blew from the river and the smooth, untrodden snow outside the city blinded the eyes. In contrast to the gleaming ice on the river and the surrounding snowy whiteness, the gloomy blackness of the coffin was all the more conspicuous. The Polish residents of the area stopped to look at the lonely funeral.

Reb David followed the carriage, holding on to its closed door with both hands, holding on to his dead baby in order not to think of anything else. But thoughts of the agunah did not depart from him.

45

At the cemetery, Reb David paid for the droshky, took his wife and son into the long wooden hut where the shrouds were sewn, then went outside to ask the gravediggers if the grave had been prepared. But as soon as he stepped out he forgot what he had intended to do, and stood in the snow-covered field lost in thought. The cemetery crouched in his mind, and the surrounding silence pounded in his ears. He closed his eyes and thought: So many righteous innocents are resting here. How good it would be if here in one of the saints' tombs he could hide from himself and from his tormenting thoughts about the agunah.

She had followed him to the *shul*; she had followed him on the street and pleaded with him to change his mind about the permission and thus save himself, his wife and children. And yet he had believed that Tsirulnik spoke in her name, and that she had sent him to demand the annulment of her marriage to Kalman Maytess. "Reb Levi Hurvitz once told me that I cause trouble wherever I turn. He's right. Reb Levi is absolutely right," Reb David murmured and heard a quiet trembling voice, as though a corpse were whispering among the trees of the cemetery.

"Rabbi!"

Reb David turned. Next to him stood a man wrapped in a quilt-like wrinkled coat, shivering with cold and fear.

"Don't you recognize me, rabbi? I'm Kalman Maytess, the seamstress' husband, the agunah's husband."

He had changed so radically, Reb David could hardly recognize him. Weeping and sleeplessness had half-closed his usually big round eyes. With hunched shoulders, yellow dough-like face, nose blue with frost, and thin voice coming feebly from his throat like smoke from a narrow chimney—Kalman no longer looked like a man in his mid-forties, but like a broken old man.

240

He told Reb David how he had been driven from the *shul* for separating from his wife and for becoming subjugated to Tsalye. Averting his face so as not to be recognized, he had wandered around the streets listening to what people were saying about the agunah. Only toward midnight did he go into a *shul* in the courtyard and sleep there with the beggars. In the morning, before the first quorum of worshippers gathered for prayers, he fled the *shul* and wandered around the streets again. He noticed that the town was preparing to attend his wife's funeral and heard people cursing him for leaving her. Men and women said that if he showed up at the funeral, they would stone him. So he ran to the cemetery, at least to watch the burial from his hiding place. He was afraid to go into the gravediggers' hut to warm up, for they knew him—after all, he had been a cemetery cantor—and would later tell the mourners of his presence at the cemetery. And therefore he had stood freezing among the trees until he had seen the funeral of the rabbi's baby.

"Rabbi, I'm not to blame for the death of your baby and I'm certainly not to blame for the death of my wife. The painters didn't let me near the exchange to look for work and Merl drove me out to round up support for you," Kalman trembled, weeping.

"For . . . me?" Reb David stammered.

"Yes, for you. When Tsalye excluded you from the quorum, Merl told me to go out and stir up the town. But who am I and what am I that people should listen to me?" Kalman told the rabbi of the anguish he had suffered until he became the assistant shamesh in the Zaretche *shul*, for he had nowhere to sleep. "And now everyone casts the blame on me and on Reb Levi Hurvitz. That's why I had to hide so that the mob won't do to me what they're planning to do to Reb Levi Hurvitz."

"What do they want to do to Reb Levi Hurvitz?"

"To bring the funeral past his house and kill him. They said that you yourself had called him a murderer, for he threatened not to let you bury your baby."

"That's a lie. Reb Levi did not say that." Reb David felt all the cold in the cemetery entering his heart and stopping it.

"I don't know," Kalman said apathetically. "They claim that you told them to kill him."

For a second Reb David stood with half-closed eyes: if only he could fall asleep now. Suddenly he started from his place and ran into the long wooden hut. The cemetery cantors dozed on their benches, waiting for the big funeral and for the invitation to chant memorial prayers. The old shroudmakers, women with veined and wrinkled hands, quickly prepared the shroud for the rabbi's baby, and then quietly exchanged remarks about their married grandchildren. The rebbetsin Eydl sat on the chair opposite the table, staring wide-eyed at her Mottele's eternal garments and huddling close to Yosefl. Reb David came in deathly pale.

"I have to go to town this minute to save Reb Levi Hurvitz. There's a rumor in town that I told them to kill him."

The rebbetsin looked dazedly at her husband, unable to emerge from her mournful thoughts or to clearly comprehend what he was saying. But Yosefl immediately burst into tears.

"Papa, don't go away!"

"Quiet!" Reb David gritted his teeth and Yosefl trembled. "Eydl, I've caused enough troubles in my lifetime. I've had the best intentions with the worst results. Therefore I don't want to be the cause of another misfortune. They will kill Reb Levi and say that I ordered it. I'm going to town."

"Where are you going?" the rebbetsin stood and her astonishment turned to anger and fear. "You're going to risk your life for the rabbi who has brought misfortune down upon us? They'll kill you, too."

"They won't touch me. I'm going to stand up for you, Yosefl and myself even more than for Reb Levi." Reb David turned to the cantors and the old seamstresses, who looked on thunderstruck as the rabbi and his wife quarreled in the cemetery. "Listen to me! I have to run down to town to save someone's life. My baby's burial will have to take place without me. Please bring the rebbetsin home after the burial. Don't leave her alone."

He ran out, shouting into the desolate wind-whipped field:

"Reb Kalman! Where are you, Reb Kalman?"

"Papa, Papa," Yosefl ran after him.

"Go back, go back to Mama," Reb David said, shaking his fist at the boy. Yosefl returned and fell against his mother who had gone outside.

"Your child isn't buried yet and you're running to the funeral of the agunah? She attracts you even in her death."

"Eydl, I swear to you I'm running to save Reb Levi. They'll commit a murder in my name," Reb David shouted despairingly and turned to the gate. "Where are you, Reb Kalman?" K-a-l-m-a-n!

echoed throughout the snow-covered cemetery, as though the dead in their graves were helping Reb David shout.

When Reb David entered the gravediggers' hut, Kalman returned to his place of concealment among the snow-covered graves. But while Reb David ran to the gate to call him, Kalman darted among the tombstones to avoid being seen by the gravediggers. He appeared only when Reb David neared the cemetery exit.

"Here I am, rabbi. What happened?"

Before the rabbi had a chance to reply, he again heard his wife's cry from the distance.

"Remember, David, I've got a weak heart. My heart will burst and you'll have a third funeral."

Reb David made a motion to return, but immediately changed his mind, seized Kalman's arm, and dragged him between the graves.

"What time is the funeral?" Reb David asked.

"They said at three. Are you going to the funeral?" Kalman tore his arm away and retreated. "I'm afraid. They said they would stone me."

"They won't touch you." Reb David took his arm again and pulled him to the path between the tree-covered hills that led to the Zaretche market. "They won't touch you or Reb Levi—unless they kill me, too."

From the wooded hills a wind howled and cast bits of thick snow at them. Reb David grabbed his hat with both hands and struggled with the vicious wind that sought to push him back to his family in the cemetery.

"You say the funeral is at three? What time is it now? Probably a little after two." Reb David waited for Kalman and caught his breath. "God Almighty, let's not be late. Do you have some money, Reb Kalman? We'll hire a droshky. Usually there are droshkies to be had in the Zaretche market."

"I don't have any money, rabbi. Not a penny. If I had money, I'd sleep in a hotel and not in a courtyard *shul*," Kalman puffed, swaying awkwardly, spreading his legs and his arms, as though he were some odd, half-human forest creature. "Ah, I can't run any more."

"Come, come," Reb David dragged him. "You won't have to roam about the *shul* courtyard any more; you'll live in your apartment, in your wife's apartment. You're her husband, and you must attend her funeral and say Kaddish at her grave."

"Rabbi, I'm afraid they won't let me say Kaddish at her grave. And where will she be buried? They say that the rabbis have ordered her to be buried next to the fence because she committed suicide."

"She won't be laid to rest by the fence, Reb Kalman. A person who commits suicide because others have persecuted and tormented him may not be disgraced after his death. The rabbis did not order her to be buried next to the fence. That's impossible. Enemies have concocted this in order to further stir up the mob."

Reb David had no more strength to drag Kalman and battle the wind whipping his face, back and legs, and blowing into his long black overcoat. Arriving at Polotsk Street, Reb David, his legs tottering, suddenly stopped and looked up at his apartment. Covered with perspiration he whispered, "Mottele, Mottele," and remembered that he wouldn't even say Kaddish at his baby's grave. But he soon took hold of Kalman's hand again and dragged him forward.

Kalman's eyes were fixed on the rabbi. As they made their way up the street to Merl's house, Kalman broke down and seized his head with both hands.

"A treasure. I had a treasure and didn't realize its worth. She took me into the house, fed me, prepared my bed, and didn't even ask me to go out and work. And I believed what that low-down Moishke Tsirulnik said about her. I don't deserve to take part in the funeral."

"Come, Reb Kalman, you're not to blame," Reb David encouraged him, scarcely able to stand on his own feet. "Neither you nor Reb Levi is to blame. I'll tell them who *is* to blame."

Supporting each other, they trod through the deep snow and descended from the Zaretche hill to the city.

46

"Better death than life," Reb Levi muttered. Since Reb Asher-Anshel's departure he sat with closed eyes, an angry smile hovering under his thick mustache. Reb David Zelver in his arrogant humility was proud that he could withstand oppression, Reb Levi thought; Reb David was ecstatic when he could show that he wasn't fazed by persecution. But Reb Levi wasn't afraid of persecutions either; not even of death.

Reb Levi heard the hidden silence whispering about him. It gradually became more tempestuous until his ears were pierced by the rustling sound of hundreds of feet, the panting of a great crowd climbing up the hilly street. He opened his eyes and glanced out the window of his study which faced the now silent courtyard. Reb Levi stood and opened the door to Tsirele's room. From the street he heard a commotion, the sounds of stormy waters crashing against boulders. The funeral had come to Shlomo Kissen's court-yard and there it had stopped. The tumult became louder and louder and exploded in a cry:

"Here's where the agunah's murderer lives."

That minute he heard a sharp, ringing sound and a cobblestone flew through his window, scattering glass across his room. Reb Levi returned to his study, donned his wide-lapelled fur coat and his sable hat, and walked out leisurely with hands behind his back, as though going to a Sabbath Afternoon Service. He stopped at the lowest step and turned around to his study, as though expecting someone else to follow. He fancied that someone had remained in the empty rooms within, but he didn't know if it was Tsirele or he himself . . . Reb Levi strode quickly through the gate.

At the head of the crowd stood a tall, pockmarked, cross-eyed youth. Holding a stone in his hand, he viewed the window from under the leather vizor of his cap. Just because he was cross-eyed, he was eager to display his accurate aim. He had broken one window and was now aiming for another. Behind him stood the broad-shouldered youths with the coffin on their shoulders and the crowd of mourners. The entire hilly street was covered with people.

Upon seeing the rabbi an angry whisper soughed through the crowd. The rows of women fruit peddlers and butchers' wives began to move and sway. The butchers, porters, and market peddlers in high shoes and knee-length boots, in leather and cloth jackets moved forward like dark clouds. Further back stood workingmen with dejected faces and shopkeepers with sparse beards; they tip-toed and peered over the shoulders of the tall, well-built youths. The crowd spoke louder and the tumult increased.

"There he is, Reb Levi Hurvitz! There's the murderer of the agunah!"

Reb Levi, his back to the wall of his house, looked wide-eyed and close-lipped at the inflamed crowd. His erect silent posture, broad reddish-grey beard and sable hat impressed the crowd. The tumult subsided to a murmur, which in turn gradually faded to complete silence. The tall, pockmarked youth holding the stone looked sarcastically at the mute crowd and approached Reb Levi.

"Say there, are you Levi Hurvitz?"

For a moment Reb Levi gaped at him, dumbfounded, unable to believe that a Jewish youth could address him in such fashion. But then Reb Levi's face glittered like polished copper; his eyes blazed, and his beard and mustache bristled.

"You brat, who do you think you're speaking to?" he said, making a quick motion with his right hand to smack the loafer's face. But the youth grabbed Reb Levi's hands, pushed him to the wall, and laughed:

"I'll squash you like a bug."

The pallbearers and the mourners were stunned. Reb Levi's shout and his lack of fear confused the youths. Only a few scattered voices urged:

"Give him what's coming to him!"

"No. I'd rather fling him back up into his window," the cross-eyed youth snickered, taking the rabbi by his lapels, as though about to magically lift him and throw him up in the air like a ball. Suddenly a short man wearing a long frayed overcoat pushed his way through the crowd and thrust himself between the rabbi and the youth. The

246

young roughneck, who until now had only been playing, as it were, flew into a rage. With one hand he fiercely pushed Reb Levi to the wall, and with the other thrust away the newcomer. Reb Levi was silent and made no effort to free himself, but the second man once again seized the edge of the roughneck's coat and shouted:

"Fellow Jews, help! You'll never be forgiven for this iniquity. I'm Reb David Zelver of Polotsk Street."

"Reb David Zelver!"

The youths carrying the coffin on their bent shoulders approached the roughneck and shouted:

"You boor, leave the rabbi alone."

The cross-eyed youth released both rabbis, stepped aside, grimaced and spat out: "Damn you! I take your part and you complain. Why don't you all drop dead!"

The mourners were shaken and astonished that Reb David had stood up for his most bitter enemy. But their surprise was all the greater when Reb Levi shouted at Reb David:

"It's your fault that the crowd wants to harm a rabbi. You, the rabbi and leader of this wild mob."

The crowd once again moved and swayed, coughed and fumed:

"The agunah's murderer has the nerve to insult us along with Reb David who's standing up for him. We won't leave Reb Levi until he begs pardon of the agunah, of Reb David, and of all the Jews."

"Men, why don't you speak up while our blood is being spilled like water?" the women yelled, their faces red from the wind and cold.

"Reb Levi Hurvitz is right," Reb David called, standing in front of Reb Levi with outstretched hands. "I'm to blame and you're to blame. Also those who are bewailing the agunah now are to blame."

"Us? You mean *us*?" came the cries from all sides. The mourners exchanged bewildered glances. "How are we to blame?"

"You!" Reb David roared, as though the torments which he had borne silently all along had now given him strength to outshout them all: "Remember Simkhas Torah in the Main Synagogue courtyard, when you people sided with me and the agunah? Then, after a complete reversal, you demanded my excommunication. I suffered persecution, and so did the agunah, but her husband, Reb Kalman, was persecuted most of all. You made fun of him, you didn't let him earn a living, and wherever he appeared you drove him away. Reb Kalman was no longer able to bear this oppression and left his wife. Now you're refusing to let Kalman attend his wife's funeral. The agunah had to commit suicide and my baby had to die in order to awaken your compassion. But even now you're looking for a scapegoat to atone for all your sins. You say the agunah's husband is to blame and that Reb Levi Hurvitz is to blame. And you say that I gave the word that he should be killed. In order to stop you from harming an old Vilna rabbi in my name, and to let the husband of the agunah come to the funeral, I was forced to run from the cemetery before the burial of my little baby."

Kalman, who had previously not dared to show his face to the crowd, felt that he could now do so. He edged out in front of the mourners and slowly slid along the length of the wall to Reb David. Now his pathetic, downtrodden appearance prompted no laughter. The women sighed, and the men, their heads lowered, wrinkled their brows. Only Reb Levi stood removed from the entire camp, following every move of Reb David Zelver's, as though suspecting that a mock Reb David stood before him and not the real one. From the rear a woman pushed her way forward, wringing her hands.

"Take our part, too, rabbi. I'm the agunah's sister. We're two orphaned sisters now, and they don't let us come near our own flesh and blood."

"She's still talking, that miserable shrew! She pushed her poor sister right into Tsirulnik's arms, pushed her to her death," the women grimaced with hatred.

But the grumbling men told their wives to pipe down. "This sister's not to blame. She's an absolute ass. Moishke Tsirulnik's to blame. But he's got a peasant's luck, lying in a hospital, guarded by doctors in white cloaks so that his sewn-up scalp won't be split open again. And what about the head shamesh with the belly-length pasted-on beard? And what about Tsalye the wife-killer? And what about the *mohel* Lapidus with the golden false teeth? Each of them added a bit of something. And now they've all scampered off to their holes and the scapegoat is the agunah's husband. And damn the painters, too! First they frightened Kalman to death and now they're all playing innocent. You heard what Reb David said. He didn't even wait for the burial of his own baby but came here to keep us from committing a sin."

The market peddlers, sick of standing in one spot, stamped their feet in the snow and elbowed one another like a herd of fenced-in oxen. Shopkeepers and artisans reminded themselves that they had abandoned their stores and not yet realized a sale. So either onward or back home. The pallbearers grumbled that they should be relieved, for the coffin was breaking their shoulders. But there were no eager volunteers. Along with the abated anger, the funeral, too, had become more workaday. The black funeral carriage was brought forward and the coffin was placed inside.

"Merke, intercede for your sisters," Golda wailed, and the women wept along with her. The atmosphere then became authentically funereal and Jewish. Both sisters and the nieces walked behind the coffin, and Kalman, too, appeared in the first row, bent, broken, but calmed. The mourners pushed closer from all sides to the carriage, so that the agunah could hear their silent requests for forgiveness. The driver urged his horses on and the funeral procession moved downhill. Reb David remained standing at the gate of the courtyard and the passing crowd looked at him with respect and wistful love. Further away stood Reb Levi Hurvitz, staring harshly at the passers-by, as though repeatedly demonstrating that he feared no one. Heads turned to him with fury-laden eyes, then looked away tight-lipped. The rabbi was hated, but the people held their tongues so as not to cause Reb David anguish. The mourners were sure that the rabbi would have gone along with them and eulogized the seam-stress, but he was afraid to leave his enemy lest people harm him. The further downhill they proceeded, the more the people were pushed and carried by the stream behind them, until the funeral turned into Zavalne Street, while the small hilly street where the two rabbis stood remained empty.

"Reb David, let's make peace," Reb Levi approached him. "I didn't argue with you for the sake of my honor, but for the sake of Heaven. But since you admitted publicly before an entire congrega-tion that you are to blame—I want to make peace with you in my name and in the name of all the rabbis."

"I did not for one minute change my mind and I do not regret my decision concerning the permission. I said I was to blame, and I *am* to blame, for I did not imagine that in your heart there would not be one spark of compassion for an oppressed Jewish woman." Reb David's eyes burned with such fierce hatred that Reb Levi immediately sensed that he would never make peace with him—neither in this world nor the next.

"You are a liar, stubborn and abnormally proud," Reb Levi

raged. "It was not me you wanted to save, but yourself, to prevent an entire crowd of Jews from pointing their fingers at you and saying: there he goes, the rabbi of the rebels and sinners, who caused a Vilna rabbinic authority to be murdered. That's what you were quaking in your boots about. And you were also afraid that I might appear greater and stronger than you and that I could die for the sanctification of God's name."

"You didn't want the sanctification of God's name, but its desecration," Reb David's lips trembled; he wanted to smile but could not. "Causing the agunah to commit suicide didn't suffice you; you also wanted poor embittered Jews to become spillers of blood. You hate Jews and you want them to sin all the more before God Almighty. Even face to face with the coffin of the agunah your heart was not moved and you did not ask her forgiveness."

"I didn't have to ask for forgiveness, for the one guilty in her death is you. You! You!" Reb Levi plucked at his beard in feeble wrath. "And I certainly won't ask for forgiveness of a man like you who publicly commits sacrilege."

"*You* are the one who publicly committed sacrilege," Reb David replied, and walked wearily down the hilly street.

47

The storm gradually abated. The winter ate its way into the thin bones of the dejected shopkeepers and bent workingmen, and the anxiety over livelihood was manifest in lightless eyes. The market women warmed their frozen, chapped hands over the coal pots, eagerly awaiting a customer, and when one mentioned the agunah, another answered with a sigh:

"She's well off—she doesn't need anything any more."

"She had a funeral like the greatest rebbetsin," the first peddler consoled herself.

The youths from the suburbs, the market dealers and the butchers who swore that when Moritz left the hospital they'd relieve him of his head, now declared that Tsirulnik didn't deserve their dirtying their hands on him. He'd remain a cripple anyway and a bit fuzzy in the head. So let him live and suffer. Moreover, the mourners couldn't understand why Reb David hadn't let them touch his most bitter enemy. They repeated what they had said when the agunah was alive:

"The religious functionaries kill each other quietly like the gangsters. But when others want to intervene and make order, they all present a solid front and stand up for each other. Let them break their own heads."

And then the street stopped talking about the agunah.

But in the *shuls* they still discussed the rabbis. Reb David Zelver's reputation suddenly soared and the pious worshippers smacked their lips in rapture and called him a great and saintly man. As Reb David was praised, so was the *mohel* Lapidus despised. They called him a quarrelmonger and an instigator, and were pleased that he did not show up in *shul*. Reb Levi Hurvitz, too, rarely came to *shul* or to the rabbinic courtroom. The young Agudah scholars in

Reb Yisroel's Shul said that Reb Levi had demonstrated his bravery in the face of a mob, but could not bear falling into disrepute among the Torah scholars. One thing, however, was clear to every one; Reb David Zelver would no longer be a rabbi in some forgotten corner, receiving a pittance for wages, but would be taken into the Rabbinic Council at full pay, like the other Vilna rabbinic authorities, and in time would become the chief spokesman at all the meetings.

Reb Levi did not mind his reduced stature among the masses and even among the *shul* Jews. But he could not make peace with the thought that Reb David would triumphantly come into the Rabbinic Council and there uninhibitedly express his opinions. The only way out, Reb Levi felt, was to leave the rabbinate. Thus he would show that at least he was not submitting to the mob and to their new teacher and guide. And if he left the rabbinate, there was no purpose remaining in Vilna—in fact, it wouldn't be proper for him to remain. After all, he was not Reb David Zelver who came running to the agunah's funeral to have everyone see him standing up for his antagonist. Reb Levi didn't want to be stared at, sighed over, or pitied for being played-out in his old age. Which meant that he would have to leave Vilna. And go where? Become a recluse in his old age in some village? But without wages from the Rabbinic Council he couldn't pay for his daughter's upkeep in the asylum . . . Nonsense! Leaving the rabbinate was impossible and impractical.

Reb Levi constantly thought of resigning, but was prepared to continue in his post in order to support Tsirele; nevertheless, it was his daughter who finally impelled him to resign. Once the tumult had subsided and the controversy with Reb David no longer confounded his thoughts, the specter of Tsirele returned to his empty apartment.

The first time he experienced this trick of the imagination was at the agunah's funeral. On his way down to face the mob of mourners, it suddenly struck him that someone had stayed behind in the room, either himself or his daughter; and henceforth these chimeras kept recurring.

Tsirele played hide-and-seek with him. She appeared while he was wrapped in his prayer shawl reciting his morning prayers. She stood behind him in the guise of a little girl and stretched out her thin pale hands to him. Swaying with greater fervor, Reb Levi prayed out loud, but she did not depart. He turned around to reassure himself that the apartment was empty. But again she stood behind him. Although she was hiding, he knew she now looked like a shriveled old woman—no taller than a child of ten, but with an old wrinkled face sprinkled with bristly hairs. Reb Levi no longer heard what his lips were murmuring. He broke off in the midst of his prayers, removed his *tfillin* and prayer shawl, and sat down in his study. He waited for Khiyeneh to come up and prepare breakfast for him.

Khiyeneh had a crescent-shaped back, a small head, and long toilworn hands that dangled and swung at her sides like two empty pails on a water-carrier's yoke. Her neighbors always asked her how she managed to get along with the rabbi who always berated everyone. Reb Levi, however, never berated her, except when she herself brought the water up to the apartment. This was actually the janitor's responsibility, but occasionally he was late, drunk, or simply remiss in his duty. Since Khiyeneh did not want the rabbi to be without a glass of tea or a warm meal, she herself brought water from the well. And for this, Reb Levi scolded her. Otherwise, she couldn't recall an instance when he raised his voice at her. Hence Khiyeneh was deeply concerned that her employer had of late been neglecting himself. When she came up in the morning she found him sitting with his head thrown back, his eyes half-closed, and his prayer shawl and *tfillin* in disarray on the table. Khiyeneh brewed tea, brought him bread, butter, salt and two boiled eggs, and waited for him to wash his hands prior to the benediction for bread. But Reb Levi took only tea. Khiyeneh asked him if he wanted some hot cereal with milk. Did he want her to bring up some hard white cheese, or perhaps a piece of herring to whet his appetite? Reb Levi shook his head. Khiyeneh went into the kitchen and discovered that the previous night's supper had also remained untouched on the stove. She sighed and began to clean the rooms.

Reb Levi sipped tea, looked into a sacred text or dozed—and his heart was desolate. He did not sense his daughter's presence behind his back and he longed for her, longed for her to the point of madness, until he felt a pleasant shudder running down his spine: she had come. This time, he knew, she was ten feet tall and had a thin, dry, hard face. Despite her silence he sensed she was hoarse, as though she were a mother who had become husky-voiced from weeping at the graves of all her dead children. Troubles have made her a vixen, he thought, and feared she might seize his throat from behind and choke him. He turned around—and Tsirele fled into her room where Khiyeneh was now cleaning.

Reb Levi recalled how Tsirele had dashed out of her room naked when the delegation had asked him to intervene in the agunah affair. He had shouted to them that his daughter was the demon who prevented him from waging holy war against Reb David Zelver and he sent her back to the insane asylum in a straitjacket. Now he saw her standing in her room, neither naked nor disheveled, but with hair neatly combed, in her white, long-sleeve, high-collar blouse.

"I told you, Papa, not to start up with the agunah." Her big smiling eyes sparkled.

"Khiyeneh, Khiyeneh," Reb Levi called weakly, wishing to ask her why she did not see Tsirele standing in the room she was now cleaning. But since Khineyeh was slightly deaf and immersed in her work, she did not hear his feeble voice. Reb Levi perked up and wiped the perspiration from his forehead. "I've gone mad . . . Tsirele is in the hospital." Reb Levi wondered why he never thought of his wife. Perhaps because she had been ill for twenty years, and perhaps, too, because he had never had much affection for her.

It occurred to Reb Levi that the best medicine for his illness would be to go to the hospital and actually see Tsirele behind the iron bars. Then he would no longer imagine that she was hiding in the house. "Nevertheless, I have lost my mind," he muttered. Didn't he know that his daughter was locked up in the hospital?

Reb Levi burrowed into his confused thoughts and could not come up with one lucid idea; he felt as though he were burrowing in hot dry sand. After Khiyeneh had gone, he remained sitting at his table, holding his head until evening fell. Then he rose, recited the Afternoon and Evening Services, and again dropped into his armchair. He fell into a deep slumber and woke up toward midnight. The starry, dark blue sky was visible through the window and the silence was so profound that he fancied he heard the shadows of the bookcases rustling. Suddenly, the sharp, abrupt sound of the gate bell. Reb Levi heard the janitor dragging himself out of his apartment to open the gate. The snow crunched underfoot as the latecomer came home. A door opened. Closed. And again silence. Reb Levi looked forward to the ringing of the gate bell. He waited in suspense, counting the seconds and the minutes, but no one rang again. Apparently all the tenants were already home. He was anxious for a baby to begin crying somewhere, or a group of youngsters to leave a friend's house. At other times, when he would hear the licentious laughter of boys and girls, he would become enraged at these libertines who were ashamed neither before God nor people. But now he yearned to hear the sound of merry laughter. Reb Levi closed his eyes—and immediately saw a woman's bare arms climbing the walls and grasping the window ledge. He saw no head, only a pair of bare arms banging on his window and fingernails scratching the pane.

"Let me in to warm up. I'm cold in the cemetery. Freezing."

He recognized the voice of the woman who had once visited him and later hanged herself in the woods; and simultaneously saw his daughter in his inflamed imagination.

"I told you, Papa, not to start up with the agunah." Tsirele stood in the adjoining room, her big smiling eyes sparkling.

Reb Levi jumped up, switched on the light, and began pacing about in his study: he must resign from this accursed rabbinate. He must. Otherwise, he'd go out of his mind.

The next morning, when Khiyeneh came up to the apartment she found the electricity still on. Reb Levi did not let her prepare breakfast for him, but told her to go immediately and ask Reb Shmuel-Munye, Reb Kasriel Kahana and his brother-in-law, Reb Asher-Anshel, to come to see him.

48

Reb Kasriel Kahana was the kind of man who never forgot an insult
—because he remained silent when he was being reviled. He calmly
heard what Reb Levi's housemaid had to say—and did not accede
to her request. Reb Asher-Anshel, too, did not want to go but
Khiyeneh told him that his brother-in-law did not look well and
should see a doctor. Left with no choice, Reb Asher-Anshel,
accompanied by his son-in-law Fishel Bloom, went to Reb Levi.
But the third of the invited rabbis, Reb Shmuel-Munye, ran more
than he walked. There was no doubt in his mind that Reb Levi
wanted to extricate himself from his quarrel with Reb David Zelver
and they were forced to turn to him, Reb Shmuel-Munye, to effect
a compromise.

Reb Levi received the rabbis looking like a sick man who had
come out of bed in honor of important guests. He asked them to be
seated and told them briefly why he had invited them. "I understand
that the Rabbinic Council will no longer contend with Reb David
and that he will even be invited to join the Council. But I cannot and
will not be a member along with Reb David. I am therefore resigning
from the Council and giving up my post as a rabbinic authority in a
city where a rebellious rabbi is considered a saint."

Reb Asher-Anshel's face turned ashen and his silvery beard hung
down heavily, as though it were inundated by a cloudburst. At
first he was certain that despite Reb Levi's monumental obstinacy,
he was touched that Reb David had protected him from the mob.
But it turned out that Reb Asher-Anshel still did not know his
brother-in-law. Reb Shmuel-Munye, too, was confused for a
moment, but quickly regained his composure and shrugged:

"What do you care what the town thinks? I never thought that
Reb Levi Hurvitz would be affected by what the town was saying."

Reb Levi did not reply. He had no strength to start from the beginning. Reb Fishel's full face and fleshy lips puffed up—he could no longer restrain himself, although he knew that his father-in-law could not tolerate his intervening. He, Fishel Bloom, had been waiting for years for a rabbinic post in some village and could not find one, not even on the strength of his dowry, which he was ready to present to the congregation—and here was Reb Levi resigning from a rabbinic post in Vilna, the Jerusalem of Lithuania.

"Does this mean that you have become frightened of the mob and are resigning from the rabbinate?" Fishel Bloom asked, gesturing with his short hands. "In his day Reb Akiva Eiger wanted to resign from the rabbinic chair at Posen and become a teacher in a village. His position I can understand," Fishel blushed confusedly, for in truth he himself did not know why he had suddenly got himself entangled with the Posen rabbi. "*He* had someone take his place, but nowadays there is no one to replace a Reb Levi Hurvitz," Fishel managed to conclude, wiping the perspiration from his fleshy neck.

"You'll replace me," Reb Levi smiled feebly.

Fishel's packed cheeks gleamed, as though he'd just come out of a hot ritual bath. Reb Levi was making fun of him, needling him for not having a post, completely indifferent to the fact that his father-in-law had heard the gibe. Fishel's father-in-law sat with a wrinkled brow, as though he considered Reb Levi's remark a poor joke. Only Reb Shmuel-Munye, with his little slit eyes, protruding ears and broad nose, realized that Reb Levi was actually serious. Reb Shmuel-Munye combed his soft white beard with all five fingers, as though it had suddenly become an elf-lock. All his limbs quivered as politics seethed in his mind like water in a covered pot: Reb Asher-Anshel was Reb Levi's brother-in-law, and Fishel Bloom was Reb Asher-Anshel's son-in-law—which meant that Reb Levi wanted to hand his post over to his nephew. But he, Reb Shmuel-Munye, would not permit this. He too had two daughters of marriageable age for whom he could get no husbands for lack of a dowry. But if he could offer the post of a Vilna rabbinic authority as dowry, then the finest yeshiva youths would flock to his house. And, anyway, by what right should the post go to Reb Asher-Anshel's son-in-law? But never mind, he would outwit both Reb Asher-Anshel and his son-in-law—politics was his specialty, thought Reb Shmuel-Munye and stretched out his hands to Reb Levi.

"We Vilna rabbis have always walked hand in hand with you, and with God's help we will continue to walk hand in hand with you. The law is on your side, justice is on your side, and we are on your side."

"Good," a bitter smile flitted on the corners of Reb Levi's lips. "I agree to remain in the Rabbinic Council, but on condition that Reb David Zelver be excluded from membership until he regrets all his deeds."

"God forbid! We dare not start up again with Reb David," Reb Shmuel-Munye withdrew his hands as though from fire.

"Of course not," Reb Levi laughed without anger. "I too hold the view that if one of us has to resign—for I won't sit on the same Council with Reb David—it is I who must resign, not he. The town is on his side, and me they have always hated, especially now. Reb David cannot resign even if he wants to. He has a wife and a boy of bar mizvah age, but I have no one."

"You have a daughter in the hospital," Reb Asher-Anshel inspected the tips of his fingers. "We have an all-merciful God and Tsirele can still be cured. But if you leave the rabbinate she will have no home to return to, and you will not be able to pay the hospital."

"You'll pay and she'll come back to your house," Reb Levi told Reb Asher-Anshel, and began pacing the room. "After all, my Tsirele is your niece, so why shouldn't you shoulder some of the responsibility?" Reb Levi's lifeless face quickened, as though the argument had given him strength. "Do you think I want to become a recluse in my old age and rove about homeless? Still, being a recluse and even a wandering beggar would be preferable to seeing the honor of the Torah dragged through the dust and avoiding my obligation by declaring that I don't bear any responsibility. And, besides, my wife's family should also be concerned with Tsirele. If your son-in-law takes my place, you can certainly set aside part of his salary for your sister's daughter in the hospital," Reb Levi stopped next to Reb Asher-Anshel. "So that's my decision. I'm resigning."

"I do not agree, and the other members of the Council will not agree, either," Reb Shmuel-Munye fumed; but it was hard to determine whether his disagreement was over Reb Levi's resignation or over Fishel Bloom being his replacement.

"I haven't agreed yet, either," Reb Asher-Anshel reassured Reb Shmuel-Munye. But Fishel was unable to utter a word. He sat there like a statue, his cheeks steaming. Fishel saw that Reb Levi was perfectly serious about him becoming the old rabbi's replacement as a rabbinic authority in Vilna.

"I am resigning," Reb Levi faced the adjoining room as though addressing someone who stood listening behind the closed door. He sank again into his chair, groaning and in pain. "Gentlemen, please don't bargain with me and let me rest now. Leave me alone."

This time Reb Shmuel-Munye was not insulted by Reb Levi's request to leave; on the contrary, he was pleased. The brothers-in-law might well claim that their decision to have Reb Fishel replace him was made in my presence and with my consent, Reb Shmuel-Munye thought, and was the first to leave the apartment. Seeing Reb Levi's condition, Reb Asher-Anshel wanted to remain, but was afraid that his brother-in-law might repeat his usual recriminations. Reb Asher-Anshel winked to Fishel and both slipped out silently. Reb Levi closed his eyes and threw his head back immediately, waiting for his spell of madness. No sooner had Reb Asher-Anshel and Fishel gone, than Reb Levi already heard Tsirele's silver bell-like voice in the adjoining room.

"Papa, you didn't tell the truth. You're not resigning because of Reb David Zelver but because of me. You want to run away from me."

"Because of Reb David, only because of him," Reb Levi whispered. If he made peace with Reb David perhaps the mad notion that Tsirele was in the other room would disappear. But Reb David would not forgive him until he, Reb Levi Hurvitz, agreed that the agunah had been permitted to marry. "He'll never live to see the day," Reb Levi laughed. He would never admit that he and all the codifiers were wrong and that the right lay with this insignificant little rabbi who had no Torah but only the boorish mob on his side.

He remained wrapped in a mist of thoughts which drizzled like a light autumnal rain. He would no longer be able to remain the rabbinic authority over agunahs, for people considered him cruel, and sooner or later the Rabbinic Council would replace him. But if he resigned, they would see that he had the courage to lose. One also had to know how to lose. No one would miss him—not the worshippers, not his colleagues in the Rabbinic Council, not his wife's family. On the contrary, the family would be happy to see Fishel Bloom becoming a Vilna rabbinic authority. The only one who would miss him was Reb David Zelver, who would have no one to triumph over at the rabbinic conventions. And he, Reb Levi thought, would not miss his brothers-in-law, either. The only thing he would miss was the mad delusion that his daughter was in the other room.

Reb Levi's tear-filled eyes roamed about the room, as though already bidding farewell to the apartment; his gaze remained fixed on the large bookcase. He wouldn't even miss his books. In his youth he had always been immersed in learning. After his wedding and after the birth of Tsirele and his wife's removal to the insane asylum, he became more engrossed with his books, devoting himself only to them and to his baby daughter. But since the onset of Tsirele's illness he rarely studied. He decided he would sell his library along with his other household possessions and make a large advance payment to the hospital. He would also demand compensation for stepping down from his tenure position, whether his substitute would be Reb Asher-Anshel's son-in-law or anyone else. This would leave him a small sum of money which would insure his independence in his old age.

Khiyeneh entered and asked the rabbi what he wanted to eat. "Eat?" Reb Levi repeated, thinking: this old woman I will miss. She would have to look for a new job and toil for a large family. She was deeply attached to his house and it distressed him greatly to have to grieve her with the news.

"What will the rabbi eat?" Khiyeneh asked again.

"Whatever you give me." Reb Levi heard her trudging to the kitchen. He'd have to tell the old woman later; now he had no strength. The books and the furniture he would sell, but the kitchen utensils and bedding he would leave for her. Reb Levi sensed that he was falling once again into the sweet numbness of a semi-conscious sleep. Suddenly, through his half-closed lids, he saw Tsirele bursting out of her room completely naked; and before he had a chance to move, she breezed by him and ran out laughing:

"Aha! Slipped by you!"

"Catch her! Catch her! She ran out naked." He jumped up. The slightly deaf Khiyeneh heard his outcry in the kitchen and ran in frightened.

"Rabbi, rabbi, what's the matter? I'll call the neighbors."

"Nothing's the matter," Reb Levi fell back into his chair with glazed eyes. "Nothing's the matter. Absolutely nothing," he attempted to calm himself, then burst into tears. "A man with an impure, shameless daughter should not be rabbi. I'm resigning from the rabbinate. Resigning."

49

During the seven days of mourning when prayers were held in Reb David Zelver's house, the Zaretche congregants tried to bring him good news. He had already been informed that he would be made a member of the Rabbinic Council with full wages, and the congregants asked if he would move into town or remain in the suburb Zaretche.

Reb David listened with a distressed look on his face, but made no reply.

Throughout the day, when the house was not taken up by the quorum, women would come in. Although the rebbetsin received them lying in bed fully clothed, the women, understanding her plight, were not offended. They brought packages, sat with her and comforted her. The rebbetsin moaned softly and whispered expressions of gratitude. Reb David would sit in a corner on his low mourner's stool, staring wide-eyed into the Talmudic tractate, *Mo'ed Katan*, which one was permitted to study during the seven days of mourning. But he did not turn a page or read a line; finally this depressing muteness drove the women from the house. Even when there were no guests he sat in a stupor without saying a word to his wife.

On the final night of the seven days of mourning, Reb David suddenly interrupted a conversation of the congregants and inquired about Kalman Maytess. They quickly replied that for the seven days of mourning Kalman had a large quorum of worshippers daily in his wife's apartment, where he would continue to live, since his wife's sisters were not demanding her possessions as an inheritance. Attempting to make the rabbi even happier, one congregant reported that Tsalye would no longer lord it over the *shul*. He still lay in bed nursing the wounds he had received after being thrown out of the *shul*; his fifth wife would most likely bury *him*. The listeners gestured to the congregant to hold his tongue. If the rabbi had run to save his worst enemy, Reb Levi Hurvitz, he might also be grieved to hear that that old crook Tsalye had been beaten up. But Reb David, his brows wrinkled, said absolutely nothing.

When the congregants left, the rebbetsin wanted to tell him that he was making himself miserable once again. Eydl was ready to forget that her husband had left their unburied baby to save Reb Levi; she was ready to forget, for this deed had won him the entire town's esteem. But if he were unfriendly to the congregants, she wanted to cry out, they would cease being concerned with him and his enemies would once again predominate. Nevertheless, she did not say a word, sensing in him a strangeness, a wrathful impatience, as though he had become disgusted with life.

After the period of mourning, Reb David began to go to the *shul* morning and evening. He would return late, after the Evening Service, wrapped in darkness, as if his shoulders bore all the shadows of the dark empty *shul*. He wasn't even bothered that his Yosefl, protesting his teacher's unfairness, still had not returned to *cheder*. The rebbetsin declared a war of silence against him, saying nothing even when the last of the gift packages had been consumed. She was possessed by a furious curiosity to see what her husband would do.

Early one afternoon Reb David came home, placed some paper money on the table and said:

"Here are my wages from the Rabbinic Council. Reb Levi Hurvitz has resigned from his post."

From the way he threw the money down on the table and snatched away his hand, the rebbetsin realized how sorry he was that he too could not resign his post. She clenched her teeth and did not ask why Reb Levi had resigned.

In the Council Reb David had learned about the rabbis' argument with Reb Levi not to resign. But that same day Reb Levi's maid came running to Reb Asher-Anshel, informing him that Reb Levi had fallen to the floor with the cry: "Catch her! Catch her!", having fancied that his hospitalized daughter had run out of the room naked. After Reb Asher-Anshel had summoned doctors to his brother-in-law's apartment, the family decided that since Reb Levi was subjected to such hallucinations, it would be best for him to resign from the rabbinate and move from his apartment.

Reb David paced in his rooms, talking to himself: "Reb Levi

doesn't want to admit that he accomplished nothing with his heartlessness. And since he doesn't intend to be compassionate in the future either, he has decided to resign. Moreover, since he believed that I was proud of being persecuted, he wants to show me that he can be rejected, too."

"Don't worry! I won't follow Reb Levi. I won't resign from my post," Reb David reassured his wife.

"Why don't you? Resign!" she laughed, then sighing, turned to the wall, as though realizing that a war of silence was not worthwhile, either.

Eydl's brief reply and bitter laugh confused Reb David. He gazed at her, not daring to approach her bed, for fear she might drive him away. He turned around, recited the Afternoon Prayer, and only then drew near and asked if she wanted to eat. Eydl lay with her head pressed to the wall and did not answer. Reb David paced some more, troubled and anxious, then suddenly began to talk as though tearing pieces from himself. He stood with his head thrown back and gave vent to the pain in his heart.

"I've become a somebody. They're paying me the wages of a Vilna rabbinic authority; they honor me and everyone feels guilty about their past behavior toward me. But really *I* am the guilty one. I didn't foresee how much trouble my permission would cause that tormented woman. In order for the city to side with me she had to sacrifice herself. As a result of her tragedy I've become famous and important. I've blossomed on her grave."

"And I suppose I haven't paid dearly!" the enraged rebbetsin cried. "It cost me my baby, my Mottele. You say that the agunah sacrificed herself for you. But you sacrificed yourself for her first. But why did I have to sacrifice my child? You feel compassion for the agunah. But don't you feel compassion for your wife and only remaining child? Make sure that the time doesn't come when you'll have to bemoan your wife and child the way you now bemoan the agunah."

The rebbetsin turned once more to the wall and sobbed, her shoulders heaving. Reb David did not know what to do. Yosefl came into the house frozen, hungry and exhausted from playing outdoors. Happy to see him, his father caressed his head and told him to sit down to eat. Yosefl wondered why his mother didn't turn to look at him, and why his father of late had completely disregarded him; but now his father was urging him to eat more and then led him to his bed to sleep. Yosefl understood that something had happened between his parents and that he had to be quiet. He undressed, recited the bedtime *Shema Yisroel*, and covered himself. Reb David sat at the edge of his wife's bed, and the rebbetsin, as though sensing his fatherly concern, turned her agonized face toward him. She caressed his sallow cheeks and his now thoroughly grey beard.

"It was nice of you not to go to the *shul* today and leave me alone," she huddled next to him. "My heart, too, pains me for the agunah. She ran to the doctor for our little baby, lent us money, ran to the market to shop for us—and I drove her out. My heart told me that nothing good would come of this. I don't know what prompted her to smash a bottle over the market dealer's head and then commit suicide. But I can't forgive myself for taking his word that she sent him to ask you to annul her marriage. You say that it's our fault she died young. God is my witness that I didn't want our salvation to come about in that fashion."

Reb David, wrapped in gloomy silence, adjusted the pillow under his wife's head. She huddled closer to him and covered him with a part of her shawl, as she had covered Yosefl when he slept next to her.

"David, did Reb Levi Hurvitz resign because of you?"

"Yes."

"David, I'm just a foolish woman, but why don't you make peace with him? Everyone is on your side now, so it shouldn't bother you to become reconciled with him. I feel very sorry for him. What will he do now in his old age without a position?"

"He won't make peace with me just because the town is on my side. He *would* make peace with me if I were to proclaim that the agunah had not been permitted to marry. But I will never declare that she was a married woman who wasn't permitted to marry again. In my eyes she was a saintly woman."

The rebbetsin heard him silently, her face strained, her eyebrows arched over her lowered eyes. Although the agunah had been a fine person, it distressed her greatly to hear her husband praising that woman.

Reb David went to a corner and immersed himself in silent devotion. His lips whispered the blessings, but his heart wept its own prayer: "Master of the Universe, ask the agunah to forgive me. Be my witness that I wanted to ease her lot so that a Jewish woman would not consider your Torah heartless. Ask her to forgive me and my wife for temporarily believing the evil reports about her. And if she refuses, remind her that she lies buried in the same cemetery as our baby."

Eydl heard his silent weeping and felt better, as one does on the Eve of Yom Kippur when man and wife ask each other's pardon before departing for *shul*.

The flame in the memorial candle had gone out, but the light in the house became brighter. A host of clouds passed their window and among them floated the huge silver moon. The clouds scudded by with secretive speed; but the moon remained suspended over the window, illuminating Reb David still praying in the corner. The rebbetsin thought she saw the agunah's face in the moon. "Now all is well with her," she sighed. "She has been redeemed and cleansed of all her suffering." And the moon, radiant with the light of distant worlds, beamed into all corners of the rabbi's house.